INSIDE
MAN

ALSO BY JOHN McMAHON

THE HEAD CASES SERIES

Head Cases

THE P. T. MARSH SERIES

A Good Kill

The Evil Men Do

The Good Detective

INSIDE MAN

A HEAD CASES NOVEL

JOHN McMAHON

MINOTAUR
BOOKS
NEW YORK

First published in the United States by Minotaur Books, an imprint of St. Martin's Publishing Group

EU Representative: Macmillan Publishers Ireland Ltd, 1st Floor, The Liffey Trust Centre, 117–126 Sheriff Street Upper, Dublin 1, D01 YC43

www.minotaurbooks.com

Designed by Omar Chapa

The Library of Congress Cataloging-in-Publication Data is available upon request.

ISBN 978-1-250-34832-6 (hardcover)
ISBN 978-1-250-34833-3 (ebook)

Our books may be purchased in bulk for specialty retail/wholesale, literacy, corporate/premium, educational, and subscription box use. Please contact MacmillanSpecialMarkets@macmillan.com.

First Edition: 2026

10 9 8 7 6 5 4 3 2 1

There is a confidence that older brothers provide to younger brothers that turns into power. So this book is dedicated to my brother, Andy McMahon, my friend, roommate, and hero growing up.

INSIDE
MAN

CHAPTER ONE

PATTERNS.

If you're like me, it's all you see in the world.

Fibonacci sequences appear in the flowering of an artichoke. The golden ratio recurs in the forms of flowers. And spirals and stripes develop in hundreds of species, both to hide from prey but also to attract mates.

Put simply, we all want to be seen—to be courted.

And sometimes even—to be caught.

But it wasn't until five years ago that the FBI green-lit a team dedicated to studying how identifying patterns could lead to perpetrators.

I opened the door to the double-wide, and the effect was like a vacuum. The smell of the nearby forest disappeared, the scent of dogwood and confederate jasmine replaced with the odor of perspiration and rotten food.

And something worse. A scent like rotten eggs.

"Mr. Pecos?" I called out.

My flashlight moved through the dark, its beam picking up

specks of dust that flitted about the mobile home. Across the stream of light, I saw the flap of an open pizza box, a curl of congealed cheese stuck to the cardboard. Then a melamine card table with an antique flintlock rifle atop it.

Behind me, the night was pitch black, and my partner, Joanne "Shooter" Harris, moved into the dark space.

"On your three," she said.

Shooter's flashlight moved right while I moved left.

"Freddie?" Her voice rang through the darkness. It sounded friendlier than mine, but I knew Shooter's voice and could sense her concern.

I turned toward the kitchen, and a cockroach passed through my flashlight beam. On the counter sat two six-packs of Yuengling lager, each with a bottle missing.

"Uh, Gardner," Shooter said, her voice coming from my right. "I don't think Freddie's living his best life anymore."

I turned my flashlight toward her voice and took in Freddie Pecos.

Our confidential informant was white and thirty-five years old. His six-foot-two frame was sunk into a threadbare couch, his hands splayed at his sides, a bottle of Jack Daniel's in the crook between his right elbow and his stomach.

And then there was the blood.

"I mean, if we're being honest," Shooter said, "maybe his best life wasn't working for us or living here. But, uh . . . this is definitely worse."

Shooter did gallows humor 24-7, which is the opposite of me. I manage a solid joke twice a year.

I stepped in the direction of the body, and Shooter blasted him with light.

Freddie Pecos was dressed in camo pants and a white T-shirt. The collar of the tee was sprayed with a red pattern that suggested he'd either coughed up or vomited blood. Six and a half inches below that—across the center of his shirt—was a wide oval of crimson.

I'd read recently in a management manual that in times of stress, it is advisable to make small talk. I kept my light on Pecos but considered a few options.

"So, what'd you do last night?" I asked Shooter.

"Hot date," she said.

I nodded, still facing Pecos.

"Threesome, actually," she continued, and I turned to face her. "Gun range." She flicked her eyebrows. "Me. Two guys named Smith and Wesson."

I made a mental note to attempt this tactic at another time—with someone not named Joanne Harris.

Then I turned back to the body and crouched. Using a gloved hand, I lifted the tee. Under a wrinkle in Pecos's shirt was a gun wound the size of a cigar burn. It varied in color from black in the center to brick red near the edge.

"Shit," I said. And I rarely curse.

It wasn't by accident that we'd descended upon this trailer in the dead of night. Freddie Pecos was our confidential informant in a case we'd been chasing for three months in Hambis, Florida, ninety minutes northwest of Miami. We had not heard from the C.I. in forty-eight hours, but someone had paid Freddie a visit.

Did they figure out he'd gone to work for the FBI?

"Single-barrel smooth-bored firearm," Shooter said.

I squinted back at her silhouette, beyond the ring of light. Shooter wore the same outfit nearly every day: a white sweatshirt and blue jeans. But for tonight's mission, she'd donned all black.

"You sure?"

Certain wounds are telling in terms of distance, number of shots, and position, and an ME specializing in GSW is often the best judge of those elements. Shooter, however, was an anomaly in many ways. She'd grown up in Alaska, where her father forbade television, replacing it with outdoor activities. He'd taught her to track animals from the age of six and shoot from the age of eight. She'd even been part of an Olympic shooting team before joining the FBI.

"Projectiles follow the path of least resistance," she said. "The tissues of least resistance, in Freddie's case."

It was a lot to surmise so quickly, but Shooter lowered the light so I could see her face. She'd been growing out her bangs, which were a strawberry-blond color. Now she swiped them off her forehead and walked exactly two paces back, measuring distance and angle.

"The perp was here." She motioned at an area ten feet from Pecos, then moved back toward the victim and took out a pocketknife. Crouching beside me, she picked at the flap of skin that made up the wound. "The shot was taken from an angle, not straight on. When we get him on the table, I think you'll find his ticker's in three pieces."

I looked back at the weapon, laid out beside the pizza box.

"That rifle," I confirmed.

"A hundred percent."

I examined the area where Shooter had been standing. In other words, the weapon was fired from straight on, but the trajectory had changed just slightly, even over that small distance, based on the inaccuracy of a rifle with no grooves inside.

Or a killer unused to firearms.

Or both.

Which is why Shooter had guessed that Pecos's heart, which was northeast of the entry wound, would be pulverized into fragments.

I sniffed at the air. The first stage of human decomposition is called autolysis, which literally translates to "self-digestion." The body's cell membranes eat themselves. When Shooter picked at the bullet wound, a sulfuric gas had been released—the kind that had been building up inside Freddie's abdomen and breaking down his skin.

"Pheff," I said, standing up.

"I know, right?" Shooter smiled. "I used to date a guy who worked at the morgue. Came home like that every night." She shrugged. "Eventually he decided it was a dead-end job."

I looked at Shooter. Most days, it was better to ignore her jokes.

"I'm going to inspect the bedroom," I said. "Maybe you can take a look at the weapons."

"Aye, aye, Captain," she said, and I moved out of the main area of the trailer.

Shooter and I work for an FBI unit called PAR, which stands for Patterns and Recognition. In addition to being her partner, I lead the group, which contains us and a second team, Richie Brancato and Cassie Pardo. Our job is to identify peculiarities in cases that have stalled or gone cold. To uncover details that others have missed, then hand the case off, either back to the field office that sent it to us—or to a team in Quantico.

When people speak well of us, they call us puzzle-solvers. When they don't, we are thought of as oddballs. Freaks with a bent toward data. Often, they call us "head cases."

To be fair to my team, the more negative comments are usually directed at the oddest among us: Me. The team leader. I try to fit in. Adjust my work style and personality. But much of who I am is simply built in. Unchangeable.

Our current investigation began ninety days ago, with an email

from the attorney general's office to Craig Poulton, the director of
the FBI. An analyst working for the Florida AG had come forward
with an odd finding: 11,600 unemployment claims had been withdrawn in the last year from the same thirty-two ATM machines.

Unemployment in Florida is paid by either check or debit card,
which raised a question about population density. Was it possible
that 11,600 unemployed people lived close enough to each other to
use this few ATM machines?

It was a question that did not seem like a question to me. Everyone
knew the answer was no. They just didn't know what to make of it.

A month into studying the patterns, I had widened our search
area to two states—and narrowed it to eight large clusters of withdrawals, four in central Georgia and four in South Florida. And what
had begun as an analytical operation in PAR's Miami office moved
northwest to the city of Hambis, where the Florida money was being
pulled out. There, a group of thieves was submitting false applications
for unemployment benefits, all with the help of an employee in the
Florida reemployment office who was rubber-stamping the claims.
When the amounts withdrawn topped two million, we packed the
case up—ready to go back to the attorney general. There was fraud.
Racketeering. Interstate commerce violations. A lot of cash moving
around.

And for us, the case was over. Florida law enforcement would
step in.

Then, on the day we were about to send the files over, something
unexpected happened. A man named Freddie Pecos was arrested for
assault. Pecos's name had been flagged as part of our investigation,
and we had an opportunity to step in and speak to him.

Pecos did not want to go to jail for assault, so he made a deal,
telling us the goal of the unemployment scam: to support a domestic

militia group run by an arms dealer named J. P. Sandoval. This was something we had no idea about. And suddenly, all those boxes were unpacked, because now we had a different case. One the FBI was not turning over to anyone.

In the interview, Pecos told us that Sandoval was also using the cash to amass a supply of unmarked weapons with no serial numbers. To be used against law enforcement, specifically.

"Kill a cop. Drop the gun. And walk away," the gang's leader had allegedly told his men, including our C.I., Freddie Pecos.

I examined the disarray that made up Freddie's bedroom. Six shirts and eight tees were on the floor. A leather jacket. Nine empty beer bottles on the dresser. But like the living area, the place did not look as if it had been rifled through. What I was looking for, in fact, was right in front of me, at the far end of the eight-by-twelve space. Three stacks of white plastic boxes, the translucent kind sold at your local Container Store.

I flipped the lid off the highest one. Ran my fingers across the tops of a hundred envelopes. Picking one out, I transferred the penlight to my mouth. On the outside of the envelope was a series of numerical notations, each in descending order, with the top two amounts crossed off:

- $~~$1100~~$
- $~~$700~~$
- 300

Below the list, written on each envelope, was a four-digit ATM passcode. I flipped the top flap off the envelope and saw a bank debit card inside.

Sandoval's men had set up false claims and chosen the debit card option for unemployment, allowing each card's balance to build for four weeks before reporting that a job had been obtained. Then it was Freddie's job to drain the debit cards over three successive withdrawals, each of which was noted on the envelopes.

Which meant that each card in this box still had three hundred dollars on it.

I studied the room. Considered how we'd found Freddie.

And something did not make sense.

"Inventory's still here," I hollered to Jo.

Shooter shuffled into the bedroom and stood behind me, the glow of her flashlight adding depth to mine. "Huh," she said in a surprised tone.

She turned her body, looking both ways, in at the debit cards and out toward Pecos.

"If he's dead . . ." she said, rotating back to the clear boxes of cards. "And his own people did it because they found out he was working for us . . ."

"Then these should be empty," I said. "Taken by whoever killed Freddie. But they're not."

"And the grand total?"

I glanced at the plastic containers. Three stacks of boxes. Twelve boxes per stack. One hundred envelopes per box. Three hundred bucks left on each card.

"One million, eighty thousand," I computed.

Shooter whistled. Again, I looked around the room. Beside the bed was a bucket filled with monofilament fishing line, a heavier weight than normal. Nothing else seemed out of place.

"Freddie's injury was obviously lethal," Shooter said. "But the way he's sitting out there with the bottle of Jack beside him . . ."

"He didn't see it coming," I finished her thought.

The front door had also been unlocked, and whoever had shot Freddie hadn't taken the antique rifle or the handgun we'd seen on the card table.

I followed Shooter out of the bedroom. She pulled a chair up to the table and sat down, inspecting the handgun.

Crouching beside Freddie, I patted my gloved hands down the side of his body. His limbs were stiff, and I tapped at a bulge on his right side. Reached down and removed his mobile phone. It was dead.

I stood up and walked back to his nightstand, where I'd seen a charger. Grabbed it and came out, looking for a plug.

As I moved across the room, I passed a full-length mirror and caught a glimpse of myself. Like Shooter, I was dressed head to toe in black, but my brown hair had gotten wavy and looked unkempt.

"Right there," Shooter said, pointing at an outlet by the sofa.

I plugged the phone in and sat on the arm of the couch, ten inches to the right of Freddie.

As the phone fired up, Shooter spoke aloud.

"Venera." She held the handgun in her gloved hands. "It's a Czech brand, but manufactured in the US. What are the odds you have their production codes memorized?"

Every handgun is imprinted with a serial number, and hidden among those numbers is information about the production date of the weapon.

"One hundred percent," I said.

The whites of her eyes disappeared, and Shooter fingered the letters and numbers along the gun's slide. In the dark, her hand moved over the raised ridges of the flat black metal.

"*B*," she said, and I pictured the FBI binder on this particular manufacturer. An Excel chart on page 38. Right side.

"April," I said. The month of manufacture.

Her fingers moved to the next grouping. "*HH*."

"Nineteen sixty-five," I replied.

Shooter's eyes flicked open, and I realized what I'd just said did not make sense. Venera firearms were not marked this way in 1965. But Shooter did not ask me if I was sure about the numbers. She knew better.

The phone came to life, and I began scrolling through Freddie's texts.

> Where the fuck are you?

This was sent twice, the first one a day ago.

The same number, twelve hours later, showed another message.

> Regnar says you missed a drop.

Then there were a series of newer texts from a different number. The area code was 478.

"Macon," I said to myself, referring to the city southeast of Atlanta. I had committed every three-digit code in the country to memory years ago.

> JP said to come down and check on you. Be there by four.

I scrolled to a text sent even more recently from the same person.

> An hour out. You better not be dogging us after this drive.

A flash illuminated the mobile home, and I glanced over. Shooter was taking pictures of the firearms.

"He's not blown," I said, my voice sounding confused as it echoed off the mobile home walls.

Shooter's face contorted. "Freddie, you mean?"

"They're wondering where he is—as much as we are."

"Sandoval's guys?" Shooter confirmed, and I nodded.

J. P. Sandoval, the mastermind behind the unemployment scam, owned a series of firearms shops near the Florida-Georgia line. But after hours, we suspected he was connected to two militia groups. Most likely, he was their leader.

"They're coming here," I said.

"When?"

I looked at the time the last text was sent. The one saying they'd be here in an hour. Fifty-one minutes ago.

"Now."

"*Now* now?" Shooter stood, her voice moving up an octave.

"At three a.m., they said they'd be here by four."

Shooter looked at her phone, and her face tightened at the recognition that a carful of armed men might be rolling up at any second. She pulled her Glock from the holster at her waist.

"We should go, Gardner. These guys show up and see us? Three months of casework is blown."

I remained on the arm of the couch, Freddie's phone in my lap. All four of us at PAR had been working this case, but it was my job to assimilate the details and set strategy.

"If we leave like this," I said, "they're going to take the guns and the bank cards and torch the place with Freddie's body in it."

The Sandoval gang had been deliberate in destroying evidence via arson and murder, and this mobile home was remote, planted ten miles outside of Hambis on a piece of land owned by Pecos's aunt. The structure would burn quickly, and the fire would not be seen for hours.

"So we do it first," I said.

"Burn the place down?" Shooter's voice spiked.

I held my partner's gaze. Our team member Cassie had already linked two Hambis cops to the criminal ring, so trusting local police was not an option.

"Gardner," Shooter said, focusing me.

"I'm going to grab the containers with the bank cards," I said. "Then bag up his trash in case there's anything valuable in it. In five minutes, I'll have everything over to that hedge we snuck through by the highway."

Shooter stared at me, nodding as she followed my logic. "So Freddie was drunk," she said. "He fell asleep. Woke up amid the smoke, but couldn't get out?"

"I'll rig the door," I said. "Break his key off in it."

"And me?" Shooter asked.

"We can't have locals thinking he died of a GSW," I said. "You've got five minutes to cut him open and remove any bullets."

Shooter squinted at me. "Upper management at the Bureau, Gardner . . . they're not gonna be happy about this." She motioned around the mobile home. "No fingerprints, DNA destroyed in a fire, no bullets."

"Right," I said. "Take the bullets with you."

I got up to leave, but Shooter was shaking her head.

It was not uncommon for others to react to me in this way. As if I were all logic and no feelings. When I was younger, my mother told me that my mind "just worked differently than others'." That my affect was simply "a bit lower than normal." But I'd learned it could be an advantage to not be bothered by emotional details.

"Freddie has no wife or kids, Jo," I said. "No relatives in the area. If local police are compromised, this is the logical thing to do. Let the fire department find the body. We find a new informant."

"All right." Shooter nodded in understanding, then flicked out her pocketknife and stared at Pecos. "Okay, Freddie."

She eyed the filthy trailer. "Did you hear the one about the germ? Never mind. I don't want to spread it around."

Shooter went to work, and I hustled into the bedroom. Grabbing the first stack of boxes, I walked out the door, examining the countryside around me.

3:54 a.m. and quiet.

At least for a few minutes.

I hurried across an open patch of scrub brush to a hedge of dogwood. Our sedan was parked in a grassy ditch off the local state highway, just on the other side of this strip of woods. I moved through the forest, angling between the vertical lines that made up the dark trees at night. When I could see the car, I placed the stack of plastic containers in the dirt and ran back for more.

3:56 a.m.

Back at the mobile home, Shooter had paused after making the first incision. She had her phone out. Before we burned the body, she was doing the smallest of autopsy reports.

"Dead body of known male, Frederick Pecos, found in his home by Agents Gardner Camden and Joanne Harris," she dictated.

"No time," I said.

She glared at me. "I can do it." Turning back to Freddie, she continued, "The body is stiff at the joints, the hands clenched and smeared in blood. Postmortem lividity cannot be fully appreciated given the . . . particular time constraints. But it appears as if he's been dead a solid day."

I moved past her and into the bedroom. Grabbed another stack of boxes.

3:57 a.m. with an ETA of 4:00 by the Sandoval gang.

"Oval lacerated entry wound," Shooter said as I passed. "Slightly charred, with blackening around it."

I ran out the door.

3:58.

I got another stack over to the edge of the forest by the road. On my trip back, Shooter had concluded her oral report and was struggling with her pocketknife.

"No bullet yet," she said.

I glanced at my phone. 4:02.

I ripped a Hefty bag from a box under the sink and dumped Freddie's trash in it. Threw in the receipts from the pizza boxes. Anything to help build a timeline of when he was alive and when someone had gotten to him.

And the big question: If it wasn't the Sandoval gang, who the hell had shot our C.I.?

I ran the trash and more debit cards over to the tree line. Popped the trunk to the sedan and tossed in the Hefty bag. Under my black Gor-Tex, I was coated in sweat.

Back at the mobile home, I grabbed a wire hanger from Freddie's closet and straightened it, standing near the door.

"Got the bullet," Shooter yelled, holding up a bloody chunk of metal.

I took the wire hanger and stuck it in the locking mechanism, attempting to jam it.

4:05 a.m.

"See if he's got keys," I said, and Jo searched the body. She found a set and tossed it to me. As I caught them, I eyed my phone and saw the time.

"We gotta go."

I stepped outside, determining which key was for the mobile home. Hearing a noise, I froze. It was a semitruck, downshifting on the highway. I took the key off the ring. Tossed the others inside. "Push him off the couch," I yelled.

"What?"

I bent my head to see inside. "Onto that rug." I pointed. "So we can drag him over here."

"Right," she said, toppling the body onto the rug. "Staging the place."

I moved closer to Shooter and unplugged Freddie's cell phone. Pocketed it. Then we dragged his body over until he nearly blocked the door. Stepping over him, I opened a liquor cabinet that I'd seen when we first got there. Found two bottles of Everclear. Dumped the 189-proof grain alcohol all over his body.

Shooter took a picture of Freddie. Spun in a circle and captured a few more shots with her phone.

I checked the time again. 4:09 a.m. Still quiet somehow.

"Should we . . . say something?" she asked.

I looked up. "About what?"

"A prayer, Gardner." Then a beat while I squinted. "For Freddie."

"Oh," I said. "Quickly."

Shooter looked down, wiping her bloody gloves on her pants. "You lived life fast, Freddie," she said. "You deserved . . . slightly better than this. But not much."

"Good," I said. "Honest. Heartfelt. Let's go."

Shooter stepped outside, and I turned on all the burners to the stove. I lit the pizza boxes and the threadbare couch on fire with a lighter.

I watched as the flames leapt two feet into the air, then closed the mobile home door, careful to catch the locking mechanism that I'd been manipulating. Taking Freddie's front door key, I snapped it off, breaking it in the lock. When I tried the knob, it wouldn't open.

We headed out fast, scrambling up the hillside toward the car. When we got to the hedge, I heard a boom and turned.

A TV antenna on the roof of the mobile home had fallen into the scrub brush at the rear of the property. A plume of gas escaped through an exhaust hole in the top of the home, and the blue vapor lit an orange flame that danced across the roof of the structure.

"We had this informant back at ATF," Shooter said. "He got pneumonia and died. Seven agents attended his funeral, Gardner. Three were pallbearers."

I made eye contact with her, and the message was clear. Burning up a C.I. might be considered over the line. But with Sandoval close, we had no choice. Right?

CHAPTER TWO

AS WE HEADED THROUGH THE TREE LINE TOWARD OUR car, a set of lights shone on the curving state highway in the distance.

They were squared off and wide, like a pickup truck, and I stepped back into the greenery and placed a hand on Shooter's shoulder to hold her still.

A rusted F-150 flew past us, and we emerged from the bushes a few feet from our 2019 Ford Taurus. I placed the containers I'd left in the dirt into the trunk.

As I closed it, another set of lights flickered in the distance. They were rounded, like a sedan. A second set followed close behind. When the first car took the turn at the hilltop, it did so at high speed. The second sedan turned after it, a thirty-foot following distance.

Shit.

Shooter was turned away from me, staring back at the mobile home, as the flames climbed into the sky.

"Down," I yelled.

We dove to the ground, our faces in the dirt, our bodies buried in the leaves that covered the forest floor.

"If this is poison ivy . . ." Shooter mumbled before going quiet.

On the highway, the two sedans zipped by us. *Ffft. Ffft.*

The sound of their engines faded, neither of them slowing to look over at our Taurus, which was parked off the shoulder, obscured by the same greenery we were hiding in.

Shooter stood up then, and we crept back toward the tree line. The live oaks and mahogany provided cover, and we watched the first sedan pull in outside of Freddie's mobile home. Then the second.

The door to the first car opened, and two men got out. One of them hustled over to the mobile home and grabbed the door handle. He yanked his hand away, as if the metal had burned him. The next man wrapped his jacket around his palm and tried it, but the door didn't budge.

"Freddie!" they hollered.

Shooter and I stared, transfixed, as the flames inside the mobile home filled the two windows.

"You're gonna have to answer for this," she mumbled. "You know that, right?"

My eyes moved from the fire to her.

Lately, I have experimented with being positive in the face of uncertainty. With saying an untruth, purely as a leadership gesture.

"We'll find another C.I.," I said. "I'm sure of it."

A noise sounded then. First a pop. And then something that sounded like a sonic boom. The gas pipe must have ignited inside, because the fire shattered the mobile home's windows and sent the two men onto their backs. The men from the second car got out and ran over. Pulled their buddies away from the burning structure.

I dialed 9-1-1 on one of Richie's burners and called in the fire. Then I took the SIM card out and broke it in half, scattering the pieces among the greenery.

CHAPTER THREE

"YOU INCINERATED THE BODY OF A C.I.?" CRAIG POULTON asked, his voice spiking.

I was seated across from the director of the FBI in his office on Pennsylvania Avenue, between Ninth and Tenth. I had grabbed the first flight out of Miami. Showed up in D.C. without an appointment and waited an hour and eight minutes to get time with the boss.

"Our C.I. was already dead," I said. "Nothing was going to change that."

"So we burn them now?" Poulton asked.

Craig Poulton is fifty-four. He is six foot two with a muscular frame and dark hair spiked up with product. At its apex, his hair gel had crystallized into two yellowish peaks, exactly nine millimeters high.

Fifteen months earlier, I'd watched Poulton outplay and then succeed William Banning, the industry veteran who had run the FBI for over a decade.

At the time, I became one of Poulton's direct reports, a move that offered me a front-row view of the new Bureau director—a man who balanced average intelligence with extraordinary political skill and a keen understanding of pressure points and leverage.

"We were sixteen minutes and ten seconds from having a case blown," I said. "One we'd worked on for three months."

Poulton leaned back in his chair. "Why not take the body with you? Sounds like everything else from that mobile home ended up in your car."

"There were corrupt local cops," I said.

"You know that for a fact?"

"We've identified two men. Bryant and Lyle."

Poulton had craggy features: a sharp jawline and a hook nose. When he cocked his head, small pockmarks on his cheeks took on shadows.

"Why hasn't Justice stepped in with the locals?" he asked. "Had them arrested?"

"We haven't yet determined the extent of who's dirty and who's clean."

"So if locals opened the mobile home and didn't find a body or the debit cards—" Poulton paused for me to finish his thought.

"The dirty cops would assume Pecos had turned," I said. "Or run. They'd tell Sandoval. Who might get spooked."

"But if they found him locked inside"—Poulton nodded—"his body and gunshot wound burned beyond recognition—"

"One of their own," I said, "lost in a tragic accident."

Poulton sat back, considering this.

His right eye was two millimeters larger than his left. Was he aware of this?

"And you grabbed the debit cards?"

"Nine hundred and eighty-one thousand worth," I said. "I dumped the last two cartons in the bedroom. Created enough melted plastic for the dirty cops to report back to Sandoval. They'll figure *all* the cards got burned."

Poulton stared past me, his teeth biting his lower lip. He had a toy on his desk, a Newton's cradle, with five small stainless-steel balls hanging from thin wire. He took a pencil and tapped the side of it, and the balls began clicking against each other in perpetual motion.

"You know, Camden," he said, "after 9/11, we had to look differently at how we leverage informants. They're a lifeline to our best intelligence."

I stared past the shiny balls at Poulton, thinking about Shooter's story of the dead ATF informant. The agents who served as pallbearers.

"Freddie Pecos was convicted of burglary," I said. "A pending assault wrap. He served six years at Polk for—"

"Some case agents," Poulton interrupted, as if I hadn't spoken, "they see C.I.s as an extension of their own team."

"Not me," I said. "And not you."

Poulton glanced up, his mouth turning into a smirk. "Oh, you know my feelings on the subject?"

"Freddie Pecos had a habit of beating his girlfriend with a wet towel," I said. "I put this in my report when I proposed working with him twenty-nine days ago. You signed that report seven minutes after I emailed it over."

Poulton held my gaze but said nothing.

"So I doubt you feel like Pecos was a member of PAR," I continued.

The balls kept clicking, and the repetition felt calming. Did others become agitated from the sound?

"You're right," he said. "I *don't* care about Pecos. But you didn't fly all the way to D.C. to tell me this. Surely you and your band of brilliant fr—"

He caught himself, but I knew the end of this sentence. Poulton had called PAR "a bunch of brilliant freaks" a year ago in this same office, back when he was deputy director.

"Surely you and your brilliant *friends* at PAR know how to deal with an operation gone wrong."

"We do," I said.

"So our conversation this morning has been what so far?" Poulton asked. "An appetizer? A test?"

I stared at the director. "This investigation began when money was skimmed from the State of Florida," I said. "That money was used to purchase weapons for a militia group. Legal gun purchases, but from an illegal source of income."

"Check," he said.

"It was our C.I.'s job to track those weapons for us. Where they were being held. When and where they were being shipped."

"And now you've lost both those things," Poulton said. "Is that it? You have no C.I. And no leads on where the weapons are?"

His statement was true, but it wasn't where I was going with Poulton.

"The day before Pecos went quiet," I said, "he and Richie Brancato had an exchange. They discussed two new pieces of intelligence."

"Okay?"

"A hundred and eighty-six guns were loaded onto a truck. Shipped somewhere."

"Where?"

"We never found out."

"And the second thing?"

"Pecos was in a room with J. P. Sandoval," I said. "He saw an invoice for two thousand firearm kits. Pre-built striker-fired pistols."

The director's eyes had wandered to his laptop, but now he met my gaze.

The gun industry had been surging in the last three years, with five major weapons manufacturers selling more than 70 percent of the guns on the market. And as much as the federal government didn't love monopolies, some had their advantages. Having direct liaisons at these five companies offered law enforcement the ability to quickly track weapons after mass shootings. Even if that action was in the rearview mirror, after the bodies had piled up.

This wasn't true, however, of what were referred to as PMFs, or privately made firearms. What the media called "ghost guns."

Those weapons? We tracked less than 1 percent of them. Which made them guns of unknown origin: silent killers.

"An invoice for two thousand ghost guns?" Poulton asked. "From a manufacturer?"

"Yes." I nodded.

"Which one?"

"We never found out," I said. "But Richie heard they could turn the order in a week. A single requisition of that quantity . . . it could only be fulfilled that quickly by certain sized companies."

Poulton sat back, considering the credibility of what he was hearing in the same way that I had when Richie first told me.

In the last few years, the laws concerning firearm parts had shifted. At stake was the definition of what was considered a gun, versus a gun part. Was a frame or receiver that was 80 percent pre-built a gun? Or simply a gun part? If there were no holes drilled yet for the trigger or hammer pin but instructions online directed a buyer how to do it, was that a gun?

The ATF said yes. To them, it was a way to corner bad actors in the industry. To force rogue part manufacturers into the light as *gunmakers*.

And if you were a gunmaker, there were rules to follow. Serial numbers to be placed on weapons. Background checks to be run on anyone buying your PMFs.

Since the law had changed, the ATF had already raided smaller part-makers. But the idea that a major weapons manufacturer might be in on the production of these kits was a bombshell.

That these silent killers were being made for a domestic militia group? That would convene Congress.

"Two thousand buy-build-shoot kits?" Poulton leaned forward. "Made by one of the big five? Why didn't this find its way into your report?"

"We don't know if it *is* one of the big five," I said. "And it would have been in my report. This week. But we never heard back from Freddie."

Then I repeated the line that Freddie had heard Sandoval use:

Kill a cop. Drop the gun. And walk away.

"Jesus," Poulton said. "We have to bring in ATF. Tell them about this."

"That's a bad idea."

Poulton pursed his lips. "Well, I'm full of them." He glared at me. "Why?"

I explained that the Bureau of Alcohol, Tobacco, Firearms, and Explosives was too close to these manufacturers. "We have no idea yet which gun company it is," I said. "Or if it is, in fact, one of the big five. If someone tips them off now, we'll have nothing."

"Let me get this straight," Poulton said. "You were following a shipment of guns, but you lost track of them. Then you heard something shocking only your C.I. could verify, but you lost track of *him*.

And when you finally found the guy, you burned up his body and any evidence in his trailer?"

The summary was accurate, so I nodded. "Yes."

"So next week, we could be dealing with a shooting at some elementary school? Innocent kids dead. And the shooter might have used one of the unmarked guns your informant was tracking?"

"Yes."

"And we'll have nothing on where it came from? No serial number? No seller? Just a bunch of dead kids?"

I swallowed, not answering this time.

"Camden," he said. "Do you have *any* leads on a new C.I.?"

"The team is working on it."

Poulton sat back, his frustration unmasked. "Forty-eight hours," he said. "Find a new C.I.—I don't care how. And get me an answer on these ghost guns."

"And if we can't?" I asked.

"Then I guess PAR is not as valuable as you and I think."

CHAPTER FOUR

BY THE TIME I BOARDED MY FLIGHT BACK TO MIAMI, I KNEW
it would be too late to assemble the team in Hambis, where we'd been
working. So I messaged them to meet me at 4:30 that afternoon at what
had become my new home in the last twenty days: the Rio Rio Hotel.

Fifteen months ago, the Bureau paid for me to relocate to Miami,
where my daughter, Camila, had been living with her grandmother,
my former mother-in-law. I rented a two-bedroom condo, and
Camila moved in with me. That was just before her eighth birthday,
and it was the first time my daughter and I had lived together since
her mother had gone away.

Together, we made a home of the place. Camila put up her drawings. We got permission to paint the condo in bright colors that reminded her of her Grandma Rosa's house. And Rosa and I worked
out a system. Monday through Wednesday, I would pick up Camila
from school. Thursday and Friday, Rosa would. Rosa even agreed
to stay the night in the condo whenever I traveled. She had just one
request: that when she was there, I was not.

Then, three weeks ago, a leak sprouted in the ceiling above the kitchen. The owner brought in a plumber, who chased the pipe into the next room over, cutting a large hole in the wall. A week later, the owner moved us into the Rio Rio, a Miami art deco hotel that for some reason is named after the word *river* in Spanish. Twice.

I walked into the hotel lobby at 4:21 p.m. and approached the front desk, a curving waterfall-style counter, where Alberto, the day manager, stood. Today, he wore a zebra-striped shirt and black leather pants.

"Your messages, Mr. Gardner," Alberto said.

Camila spent her afternoons creating art and puzzles and leaving them with Alberto. It was our custom that I solve these before going upstairs to our suite on the third floor.

I took the pile of construction paper to one of twelve shiny high-tops, where, in the morning, continental breakfast was served. Camila's first note was on green paper with red writing in marker. "Give me a drink, and I'll die," it read. "Feed me, and I'll get larger. What am I?"

I smiled gently.

My mother and I used to play games like this.

I clicked my pen. Wrote the word *fire*.

The next one had a maze on it, and I drew my way through the small, uneven channels that Camila had made. At the end, it read. "Who ♥s Dad?" with six spots for letters.

I wrote, "C-A-M-I-L-A."

The last one was an ornately folded piece of paper—what was called a *cootie-catcher* when I was young. I put my fingers into the folds and moved them back and forth, seeing that the words in each area formed a request: "Put a riddle here."

I clicked my pen again and wrote a puzzle for Camila to solve. *What question can you never answer yes to?*

I folded up the papers and took the elevator to 3. Rosa had texted five minutes before I arrived, and I'd told her she could go.

At room 312, I tapped out our special knock on the door. "Camila?"

My daughter opened up. She wore a purple shirt and denim overalls that stopped above her knees.

"Permission to pass," I said, and she grabbed the papers.

Camila has long brown hair like her mother, Anna. Her complexion is a mix of my lighter skin and her mother's olive color. Over the last year, brown freckles have formed on her cheeks.

"Correct," she said, dropping the green paper with the riddle on it onto the carpet as she walked. "Correct again," she repeated, looking at the maze while she followed me into my room in the two-bedroom suite.

"I'm meeting the team downstairs," I said. "I'm just here for a minute."

Camila dove onto my bed, which this morning had been made with a perfect hospital tuck.

"Can I come to the meeting?" she asked.

I looked at my daughter through the mirror. The last year had been so different from the years before—when I'd felt more like a visitor, coming on the weekends to Rosa's—rather than her dad. But now Camila and I were a team. "Us against the world," she'd say. And I would smile without forcing my lips to turn. I'd feel something. Real emotion.

"Sorry, hon," I said.

She rolled onto her back, the cootie-catcher in her hand. "Why not?"

"Case meeting."

"Interesting case or boring case?" she said, studying the riddle I'd left for her.

I thought of how the meeting with Craig Poulton had ended. The threat of anonymous, untraceable guns on the street. *What if Camila's school was the one that got shot up?*

"Irrelevant," I said, knowing Camila could not attend.

"Will there be discussions of murder and intrigue?"

Camila had learned to speak early and was currently reading three grade levels above her age.

"No intrigue," I lied. "Just office politics."

"Bo-ring," she complained.

I took a wet towel and wiped at my face. My blue eyes were blood-shot from being up half the night, then catching the first flight to D.C. "I'll be back in an hour."

Camila held up the paper with the riddle. "I don't know this."

"That's the point," I said, kissing her forehead. "And no googling."

She turned and headed out to the living room. "I'm setting my timer," she hollered. "One hour. A second more, and you're grounded."

As I passed her, she was grinning. "Smile," she said. "It was a joke. That's what people do."

I made a smile for her, then turned. Felt it fall.

When I got downstairs, Richie Brancato was seated at the same table where I'd unfolded Camila's riddles, a six-pack of Red Trolley in front of him, drops of condensation thick on the sides of the beer bottles. He was taking in something on his phone.

"What's new?" I said.

Richie ran his fingers through his dark hair, which was spiked up. He has a Mediterranean complexion, with angular cheekbones and thick eyebrows. "This lady's griefing me about a boat I took out two weekends ago with some friends. Says it's got a ding on the star-board side."

He saw my face and stopped. "Oh, you meant with the case."

I had. But I remembered a line my mother had repeated when I was growing up. *A full life is full of people, not facts, Gardy.*

"No. Go ahead," I said, remembering my resolution to make more small talk. "What happened with this boat?"

"Well, I didn't do shit to it," he said, putting his phone away. "But she says there's six hundred dollars' worth of damage."

Richie could pass for twenty-one, even though he was twenty-six. He'd joined PAR straight out of the Academy. It was a different path from the rest of us, who had all come from some dead-end assignment where we'd been exiled after making a mistake elsewhere at the FBI.

It was the dream of Frank Roberts, the man who started PAR, to build a small FBI team of experienced puzzle-solvers, not take on new agents fresh out of Quantico. But so far, Richie had proven he belonged.

"I was thinking of going down to the harbor," Richie said. "Flashing my badge at this lady."

"No," I said.

Richie ran his palm along his jawline. "Throwing some weight around?" he suggested.

"No," I repeated.

He squinted at me. "And just out of curiosity, why not?"

"Because two weeks ago Monday, you showed up in an Uber, not your Jeep. We met at the office, and you took four Tylenols. Two at 9:32 a.m. and another two at a noon lunch at the Chili Shack in Hambis."

"So?"

"So odds are you were hungover," I said. "It's likely that your friends, who statistically are probably less successful than you,

dinged up the boat—that is, if you didn't do it yourself and can't recall because of intoxication. Either way, if your name is on the rental
agreement, you're liable."

The automatic front doors slid open then, and in came Shooter.
She was back in her work uniform: faded blue jeans and a white
sweatshirt with no logos on it, her strawberry-blond hair loose at
her shoulders.

"I thought this was a work meeting," she said, grabbing a longneck from Richie. "We getting drunk?"

Richie slid the six-pack toward her. "Take 'em all," he said. His
eyes moved defensively to mine. "I no longer feel like drinking."

I walked over to Alberto at the front desk and borrowed the key
to the business office.

As I did, Cassie arrived. She is the fourth member of our team,
and was, until last year, my partner on PAR. She was dressed in a
black pencil skirt and a white blouse that contrasted with her dark
skin.

I considered the events of the last seventy-two hours. How we'd
lost track of a quarter-million-dollar gun shipment. Then found our
C.I. dead, but not at the hands of the people most likely to kill him.

"C'mon." I motioned to the team. "Let's talk in private."

We held any conversation until we were assembled in the hotel's
business office and I'd closed the door. Along the north wall was an
overstuffed couch and a marble coffee counter. Cassie sat on a bar-
stool near the cappuccino machine and fired it up.

"Gardner," she said, swiping her dark hair out of her eyes. "You
look crashy. How 'bout some liquid ingenuity?"

I made eye contact with her and nodded. Then glanced at the rest
of the group. The problem on our hands was difficult to solve, but
easy to understand. There were two shipments of guns. One we had

lost track of: we had to make sure those didn't end up in the wrong hands. The other, which was still on order, was even more dangerous: unmarked weapons for the express purpose of killing cops.

Say something positive.

"What's the latest on Pecos?" I asked.

"We're starting to build a timeline," Richie said.

We didn't have time for a timeline.

"And?"

"The first few days," Cassie said. "Meaning seventy-two hours out from his death . . . Freddie went off."

Cassie Pardo is only five foot three but is a dynamo of energy. She also uses the slang of a twenty-year-old. "Out all night Thursday and Friday," she said. "Saturday, a dayger."

A *dayger*, I'd previously found out, was slang for a daytime rager.

"He partied?"

"We got him in two places in Hambis," Shooter said. "Bought rounds for the house with fresh cash."

"ATM cash," Cassie clarified. "But no answers so far on who killed him. Richie's focusing on his last twenty-four hours."

"What about a new C.I.?" I looked at Cassie. "You emailed two hours ago. Said you wanted to talk through something live?"

"I do," she said, looking around and smiling. "*We* do," she clarified. "And we think it slays."

Slay is big with Cassie. Sometimes she uses it as a noun. Or a verb. Even a direct address. She has texted me the words, *Hey, Slay.* Which, as the most statistically productive agent in the Miami office, I accept as a compliment and respond to.

"Let's hear it," I said.

"Travis Wells." Cassie hit the button to stop the cappuccino machine from pouring. "He's one of Sandoval's guys. Travels back and forth from Florida to Georgia. He's also a two-striker, Gardner. Under Florida's 10-20-Life Law, his next pull is life in prison."

"So how do we turn him?" I asked.

"That's the thing," Richie jumped in. "We've got nothing on Wells. From what we understand, he doesn't transport weapons or cash, either."

Cassie took a carafe of milk from a mini-fridge and placed the steam wand into it.

"He just drives from Georgia to Florida," Shooter said. "Checks in on the operation for Sandoval."

"I'm not following," I said.

"Travis has a cousin named Matt." Cassie pulled the wand from the milk, poured the thickened cream atop the coffee, and placed it in front of me. "He lives in Portolare, four miles from the hotel where we've been staying in Hambis. The two of them get shit-faced twice a month when Travis is down here. Like CEO of the bar, you know? Total throwdown. Richie witnessed it two weeks ago."

I glanced at Richie, who nodded.

"Then Travis drives drunk to Matt's place a few miles away and crashes," Shooter said. "Next morning, he makes the trek back to Macon."

"We're gonna tip a local cop," Richie said. "Get Travis pulled over for driving drunk."

I nodded, but something was wrong. "Guys," I said. "A DUI isn't considered a third strike."

Shooter pointed with her longneck. "Now that depends on where you live, boss."

Cassie sat down across from me and took a sip of the cappuccino she'd just made. Slid it back in my direction. Around her eyes, her makeup was done in a way that Camila once called "smoky cat eye." She told me it was for when women have a hot date.

"There's a DA in Farner County, Gardner," Cassie said. "He's making a name for himself by prosecuting DUIs as third strikes. He's got two that have stuck."

I sat back, understanding their plan now.

"You want to take advantage of a particular jurisdiction where this district attorney is handing out life sentences," I said.

"Now we're tracking," Cassie said, pointing at me.

"And when the DA pushes for life, we swoop in and take Travis Wells off his hands? Make him our C.I.?"

They all nodded.

"What's the DA get?" I asked.

Shooter flipped over her cell and took a bank card from a flap at the back of her phone case. Held it up. "A million-dollar fraud case." She smiled. "Poulton won't care if we trade it away, right? As long as we close the gun investigation?"

I thought of Poulton's tone in D.C. and the threat of guns showing up at some school.

"You have a sting worked out?" I asked.

"We've got some beige to iron out still," Cassie said. "Then we'll get the paperwork to Justice."

Beige was Cassie's expression for "details." Boring stuff.

"So whadaya think," she said, "are we green-lit?"

I stared at the team, landing on Cassie Pardo. By trade, she is a mathematician. More specifically, she is an expert at what are called imaginary and unknowable numbers. But this specialty has an odd extension within PAR. She is often tasked with finding creative solutions to impossible situations. Like finding a second C.I. in forty-eight hours, three months into a case.

"How do we know Travis Wells is still in town?" I asked.

"That part's a little ironical," Shooter said, purposely messing up her grammar. "We started researching him. Pulled his credit and noticed something. Travis spent the night in the local ER. He had burns on his hand. Temporary loss of hearing."

I turned to Jo, surprised. "*He* was one of the guys who got blown backwards from the trailer?"

"It's the universe." Shooter smiled. "Giving us a sign."

I looked at the team. The calculus on this seemed simple.

No C.I. . . . no information on Sandoval's operation.

No information on the operation . . . no leads on the missing guns.

"Consider yourselves green-lit," I said.

CHAPTER FIVE

ON TUESDAY AT 2:38 P.M., WE CHECKED OUT A CHEVY Express van from Tech. It came with an operator named Vincent, a New Yorker who had transferred to the Miami office ten months earlier.

We still didn't know how someone had come upon Freddie Pecos and why whoever killed him had left two weapons and a million dollars' worth of debit cards inside his mobile home. So we left Richie at the office, looking into those crucial twenty-four hours before Freddie's death.

The rest of us hit the road with one goal: to enlist Travis Wells as our new C.I.

Vincent, our tech, was a thick white guy—five foot six with long, brown sideburns and a black T-shirt under a white polo. His skin was pale, almost bloodless. As we got in the van, he pointed toward a swiveling captain's chair in the back.

"Grab some wood right there, Agent Camden," he said, his accent thick on the word *there*. "That's the primo seat in the house, and you're the boss, am I right?"

"You are right," I said.

I told Vincent we needed to move, and he nodded.

"Just gotta put on my lucky surveillance hat," he said, grabbing a Yankees baseball cap from the glove box. "Nothin' ever goes wrong with this bad boy on."

We drove diagonally out of the Pembroke Pines area to Farner County, an hour northwest. The sky was pale blue, and all around the highway were marshes that looked like mile-wide prairies, with osprey and snail kite perched on branches that protruded above the sawgrass.

Shooter sat up front with Vincent. "How long you been in the undercover game?" she asked.

"Oh, I'm just the tech guy, Agent Harris," he said. "I don't do undercover."

"But we're headed to a bar," Shooter said. "When we get there, you're gonna go inside, right? Set the cameras up?"

Cassie flicked through pictures of the bar's Instagram on her phone, and I looked over her shoulder, half listening as Shooter tried to get Vincent to tell her stories about his best undercover work.

"I'm known for my discretion," Shooter said, and Cassie snorted.

We passed a grove of weeping banyan, their husky aerial roots dropping down from the branches overhead and forming thick trunks of wood that plunged into wide swaths of standing water.

Turning farther west, we drove inland through farm country. Along the highway, giant poles strung electrical wire from a series of towers, the larger ones on my left turning to parts unknown, where residents use boats to get around, more than cars. I opened my laptop and finished a report for Poulton.

A moment later, Cassie nudged me as a structure came into view.

The Rotten Coconut was a one-story bar with a wavy metal

overhang that jutted six feet out from the top of the building and was painted teal. Mounted atop the metal was the bar's name in yellow, flanked by a pair of circular objects painted a cream color to look like coconuts. Through the two large windows, neon signs advertised Budweiser and Miller Lite.

Vincent brought the van to a stop in the parking lot and turned to Shooter.

"You wanna come with?" He motioned at the bar. "If I have to do it myself, it's gonna take longer, 'cause I gotta order a drink. Wander around. Act like I'm going to the bathroom."

Shooter looked at me.

"These are pin cameras you're placing?" I asked.

"Not more than an inch wide," he said. "Built-in networking equipment. State of the art. Primo stuff."

I nodded at Shooter, and Vincent leaned over the bank of seven-inch monitors that faced Cassie and me. He turned on three of the four screens, which all showed static.

"Those'll be up quick," he said and turned back to Shooter. "If you can talk up the bartender, I'll wander around. Quietly place the cameras."

They got out and walked over to the front porch. Moved inside.

The FBI has long engaged in undercover operations, and the techniques are considered standard in detecting and prosecuting all sorts of activity, from terrorism to public corruption, drugs, and organized crime.

Cassie turned to me. "You got plans this weekend?"

"Camila has a science project," I said. "There's an event at the school on Friday."

"In other words," she said, "*you* have a science project to finish sometime this week?"

I noticed her smile and turned up the corners of my mouth in response. Today, Cassie wore black jeans and a white blouse that became sheer along the sleeves.

"It's a display," I said. "A series of homemade fly traps. Camila's been saving water bottles and cutting them in half. She takes the top and sticks it upside down into the bottom."

"I've seen those at my niece's school," Cassie said. "She's testing different types of bait?"

"Four," I said. "Molasses, maple syrup, and honey. Then there's a wild card. She's been rotting beef in the hotel room's mini-fridge."

"Eww." Cassie cringed. "Lucky you." She cocked her head then, smiling. "Need a math expert to help?"

"No," I said.

I realized right away that I had answered too quickly. But when I examined Cassie's face, she did not seem offended.

I studied her as she looked back at her phone. For years, Cassie and I were partners. And she was always a terrific teammate. Always willing to listen to my ideas or brainstorm. Day or night, I'd call, and she'd come by. But after the big case we closed fifteen months ago, she asked me a question at a retirement party. And it dawned on me that maybe she was more than a work friend. That a relationship might be had between us.

But that was the same week that Frank Roberts, our former team leader, left PAR: the week I became head of the group. Trying to navigate this was fraught with politics. And I fail at politics.

So as we rebooted in Miami, I partnered with Shooter and let Richie and Cassie work as a team. When Cassie asked me why I'd made the change, I told her that what Richie needed most was a teacher. Which was true. And that she was our best mentor. Which was also true.

But neither were the reason for the reorganization.

Did she understand the real reason? I don't know. We never spoke of it aloud. I never allowed myself to give anything between us a chance. I was the new Frank, after all.

The first monitor came to life. Video only. No sound. A fish-eye view from a pin camera that Vincent had stuck to a window. In the background, I could see Shooter flirting with the bartender on duty, while Vincent crossed the large open space, which at this hour was devoid of customers.

The second screen came to life, then a third. The second showed the main area of the bar, a collection of nine red leather booths. With the afternoon sun pouring in, the place looked white hot and worn down.

My eyes moved to the third monitor, where two pool tables were situated.

On screen one, Shooter high-fived the male bartender. A few minutes later, Vincent came out of the restroom, and she followed him out of the bar.

And that was it.

That would be the extent of our work inside the Rotten Coconut. From here, it was a waiting and watching game. Waiting for Travis Wells to show up with his cousin. Watching as they got drunk. Then tipping off a local cop to pull him over.

"Quick work," I said when Shooter and Vincent were back in the van.

Vincent got behind the wheel, and we picked up food from Jimmy Roo's, a local chicken place, before heading back to the bar.

"What do we know about Travis Wells's cousin?" I asked as Vincent drove.

"Matt?" Cassie said. "Thirty-three years old. Works construction. A drywaller."

"Criminal charges?" I asked.

"None," Shooter replied. "Unless consorting with his shitbag cousin counts."

Vincent pulled the van back into the lot at the Rotten Coconut, parking in a spot where we would go unnoticed. Sandwiches and chicken fingers were passed around. As I ate, I recalled other undercover operations I had done as a rookie. The feeling was familiar. Waiting. Waiting with seemingly nothing to do.

The sun went down, the bartenders changed shifts, and the parking lot lights came on. I texted Camila, who was with Rosa, to make sure she was doing her reading. A text came back fast.

> Done and done. Watching Soy Tu Duena with grandma.

A rerun of a telenovela Rosa had seen years ago.

I turned my attention to the screen farthest to my right. Vincent had stepped outside a few minutes earlier and set a pin camera on a fence post outside the bar. Now an image of the parking area filled the final monitor.

At 9:15 p.m., the 1983 Chevy Camaro that belonged to Travis Wells pulled into the lot, parking four spaces down from us. The car was white with a gray rocker panel. Two black stripes ran down from a vent that protruded from the hood.

We were set up in the back of the van, and Vincent had laid a reflective strip across the front window to create a dark cube of space inside.

"That's a classic shape, huh?" he said, motioning at Wells's

Camaro. "Chevy never strayed back then. Same car for decades, am I right?"

"You are wrong," I said, my eyes not moving off the screen. "In 1983, Chevy added a five-speed manual transmission as standard equipment on the Z28. Two years later, they added the IROC-Z package. They were constantly changing things, and they did well financially until '87."

Vincent turned to me. "You a car guy, Agent Camden?"

"No, he just knows everything," Shooter said. "It's a blast on long assignments."

Out of the Camaro's driver's-side door emerged Travis Wells, our target. He was six foot one with the broad, muscular shoulders of a tight end. He wore a long-sleeved flannel, and his hand was wrapped in a tan elastic medical bandage.

I looked at Wells. PAR needed this guy to work out. *I* needed him to work out.

And all he had to do was get drunk.

"Here we go," Cassie mumbled.

But her face changed when the passenger door opened.

"Wait," she said. "That's not his cousin Matt."

We crowded in close to the farthest monitor on the right. A man stood beside the Camaro. Thirties and heavyset, with a beard and dark, slicked-back hair.

"I've seen him." Shooter pointed.

"We all have," Cassie said. "His name is Daniel Horne."

I recalled this man. At first, we'd thought he was a soldier in Sandoval's gang, but when Richie had tailed him two weeks ago, he discovered that Sandoval used Daniel Horne as an errand boy. In his report, Richie had described Horne as "a bit slow."

The two men moved inside, and we followed them from camera

one at the bar to camera two in the large room, then on to camera three as they grabbed a booth by the pool tables.

"This changes nothing," Cassie said. "Travis gets drunk. Travis gets pulled over for a DUI."

A waitress appeared, and the men ordered. But when the drinks came, the one in front of Travis was in a tall iced tea glass.

"I thought these guys did shots all night?"

"Give 'em time," Shooter said. "They'll get doused."

For the next half hour, though, it was the same routine. The two men talking, traffic at the bar light. I squinted at the screen. For the third time, Travis stared over at the door.

"Not for nothin'," Vincent said, motioning at the monitor as Travis finished his second drink, "but I don't think that's a Jack and Coke." He tapped the screen with his finger. "Look at the color. I think it's a Coke. Straight up."

Cassie had taken the captain's chair, and she swiveled it in my direction.

"Ideas?" I said.

"Could be he's fresh out of the ER," she replied. "On meds and not drinking. If so? We come back tomorrow."

"If patterns hold, though," Shooter said, "tomorrow Travis Wells drives back to Georgia."

I sorted through other options in my head.

"We could go in," Shooter said. "Sluice the machine. Buy a few rounds for the bar. Not that many people in there."

"That could piss backwards on us," Cassie said. "If we get in a room with Travis Wells's attorney, and we're the ones who got him drunk?"

"How's your pool game these days?" I asked Shooter. I'd once watched her and our old boss Frank play nine ball for three hours at a bar in Jacksonville.

"I can play," she said.

"Cassie was looking at the bar on Instagram," I said. "They do a midnight tournament tonight."

Cassie opened the app on her phone again, and I asked her to page down.

"There," I said. "Zoom in."

She used her fingers to drag the post wider. And there was Travis Wells, along with a silver trophy on a pool table.

"You're thinking what?" Shooter asked. "We start playing? Look cute? The two boys wander over?"

I shrugged. "There'd have to be ground rules," I said. "You can't buy them a drink."

"Easy," Shooter replied.

"You can't *tell* them to drink."

"Still easy," Cassie said. "They're men. We'll just rebuff them."

I blinked.

"We say no." Shooter looked from me to Vincent. "Your gender doubles down."

I turned to the tech. "I'd need audio."

"Oh, my turn to talk?" Vincent smiled. "Sorry, this is fun." He looked around. "I mean, I could wire someone up, but . . . it wasn't in the package you requisitioned."

I narrowed my eyes at the tech. "We're sort of a specialty group, Vincent. You've heard of us, right?"

"Some things," he said.

"We're assigned cases that others can't solve. It requires a different way of thinking."

"I feel that," he said. "And I mean—I got ideas if you're open, Agent Camden. Good ones. They're just more legal-*ish* than legal."

"Like what?" Shooter asked.

"Like I could tap into your cell phone." He turned to her. "Use it as a listening device."

Shooter pulled her iPhone from her back pocket. "I got no objections. This is for Agent Camden to listen, not for court."

Vincent looked at me, and when I nodded, he pulled a backpack from under the passenger seat and removed a laptop. Plugged Shooter's phone into it.

A minute later, he unplugged it.

"Done," he said. "Your microphone is now my speaker."

Vincent attached a dongle to his laptop and connected the other end to the bank of screens in the van. "Say something."

"Something," Shooter said, and her voice warbled out of the speaker above the monitor.

I looked to her and Cassie. It was go time.

CHAPTER SIX

THE MAIN BAR AT THE ROTTEN COCONUT FEATURED A faux-thatched roof with shaggy palm fronds that hung down in irregular patterns. An attempt to reinforce a Key West theme, even though we were 320 miles from the vacation area.

On camera one, Cassie ordered two longnecks of beer and two shot glasses filled with something clear.

My eyes moved to Shooter, who slowed in the large room near camera two. I scanned the seven-inch color screen, counting nine four-tops. On the wall above a jukebox were two large inflatables, a coconut tree and an oversize duck with a female blow-up doll atop it.

Shooter passed in front of camera three and placed her purse in a booth next to Wells, leaving her phone strategically near the edge of the table. The pool tables were empty, and she grabbed a stick. Racked some balls.

"All right," I said.

But as I glanced at the four screens, something caught my eye. The camera that showed the parking lot. A black Escalade had pulled up outside the bar. A second identical SUV pulled in behind it.

And that's when I saw him. For the first time outside of a digital photo. The man at the heart of our investigation.

J. P. Sandoval was tall and athletic with wavy brown hair and a model's face. He was mid-forties but moved like a man ten years younger.

I pulled out my cell and called Cassie, but she didn't answer.

"Turn on that speaker, Vincent," I said. "That's our whale."

My eyes followed Sandoval and three burly men toward the front door of the Rotten Coconut. Then on to monitors number one and two.

Vincent tapped at the third screen, where Shooter stood, chalking a cue. "You're pulling them out, right?" He motioned, his voice rising an octave. "You guys aren't an undercover group."

"The speaker," I said.

Vincent switched on a button and adjusted the volume. The sound of Wells and Horne talking at the table came in clear, the din of rock music behind them.

But the men went quiet almost immediately, and we saw why. Sandoval was standing beside their table, his men flanking him.

"Gentlemen," he announced, sounding as casual as a man bumping into an old friend.

A female voice chirped, "Can I get you fellas something?"

Sandoval turned to a waitress, who stood between their booth and the one where Jo had placed her phone.

"Pack of smokes for me, darlin'," he said. "Marlboro Lights if you have 'em."

"And you three?" she asked Sandoval's men.

The trio shook their heads, and the waitress left. As she did, I caught a glimpse of Cassie and Shooter, taking in everything while warming up at the pool table.

I studied Sandoval. Not only was he in charge of the militia, he was profiting off it. He was the one exchanging the cash for guns, his weapons and ammunition businesses flourishing.

"Trav," Sandoval said. "You mind taking a break for a few minutes? I need to have a conversation with Daniel."

Travis Wells shot up, and we watched him move across monitor two. He saddled up to the bar on monitor one and waved his hand at the bartender, who set a shot in front of him.

Sandoval took Travis's place, his back against the booth where Shooter's phone sat. "How you doin', Daniel?" he asked, his accent Southern, but neutral.

"I'm okay," Horne said, the pattern of his speech slow and thick. "How are you, JP?"

"Me? I am *not* okay, Daniel," Sandoval said. "See, I lost some inventory recently. Not sure you heard?"

"Yeah," Horne said.

"One of my best men, too," Sandoval continued, his voice intense. "Then this morning, I get a call from my attorney telling me *you* got arrested. I start thinking—maybe I need to spend more time in South Florida."

Daniel Horne visibly swallowed.

"Am I to understand that you left a gun on the dash of your truck?" Sandoval asked. "At a Twistee Treat?"

Horne didn't answer the question. On the screen, we could see a three-quarter angle on Sandoval's face, but only a slice of Horne beyond him.

"My daughter *loves* the shakes at Twistee Treat," Sandoval said, his words almost a chuckle. "You like their shakes, Daniel?"

"They have good shakes, yeah."

"But here's the thing." Sandoval shook his head. "I cannot tell you a time I've been there when I did not see at least one cop car in the parking lot. And you had one of *my* guns? Up on your dash?"

"I told the lawyer at the bail hearing," Horne said, "it was an accident."

"Yeah, he passed that on, Daniel. But to me, it sounded more like a lapse in judgment. And it got me thinking—*Does Daniel* have *good judgment?* 'Cause you're privy to a lot of my operation."

The waitress returned with Sandoval's cigarettes, and he grabbed at the plastic strip to open them. But after a moment, he looked to Horne. "I tore the strip," he said. "You keep a knife on you, don't you, buddy?"

Horne reached into his back pocket and produced a switchblade, which Sandoval flicked open. He sliced at the Marlboro packaging and pulled a smoke from it. Lit up.

"The word you used with my attorney, though," Sandoval said. "*Accident.* That's more interesting than my word. See—*accident*, Daniel, that encompasses a lot of subcategories."

"Encompasses?" Horne said, his forehead furrowed in confusion.

"Includes," Sandoval clarified. "Car crashes . . . poisonings . . . ODs. There are age groups, Daniel, where accidents are the number one cause of death. Did you know that?"

Horne shook his head, and my phone buzzed. Richie calling. I silenced it.

Sandoval pressed the button, and the switchblade flew open. *Flick.*

"See, Daniel," he pointed with the knife, "I got my master's at Duke in interdisciplinary data science. I spent a lot of time getting to know uncertainty. Studied topics like risk tolerance and mitigation. Y'ever heard of those things?"

"I heard of Duke," Horne said. "Not that other stuff."

"There's an age, Daniel. This is awful, but . . . a toddler doesn't have enough strength in his neck. He drops a toy in a toilet and goes after it. Leans his head in. Drowns in there." Sandoval shrugged then, his voice becoming lighthearted. "But you know . . . it's just an accident, right?"

Horne said nothing, but his eyes moved to Sandoval's heavies, looming on each side of the table.

"Whatever I can do to make it up to you, Mr. Sandoval—"

Flick.

Out came the knife again.

"Well, I'm gonna think on that, Daniel. But maybe *you* got ideas. I could leave a few guys here to brainstorm with you?"

"Okay," Horne said, his voice turning optimistic.

Sandoval stood up then, and the waitress came by.

"You all right, hon?" she asked.

He held up his cell. "Business call, actually. No rest for the weary, right?"

He pressed a hundred-dollar bill into her hand, and I watched him walk off, passing across each screen. His movements were effortless, his gait that of a man floating. He reached the outside and got into one of the Escalades. Took off.

When I looked back, the booth was empty, the knife taken by Sandoval.

I turned to Vincent. "Where's Horne?"

"Bathroom, I think." He pointed. "Past the pool tables."

On camera four, the second Escalade pulled up to the red curb outside. I called Cassie's phone. "Cass," I said, "you see the bodyguards?"

"They split up."

She hesitated, and I watched her turn. Search the place.

"One's by the inflatables," she said.

I found the guy. Looked from screen to screen for the others. But the place was getting crowded, and it was hard to pick out individuals on camera.

On monitor one, Travis leaned over the bar. He lined up another shot. Threw it back.

"I'm tracking a guy to the exit," Cassie said. "I think the third just came out of the bathroom."

On the outside camera, one of the big men got in the second Escalade.

Horne, I thought. *Shit.*

"Get into that restroom," I said to Cassie.

I saw her move toward the corner of the screen, past the pool tables and out of my view. On screen four, another man got into the second Caddy, which took off.

"It's a men's restroom, Gardner," Cassie said, even though I couldn't see her on camera.

"Just go," I said. "And stay on the phone."

I heard her knock. Then the creak of a door hinge.

"There's someone in a stall," she said to me. Then louder, "Hello?"

There was silence, and another creaking sound.

"Oh my God."

"What is it?" I asked.

"He's sitting on the toilet, Gardner. Fully clothed. But . . . I took his pulse." She exhaled loudly. "Nothing."

"His head and shirt are soaked?"

"Yeah," she said, not having heard the audio that Vincent and I had. "Why is that?"

"Shit," I said. We had two agents and three cameras in the bar, and a man had been drowned in the toilet, right under our noses. I thought of what Poulton would think. Then I thought of what the director would do if *he* were here, trying to preserve an undercover op.

"Close the stall door," I said. "Put on your game face and grab Shooter."

"And Horne?"

"Leave him," I said. "Take the pin cameras with you and go. We're done for the night."

Cassie and Shooter settled their bill and made their way to the parking lot. I told Vincent to get up front, ready to leave. When everyone was in, we took off, heading toward the interstate.

A man had been killed on our watch, and the mood was quiet. Vincent drove without making small talk, and I had my laptop open but wasn't typing anything. Just thinking about J. P. Sandoval. He'd made sure the waitress knew he left, well before Horne would be found dead in the bathroom. And he'd disarmed Horne in advance of his men drowning him.

"What are you thinking about?" Cassie asked, her breath smelling of rum.

"I dunno." I motioned at my laptop. "I was gonna read up on Justin Seethers, the DA." This was the guy who'd been prosecuting DUIs as third strikes. I closed the lid of my computer. "No point now, I guess."

Vincent made his way through swamp country, and the shadows of giant cypress trees fell across the road.

At PAR, one of us usually came up with a solution. But right now, Shooter and Cassie were both quiet.

"The plan with Travis was sound," I said. "Until it wasn't."

"Travis," Shooter huffed from the passenger seat. "No wonder he wasn't drinking. He was the setup man. He brought Horne there to die."

I glanced at the time on my phone. Thirty-eight hours and ten minutes had passed since Poulton gave me a forty-eight-hour warning. And we had nothing.

"What a shit show," Shooter huffed, and I thought of what the director had said about PAR.

"The night wasn't a complete loss," I said.

"How's that?" Shooter asked.

"There is value in seeing your enemy up close," I said. "It helps you predict what he'll do next."

And I had seen something in Sandoval tonight. He was smart. Cool under pressure. And he discussed matters of life and death with unusual ease. When he'd turned to leave the bar, I'd caught a glimpse of him straight on.

Dead eyes.

He would sell out every one of his men to save himself.

But it didn't change the fact that we were almost out of time. And we had nothing.

CHAPTER SEVEN

BY 12:53 A.M., WE'D MADE OUR WAY BACK TO THE MIAMI office, the glass building with its diamond-shaped metal sunscreens a dark shadow against the night sky. Vincent pulled the van into the subterranean loading dock.

A slight figure was asleep in a folding chair by the back door, a sweater wrapped over his head. As the van turned off, Richie got up from the chair.

"Gardner," he said as I came out of the van's side door. "I called you like three times."

"I figured you'd gone home already," I said. "What is it?"

"I mean—like—maybe everything?" Richie's voice cracked. "Like possibly the break we've been waiting for."

PAR's youngest member tended to be overly enthusiastic, but after the night we'd had, I wasn't sharing his positivity. . . . I placed my bag on a worktable used by tech staff to unload equipment. "Start at the beginning."

"Sure," Richie said. "So I've been following Freddie Pecos's every move during the last twenty-four hours of his life, right?"

"Right," I said.

"I hit a wall. Decided to switch gears. I looked at the amount you seized in debit cards from the mobile home."

"The nine hundred and eighty-one thousand dollars?"

"To that, I added the amount of cards that you and Jo burned up in the mobile home fire. Guess what?"

"It didn't match with what you knew Freddie had on hand," I said.

Richie stared at me. "How did you know that?"

"Freddie was a criminal," I said, grabbing my bag. "He was skimming, Richie."

Cassie moved past us, up the concrete steps that led toward the bowels of the building. "A little for the Sandoval gang," she lilted, her voice singsong. "A little for me."

"But you don't know *where* he was skimming, do you?" Richie looked at us. "You don't know how?"

"Just tell us, rook," Shooter said, coming up behind Richie. We were all exhausted from the sting gone wrong and the drive back.

We moved in a group toward the elevator.

"Well. I knew Freddie pretty well," Richie said. "And he was lazy. I mean, real lazy."

Cassie slowed to listen. "Don't tell us he was skimming at the same ATMs he used to pull money out for Sandoval."

Richie nodded, smiling. "I took a field trip to his three favorite banks."

"You contacted the managers at Twenty-First Street, Forktree, and Seventh?" I asked.

These were the ATMs the gang preferred because the machines were older and the equipment in them suffered from ailments that befell all ATMs of that generation: color cameras that lacked dynamic range or failed to operate well in high or low light, resulting in back-lit silhouettes or overexposed images.

"I did," Richie said. "Checked out the security feed. And I watched Freddie make withdrawals, card by card. He turned to leave, but something happened. He started talking to some guy."

I had been building my mental to-do list for tomorrow, but now I stopped.

"What guy?" I said.

"Which ATM?" Cassie asked at the same time.

"Seventh Street," Richie said. "And I know what you're thinking. It's a solid neighborhood. No one should be around at 2:39 a.m. on a Sunday. Let alone Freddie and some other dude at the same time."

I slowed as we approached the elevator. "You have a picture?"

Richie had been carrying a manila folder, and now he pulled a photo from it. It was overexposed, but we could see Freddie in the center. A few feet away stood a slender man with a baseball hat pulled low over his forehead. Richie took a second photo from the folder, this one a close-up of the man in Freddie's peripheral.

"Not much to see," Richie said. "But it's no one I recognized from the Sandoval crew."

Cassie took the printout and scanned it. Handed it to Shooter.

"That's not the end of it," Richie said. "I rewound the tape. This mystery guy backs his sedan in. No plates on the rear. He pulls down the bill of his hat as he walks over. He purposely avoids any ATM cameras."

"What makes you think this is our big break?" I asked. The photo could be of anyone.

"This ATM, Gardner," Richie said. "It's one of two we placed an *extra* camera on for our debit card case. A secret camera on a pole in the parking lot."

He pulled another photo from the file. From the direction of this shot, we could make out more of the man's face. The night was dark, and the photo was black and white. But we could see that he was either white or a light-skinned Latino, with some sort of Band-Aid on his chin.

"I didn't recognize him, so I fed the picture into the system," Richie said.

"You got a match?" Cassie asked.

"Not at first," Richie said. "But Lanie in Quantico told me about this new beta software they're testing out. Combines facial recognition with AI."

The elevator doors opened, and we stepped inside.

"It matched," Richie said. "But not to any photo in the system. It matched a facial composite."

A facial composite wasn't a photo. It was a graphic representation based on multiple witnesses' descriptions of someone's face—essentially a combination of several sketches into near photographic form. It was usually developed by law enforcement to get an image out to the public. Which meant the composite was a person of interest in some other case.

"Where's mystery guy's close-up?" I asked. "If he was there to use the ATM, he should have his own photo from—"

"That's the other weird thing," Richie interrupted. "Once he spots Freddie, our mystery guy decides *not* to use the ATM."

That wasn't just weird. It was the behavior of someone avoiding being seen in a close-up. I stared at the grainy photo from the parking lot. Then at the composite and the ATM photo. In the upper-right-hand corner of the bank picture was the timestamp Richie had mentioned.

2:39 a.m. Sunday.

Shooter and I had arrived at 3:36 a.m. on Monday morning. When she'd performed her mini autopsy in the mobile home, she'd estimated Freddie had been dead for one day.

I looked at Richie. "Twenty-four hours before our arrival was 3:36 a.m. Sunday," I said. "That's less than an hour after this photo was taken."

"I know," Richie said, beaming. "I did good, right?"

The elevator doors opened, and we all stepped out.

Richie had indeed done well. The man at the ATM was likely the last person Freddie Pecos had seen alive.

I re-scanned the facial composite. Then the parking lot picture. There were subtle differences in the man's mouth and nose. But the two images looked similar.

"Who put the composite in the system?" Cassie asked. "Hambis police?"

"Nope." Richie smiled. "The Federal Bureau of Investigation." He waited a beat to see our reaction, then surprised us a second time. "The Jacksonville office."

We turned to each other. That was *our* old office, where PAR was started.

"You call them?" Cassie asked, raising an eyebrow.

"I did," Richie said. "And guess what? An agent told me that they asked for PAR's help on this case already." His eyes moved to mine. "You turned them down."

There is a process by which cases are sent to PAR. To put it simply, I knew every case that we had considered, turned down, or accepted. This one didn't sound familiar.

"So I guess we *all* did good tonight, huh?" Richie smiled.

"Speak for yourself," Shooter said. "Travis Wells was a bust."

Richie cocked his head. "I don't understand," he said. "We put his name in the system so the DA would call us."

"Yeah," Cassie said. "That guy won't be calling."

"He already did," Richie replied. "Five minutes before you guys got here."

I squinted at Richie, confused. "What do you mean?"

"Travis Wells left the bar drunk, and a cop in the parking lot saw him get into his Camaro," Richie said. "Pulled him over a block away."

I recalled Travis, up at the bar doing shots, probably trying to forget what was happening to his buddy on his watch.

"So whatever you guys did," Richie said, "we got our potential C.I."

CHAPTER EIGHT

TRAVIS WELLS HAD BEEN BOOKED AT 2:12 A.M. AND WAS currently sweating it out in a holding cell in Farner County.

But according to my early-morning phone conversation with DA Justin Seethers, we had to wait seventy-two hours to approach him. Only then would a reasonable defense attorney take the DA's claim of a third strike seriously.

"Three days?" I said to Seethers. "You can't make a deal sooner?"

"It's not like that," the DA said by phone, his accent ringing of a youth spent in Georgia or Alabama. "See, this approach to the law is fairly novel, Agent Camden. Far as I know, it's just me and one other fella prosecuting this way."

"So you charge these guys under Florida's 10-20-Life Law and get a big bail assigned. Is that right?"

"Yes, sir," he said.

"On day one in jail, they think you're bluffing about life in prison," I said. "But by day three—"

"I make a believer out of them," he finished my sentence.

After the call with the DA, I jumped in my car to head to the Miami airport. I texted Richie to grab his go bag and do the same. If we had three days before Travis Wells got out of jail, we had time to go to Jacksonville. We could check out the case on this mystery man—and possible killer—who'd interacted with Freddie Pecos at the ATM.

More than that, if we wanted to keep a second C.I. alive, it would help to have clarity on who had murdered our first one.

At the airport, I emailed Craig Poulton, carefully choosing my words to communicate that a new C.I. was on the horizon, but it would take time to lock him down.

Then Richie and I got on a last-minute flight. By 10:45 a.m., we had landed at the Jacksonville airport. We rented a Ford Edge and came down toward 95, the clouds bright white against a pale blue sky.

As we drove, Richie filled me in on the timeline he'd constructed for Freddie Pecos's final hours. He walked me through his process: how he'd painstakingly documented every pizza delivery receipt in Pecos's trash and examined every text our old C.I. had received and sent. All of this had helped him narrow down Pecos's time of death to a slot between 3 and 4 a.m. on Sunday, which confirmed Jo's initial estimate.

"How far was the ATM from Freddie's mobile home?" I asked.

"Fourteen miles," Richie said. "I estimated his ETA that time of night. To cross town and get there—twenty-seven minutes."

I bit at my lip. The time window between this unknown subject seeing Pecos at the ATM and Freddie's death was tight. Which made it more likely that he *was* Freddie's killer.

"You showed us pictures of this mystery guy," I said, "but I presume you looked at Freddie as well? Video of this moment?"

"At the ATM, you mean? Yeah, of course," Richie said. "I studied his eyes and facial expressions. He showed surprise, Gardner. But also familiarity."

"So Freddie knew him?"

"I believe so," Richie said.

"And your theory?"

As the newest member of PAR, this was part of Richie's training: Come up with a theory of the crime; be specific in details and resolute in his belief system—yet flexible enough to abandon it when new information arrived.

"Well," Richie said, popping a piece of gum in his mouth, "I figure that this unknown guy—maybe he and Freddie grabbed some beers. Agent Harris said there were two six-packs on the counter in the mobile home when you guys arrived. A bottle missing from each."

I switched lanes. After four years in Jacksonville, I drove unconsciously toward our old office, noting that the project expanding the freeway only appeared to be 11 percent further along than it had been fifteen months earlier. A giant swath of dirt stretched between the north and south sides of 295, with splotches of mud six feet wide covering the eight unmanned construction vehicles parked there.

"And?"

"They're drinking back at his trailer," Richie said. "They have beef, and a fight breaks out. This mystery guy grabs the rifle and shoots Freddie. But he doesn't know what Freddie was into with the debit cards. So he leaves them there. Takes the cash."

To my right, loomed the enormous freight loaders at Dames Point. We drove up and across the bridge, the harp-stay arrangement of cables rising 471 feet in the air.

Richie stopped speaking, and I waited to see if there was more.

There was not.

I took the exit off 295 to the Jacksonville office. If two criminals had beef with each other, and that's all that had happened between the ATM moment and Freddie's death at his trailer, we wouldn't be chasing this lead in Jacksonville for long. But it wouldn't be productive to tell Richie this. He was still learning, and he required encouragement and motivation.

"You've been a key part of a seven-figure fraud case," I said to Richie. "A two-month-long undercover operation."

"Yeah," he said. "I appreciate that."

"And we're willing to trade away all that intel—three months of work—to a local DA. Why?"

"Because we're after something bigger," Richie said, palms up, as if the answer was obvious. "Illegal guns. A militia group stockpiling semiautomatics."

"Exactly," I said. "That's domestic terror, Richie. That's more than a crime. It's a mission."

"Got it," he replied. But his face showed something else. Skepticism? Confusion? I could sense he was wondering why we'd come to Jacksonville at all, then.

"We look at patterns, Richie. Analyze what should exist and what shouldn't."

He nodded. "And sometimes what we *don't* understand is more important than what we do."

"Precisely," I said, tightening and loosening my fingers on the steering wheel. "So we look at statistics. Is there some estimable reason why a man who is wanted by the FBI in Jacksonville would be hours away in South Florida at this ATM?"

I passed a row of furniture stores and turned into the lot at our old office.

"I don't know." Richie shrugged.

"If this mystery guy is so dangerous, why did Freddie invite him back to his trailer? Why break out the beers and the Jack Daniel's?"

"Don't know that, either," he said.

I held up my ID for Anthony, a security guard I knew from my time at this office. He raised the gate to let us into the parking lot.

"We have three days before our new C.I. is up and running," I said, pulling into a space behind the building. "That's our time to look into whatever this connection is."

Richie nodded, and we got out.

As we walked down the curving path that bordered the back lawn, I pulled the composite sketch from my bag. "Back in 2019 when the FBI was called onto this case, who was the lead?"

"A guy named Ed Offerman," Richie said. "But he retired. I spoke to his old partner, Ray Chizek."

I nodded, and Richie cocked his head. "You know them?"

"Offerman I knew a little," I said. "Chizek, no."

Inside the building, we made our way to the third floor.

Ray Chizek was camped out in a conference room, next to a table piled with file boxes, each with their tops off, revealing thick manila folders with color-coded tabs on the sides. He was in his forties and five foot seven, with the thick, muscular body of a three-down running back.

Chizek looked up as I got to the doorway.

"If it ain't the special people who left us for the soft confines of Miami Beach." Below his bushy brown moustache, his lips curved into a smirk. "Gardner Camden, right?"

I had never met this man before, but Cassie once told me that everyone in the building knew who I was. I extended a hand, and we shook.

"Ray Chizek," he said. He turned to Richie. "You must be Brancato. You even look like a nepo baby."

I glanced at Richie, but he didn't blink at the comment, which referred to his grandfather, a man who had once run the FBI. I pointed at the file boxes. "I assume those are ours to go through?"

"Pfft." Chizek blew out a gust of air. "No, no, no. The case *you* called about—the missing women who turned up dead? There's not this much meat on the bone."

He waved for us to follow him. As we moved through a maze of cubes, I noted that Chizek favored his right leg as he walked.

We emerged by a windowless office. He grabbed a file, no more than an inch thick, off the desk. "This is it," he said, hiking up his dress pants with his free hand as he gave it to me.

I flipped through the file, seeing twelve pages of notes, along with DMV pictures and two typed witness interviews. In the case summary, I read the names of three women whose bodies had been found in a town west of here called Shilo.

The case notes were initialed by retired agent Ed Offerman. After them were photocopies of multiple sketches, each drawn in pencil and heavily shaded. Following the fourth drawing was the composite Richie had obtained, which we could now see was a combination of the previous drawings, put together by software.

"You mentioned this case had been sent to PAR for consideration," Richie said. "But Agent Camden doesn't recall that. And his memory is kinda . . . legendary."

I glanced from the file to Chizek.

"Yeah, my old partner knew Frank Roberts pretty well," Chizek said. "Every time he saw Frank in the elevator, he'd hit him up to take this thing on."

"Did Offerman ever make a *formal* request to PAR?" I asked.

"Formal?" Chizek said, blinking. "I mean, we were all coworkers, weren't we, Camden? One happy family?"

The attitude toward PAR in Jacksonville was not what I would characterize as happy. It was in this office that the moniker "head cases" had been invented. And it was one of the nicer things said about us.

I stared at Chizek until his face changed.

"All right," he said. "Ed was an A personality. He crossed swords with a lotta people and rarely did anything through . . . *official* channels."

We had wandered halfway back to the conference room while talking and were standing in a hallway. Twice now, I'd seen Chizek pause and tap at both pockets. I stared at the yellow marks on his teeth. He was a smoker, jonesing for a cigarette.

I glanced down at the notes again. There were two memos between the FBI and the city of Shilo, both dated after the women went missing, but before any bodies were found.

Why would the FBI even be on the investigation at that point, especially with the scant amount of information in this file?

"Was Offerman working this case off the clock?" I asked.

Chizek hesitated. "Ed never knew his birth mom." He shrugged. "About the time of this case, he did one of those genealogical research things." He stopped and looked around. Hiked up his pants again. Tapped his pockets. "He found out his mom was a pro."

"A sex worker?" I confirmed, using the correct term.

"Yeah," Chizek said. "And one of the gals missing in this case was a . . . sex worker. Ed sorta felt for her. Thought no one was going to look into the case if he didn't."

"Sounds like a good partner," Richie said, going for rapport. "You stay in touch?"

Chizek made a face. "Ed moved to some godforsaken part of Mexico called the East Cape." He flicked his eyebrows, addressing Richie more than me. "Lives *off the grid*. Water shipped in on a truck. Solar power. Not exactly easy to grab a beer."

"Is there an office we can sit in?" I asked. "Go through these notes?"

Chizek swiveled his head to me, annoyed at my interrupting his reverie about his old partner.

"You're welcome to use my office, Camden." He pointed back at the windowless room. "Or if you want to go back to your old floor, you could sit in the break room." Again, he flicked his eyes at me. "Some agent trashed the place a year or so ago. Punched holes in the walls. But it's been patched up since then."

I kept my eyes on Chizek, my reaction flat.

"Good news is," he kept up, "we sent those people away. Big office like Miami . . . you can be Special Olympics and go unnoticed, I figure."

CHAPTER NINE

CHIZEK'S PARTING SHOT ABOUT "THOSE PEOPLE" AND "Special Olympics" referred to PAR, and the agent who had trashed the office was me. But this was not the attitude of 90 percent of federal agents I'd worked with. So I ignored the dig and told him we'd be happy to use his office.

Richie and I made ourselves comfortable then. I sat down at Chizek's desk and removed the notes and sketches from the two-hole punch. I'd start reading at page 1, I told Richie, then pass the pages to him, so he could read them next.

He grabbed a cup of coffee while I began, moving through the details of what Offerman had documented.

On October 14, 2018, a Baptist preacher in Shilo, Florida, reported two women had gone missing. Their names were Maria Elisandro and Rana Delgado, and both were congregants at the Reverend Jerry Webber's First Church of the Almighty. Elisandro had been a sex worker, although according to Rev. Webber, she had left the profession and was working as a hostess at a family restaurant.

Rana Delgado, on the other hand, had worked two jobs, one as a cleaning woman, the other as a waitress at a roadside diner called Scottie's.

The police put out the appropriate BOLOs on the women, but nothing came of the cases. When a third woman disappeared three months later, the city of Shilo reached out to the FBI for a consultation. The case of the three missing women was assigned to Ed Offerman in the Jacksonville office, who made the seventy-minute drive to Shilo on January 22, 2019.

Offerman connected with Shilo detective Warner Quinones and examined what evidence there was on the missing women, but that was it. The Bureau could offer little more in the way of help at that time.

Seated in Chizek's office, I flipped to the next page of the file, leaving each sheet for Richie, who picked it up after me and read it.

Four months later, in May 2019, as construction workers dug for the Sandalwood Johnson Public Housing Project in Shilo, three bodies were found, each victim buried three feet from the next, in a perfect line.

The media dubbed the women "the Shilo County Three," and Offerman returned to town. The first two missing women, Elisandro and Delgado, were among the victims found, but the third body did not match the third missing woman. It was soon identified as Susan Jones, a woman who had managed a small hotel on the edge of Shilo and had no connection to sex work or either of the first two women.

Offerman tried to connect with friends and families of the victims, but Elisandro was known mostly by other sex workers, and Delgado was an immigrant with no family in the States. He also checked in with churchgoers, but the other congregants only knew the women to say hi or bye. Still, Offerman dug in, finding at least two people who knew each of the three women. And witnesses described a man who'd picked up Delgado and Elisandro for dates in the last week before they went missing.

My eyes moved to a typed Q and A, taken from an interview Offerman had conducted with a friend of Elisandro's, a woman who was also a sex worker.

Q: Maria was supposed to go on a date with this guy?

A: Yup.

Q: A date like I'm imagining?

A: I don't know what you're imagining.

Q: A real date?

A: Exactly. Like real people go on.

Q: You go on a lot of . . . real-people dates, Denise?

A: Not me, no. I ain't getting in someone's car without seeing some bills.

Q: But Maria Elisandro did?

A: Maria said this was different.

Q: Different how?

A: *Like someone nice. That's what I'm saying. A real date. Maria had moved on, you know?*

Q: *She wasn't a working girl anymore?*

A: *That's what I'm telling you.*

I stared at the interview, remembering a conversation I'd had with Frank back in 2019. Someone in the office had called Ed Offerman "straightforward." In response, I had asked Frank a simple question—"So he's like me?"

My boss shook his head. "You're straightforward, Gardner, for sure. And sometimes you say things you shouldn't. But Offerman? He's callous. There's a difference."

I scanned the notes I'd been writing, then flipped to an interview Offerman had conducted after the bodies were dug up. This one was with Mila Jones, the sister of Susan Jones, the dead hotel manager. In the transcript, Mila reported that a man had come into the hotel office twice that week to talk to her sister, a man that Mila believed was not a hotel guest.

When Offerman tried to obtain more information from long-term hotel residents, he got nothing except a vague description of a white or Hispanic man. Eventually he called on a local artist, who drew multiple pictures of the suspect, each based on the testimony of the few eyewitnesses who could be cajoled into talking.

I laid the last page of notes flat on the desk and splayed out the four sketches to my right.

The job of a forensic sketch artist is nothing like that of their counterpart inside a courtroom. A courtroom sketch artist has the benefit of staring at a witness as they testify. A forensic artist must elicit details from people's memories, pulling specifics from the worst day of a victim's life.

The sketches I was examining, however, were not drawn from the words of a victim but from third-party eyewitnesses: friends and family who saw this person of interest just one time but were not in jeopardy themselves.

"You're thinking of something," Richie said. "A question."

I glanced up. "I am," I said, cocking my head to encourage him to guess.

"How is this unknown male who's wanted for three murders in Shilo," he said, "connected to our dead C.I. down near Miami?"

"And?" I asked.

Richie put up both hands. "It's like my dad says about the check at a nice restaurant: If you want to know the amount of the bill, you gotta pay for the meal."

I smiled at Richie. It was nearly impossible to dislike him. He was too earnest. And I got his meaning: If we wanted to know more, we had to pause on Freddie and the guns and look into this.

"We're gonna investigate this case, right?" he said. "Whether it's small time compared to the ghost gun kits or not."

"We have two and a half days," I said.

"So we stay up here," Richie said. "Grind on this 'til that DA's ready?"

I nodded. "But when he is, Richie, you gotta understand that those guns take the A spot."

"Sure." He shrugged. "But this is connected to that. I'd put money on it."

My eyes returned to the sketches. I slid two of them apart from the others. "These men look alike," I said. "The other two are also similar to each other, but different from the first pair."

I looked at the far-right image, which was the composite by FBI software.

"You think a couple of these aren't accurate?" Richie pressed.

"People are unreliable," I said. "Memories even more so."

I opened my satchel and grabbed the photo of the man who had approached Freddie Pecos in the dark outside the ATM. Then glanced back at the sketches. I took the face in pieces, looking from mouth to mouth, then the bridges of each nose. Finally, at what little I could see of the eyes, given the man in the photograph wore a brimmed hat pulled low.

Portions of different sketches matched the man in the picture to a T, yet none of them matched him in total. The parts, oddly, were greater than the whole, rather than less than it. Taken in full, none of the sketches looked exactly like the parking lot photo.

"Maybe these are the same person," I said. "Maybe not. But something about the sketches is off."

At the bottom of each drawing was Ed Offerman's name, and below that, a signature that read "W. C. Walker." The sketch artist's name.

I glanced at the last page of the file, which was more of a catalog of names, detailing other women who had been reported missing after the news of the first two bodies had surfaced. The list was made by Offerman, but he referenced the local lead, Detective Quinones, who had detailed files on each missing person—available if the investigation showed promise in the future.

Looking back at the last paragraph on page 18, I reread the final sentence from Offerman, who noted that between mid-2018 and mid-2020, Shilo County had more missing women per capita than any other county in Florida.

Richie had been taking notes on his phone. Now he set it down on the desk. "So," he said, "next steps?"

Our potential new C.I. was sitting in jail for at least two days. After that, Director Poulton would not care about a cold case involving three dead women in North Florida. Not unless we could tie it directly to J. P. Sandoval and guns.

"Let's take a drive," I said, grabbing the notes and sketches and dropping them back onto the two-hole punch in the file.

I headed for the elevator, but Richie was moving in the other direction.

"Shouldn't we swing by and say goodbye to Agent Chizek?" he asked. "Thank him?"

"Thank him?" I turned to Richie. "For what?"

CHAPTER TEN

WE HEADED WEST ALONG 10 OUT OF JACKSONVILLE, BUT
quickly transitioned onto rural state highways 23 and 21.

The diversity of plant life and habitat in Florida's interior is like
few other places. I remembered canoeing through the swamps in this
area with my Uncle Gary, two weeks after my ninth birthday. The
surface of the water was the color of celery, the riverbanks crowded
with sweet gum and cypress trees. We emerged onto a sinkhole where
otters played and a group of eighteen Black women were holding a
baptism, their clothes as white as the inside of a coconut before they
entered the green water.

I looked over at Richie, who was studying the landscape out the
window. I rarely felt the need to fill an empty space, but intellectually,
I knew others appreciated it.

"You all right?" I asked.

He nodded, turning to me. "Where I grew up," he said, "inland
from San Diego? People don't think of it as farm country, but it is.
A lot of horses and crops. New subdivisions poppin' up all around
them."

"Did you grow up on a farm?" I asked.

"No," Richie said. "But my sister rode horses. We had a field behind our house with avocados and orange trees." He motioned around us. "Like Florida, California is a lot more rural than people think."

Richie and I were almost in Shilo when I veered off State Route 21. It was 12:08 p.m., and my gas tank was close to empty. I pulled into an Exxon that shared a parking lot with a Dollar General and a Tropical Smoothie Cafe. Richie got out, telling me he needed to use the head.

As I filled up, I stared at the storefronts on the opposite side of the street. One-with-God Church. Rent-2-Own Furniture! Pawn4Cash. I topped off the tank and put away the nozzle.

"What are you thinking about?" Richie asked, following my eyes across the road. He stood to my right, shoveling gum into his mouth from a paper bag.

"The odds," I said. "One shopping plaza with numerals in all three shop names."

Richie often chewed gum, but this time it was a baseball-themed brand for children, packaged in the kind of paper pouch I had not seen since my mother forced me to play Little League.

"And those numbers?" he asked.

"One-point-four percent," I said. "But the margin of error is higher than I prefer."

Richie stared at me, nodded, then got in the car.

Twenty minutes later, we were sitting with Detective Warner Quinones from Shilo Police Department. Quinones was five foot eight and stocky, a Latino with a five-o'clock shadow and wavy hair.

Per our plan, Richie and I held back talking to Quinones about the weapons case, which left the fraud investigation as the only context we'd shared.

"So you guys are here why?" he asked. "You wanna reopen an investigation into these murders?"

There was an edge to his voice, and I studied his office. Quinones used a wooden side table as his main desk, which created enough space for a seating area with an armchair. My eyes moved to his bookcase, which was not standard fare for cops. On his shelf, I saw the *DSM-5* and *Portrait of an Addict as a Young Man*. He was a thinking man's detective.

I turned back to him, surer now of my approach.

"We'd like to go through the missing women's files," I said. "Look at anything that didn't make its way into Agent Offerman's notes."

"Huh," Quinones said, a slow burn of surprise.

It was an unusual reaction from a local cop who had previously invited the FBI into his investigation. Technically, didn't we still have jurisdiction?

"Sounds like you wanna make sure my pesky little murders aren't messing up your fraud case," he said, sitting back and crossing his arms.

As it pertained to Craig Poulton's goals at the Bureau, Quinones was not far off. In the new director's FBI, local murders, even if they rose to the level of a serial, were usually best left with locals.

"I run a group called PAR," I said to the detective. "It stands for Patterns and Recognition. When cases are particularly puzzling and police departments or Bureau offices cannot solve them, we are sent those files. From all over the United States."

"Except you're not coming here for that reason, are you?" Quinones said. "My murders are long cold."

I thought of Frank in the elevator with Offerman years ago.

"True," I said. "But perhaps we should have come here a long time ago, instead of Ed Offerman."

Quinones pursed his lips. "You're a little different, aren't you?"

I hesitated. I don't particularly enjoy it when people point this out. But I don't get emotional about it, either. "Yes."

"And this PAR—it's full of people like you?"

"In a manner of speaking."

"Okay," he said, his attitude relaxing. "I don't mind that. So what do you need?"

Richie jumped in. "Copies of everything," he said. "Every missing person's report. Notes from every interview. Suspects you considered. Crime scene photos. All of it."

Quinones stood up. "Last time your people left, I knew it wasn't over. We had one of our admins make a clean copy of every paper. I have a box downstairs."

CHAPTER ELEVEN

RICHIE AND I SAT IN A SMALL CONFERENCE ROOM AT SHILO
Police Department, and I read every interview that Offerman and
Quinones had conducted. As Richie looked through a list of locals
brought in as suspects, I spread out a county map—a clean one I'd
requested from Detective Quinones.

I was marking points on it, using the file as a straight edge and
extending property lines. Noting public and private roads. Waterways and floodplains.

Quinones popped in his head. "Questions?"

"Do you have a couple shovels?" I asked.

"Not on me."

He smiled, but his face went serious as he stared at the twelve
circles I had drawn on the map, with lines in red running tangent
to them.

"I can ask facilities," he said.

When he came back ten minutes later, I had punched a set of
coordinates into my phone. "We need to go here," I said.

Quinones used his thumb and index finger to zoom in and out

so he could see the area better. "That's right on the border of us and Putnam County," he said. "Unless I'm wrong, all you're gonna find there is a pile of dirt, Agent Camden."

"Dirt is where I expect to start," I said. "That's why I wanted a shovel."

Quinones stared at me. "Can I ask how you arrived at those coordinates?"

"I began with the housing project where the three bodies were found," I said. "It had been purchased by a real estate investor, correct?"

"Yeah."

"And that purchase occurred in between the women going missing and the three bodies being found?"

"Why does that timing matter?" he asked.

"Before the sale, that land was on the border of two spaces," I said, "public and private. Neither of them was fenced off. Do you know what the company was doing the day they found the bodies?"

"Grading the land, I think," Quinones said.

"They were digging for a retaining wall," I corrected him. "To block off water that naturally overflows from the Sestes River."

Richie spoke up, his eyes on his phone where he took notes. "We looked at land with similar attributes, Detective. A floodplain. The edge of public and private land. And like the other parcel, up against the county line."

"You have a theory?" Quinones asked.

Richie looked to me, and I nodded for him to keep going.

"Someone is burying bodies in naturally fertile areas," he said, tapping at the map in front of me. "Areas that might have disputed jurisdiction."

"Half this county is naturally fertile," Quinones said, shaking his head.

"Not this much," I said. "Here, a body could be buried in just thirty inches of hard dirt and still rot quickly."

"And it'd be far enough down to not rise up," Richie added.

I tapped at the map. "This area gets drained multiple times a year from the Sestes River. If someone buried a woman there, the land would have heavy growth on the topsoil in under ninety days. It would provide quick cover."

Quinones pursed his lips and nodded, his eyes narrowing as if in thought.

"The bodies found last year," I said. "They were thirty-six inches apart, correct? Buried in a straight line."

"Yeah," he said. "What's that mean?"

"People familiar with planting patterns might naturally walk off that distance," I said. "Statistically, twenty-four and thirty-six inches apart are the most common recommended distances for planting vegetables."

"Vegetables." He snorted. "Right. That sounds important."

My affect was not so low that I didn't notice the sarcasm. But did I care? Not at all.

"You get the shovels?" I asked.

"Three," he said.

I gathered my things and placed the files and maps into my satchel. "Then let's go."

We piled into my SUV and headed fifteen minutes southeast. Quinones said little as I drove, and neither Richie nor I filled the silence.

As we traveled along a small state route, the Sestes River passed

under the road. We moved over a bridge and watched it flow back
the other way. Along the roadside, someone had constructed a barn-
like structure from shipping containers, cutting the sides off each
one and piling them atop each other. Under the giant structure, I
counted forty-three propane tanks.

The road turned, and islands of longleaf pine rose up. In the sliv-
ers of light that came through the trees, the river turned with the
road and away from it. The water was a pea-green color, and Richie
held my phone out, directing me. "There," he said, pointing down an
embankment off the state highway.

The trees pulled away from us, and I moved onto a gravel path
that took us five hundred feet down an incline. As I glanced over, my
phone directed us to the coordinates.

Nine hundred feet away.

Five hundred feet.

One hundred.

I turned off the ignition, and we got out, heading to the back of
the SUV and grabbing the shovels. The sun was still high in the sky,
and a slight wind was moving from the southeast.

"Give me a second," I said, walking forward, my phone and shovel
in hand.

The area where we'd parked was an open field, and the ground
was a mix of wetland grasses and sandy dirt, which had a silty tex-
ture from the overflow of the river. Far in the distance, the greenery
got taller, and I could see a line of magnolias. Close to us was a fence,
marking out the confines of private property.

As I paced off an area near the fence line, I could hear Quinones
telling Richie that he had looked up PAR and come to the conclusion
that we were "the real deal." I wondered how long that would last
once I put him to work digging holes.

When I had the area mapped off in my head, I motioned Richie and the detective over and paced off seventeen feet. I told Richie to stand there. Then I asked Detective Quinones to step two feet over and six feet back. I walked to a third spot.

"I'm going to ask you each to dig four holes," I said. "Thirty inches deep. Can you do that?"

Richie glanced at me. "Hey, I work for you."

I looked at Quinones.

He shrugged. "Why not."

Still, he didn't look prepared to dig. "Do you have a question?" I asked.

He shook his head, and we all began. Richie dug, then moved, as did Quinones and I. As we got deep, we had to go wider, and the process took time.

"If you hit nothing," I said, "move two feet to the east for your next hole. If nothing's there, two feet south. Then east. Then south."

We each finished our second hole and moved.

As we started our third, the detective began speaking. "The way I see it," he said loudly, "you fellas gotta start back at the beginning. Talk to witnesses. Look for new leads."

Others might have been frustrated by Quinones's complaints, but I was blocking the noise out. Thinking of a time when I was eleven and my mother had taken me panning for gold. It was a trip to Arizona that I'd begged to go on, but upon arrival at the location, it was clear the place was a tourist trap. Still, I stayed out every night until 9 p.m., convinced the statistics were on my side. That I would find gold and make us a fortune.

"I'm at depth," Richie said.

He was going faster than Quinones and I were.

"Just wait for us," I said, "so we're all moving in tandem."

"These are folks from marginalized communities," Quinones continued, still digging. "Prostitutes. Illegals. But that doesn't mean someone didn't see something."

"I'm ready to move," I said to Richie, and we all shifted.

A moment later, I heard a noise and looked over.

Richie stood there, frozen.

He'd hit something.

CHAPTER TWELVE

RICHIE'S SHOVEL WAS EIGHTEEN INCHES INTO THE ground at the fourth spot, and the sound we'd heard was the blade connecting with an object that was hard, yet gave off a dull thud.

I turned to Quinones. "The three women were wrapped in cloth, correct?"

The detective nodded, but his face barely moved. "Yeah," he said. "Like—strips of it."

"Mark where you are, Detective," I said. "I'll do the same. Then we'll both help Richie."

I made an *X* with my shovel blade and moved to an area two feet from the rookie.

I began on one side of the hole, noting the bushy growth of grass in the area. Quinones started on the other, the two of us digging smaller holes around Richie. When we hit nothing, we adjusted course until we heard the same sound.

After fifteen minutes, we had dug a trench around a shape, two feet by six. I walked over to my SUV and opened the back. Grabbed a set of gloves, a sweatshirt, and a pocketknife from my bag.

Gloving up, I crouched near the hole. Using my sweatshirt as a broom, I swept the dirt aside, pulling it up and out of the hole. Then I dug with my hands. Slowly, more of a shape came into view. Little bits of dirt poured back over the edges into the hole, but I kept wiping them out and away while Quinones waited for the cloud of dust to pass.

When I was ready, I flipped open my knife and made a cut through a strip of dirty brown fabric at one end of the hole. Reaching inside with my hand, I felt more dirt, which I moved aside, my fingers finally locating something solid.

Quinones took a step back. The dust cloud cleared again, revealing what I'd already assumed from touch: a human skull.

"Son of a bitch," the detective said.

I stared at it. "Rounded frontal bone," I said. "Smooth supraorbital ridge. And a pointed jawline that slopes gently toward the ear. All of which makes this likely an adult female."

Quinones was shaking his head and pacing. "I can get a tractor out here in an hour. Dig up this whole area."

I handed the skull to Richie, who had gloved up, too.

"That's unlikely to produce results," I said.

"What do you mean?" Quinones said. "The other bodies were found in a line. Remember? Vegetables? Planting patterns?"

"There's no space in that direction," Richie said, pointing at the fence. "If you go the other way, the dirt gets too hard. This way, too soft and close to the river."

Quinones looked frustrated.

"There are other areas we suspect may be relevant," I clarified. "From your county map. But they're larger and more difficult to survey. This was the small one. To test out our theory."

"Other areas with bodies?" Quinones's voice spiked.

I nodded, and my phone rang. "One second, Detective."

I walked a few feet away. "Mr. DeLillo," I answered my phone. "Thank you for returning my call. Your timing is perfect."

Tristan DeLillo was a camera specialist who lived a half hour west of Jacksonville and had consulted with me on a previous case. Twelve years earlier, he'd been among the first to attach a camera to a drone. For some time, he shot commercials. But the business got crowded, and DeLillo moved on, connecting increasingly more advanced tech to his drones. I had texted him an hour ago.

"Are you still running airborne search teams?" I asked.

"Yes, sir," he replied.

DeLillo's team was contracted for various types of rural search, but the technology I wanted to use was different.

In recent years, scientists had discovered that as bodies decompose, they produce so many nutrients that the soil around them dramatically alters. The expression for the mass that is created as a victim rots is a cadaver decomposition island, or CDI. DeLillo's drones, mounted with near-infrared sensors, or NIR, could detect human remains by searching for these islands.

"This job will require NIR and may take a few days to get funded," I said. "Can you start sooner, before a formal purchase order comes through?"

"I thought you moved to Miami," DeLillo said. "There's fellas in your area that can—"

"I'm back up in *your* area," I interrupted him. "In a town called Shilo."

DeLillo was familiar with the city. He told me to send him detailed information about where his team would be searching and what type of cameras were required.

In addition to NIR, I intended to leverage traditional infrared imaging. These sensors could be calibrated to detect the chemical signature that extra nitrogen, released from the dead bodies, had on the growth of plants directly atop a body dump site. This was something that would be relevant with victims buried less than thirty-six inches from the surface and wrapped only in cloth. The plant life growing there would reflect infrared in a way that other plants in the area would not. A drone flying overhead could register the contrast between both areas.

By the time I hung up, Richie and Quinones had pulled more dirt away from the hole, revealing a full skeleton, wrapped loosely in strips of either linen or bamboo.

Bones go through their own decomposition process, which is called diagenesis and can last a year or two decades, depending on what part of the bone degrades first, the protein of the structure or the minerals. Temperature and the amount of water in the ground also play a role. We would need to study the bones carefully, looking for tiny cracks or flakes—areas where minerals from the soil had filled in miniscule voids in the bone structures and fossilized them.

"You think we'll find other skeletons?" Quinones asked, breaking me from my thoughts.

"Yes."

"Son of a bitch," he said. But his tone had changed. Something more serious had set in.

I thought of the reality—that despite this finding, we might not be on this case for long. Not if Director Poulton wanted us on the gun investigation.

"I'd recommend you have a coroner take this body in quietly and not alert the public," I said. "If your killer lives locally, you don't want him to think the Bureau is back and finding anything."

Quinones made a call, then told us he'd stay with the body to wait for the coroner and forensic team while we headed back to the station to prepare for a bigger survey of a second area. As we spoke, Richie moved off to the side and phoned Shooter and Cassie. Told them to grab the first available flight in our direction.

On the way back to town, Richie filled out the paperwork for us to hire DeLillo, submitting it up the chain of command on my behalf. He also reserved a handful of rooms at a nearby Homewood Suites.

We made our way toward the station, and in my mind, I pictured the county map and the notations I'd made on it so far. But before we arrived back at the precinct, my phone rang again.

It was Craig Poulton.

"Did your C.I. talk already?" he asked.

"I sent you a note," I said. "We're letting him sit in jail."

"But you have a lead? Some weapons cache?"

Was there an update from Shooter or Cassie that I hadn't seen? Surely they wouldn't have communicated directly with Poulton.

"The IR request," Poulton said. "The flyover money, Camden."

He was referring to the requisition Richie had just put in, but it was obvious the director had not read any of the details. He had just seen the word *PAR* attached to it.

I explained what we'd found with Freddie Pecos at the ATM and how it had led us to Shilo. But Poulton did not seem intrigued.

A year ago, when he took the lead spot at the FBI, the director made it the new priority of the Bureau to focus on four areas: fraud, domestic terrorism, human trafficking, and the proliferation of child sexual abuse material. Criminal investigations that included homicide, unless they crossed state lines or were the source of "opportunity press," as Poulton called it, were better turned over to local police or state investigators.

"We've got two days until we get our hands on this new C.I.," I said. "This case could be connected."

"But you don't think it is," the director said.

"I wouldn't be here if I didn't."

Poulton snickered. "This is where you usually mention the odds, Camden. Seventy-six-point-something percent chance. Where you tell me you don't pursue low-probability outcomes."

I hesitated. "A man who killed our C.I. led us to a serial murderer operating in Shilo, Florida. You follow that, right?"

"You know I do," he said, his tone sharpening.

"And this murderer," I continued, "he's the only lead we have in the death of Freddie Pecos, our C.I. on the gun case."

"You mean the C.I. that you and I don't care about," Poulton said, referencing our conversation in his office two days ago.

"Sure," I said. "But we have no idea how this mystery guy got to Pecos. Or if he's tied to Sandoval. That doesn't sit well with me."

"Leave your team there to look into it," Poulton said. "Get on a plane."

"Where am I going?"

"D.C."

I wasn't following him. "Is there a press conference or—?"

Poulton began laughing. "You think I'd let *you* talk to the press, Camden? No, no, no. If you have extra days to spare, we'll bring in ATF early on the gun case. Me, you, and Barry Kemp. Nine a.m. tomorrow."

Barry Kemp was the deputy director of the Bureau of Alcohol, Tobacco, Firearms and Explosives. Above Kemp was the ATF director, who was Poulton's counterpart.

"You want ATF to use the next two days to get up to speed," I said. "Then they'll be ready when our C.I. realizes it's time to talk or he's going to prison for life?"

"Now we're tracking," Poulton said.

I agreed and hung up, telling Richie to change direction and drive to the Gainesville airport.

"So we're doing this one without you?" he asked.

"At least for tomorrow," I said.

I considered the two cases. One thing was clear: There *had* to be some connection between the mystery man at the ATM and Freddie. There was too little time between their meeting and our C.I.'s death.

Could Freddie have known something about these murders up north?

Did he die for that reason?

"What are you thinking about?" Richie asked.

I glanced over at him. The problem was that if a connection existed, we didn't have a clue what it was.

"Nothing," I said.

We reached the airport in fifteen minutes. On the way, I told Richie that he would run point here in Shilo until Cassie and Shooter showed up.

"Can you handle that?" I asked.

"No problem," he said.

But as I pulled in and gave him the keys, my phone buzzed. I stared at the incoming text, frozen in my seat.

"Agent Camden?" Richie said to me.

I glanced over, but didn't answer.

"Everything okay?"

"Yes," I said.

But I wasn't sure that was exactly true.

I got out of the SUV and grabbed my bag. When I entered the airport, I ignored the line to check in for D.C. and found the American

Airlines counter. Booked a flight to Dallas instead and waited at the terminal, my phone turned off and my eyes closed.

Impossible, I thought, my throat going dry and my pulse quickening.

But sometimes the impossible happens.

CHAPTER THIRTEEN

I STOOD AT THE THRESHOLD OF THE HOSPITAL ROOM AND stared inside.

"Looks like *someone's* got a visitor," said the nurse, positioned to the right of the single bed in the room.

The bed that contained my mother.

She opened her eyes and stared at me. Awake. Conscious. Responding to directions.

"Mom?" I said. The single word encapsulated not just the title for the woman who had raised me but my surprise at seeing her eyes open after fifteen months in a comatose state.

She was positioned half sitting, her eyes huge under a wave of unkempt white hair.

"Is that your son?" the nurse asked, pointing in my direction.

I waited, but my mom made no move to acknowledge me, her cool blue eyes landing on a point beyond me, out in the hallway.

My body was filled with emotions I was not used to. Anger. Guilt. Happiness.

Fifteen months earlier, I was chasing a suspect in the biggest case of my career. When I pushed him too hard, he broke into my mother's nursing home and poisoned her with a paralytic called vecuronium.

"How do you feel?" I asked, my throat tight, the words struggling to escape.

Her eyes moved to the nurse. "I had a stressful dream."

Fifteen months of silence, and her voice sounded the same. Slightly hoarse. Maybe a touch weaker. But the doctors had warned me that she would probably never open her eyes again. Never speak again.

My mother glanced around. Was she searching for something familiar? After the attack, she had been airlifted from her nursing home to a trauma center. Weeks later, I moved her here—to a long-term care facility.

I pictured the last time I had seen my mother awake and in person. She had helped me solve something complex. Then, a minute later, she'd disappeared into the void of Alzheimer's.

Because of her age and condition, the doctors had made the decision to anesthetize her after the attack, in an effort to stabilize her. But last month, I had worked out a plan with her physician, Dr. Eastman, to begin withdrawing the anesthesia. He told me there was little guarantee she would wake up.

"I was somewhere else," my mother said, her voice hoarse. "A beach in South Carolina."

I swallowed, controlling my breathing. When I was a child, we'd travel to Kiawah Island every summer. I would stay on the beach until the sun dropped below the horizon and the sand grew cold under my feet. Then I would climb onto my mother's lap, where she'd cover me in towels and blankets so we could stay out even longer.

"You've been asleep," I said, walking closer to the bed. "For fifteen months and nine days. It's not unusual to have strange dreams."

"Fifteen months?" My mother blinked.

The most common scoring system for the condition of a comatose patient is the Glasgow Coma Scale. The GCS measures responsiveness over three areas: eye opening, verbal response, and motor activity. One of those is rated on a 1–4 scale, the next on a 1–5, and the last on a 1–6. Dr. Eastman had totaled up my mother's scores ninety days ago and landed on a five, which was only two points above complete unresponsiveness.

My mother began whimpering, and I moved closer to take her hand. It felt cold and small. The skin on her fingers was loose against my wrist.

This was the reason I'd put a plan in place to try to wake her up. According to her doctor, my mother's system would not tolerate another two months of muscle loss or respiratory decline.

Dr. Eastman came into the room. "You got here fast," he said. "When you're ready, we should talk."

I spent a few more minutes with my mother, then found the doctor in his office just past the nursing station. Eastman was five foot eight, with wavy white hair and sun-wrinkled skin. He wore a tailored suit jacket over a blue shirt, a look that read more aging European fashion model than geriatric specialist.

"So," he said. "What do you think of our patient? Remarkable, isn't it?"

The sun had gone down while I traveled west, and looking out the window, I was reminded of the flatness of Texas. "Does she remember anything?" I asked.

Eastman squinted at me. "Mr. Camden," he said, "we opened a

bottle of champagne. Nurses were crying. A man of your intelligence must understand how rare this is."

"Do you have a plan?" I asked. "She appears to be nineteen pounds lighter."

Eastman glanced at his desk, picking up my mother's chart. "Eighteen point five, actually."

"You'll get her going with therapy, then," I said. "PT to start. A diet regimen?"

"She'll have a different therapist every hour," Eastman said, his face forming a gentle smile. "Even psychiatric. It's not every day that a well-regarded behavioral expert goes up against one of our own."

Years ago, my mother was a respected figure in the psychiatric community. Before she retired and moved west, she was on retainer with the Charleston Police Department. There, she consulted on dozens of investigations, including two well-known serial murders.

"But let's take a moment," Eastman said, "to be positive."

I wasn't trying to be pessimistic, but I knew the statistics on patients who woke from a comatose state. Short-term memory loss. Word-finding problems. For someone with advanced Alzheimer's, these would be even more severe.

"Of course, yes." I forced a smile. "Thank you for reminding me how rare this is," I said, even though I was the last person who needed a recap of anything statistical. I moved back to business. "Do you imagine she'll remain conscious?"

"Oh, absolutely," he said. "Progress only moves in one direction, my friend."

We spoke for a minute more, but the doctor continued to focus on celebrating the moment, while I locked down a plan for recovery. I informed Eastman that I had jumped on the first flight, but would have to leave shortly and return several days from now for a longer stretch.

"Can I spend the night in her room?" I asked.

"Yes, of course," he said. "We'll roll in a cot. Normally we wouldn't all be here at eight o'clock on a Wednesday night, but . . ." He grinned again, pointing in the direction of my mother's room.

I grabbed a water from the Coke machine. By the time I was back, an orderly had set up the cot next to my mother's bed, and Mom was resting. I studied her vitals, observing that her breathing was normal. Her heart rate was 124 beats per minute. Toward the high end of the range for her age, but not out of bounds.

I placed my hand on her arm, thinking of her as a younger woman. When I was growing up, my mom would put on music every Sunday and twirl around the house in a sundress. She would dance around me, delivering advice that her son, who was not like the other boys, needed for life.

She taught me never to compare myself to anyone else. That I was different, and that was that. *End of chapter*, she would say. *End of story.*

She also told me that it was beautiful to be unlike others. That if I kept learning, I would always be needed by one person and one organization. Between the two, that was enough for life.

Years ago, when I began working at the FBI and met my ex-wife, Anna, I thought I had found both of those things. Anna was the daughter of Saul Moreno, my first partner at the Bureau. She brought out something in me that was strange and enjoyable, even if it was uncomfortable. Real feelings. And for a while, our life felt delightfully predictable in ways that pleased me.

But things did not go as planned. When Camila was just one, my wife was arrested for RICO violations and sent to prison.

And I was the one who made the phone call to the police.

I fell asleep on the cot. In the morning, when I awoke, my mother's eyes were wide, and there were tears on her cheeks. I folded up the cot and turned her bed at an angle, so she could see the sunrise coming up over the hills.

"Are you my nurse?" she asked.

I smiled at her. "For the morning at least."

"And tell me your name again, dear?"

I pursed my lips, answering slowly. Then I helped my mother into a wheelchair and pushed her out the door. We took the elevator down to the grounds, and I moved her around, watching as she surveyed the gardens behind the facility for the first time.

We got to the far side of the looping path, then headed back toward the building. Some urge pinged at me from within, a need to tell my mother that I had violated one of her key rules for life: *Never use my intellect as a weapon.* It was this violation that had driven a madman to visit her nursing home and inject her with a deadly medicine.

But she would not understand any of this, and none of it would be productive for her recovery.

We took the elevator up to her floor, and I got my mother back into bed. As I pulled the covers up to her neck to keep her warm, the orderly brought in breakfast, and my phone rang. It was a number from the Bureau, and I stepped into the attached bathroom to answer.

"This is Olivia," a voice said. "I have Director Poulton for you."

I waited a beat, and the director came on.

"What the hell, Camden?" Poulton said, his voice ringing with annoyance. "You're not in D.C., and you're not in Florida, either?"

Late last night, I had penned an email to the director, telling him

I would not make the 9 a.m. meeting with him and ATF Deputy Director Kemp—due to personal matters.

"I'm in Dallas," I said.

"Jesus, are there missing women there, too?"

"Well, statistically speaking, I'm sure there are—"

"Don't be a smart-ass," Poulton cut in, and I realized the structure of the joke I had inadvertently constructed.

"My mom woke up," I said, and Poulton went quiet. He'd had a front-row seat on the day my mother was attacked. It was Craig Poulton, in fact, who had pushed me on that case, driving me out of my comfort zone. It was something my mom had done all my life, so I'd accepted the shove. But I didn't see until it was too late that I had goaded our suspect past a line. I'd made it personal between him and me. That's when he took his rage out on my mother.

"Shit," he said. "How is she, Camden?"

"Coming along," I said, though this felt like a lie.

"Well. You got a lotta irons in the fire, Agent," Poulton said, his voice calming. "I read your note about the body you found last night. Feels like I should put another team on one of these cases."

"The case in Shilo *had* another team on it," I said. "Left a sour taste in the locals' mouths about the FBI." I watched from the bathroom as a nurse spoon-fed my mother tapioca. "I'll make it to D.C. this afternoon. Then come back to Texas in a week. Take a few days off at that point to be with my mother."

"You think this gun case will be over in a week?"

The odds of both investigations being completed in a week was single digits, but I was learning that brevity was the better part of most things when it came to answering Craig Poulton.

"Leave it to us," I said.

Poulton hesitated, waiting for more. But I kept quiet.

"When you're ready, call for a jet instead of flying commercial," he said. "I'll let Olivia know."

Poulton hung up, and I called Richie. Got a summary of what was going on in Shilo and what the plan was for the search that day.

Next, I rang up Tristan DeLillo, asking him if he had questions about the areas that I had marked on the map on the plane ride to Dallas.

All the while, I kept the door ajar, my eyes on my mom.

When I was done, I stepped back into her room and checked to see how much she'd eaten. Two cups of tapioca were empty, as was a tiny dish that had held a mandarin orange mush. The nurse took it away and nodded to me.

"You were a good eater today," I said to my mom.

"My drink tastes funny," she replied.

I glanced down, seeing a cup filled with water. It had been mixed with thickener.

"They'll test your swallowing later," I said. "Until the therapist says different, this is what you drink. For your own safety."

"Are you leaving?" she asked.

I had to go, and I was not going to lie to my mother.

"Yes," I said.

I turned away from her and moved into the bathroom. Stayed there a moment and ordered an Uber on my phone.

That's when I heard it. A single word.

"Gardy?"

It was a nickname that only one person in the world used for me.

I walked back into the room. Looking down at my mother, I swallowed, but said nothing.

"You caught him, right?" she said. "The man who did this to me?"

"Yes," I said. "I caught him."

"Good," she said. "There are some things—" She paused and glanced around. Was she about to disappear again? As she would before the attack, when the Alzheimer's would take hold. "Some things you cannot leave for others to solve. Is that where you're going now, Gardy?"

"Yes."

"Then go."

I kissed her on the forehead and told her I'd be back in a week.

As I pulled away, she was squinting at me. I left quietly. I couldn't bear to ask any other questions and find out that I'd receded in her memory once again.

CHAPTER FOURTEEN

BY 2:30 P.M., I HAD LANDED IN D.C. UPON ARRIVAL, I NOTED no new emails from my team. I had sent Cassie a note last night about my mom, so there was a possibility that my colleagues were leaving me alone, believing I would take some time off.

Barry Kemp from ATF had texted, though, telling me that if I got to Washington before three, he'd meet me for a late lunch.

As I took an Uber to the address in the Adams Morgan neighborhood that Kemp had given me, I saw a text from the owner of the condo that I rented for Camila and me. He was considering selling the place. I bit at my lip, but did not respond. Too much else going on.

I got out of the Uber in front of a restaurant called the Federalist Pig, a barbecue place that Frank had brought me to on a trip to D.C. years ago.

Inside, I introduced myself to Kemp, who was six foot three, with a sturdy, muscular figure. He ran 250 pounds but carried it well in a dark blue suit, white shirt, and red tie.

"Why don't we order, and we can sit out on the patio and chat?" he said, directing me to the woman at the counter.

I ordered a brisket sandwich with beans and brussels sprouts. Kemp asked for a jalapeño sausage with a side of mac and cheese. We made our way outside and sat across from each other at a table made of butcher block.

Kemp had avoided meeting in his office at ATF, then sent me to a restaurant fifteen minutes away, well past the lunch rush when no one was around. Since my concern was loose lips at the ATF on our weapons investigation, I appreciated his approach.

"So," he said after we got our food and made the requisite small talk, "you can imagine my disbelief at the idea that a major arms manufacturer is making a buy-build-shoot kit."

"I never said it was a *major* manufacturer," I replied. "Director Poulton asked that, and my answer was that we never found out."

Kemp had a wide face with a big jawline and no facial hair. "Before your C.I. was killed, you mean?"

"Precisely," I said.

"And you don't know who killed him?"

"Not yet," I said, "but we don't think it was one of J. P. Sandoval's guys."

I gave Kemp background on the texts we'd seen on Freddie's phone, detailing how the gang didn't appear to know he was dead. How when we found that out, I made the call to light the mobile home on fire.

As I described that night, Kemp laughed and shook his head, speaking in an accent I placed as Oklahoman.

"You're one cool customer, Camden," he said. "Your team has a great reputation. 'Course, we know Jo Harris from when she was one of ours. A lot of people thought she was a ballbuster, but the guys I talked to said it was a big loss when she pulled that stunt and got sent away."

Six years ago, Congress's lack of funding for ATF had upset Shooter. While at a federal gun range, she'd used her incredible fire-arms accuracy to write F-U-C-K C-O-N-G-R-E-S-S in bullet holes across a series of targets. On the same day, a senator from Massachu-setts was getting a tour of the place. Same hour, in fact.

Jo was transferred to a remote ATF outpost shortly thereafter. A year later, like me, she was recruited to join PAR.

"If you scratch the surface of any of us at PAR, you're going to find a story like that," I said.

We dug into our food then. As we ate, Kemp asked about PAR's mission and how we judge success. I shared with him the fraud part of the case that got us started in Hambis and how we planned to trade that to a DA in Florida.

"And Craig's all right with that?" Kemp squinted, referring to Poulton.

"I haven't told him yet," I said. "I'll inform him later."

"Oh, man," Kemp laughed. "You're gonna be in hot water, Camden." He poured red sauce over his sausage. "I'll keep that part to myself."

He finished his meal quickly and examined me. "So," he said. "You're a smart guy. Straightforward. You got concerns about my team?"

"You have to liaise with firearms companies on a regular basis. I would say monthly, but with the number of active shooters lately, I know you're talking with some of them every week."

Kemp wrinkled his forehead. "And you think what—one of our guys is cozy with them? Gonna tip 'em off?"

"Some things are human nature," I said. "The urge to protect those you work with."

"Sure, it's a fair concern."

I waited to see if he would say more. After a moment, he did.

"How about this?" he suggested. "You keep the case with your team, but have your finger on speed dial. My number specifically."

I was surprised by this response, which only made me more convinced that Kemp was also concerned someone in his organization might tip off a weapons company.

"Okay," I said. "Call you before it heats up?"

"Not a minute too late," Kemp said. "Can I trust you on that?"

"Absolutely."

"When you ring me, I'll have an agent ready."

"And if it turns out there's a domestic manufacturer involved?"

"If it's S&W or Remington?" Kemp shrugged. "Congress is gonna shit a purple Twinkie. Convene hearings and drag their execs in. But there's foreign companies making guns here, too. German subsidiaries. Czech firms."

"And if the whispers turn out to be nothing?"

"If you're satisfied, and I am, too? Then no harm, no foul. I'm not angry about spending a few hours on this."

When we finished, Kemp offered me a ride to the airport. As he drove, he asked about my mother's status; Poulton must've informed him.

"You got other family?" he followed up.

I was sure Kemp had done reconnaissance on me, and it didn't take much work to find out that I had sent my own wife away, a woman whose father was a legendary federal agent.

"I'm divorced," I said. "One daughter."

He pulled up to the curb at Dulles. "Well, let's keep the next generation safe. If anything comes up, you text me direct, y'hear? Not a minute too late."

I nodded and thanked him for the ride. Then grabbed a flight to Gainesville, where I took an Uber to the Shilo police station twenty miles away. It was 8:45 p.m., and Camila's bedtime was approaching fast. I called her, walking through the parking lot as we spoke.

"Where are you?" my daughter asked.

"A small town," I said. "An hour from my old office."

"Are you coming home?"

"Not tonight," I said.

It was Thursday, and Camila's science fair was the following night. She hadn't yet asked if I'd be back in time, but with our current case volume, the answer didn't look good.

"What are you doing?" I asked.

"Reading *Ramona*," she said. "Grandma says if I read three chapters, we can do karaoke."

Camila had read the Beverly Cleary *Ramona* books when she was five, and I knew they were comfort food more than hard reading.

"What are you going to sing?" I asked.

"Pfft," she said as if the answer was obvious. "Taylor."

"And your nana?"

"Some sappy Luis Miguel song probably," she said. Which cracked Camila up.

"I have to go."

"*Te amo*, Daddy," Camila said, telling me she loved me.

"*Te amo* more."

I walked inside the station. Not seeing my team on the floor where Detective Quinones's office sat, I texted Richie. His response came back fast.

Come to the basement.

I took the elevator down to B. As I entered the medical examiner's suite, I slowed, seeing the room was crowded with tables. Among them was the stainless-steel type every ME uses to evaluate victims. But those had been run through quickly, and four bodies had been laid atop folding card tables, the kind sold at every home improvement store.

On each table was a skeleton, covered in dirt and debris. Six in all.

I threaded my way through the maze, and Quinones turned as he saw me.

"You said to keep things quiet," he said, his voice low.

My eyes moved from body to body. The pelvic bones were wide, the rib cages broad and curved. Each of the skulls was delicate.

"Shit," I said softly.

The bodies were in various states of decay, some indicating a death months ago, with fatty tissue turned to wax still clinging to the cheekbones of one skull. Others appeared to have been in the ground for years. One looked like it had been buried less than three weeks ago.

I scanned the length of the bones, my eyes stopping at the epiphysis on the sternal end of each body's clavicle, which usually fused around the age of thirty or thirty-one. In all the victims, they were unconnected.

Six bodies. All women around the age of thirty or younger.

Slain and hidden in the dirt.

When I'd left Florida twenty-nine hours ago, there was one new victim on this case. Now the room was crowded. Which meant our potential suspect in the death of Freddie Pecos hadn't just killed our C.I. and the three women that were discovered years ago.

He was a serial murderer, with at least ten kills to his name.

CHAPTER FIFTEEN

"TELL ME WHAT YOU KNOW SO FAR," I SAID, STARING AT my team.

We had assembled on the roof of the police station, and Richie was smoking. I wondered if the stress of the case had pushed him to this, or if he'd always been a smoker and I had simply not been aware.

"We've only ID'd two of the bodies," Richie said.

"So far," Cassie added.

"So far," Richie corrected himself.

The wind whipped around the roof, and Shooter spoke up. "You remember Ingrid Santos from Jacksonville, right? We called her Santos Santos?"

This was the ME from our old office, a woman who had a habit of repeating words at the end of every sentence.

Cassie shook her head at Shooter. "*You* called her Santos Santos. No one else did."

Shooter continued, undeterred. "Shilo lost their coroner six months ago, Gardner. They've been using a mortuary employee to fill the role."

A fairly common practice in small communities, but we couldn't rely on a skill set like this for a complex case. "You called Santos?" I asked.

Shooter nodded. "She'll be here at eight a.m."

Richie's eyes moved from face to face in our small circle. "Is she good?"

Cassie looked to me.

"She's the only one available," Shooter said.

"We also reached out and booked Patsy Davitt," Cassie added.

Davitt was a facial reconstruction expert who did contract work for the FBI. She was an artist who specialized in the Gatliff–Snow tissue depth method. She glued soft plastic markers to a skull before spreading clay atop it. From there, she could add prosthetic eyeballs and wigs or complete the same process digitally. Either way, we'd arrive at a likeness of the victim—one good enough to show to the public.

"How fast can she get our first victim clayed up?" I asked.

"A day maybe," Cassie said. "Davitt's gonna work on-site, and we've got pictures of a number of the missing women. If we're lucky, maybe we get a couple IDs on day one."

"And how did you identify the two women whose names you know?"

"Jewelry," Richie said. "One had a necklace with her. The other had a pin, custom made by her mom. Detective Quinones knows these cases inside and out. He recognized both of the items immediately."

I thought of the short time we had before our gun case got hot—and how important it was to make some connection to the man at the ATM. Some of these women might have been in the ground for years, and identifying them, while critical, was not time sensitive. But identifying the man in the sketch was. He was tied to an active investigation, even if we weren't clear on how. And he was a killer.

"The two identified women," I said, "did you reach out to family members yet?"

"No," Shooter said. "We got back here ten minutes before you."

"Well, that's the first order of business tomorrow," I said. "We need family members looking at our sketch. If either of them recognizes this suspect, we dig in fast."

In the distance, a plane flew overhead, and my eyes followed it toward Gainesville. "We start early tomorrow," I said. "I need to make a phone call."

The team broke up, and Richie said he'd give me a ride to the hotel, where he'd secured rooms the night before. "I'll be there in a minute," I told him.

I looked at the time. It was late. Past 10 p.m. I took the stairs back down to the basement to examine the bodies again myself.

Cases like this spun a community out, and I could see that happening in Shilo. The knowledge that some madman had been in town for years, attacking women . . . every parent and husband would see their worst fears come to life. And every woman would be afraid to go out alone.

I shot a photo of the six bodies. Texted it to Craig Poulton. Thirty seconds later, the director was calling.

"Tell me that's not what I think it is."

"The original body from yesterday, plus five more."

"Jesus H. Christ on a grain of rice. All in that shit little town?"

"The team has identified two bodies so far," I replied. "The rest we're hoping to ID soon."

"Well, you got tomorrow and not more," he said. "Tell me, Camden. Who's your number one?"

"Not sure I follow."

"You were Frank's number one. Who's yours?"

I considered Shooter versus Cassie. "Well," I said. "Agent Harris is more physical, while Agent Pardo is more intellectual."

"Okay?"

"Harris is more of a rational problem solver, while Pardo is more emotional—"

"Jesus, Camden," Poulton interrupted. "Who do you count on the most?"

"Cassie Pardo," I said.

"You and she function as a team? Or you split her up? Put her with the rookie?"

I had, in fact, teamed Cassie up with Richie. But not for the reasons Poulton was implying. "She works with Richie Brancato."

"Well, for right now, she works with you."

"Sir?" I said, a question more than an answer.

"You and Pardo peel off and fly to Miami by seven p.m. tomorrow. I want you fresh in Hambis the following morning. Kemp called me from ATF. Said he liked you. Gave you free rein."

"Yes."

"I wouldn't have made that decision."

I said nothing, and Poulton waited.

"I need to know that you hear me, Camden," he said. "Before we get any deeper. You. Tomorrow night. Flying to Miami."

I wasn't hesitating because I planned to defy Poulton's orders. If I had known he was making this move, I would've picked Shooter instead of Cassie. Because of her experience, she'd be stronger on the weapons case. But knowing the director's personality, switching personnel now would be perceived as weakness or indecision.

"I hear you," I said.

"Do you? 'Cause I think you're in Hambis the other day, and you're outside my office here in D.C."

"It was my belief that—"

"Then I think you're in D.C.," Poulton cut in. "And you email me that you're in Texas."

"Sir," I said. "There are innocent women who—"

"Tomorrow night," he interrupted, "I don't want to find out you're somewhere other than Miami. And there's one way I make sure of that. Someone else starts project-managing you."

"Director Poulton," I said.

"You have tomorrow to work on this . . . whatever it is. The day after, Miami, first thing," he said. "You manage two cases. Or I'll find someone to manage you."

"Yes, sir."

"I might find someone anyway. You four are juggling a lot, you know."

"Yes, sir," I said again. Which was usually effective for getting Poulton to stop talking.

The director hung up, and I headed off to meet Richie at the rental car downstairs. On the way, I texted the team:

> 6 am start time tomorrow.

Richie was staring at his phone when I got there.

"Everything all right?" he asked.

I nodded. Everything was all right.

Except for Poulton.

And the fact that my team had dug up six bodies in the last twenty-four hours.

And we had one day to solve an active serial murder case. One that was somehow connected to Freddie Pecos, even though we still had no idea how.

CHAPTER SIXTEEN

"BY SEVEN P.M. TODAY, CASSIE AND I WILL BE ON A PLANE to Miami," I said.

It was 6:20 a.m. on Friday, and we had regrouped in the main conference room at Shilo Police Department.

"What for?" Richie asked.

"ATF is preparing to join us on our gun case down in Hambis," I said. "So we'll be splitting up the team. Cassie and I will work together today. Then roll off. Back to the gun case down South, which we'll hopefully have a new C.I. on, right?"

"Right," everyone said.

"In the meantime, Richie, you'll team up with Shooter and stay here."

"Boss?" Shooter squinted at me.

"You didn't do anything wrong," I said to her. "And I realize you might have been a better choice, given your background with ATF."

"Then again, there's her background with ATF," Cassie said, smirking.

Shooter tipped an imaginary hat at her, appreciating the dig.

Then she turned back to me. "Obviously Poulton's making this call," she said. "But does he realize we have six dead women here?"

"He does," I said. "Our other choice was to give up one of the cases. But if we walk away from this one, who thinks it's gonna get solved?"

Nobody said anything.

After a moment, Richie cleared his throat. "So what's our plan today?"

I picked two thin files off the table next to me. "We start by splitting up the new IDs." I handed one of the folders to Richie. "You and Shooter take Araceli Alvarez. Cassie and I will take Melanie Nelson."

"And me?" a voice said. It was Detective Quinones, standing in the doorway.

"You're home base," I said. "Any leads that come in from our IDs will need to be checked out. You'll also coordinate with our ME and forensic artist. The artist will be ready for the first skull at eight a.m. Decide who goes first."

Quinones nodded. "Can do."

I grabbed one of the sketches from my satchel and held it up for Quinones. "This sketch artist," I said, "I want to talk to him. Can you find him for me?"

"I can try."

Five minutes later, Cassie and I were in her rental car, and I was looking through what little we had on the body identified as Melanie Nelson.

"So," she said. "Your mom . . . that's great, right?"

I had been thinking about my mother all night. Had woken up twice, restless, staring at the hotel ceiling.

"Yeah," I answered. One word only.

Cassie made eye contact. "Gardner," she said. "You're gonna have to talk about this with somebody at some point—you know that, right?"

I hesitated, and Cassie let me be. She got off the interstate and headed east.

"Her doctor," I said finally. "He wanted to break out the champagne."

Cassie looked over, her forehead creased with lines.

"Can you imagine that?" I said. "Me? Celebrating? Meanwhile, you could put your hand around my mother's wrist."

Cassie took this in. She knew me well. "He's wanting to make a toast," she said. "And meanwhile, you're calculating how many months of PT your mom will need. How far her weight has dropped."

"Eighteen and a half pounds," I said.

Cassie changed lanes. "Gardner, how rare is this? Her waking up?"

"With her GCS score," I said, "one in a hundred and eight thousand."

"That's amazing," she said. "And you thanked him, right?" Her eyebrows arched. "You thanked all the nurses and doctors?"

I turned to her. *Had I thanked anyone?*

I pulled out my phone to write a note, and Cassie turned the rental into a small neighborhood of trailers and manufactured homes. The streets were wide, and the RVs were painted in pastel colors: soft pinks and Easter yellows. I glanced at the address, then pointed at a sky-blue manufactured home with a white vinyl lattice around the base.

"There," I said.

Cassie parked the car, and we got out. Walked to the front door and banged on it. It was a little after 7 a.m., and the street was quiet, but we heard movement inside. After a moment, a blond woman answered the door.

"Rebecca Nelson?" I asked.

"Uh-huh?"

"My name is Gardner Camden. This is my partner, Cassie Pardo." I showed her my identification, and Cassie did the same.

The woman tucked a wavy bunch of hair behind her ear. She was in her late forties and dressed in a V-neck and sweats.

"We're here to talk to you about your daughter, Melanie," Cassie said.

On the way over, I'd noticed that Rebecca Nelson had been interviewed after Melanie had gone missing, but she had not been the one to report her daughter's disappearance.

"What's she done now?" she asked, her hand holding the edge of the door ajar, her body in the space in between.

"Do you mind if we come in?" Cassie asked.

"Place isn't clean," the mother said.

As she turned to me, I examined her face. She had a wide, almost square mouth and two moles the color of over-milked coffee, four millimeters to the left of her nose.

"When's the last time you saw your daughter?" I asked.

"Over two years," Rebecca Nelson said. "She left home when she turned of age."

"No phone calls?"

"I talked to her on the phone once. But that was a while back. A month after she left. What do you want with her?"

"Does Melanie live by herself?" Cassie asked.

The woman's head swiveled to Cassie, her face showing irritation that we were not answering her questions. "Your mother know where *you* are at all times, missy? Melanie ran away with a guy. Y'understand?"

It looked as if she might close the door on us, and I took out my notepad. "His name?"

"His Christian name?" She snorted. "Hell, I dunno. They call him D-O-G," she said, spelling out each of the letters, one at a time.

"Dog?" Cassie repeated. "Is he a Georgia fan or something? From that area?"

"I don't think he was studying at the university in Athens, if that's your thought, hon. Listen. Melanie ran away with a pimp. It was clear to everyone except Mel what he did for business. And if you run away with a pimp, it's only a matter of time before you work for one."

"Eighteen months ago, the police came out here," I said. "A friend had reported Melanie missing."

"Yeah, I 'member that." Rebecca Nelson waggled her eyebrows. They were so thin and reddish blond they nearly disappeared against her skin. "This good-looking Mexican cop talked to me. I told him the same thing as you. I got no idea where she is."

"We were hoping you could look at some pictures of a man," Cassie said. "See if he's someone you recognize."

She handed Mrs. Nelson the five sketches, and the woman dropped her hand off the doorjamb. Paged through them slowly.

"I don't know this guy," she said. "What color is he?"

I blinked. Was she trying to align the sketches with the man who had been with her daughter?

"What ethnicity was Dog?" I asked.

"Hispanic."

"Let's presume the sketches are of a Latino man, then. Do they look like him?"

"Like Dog? Nuh-uh." She handed the papers back. "This guy

looks big. Dog acted tough, but a solid wind could blow him over. He was thin. Cute. You know the type?"

"Certainly do," Cassie said. She asked for a list of Melanie's friends, but the mother was a stone wall.

"The daughter I know is long gone, darlin'," she said. "A day after high school graduation, there wasn't a scrap in her room. Emptied out, y'understand? I can't tell you nothing."

Cassie gave me a hard look, and I clocked the meaning of it. The woman wasn't telling us anything, and Cassie wanted me to deliver a death notification in the hopes that it would shake something loose. Increase the velocity on the case.

It was Detective Quinones's job to do this. Not us. In fact, over the last three decades, local police had developed the best procedures on performing proper death notifications. The news should be delivered in teams of two, one of which was typically a uniformed officer. And it was best done inside the family home, to which Rebecca Nelson had already blocked our access.

Still, Cassie and I only had one day on the investigation.

"Local police have discovered the body of a young woman," I said. "It's possible it could be Melanie."

The mother was inscrutable. "What do you mean it's possible?"

There was a particular vocabulary used in death notices, and expressions like *it's possible* were central to it.

"Did she get hurt in some way?" Rebecca Nelson asked, squinting. "So it don't look like her anymore?"

"We can have a patrolman come out here," Cassie said. "Bring you down to the Shilo police station. There, you could help make an identification or rule her out."

"You don't have a picture on your phone?" she asked.

Cassie did, in fact, have a photo on her phone. But it was of a set of bones.

She lifted her cell from her back pocket and scrolled instead to a photo of the necklace that Melanie's friend had identified as being on her person the day she went missing. The one found along with her remains.

"This piece of jewelry was found with the body," she said, showing it to Mrs. Nelson. "Do you recognize it?"

The mother pursed her lips then, and her cheeks rode up high on her face. Her eyes watered, but she didn't cry. "Mel's grandma bought that," she said. "For her eighteenth." She glared at Cassie. "What condition is this body in? Is it beaten up?"

"No," I said, trying to divert attention off Cassie.

But the mother didn't turn to face me.

"I see," she said, her nostrils flaring two millimeters wider, the edges of her nose turning from pink to white. "It's some skeleton, then? Like those women they found two years ago?"

Cassie's face tightened. She looked to me, but I wasn't sure I knew what to say. "If you could just come down to the station—" Cassie started.

"And what?" Rebecca Nelson said to her. "You want that I look at some bones and ID my daughter? Is that it?"

CHAPTER SEVENTEEN

I STOOD AT THE SIDE OF HIGHWAY 21, EIGHTY FEET FROM a mini-mart where Cassie had stopped to get a coffee and use the bathroom.

"This job, huh?" she said, coming out with a paper cup in hand.

We'd left the home of Rebecca Nelson twenty minutes earlier, the mother refusing a ride from us or a local cop to go to see her daughter's remains.

I studied Cassie, noticing small streaks in her eye makeup.

"You didn't need to use the bathroom, did you?" I asked.

"Jesus, Gardner," she huffed, and I estimated the chances were 82 percent that Cassie had used the gas station's facilities to cry, then reapply her mascara.

"It's okay," I said, the words coming out mechanically. "To feel sad about this case."

I had the passenger door to the rental car open and was staring at two files while Cassie paced along the roadside, the paper coffee cup in her hand.

"What are you looking at anyway?" she said finally, a frustrated tone in her voice.

I held up the files, which I'd grabbed from Richie in the morning and had been studying while Cassie drove.

One was thick and belonged to Susan Jones, the hotel manager found when the construction project unearthed the first three bodies. The other was a missing person's file on Neta Garcia, a taxi driver who had disappeared in October of 2020.

"All these missing women," I said. "They're marginalized in some way. But not these two."

Cassie came closer to me.

"You don't think a taxi driver is marginalized?" she asked, motioning at Neta Garcia's paperwork.

I looked back at the list of victims we knew, as well as the missing persons list that Detective Quinones had provided us. "One woman is a sex worker," I said. "Another an exotic dancer. Three are single moms. One undocumented woman. If our killer was picking off easy targets, these two are not as easy. Neta Garcia," I said, referring to the taxi driver. "She worked for nine years in an industry dominated by men and immigrants. She filed tax returns. Has a credit history. The motel manager." I pointed to the second file. "She owned a gun."

"You wanna re-canvass these two?"

I nodded, and Cassie spilled the contents of her coffee in the ditch. We got back in the car, and I fed the address of the hotel manager's ex-husband into my GPS.

We got back on the highway toward Shilo, then veered north into a more rural area. The road got smaller, and all around us, bald cypress towered out of the wetlands. In between were banks of dogwood, with clusters of white flowers spreading atop their canopies.

Cassie got a call from Shooter and put it on speaker.

While we met with Melanie Nelson's mother, Richie and Shooter had gone to see the family of Araceli Alvarez, the other body that had been identified yesterday.

"You get anything?" Cassie asked.

"Not much," Shooter said. "But something odd came up. Not sure what to make of it."

"What is it?" I asked.

"I talked to Araceli's mother. Ran through the last day she saw her daughter and what the girl's state of mind was. Richie pulled aside her sister at the same time. They each mentioned Araceli was depressed. Wasn't happy with her nose. I guess it kinda hooked unnaturally to the left?"

"Is this a joke?" I asked, knowing Shooter's penchant for humor.

"No joke," she said. "I had Richie call it into Santos Santos, you know, just in case . . . I don't know . . . something popped."

"And?"

"The ME examined the dead girl's skull in that area," Richie said. "Saw a nick in the bone of her face. In between the woman's nose and her infraorbital foramen."

"I'm not following," I said. "This was a natural abnormality?"

"No," Shooter said. "Santos thought it looked like something from an autopsy. Someone with unsteady hands. They slipped and nicked her bone."

Except none of these women *had been* autopsied. The ME was looking at the bodies for the first time.

"A previous plastic surgery?" Cassie asked.

"No," Shooter said. "We asked."

"On top of that," Richie said, "the sister said the nose hooked to the left, but the cut was on the right."

"A relative could've gotten that part wrong," Cassie said. "Did the family recognize the sketch?"

"Said they'd just be wild-ass guessing," Richie said. "What about yours?"

"No," Cassie said, her voice frustrated. "This ID . . . is not IDing."

This was Cassie speak. Sometimes the math was not mathing. When she looked good, her makeup was makeuping. Point was—we'd struck out twice getting an ID on our mystery man.

Cassie told Shooter we were going to meet the motel manager's ex, and Richie asked what their next move should be.

"Head back to Shilo," I said. "And split up. Jo, examine those skeletons again and find something. Richie, help Patsy Davitt get to an ID, and fast. Let me think on the nose."

Cassie and I pulled down a logging road and parked outside a small cabin. The home was no more than eight hundred square feet, with all wood on one side where the bedroom was—and all glass looking in at a combined kitchen and living room.

We banged on the door, but no one came to answer. Putting my face to the windows, I peered around. There wasn't a soul in sight.

"Fucknuts," Cassie said.

It was 11 a.m. already, and so far, we had nothing to show for our work. This was not abnormal in our line of business, but Cassie and I only had one day in Shilo before Richie and Shooter had to handle everything on their own.

"Is this the only relative?" Cassie asked.

"No." I walked back to the rental car where the file was. "There's a sister. Mila. And a mom."

My phone buzzed with a text from Detective Quinones.

Found a current address on the sketch artist.

This was the man who'd drawn the sketches that were our primary piece of evidence on our suspect. I wanted to have an in-person conversation with him. "Let's find this guy," I said. "At least we'll get something accomplished this morning."

By noon, we'd reached the address where the sketch artist lived. It was an older neighborhood in a town called Dennis, twenty minutes north of Shilo.

The garage door was slung open, and a man in his thirties was inside, bench-pressing weights. He wore black shorts and a gray tank top.

"W. C. Walker?" Cassie asked, walking closer.

"Depends on who's asking."

The man said this with a serious voice, but when he sat up, I saw the grin on his face. His biceps were covered in tattoos, and his chest bulged against his tank top. *Yoked* was the word Cassie would use if we were by ourselves. Or *swole*. *Swole* was big with her lately.

"Gardner Camden," I said, introducing myself and telling him we were with the FBI. "This is my partner, Cassie Pardo."

I studied the Ford Bronco and motorcycle parked in the garage on either side of the workout bench. California plates on both. The dates on the Bronco's stickers were expired.

"You're from out west, Mr. Walker?" Cassie asked.

"William," the man corrected her.

He followed my gaze to the front of the Bronco, then back to Cassie's badge. "Tell me the federal government ain't busting folks for expired tags these days."

"Not our line of business," Cassie said, explaining that we were here about a case where Walker had been a sketch artist.

"Those women who went missing?" he asked.

I blinked. "What makes you say that?"

"Only case I ever drew on."

We moved closer to him, and Cassie held up the file, flipping to a page that featured one of his sketches. "So this is your work?"

"Damn straight," he said. "If it looks different than other police sketches, it's probably 'cause I wasn't a regular and didn't know what the hell I was doing."

"This was the first and last time you drew?"

"For the cops, yeah," he said. "I started my career in Hollywood making Marvel posters. Work got old, so I busted a nut southeast. Did odd jobs in Alabama, Georgia, and Florida."

"How did you get involved in this case?" Cassie asked.

"I was making illustrations for a tattoo shop. Met a cop there. He told me this fed was looking for help, and Shilo Police would pay two hundred bucks a sketch."

"So for these sketches specifically," I said, motioning at the drawings. "The women who described this man—you met them at the Shilo precinct?"

"No, no. I drove around with this guy . . ." He searched for a name.

"Offerman?" Cassie said.

"Offerman." He pointed and nodded. "Big guy. Talked a lotta shit. And these witnesses were all women. Mostly poor. A couple pros. To Offerman's credit, he was smart enough to see they didn't like him. He left me there and went out for a pop while I worked."

"He went out for a drink?" Cassie said, blinking.

"I don't want to get him in trouble or nothing."

"He's retired," I said.

"Well, okay. Yeah. He'd have me text him when I was done. And he'd come back smelling like gin."

"And the witnesses?" Cassie asked.

"We'd talk for a bit," Walker said. "At some point, I'd tell 'em, 'Let me sketch you.'"

"You'd sketch the witnesses?" Cassie confirmed.

"You know . . ." He winked at Cassie. "Put the ladies at ease."

"Then you'd transition to the sketch of this man they remembered?"

"Exactly," Walker said to me. "But this thing—" He held up the last page. "I didn't know my drawings would get merged into some super-sketch. To be honest, I would've changed my approach if I did."

I wanted to know how well Walker remembered this time. "Do you recall these women, William?"

"Hell yeah." He took the file from Cassie. "The gal I interviewed for this one—" He held up one of the drawings. "The missing woman was her best friend. I'd lost my pop the year before that. The pain she talked about was real. We sat for two hours. Cried for a solid twenty minutes. Then I got to work. But she didn't remember the guy that well."

"The man you sketched?" I asked.

"Yeah." Walker nodded. "But Offerman told me if they couldn't recall the eyes or nose, I could fill it in from one of the other drawings."

Cassie gave me a look. This was not proper police procedure. It was also what had probably created some of the inconsistencies between the four drawings.

"Plus, two of the women couldn't see his mouth," William added.

"What do you mean?" Cassie said.

"He was wearing a mask."

"Like a surgical or N95?"

Walker hesitated. "Surgical, I guess," he said. "The paper kind we all wore. So I had to fill that in, too."

Cassie took the sketches back and pointed at dark areas on the face on two of the drawings. "What are these?" she asked.

"To be honest," he said, "I can't remember. But if I had to guess—scars of some type."

"Mr. Walker," I said, "did Ed Offerman ask for your impressions of these interviews?"

"My impressions?" He grinned. "You got a better vocabulary than me, brother. No, no. Impressions were not requested. My job was just to draw this guy . . . *el joven.*"

Cassie squinted, translating. "The young man?"

Walker smiled. "It wasn't that, though. But there was a nickname."

"Wait," I said. "The nickname was in Spanish?"

"Oh yeah. Most of these gals spoke Spanish. I told Offerman that, too. That he spoke Spanish."

"He who?" I clarified.

"He the whatever," Walker said. "The bad guy. Whatever his nickname was."

Cassie and I exchanged a glance. This was nowhere in Offerman's notes, and I wondered just how much he'd drunk while Walker drew.

"You're sure?" Cassie said.

"Oh yeah." Walker nodded. "Me and the ladies talked in Spanish for a while, and this one gal—she mentioned the guy in the sketch picked up her friend for a date. And that he spoke Spanish."

"How well?" Cassie asked.

Walker hesitated. "I remember asking her that—'*Como un guero?*'"

"Like a white boy," Cassie translated.

"And she smiled at me," Walker said. "Said yes, but mentioned he spoke okay, all the same."

"And you took that as what?" I asked. "The guy in the sketch grew up here, but in a Latin community? A Latin family?"

"Hell, I dunno, man. It's Florida. You can be *born* here and not speak a lick, you know what I'm saying? Or you can pick up the language along the way, am I right?"

Walker was right.

He'd also handed us our first potential break in the case.

"So he spoke Spanish," I said. "Fluently enough to communicate with native speakers."

"Check," the sketch artist said.

"And he went by a nickname. But you can't remember it?"

"Check again," he said. "And sorry."

"Tell me," I said. "If you heard the nickname . . . if someone else told us . . . would you recognize it?"

"For sure."

CHAPTER EIGHTEEN

CASSIE FOLLOWED UP WITH MORE QUESTIONS FOR THE sketch artist, asking Walker what he remembered about the women he had spoken to. But nothing else stuck.

"I'm glad y'all are looking into this," he said. "Those women didn't have much, but their girlfriends missed 'em bad. It's not fair, you know?"

Cassie nodded without speaking, and I understood intellectually how a more emotional person might get lost in this case. But for me, it was just numbers and facts. Victim's ages with no patterns. The same with occupation and social class.

My phone pinged with a text from Richie, and I stepped away. Walked halfway back to the car.

> Davitt has a solid pix on one skull. Q wants to go out to media.

Q had to be shorthand for Quinones. I turned back to Cassie and the sketch artist. Thanked him and told her we had to go.

Twenty minutes later, we were back in the Shilo PD lobby. I flashed my ID at the front desk. "We're headed to the basement," I said. "Do we need an escort?"

The woman at the desk was heavyset with enormous fake eyelashes. "You, honey"—she pointed with a long fingernail—"are hard to forget." She buzzed me in and motioned at the elevator. "Go on, handsome."

As we walked over and got inside, Cassie grinned.

"It's floor B, handsome," she said, motioning at the panel.

I ignored her and hit the button.

Getting off at the basement level, we saw Shooter at the far end of the room. She wore a head-to-toe suit made of white Tyvek material and had positioned two lights over the far end of a particular skeleton.

We came closer, examining the bones of the woman. The skull was missing, presumably with our facial reconstruction artist, whom I did not see on the floor.

"Until we have an ID, we're using numbers," Shooter said without looking up. She held a magnifying glass, which she'd trained on the woman's right femur. "Say hello to number four."

A sharp tool lay beside the skeleton's femur. Next to it was a pile of wax shavings.

"Be polite now," Shooter chided.

"Hello, number four," Cassie and I said simultaneously, knowing Jo would not relent until we did.

I turned to Shooter. "Where's Richie?"

"Third floor. Patsy Davitt wanted natural light."

Davitt was the facial reconstruction artist we'd brought in to help us identify the skulls of the six women. I looked at Cassie, who nodded.

"On it," she said and headed back to the elevator.

I glanced at the pile of shaved wax beside the femur. In humid environments like the South, a buried body can undergo a process known as saponification. The fatty tissues break down after burial and turn into a yellow material that gets whiter and more rigid over time, sometimes even preserving the bones.

"You've scraped off an adipocere formation," I said.

Shooter glanced at the pile of wax. "Four and I have spent a couple hours together," she said. "I noticed what looked to be a fracture along her femur."

"Did the ME concur?" I asked.

"She did," Shooter said. "But she also told me not to worry about it. That it's healed. Thing is . . . the bone just looks wrong, you know?"

I stared at it. I didn't know. But Jo Harris had the persistence of a bull terrier. She'd also studied kinetics and was once an Olympic athlete, so she knew the human body better than most.

"What are you seeing?" I asked.

"The wax," Shooter said, her head down again. "It's harder to see now that I've shaved it, but it was building up in a strange pattern. Right in this one area."

I moved around to the opposite side of the table, getting close to the scratch marks where Shooter had scraped off the adipocere.

"Or I should say," she corrected herself, "it *wasn't* building up in one area, Gardner. Almost in a straight line."

I borrowed Shooter's magnifying glass to study the femur. "I once met a forensic artist," I said as I squinted. "He swore he could use the gamut of color on a skeleton's fatty deposits, from white to yellow . . . along with the smell of the wax . . . to establish a rough time of death."

Shooter glanced up. "That is a particularly disgusting thought, Gardner."

I put gloves on and ran a finger along the femur. I had a theory in support of what Shooter was seeing, but I needed to prove it.

I moved out of the area and found the ME, her feet up on a desk that had once belonged to the Shilo medical examiner.

"Good afternoon," I said.

Ingrid Santos's feet came down, and she sat up. "Agent Camden," she said. "I didn't know you were here."

Santos was white and in her fifties with graying brown hair. When we had worked together in Jacksonville, her face was consistently flushed with red most afternoons, and I suspected she drank at lunch. Statistically, those with a faulty version of the aldehyde dehydrogenase 2 gene lack the enzymes to break down acetaldehyde in alcohol at the same rates as others, which can cause this kind of redness.

"Agent Harris had questions about a body part," I said. I glanced at a plate of chicken nachos in front of Santos. The cheese was congealed into a nearly flat mass, indicating the passage of at least forty-five minutes. "You *did* bring an autopsy saw with you, as I requested?"

"Yeah, of course," she said. "I was just having lunch is all, is all."

Santos had an iPad open, on which was displayed the home page of TMZ. I stood there, at first saying nothing.

"Did you start eating before Agent Harris asked you to follow up on her hunch? Or after?"

"Gyad," Santos said, exhaling loudly and standing up. "I'm moving, I'm moving."

I walked back to Shooter. A minute later, Santos arrived with a silver Mopec 5000 Autopsy Saw. In her other hand was its power supply box.

She exhaled loudly. "Where am I going with this bad boy?"

I motioned toward the bottom of the table. It wasn't uncommon for parts of the same skeleton to decompose at different rates. In this particular victim, the bones in the arm were still connected, while those in the legs had separated completely, one from the other.

"The femur," I replied. "Right side."

Santos moved closer to where Shooter had been working.

"You know lunch breaks are legally required in the state of Florida, Agent Camden," she said.

I looked at her. "That's not exactly true," I said. "Florida law doesn't require employers to provide lunch breaks specifically. It does, however, set parameters for employers around rest breaks, some of which can be used for lunch."

Santos blinked. "Where am I cutting?"

"I'd like you to measure first," I said. "One and three-quarters inches from the head of the femur. Then cut there."

Shooter handed the ME a measuring tape, and Santos marked off the distance, making a small x on the bone before positioning her saw.

"And you just want me to randomly cut the bone," she said, "right here?"

I studied the saw's power unit, which had a row of four lights. Ounce for ounce, bones are stronger than steel, and it takes four thousand newtons of force to break one.

"Slowly," I said. "If the overload light goes on, I'd like you to pull back and I'm going to turn the femur, allowing you to cut to the same depth all the way around."

"Oh-kay." Santos shrugged.

She began cutting. The sound echoed off the basement walls. Then the hum changed to a struggling whine, and the overload light flickered. I held the other end of the femur and turned it two inches. The light went off and Santos began again, this time cutting in from the other side of the bone. When it flickered again, I rotated the femur a third time.

As we got around to where she had begun, the bone broke, and I heard Shooter gasp.

"What the hell is that?" she said.

We all leaned in to see.

CHAPTER NINETEEN

A SHINY TITANIUM ROD WAS EMBEDDED INSIDE THE femur.

"It's called an intramedullary nail," I said. "The saw blade was designed to cut through bone, but not the harder metal."

"What's it for?" Shooter asked.

"Support for the fracture," the ME said, looking to me. "How the hell did you know that was in there?"

"I didn't." I pointed to Shooter. "She did. Somehow the metal rod was repelling the waxy buildup. I'll have to research why at a later time."

"Give me a minute," Santos said. "I can pull that outta there, outta there."

She left the area, then came back with an extraction tool, which she used to remove the shiny metal rod.

"The manufacturer of that will give you the doctor's name," I said to Shooter. "From there, you can ID the victim."

While Shooter followed this up, I headed off to check in with Richie and Cassie upstairs. As I waited for the elevator, my phone rang. It was Justin Seethers, the district attorney who was holding Travis Wells in jail down in Farner County. Our other case.

Seethers asked me if I was still in the area.

"No," I said, mentally switching gears to the gun case. "We're juggling another investigation. Is everything all right?"

"So far so good," he said. "You?"

The propensity humans have for small talk constantly confounds me. When I worked in Jacksonville, we had an admin who would answer emails in which I signed off with "You're welcome" with the response "No—*you're* welcome."

"My colleague and I will be there in the morning," I said to Seethers. Tomorrow would be Saturday, so I added, "Is that acceptable to you?"

"Acceptable?" He snorted. "Yeah."

I took the elevator to the third floor. Richie and Cassie stood in a corner office, along with Detective Quinones and Patsy Davitt.

"This is Gardner Camden," Richie said, introducing me.

Davitt sported a white lab coat, but it hung loosely on her thin figure. "Agent Camden and I have met before," she said. "Two years ago. Another case."

Behind Davitt were four skulls, laid out on a side table. The far-right one was placed at a distance from the other three, and I crouched to inspect the set that were grouped together. Davitt had glued red markers to each skull that approximated the depth of tissue, then laid clay in between the markers, slowly forming the contours of what was once a face.

I knew from the past case that after this, Davitt would make a silicone mold from the skulls, photograph it, digitally add hair, and color the skin.

"Have you gotten these three into the computer yet?" I asked.

Richie nodded before she could answer, flipping open his laptop. "Dr. Davitt colorized the skin an hour ago," he said. "Added shadows for the jawline."

I stared at the digital faces of three women. Two were Caucasian with brown, shoulder-length hair, and one was Latino. My eyes scanned from the pictures on the laptop to the skulls themselves, matching up each one. "And the fourth?" I asked, nodding at the skull that had been set apart.

"The more I studied this one," Davitt said, putting her hands on her hips, "the more I thought that it might be a man. Slender framed. Delicate features and thin hips, but masculine. We'll need to go back and look at the skeleton again."

I took this in, nodding. I also noticed that Detective Quinones was wearing a suit, and I speculated that he'd put it on for a press conference.

At some point in an investigation, the need to alert the public outweighs the impulse to keep a case quiet. This is especially true if police suspect the murderer is still active in the area.

"You went out to the media?" I confirmed.

"A half hour ago," Quinones said. "I've got two patrolmen taking down numbers and names as the calls come in."

Shooter walked into the office and filled the others in on the rod we had found inside the femur.

"I talked to the manufacturer," she said. "They gave me the name of the surgeon like you said, Gardner. I called his office and asked about the woman."

"So we've got a name for number four?" Richie perked up.

"Mavreen Isiah," Shooter said. "Thirty years old. In 2018, she leapt from a second-story balcony. Suicide attempt. Broke her femur."

"You talk to her family yet?" I asked.

"None I could find so far," Shooter said. "But you know my go-to move."

Shooter's philosophy was simple: You learned more about people from what they spent their money on and who they owed.

"You ran her credit?" I said.

"And here's the thing, Gardner," Shooter said. "Mavreen Isiah is alive. She works at a plumbing supply house twenty minutes away."

I blinked. "What?"

The skeletonized woman in our basement was clearly not with us anymore. Which meant that someone else was using Mavreen Isiah's identity.

Which in turn meant we had a lead.

"You sure?" I asked.

"Active income," Shooter said. "Federal and state tax taken out. This week, even."

I looked at the time. Five hours 'til Cassie and I had to be at the Jacksonville airport.

"I got an address where our supposed Ms. Isiah works," Shooter said to me. "You wanna go interview a dead woman?"

CHAPTER TWENTY

ANY WAY U LIKE IT PLUMBING WAS IN A TOWN CALLED Lideca, twenty-three minutes from Shilo, along State Highway 301.

As Shooter drove, I reviewed Richie's notes on Patsy Davitt's work, which he'd emailed before I left. I used my thumb to scan down as I speed-read them on my phone, stopping in a particular section.

Richie and Detective Quinones had gone through missing persons reports in the Shilo area, and an interesting name had popped up.

Tommy Herrera, also known as "Dog," had been reported missing on January 17, 2020. This was the pimp boyfriend of Melanie Nelson, whose mother Cassie and I had interviewed that morning. Rebecca Nelson had described the boyfriend as tiny; in her words, "a solid wind" could blow him over.

Dog's cousin had waited a full month before coming into the Shilo police precinct to report the missing person, presumably since Dog himself was a two-time offender.

All this led Richie to a theory. That the skull Davitt referred to as having "delicate features" was possibly Dog, somehow caught in the crosshairs by whoever had taken his girlfriend, Melanie.

I relayed this to Shooter, who scowled at me. "So what are we thinking?" she said. "Our man in the sketch is abducting couples now?"

"We don't know enough to rule that out," I said, acknowledging our ignorance with a frown.

Shooter switched lanes and got off the highway. The sun was still high, and the sky was streaked with red.

"You checked that this Isiah woman is at work?" I asked.

"I called before we left," Shooter said. "Told the guy I was a customer who spoke to her last week. Mavreen works the afternoon shift. He said she'd be in by now."

The area was industrial, and nearly every turnoff led into a commercial park, filled with buildings with roll-up doors and trucks covered in vinyl.

Shooter slowed the car by a sign with blue neon letters that read ANY WAY U LIKE IT. I glanced around. Across the street was a liquor store called Silver Star.

"What is it?" Shooter asked.

"Where was the surgeon?" I said. "Who did the operation on the femur?"

"Gainesville."

My mind formed a triangle between Shilo, Gainesville, and Lideca. No theory emerged. I struggled to remember a case where we had learned so much in three days yet still had no leads on a killer. Each question led to more questions.

Shooter shut off the engine. We walked inside and tapped a bell at the counter.

The lobby was small. Sixty square feet, furnished with a gray love seat and a watercooler with a stack of nine pointy cups atop it. Under the glass counter were policies and procedures, printed on paper that had yellowed over time.

Shooter smiled at me, tapping on the counter. "Lotta rules for a place called Any Way U Like It."

A woman emerged from the back. "Afternoon," she said.

She was blond and plain, with a small nose and wavy hair cut short off her shoulders, like a young boy. Shooter glanced over, deferring to me.

"My name is Gardner Camden," I said, showing her my badge. "This is my colleague Joanne Harris. We're with the Federal Bureau of Investigation."

"Okay?" the woman said, a question more than an answer.

"We've discovered the body of a dead woman in Shilo, Florida," I said. "She had a surgical pin in her right leg from a jump she'd made. An attempted suicide off a second-story balcony."

I paused, studying the woman's reaction. Her throat distended, and her pupils shrank to two and a half millimeters. She placed her hands behind her back, I suspected to keep a tremble out of view.

"The surgeon identified the pin as belonging to Mavreen Isiah," I continued. "Except—that's you, right?"

The woman said nothing, and I counted nineteen seconds since she'd visibly breathed.

Her eyes darted past us then, out to the street.

"What you may be experiencing right now is a fight-or-flight reaction," Shooter said. "But we're not here to arrest you . . . as long as you can help us."

I looked from Shooter to the woman. We could ask for her real name. Threaten her. But I wanted to get a reaction that might break the case open. I pulled the composite sketch from a folder in my satchel and laid it on the counter.

"Do you know this man?"

The woman's eyes locked onto the photo, and her face drained of color. "No?"

Again, the answer came out as a question. Shooter cocked her head, leaning her body low enough to make eye contact with the woman, who was staring at the ground.

"Ma'am, we believe the woman whose body we found was killed by the man in this sketch."

Tears streamed down the woman's face, and she breathed through her nose, her chest rising and falling. Gasping, she wiped at the streaks of makeup with the back of her hand.

"She's my sister," she said, her voice almost a whisper.

"What's your name?" I asked.

"Amber."

"Amber Isiah?"

She nodded.

"And you know this man?" Shooter said, her voice soft.

"I saw him once," Amber said. "But I don't know his name."

"Amber," I said, "let's start back at the beginning. Explain to us why you're working here under your sister's name."

She nodded, but seemed frozen. "I need a cigarette," she said, her voice breaking. "Sorry." She looked around. "There's none here. They don't let us smoke on the property."

Shooter touched the woman's arm. "I'll go across to the liquor store."

She returned a few moments later and handed Amber a pack of Camel Lights. We stepped through the glass door to the curb out-side—to get the woman some air, if nothing else. Cars passed, and Amber's fingers trembled as she lit a cigarette and sat down on the edge of the curb.

"I'm scared," she said, her voice so light I could barely hear it.

I studied her. What we lacked so far on this case was victimology, but now we had the relative of a victim. Someone who'd seen the perpetrator. We just needed to get her talking. About anything.

"Mavreen was your sister," I said to her. "Where did you two grow up?"

"Boston," she said. "Mavreen was two years older than me."

"What brought you to Florida?"

Amber took a long drag on her cigarette and nodded. "I was a few years out of high school and working at Star," she said. "That's a grocery store up north. Mavreen came to me one day saying she was going to Florida. Wanted me to come with."

"She had a job?" Shooter asked. "School?"

"No," Amber said, shaking her head. "But Mavreen was always doing stuff like that. Spur-of-the-moment trips. She was the wild one, you know? But . . . she was my best friend."

We nodded and waited for more.

"I figured I could do the same thing in Florida that I was doing in Boston," Amber continued. "But, you know, better weather?"

She went quiet, and I prompted her. "So you two left and came down here?"

"Jacksonville at first," she said. "But it was the usual. We got there, and I realized Mavreen already had some guy lined up. That's why she'd picked that place. I ended up staying with them awhile. A room in his garage."

I pulled out the sketch. "This is the guy you stayed with?"

"No," she said. "This is earlier. You asked where I was from. How I got down here."

Shooter gave me a glance, and I heard my mother's voice.

Slow down, Gardy. Give people time to tell their story. Let them own their moment.

"I apologize," I said, my words sounding hollow. "Please keep going."

Amber placed the cigarette on the edge of the curb, its tip still lit. "I didn't know for sure," she said, wiping at her eyes with both hands. "That Mavreen was dead. I thought maybe . . ."

"Amber," Shooter said. "Why were you using your sister's name?"

"That goes back to him." She pointed at my bag, where I'd put the sketch away.

"The man in the picture?" I asked.

"I don't know his name or anything, but—"

"You saw him?" I said.

"Not exactly." She looked at me. "Mavreen met this guy and wouldn't stop talking about him. Then she kinda became his girl-friend, I guess? It was weird."

"Weird how?"

"Like how she acted. Like a kidnap victim or a cult member or something."

"He had some control over her?" Shooter asked.

"Yeah," Amber said. "Some power. I dunno."

"Did they work together?" I asked.

"I don't think so," she said. "Mavreen was a CNA, you know?"

"A certified nursing assistant?"

"Yeah. And she worked in this like—office park. There were other medical offices there. Dentists and doctors. Other places, too. A cof-fee place. A café. I don't know where he worked, but they met in the courtyard one day."

"They didn't meet in *her* office?" I asked.

"No, I asked if he was a patient. She said no."

"What *did* she say?" Shooter asked.

"I was living an hour away back then," Amber said. "So we'd talk by phone mostly. She was always kind of weird about him." She squinted. "Like, holding stuff back. Thinking I'd be mad. Then she stopped working at that place, and I didn't see her for a while. She'd call me from different numbers. Like, you know how the city comes up on your phone sometimes? She'd tell me she was in that city. Just for a month."

I considered options that made sense. "Was your sister a traveling nurse?"

"No," Amber said.

"You said she called you," Shooter cut in, prompting her back to that detail.

"Yeah," Amber said. "And the last time, she sounded really scared. Told me that if I didn't hear back from her in a few days, she might be dead. I told her to get out. To run. Three days passed. Then a week. I called the number back and asked for Mavreen. The guy who answered told me she wasn't there. He said not to call again."

"This was the guy in the sketch?" I asked.

"I think so," she said. "But it was just a phone call. I couldn't see him."

"Did he have an accent?" I asked.

"Maybe?"

"Okay," I said, slowing down. "What kind?"

"I dunno."

"Was it Southern?" I asked. "Georgia? Florida?"

"No."

The sketch artist had told us the man spoke Spanish.

"Was it foreign?" I asked, not wanting to steer her toward any language yet.

"It was like . . . he was trying to talk with a voice. Like, to sound well educated."

Huh?

"All right," I said.

"I asked the guy," Amber continued, "'Is this her boyfriend?' That's when he got scary. Said he knew my name. Where I lived. Said if I kept asking around, he would come for me. Cut me."

"Cut you?" I said. "Those were the words he used?"

Amber pursed her lips together, the color drained from them. "Yeah," she whispered.

"Did you call the police?" Shooter asked.

"And say what?"

"That your sister went missing," Shooter said. "That a dangerous man had threatened you."

Amber grabbed at the cigarette at the curb and stubbed it out, even though it was long extinguished. "Mavreen was *always* into dangerous guys. She dated drug dealers in high school. The guy in Jacksonville was in a bike gang. I figured it was one more guy like that."

Except well educated?

"What happened next?" I asked.

"She'd called me from a lot of numbers, so I tried a different one the next week."

"You called a different number back?" Shooter clarified.

"Yeah," Amber said. "But the same guy answered. He freaked this time. Said he warned me, and now he was coming after me. He told me, 'Your name is Amber. You live on Oak Street.' I just . . . I panicked. Loaded up my car and left Gainesville. I'm driving around the next day, and suddenly, I'm in the middle of nowhere. I get a Coke. See this place."

"This plumbing place?" Shooter confirmed, gesturing to the office behind us.

Amber nodded. "There was a Help Wanted sign. Manager said if I agreed to work the late shift, I could sleep in this tiny house at the back of the property. I was afraid that the guy knew my name. I thought—if he killed Mavreen—who's the last person he's gonna ask for?"

"Mavreen," Shooter said.

"So I told the manager my wallet got stolen, but I knew my social. Gave him hers. They didn't even ask for my ID. I just told them I was Mavreen Isiah and they believed me."

"When was this?" I asked.

"The last call?" she said. "A year ago. I started working here the next day."

"Amber," I said. "You and your sister were best friends, right?"

She sniffed, tears coming again.

"Sisters talk," I said. "Best friends talk. We need to know anything else she might've said about this guy."

Amber wiped at her nose with her shirt cuff. "In the beginning, she said she heard rumors about him. I asked, 'What kinda rumors?' She acted like he was in legal trouble. But then she told me, 'It's not like you think. He's got money. People come to him. People who need things.'"

"What kind of things?" Shooter squinted.

"I don't know," Amber said. "She told me once—sometimes the system is broken, so people come to him. To go outside of regular channels."

"Was he organized crime?" I asked.

"I don't think so."

We needed to learn something definitive about this guy, and

Amber was going in circles. I glanced at Shooter, whose eyes ran over my posture, which was rigid, hands on hips. Taking a slow breath, I loosened up and tried to select the right phrase.

"You met him, though, right, Amber? We showed you the picture, and your face went white."

"It was on FaceTime," she said. "When they first got together. I called her one night and she was in a bar. So I saw him—yeah—well enough to know that's him. But it was over the phone. And it was dark, like a bar is, y'know?"

"But he looked like the drawing?" Shooter asked.

"Yeah." Amber nodded.

"Was he white?" I asked. "Latino? Black?"

"Not Black," she said. "White, I think. Or maybe a mix of white and Hispanic? Like I said, it was dark."

I pulled out the composite sketch and laid it on the curb. "And he looked like this?"

"Pretty close." She nodded.

I laid out the other sketches beside the first. "Which one of these is the most accurate?"

"It was only the one time I saw him, but his eyes were more like that one." She pointed at the third sketch. "The rest of his face is like the first."

"And these marks?" Shooter pointed at a dark area on the sketch.

"I dunno," Amber said. "A cut, maybe?"

"You said Mavreen met him when she worked at a medical clinic?" I looked to Shooter. "We have her sister's work history, right?"

Shooter pulled out her laptop. "Was this at Alantay Medical Group?"

"Yeah, exactly." Amber nodded.

"That's 2019, Gardner," Shooter said to me. "She stops working there in December. Between then and that call is four months."

My mind populated the dates we knew onto a timeline. If what Amber was saying was accurate, it meant that the phone call and Mavreen's death happened around April 2020.

Shooter squinted at me, her mind clocking something on my face.

"What else did your sister tell you?" I asked. "They go anywhere? Do things together?"

"Yeah," Amber said, picking out a new cigarette and tapping the end against her leg. "Mavreen got her passport. They were going somewhere."

"Good," I said, knowing we could check where Mavreen had traveled if she had left the country. "And the number your sister called you from? You could see it on your phone?"

She nodded. "But like I said, she called me from different numbers. All the time."

"You ever see the same one twice?"

"Couple times. That's how I called it back—that last time when he threatened me."

"What about after you got here?" Shooter asked.

"I never turned on that phone again. I called the neighbor from my old apartment from the office phone here. She said some guy came around, looking for me, the same afternoon I applied for this job. Girl at my old place of work told me the same thing. Same day."

"You still have that phone?" I asked.

She nodded, looking wary. "I've got it. You want me to call the number?"

"We want you to give it to us," I said. "And, Amber, have you told anyone else this story? About Mavreen?"

"No." She shook her head.

"No one at all?" Shooter asked again.

"No one."

"Good," I said. "You're going to continue being Mavreen. For your own safety. The only people who know you're not are Agent Harris and me. Now please bring us that phone."

Amber locked up the office, placing a sign in the window that said she'd be back soon. Then she punched in a code at the gate and walked toward the back of the property, presumably to the tiny house she'd mentioned staying in.

"What was I missing back there?" Shooter asked once she was gone.

"What do you mean?"

She motioned at my head. "I saw the supercomputer going. When she said those dates."

"Oh, that." I nodded. "Let's wait until we're back at the precinct and I can populate a timeline on paper. In case I'm wrong."

"You?" Shooter said.

But I nodded. Something had been unsettling me all afternoon.

Was it the dead women? It would be unlike me, but perhaps I was extrapolating my Camila—forward in age—imagining an atrocity like this happening to her.

Amber came back through the office and opened the door, handing Shooter an iPhone in a pink case. Her eyes were red again.

"I thought she was exaggerating," she said to me while Shooter inspected the phone. "You know?"

"Mavreen?" I confirmed.

Amber nodded, and I said nothing. What was there to say?

"What happened to your sister wasn't your fault," Shooter jumped in. "So don't do that to yourself, Amber. It's not true, first of all. And it's definitely not worth it."

"There was always some guy." Amber wiped at her face. "Being mean to her. Scary. Guess I got tired of rescuing her."

Amber was staring at me.

The silence grew, and I knew I should say something. But she didn't want to hear the truth: that her sister had reached out to her, and she had let her down.

And I wasn't good at handing out redemption.

CHAPTER TWENTY-ONE

SHOOTER AND I SUPPLIED AMBER ISIAH WITH OUR contact information, and Jo took the wheel, heading back to Shilo.

"You know, Gardner," she said after a minute, her voice more serious than usual. "Sometimes people are just looking for an 'It's okay.' You know how to say, 'It's okay,' right?"

"Yes," I replied. "Yes, I do."

Shooter's phone rang through the speaker of the SUV, and Richie came on. "We've got something," he said, his voice ringing with the nervous excitement we'd grown accustomed to. "Can you talk?"

"Yeah," Shooter said. "We're just driving back."

"A woman named Olive McCredey saw one of the skull photos. Came by here in person."

"This woman has a missing daughter?" Shooter asked.

"No," Richie said. "She's a retired schoolteacher. Told us one of the photos looks just like a girl she once taught. The girl's dad lives on a houseboat on Lake Garvin."

"You talk to the family yet?" Shooter asked.

"Detective Quinones said it's on your way back," Richie said. "But it's not in his jurisdiction. He's asking if you want a sheriff to meet you there."

A sheriff would deliver a death notice, but we needed to verify more details before that.

"Send us the picture you went out with," I said. "And the address. We'll check it out first."

"I could meet you guys," Richie offered. His voice was full of nerves, and I couldn't tell if he was on edge about doing his first death notification—or something else.

"It's all right," I said. "But after this, let's get the team assembled. Cassie and I need to head out soon, and I haven't eaten all day."

"Copy that," Richie said. "Why don't I pick up some chow while you two follow this up?"

"Great."

"And, guys," Richie added, "apparently the girl's dad is a little jumpy. War vet. Raised his daughter on that houseboat. Probably still waiting for her to come back."

We got off the state highway three miles down. A roadside sign advertising FLORIDA'S LARGEST CITRUS STAND offered free samples of oranges and pecan candies and sold fireworks all year long. We passed it and headed south, the road becoming a two-lane with rosemary and marsh marigold growing wild along the roadside, saturated in eight inches of standing water.

Neither of us had spoken in ten minutes.

Shooter turned to me. "What are you thinking?"

"This guy," I said, referring to the man in the sketch. "We have no idea what's motivating him. What these women have in common."

"Yet," Shooter said. Which was a rallying cry at PAR.

"Yet," I agreed.

But inside, I had a fear that comes to me from time to time. That

PAR would inherit a case that bore no patterns for us to recognize. Offered no riddle to solve. Was devoid of any real evidence.

The FBI, for what it's worth, has always been an organization full of lawyers and accountants, along with ex-cops and law enforcement types. But PAR was built from a different DNA, and the most common skill set we all had in common was data analysis. Which wasn't that helpful on cases with no data.

Shooter slowed the car, and I examined a small marina. A dock stuck out onto a green lake on which four boats were moored. Two were houseboats; the other two were sixteen-foot outboards. The rest of the marina contained open slips for boats to motor in for gas or bait.

The two houseboats were connected by a small plank walkway, and faded signs with arrows pointed to each side: GILLIAM'S BAIT SHACK and GILLIAM'S HIDEAWAY.

I opened the text from Richie.

Julie Gilliam. Missing since March 2020. Dad: Bud Gilliam.

I held it out so Shooter could see it, and she pursed her lips, nodding.

As we glanced at the phone, a second text came in, this one containing the computer-generated image that had gone out to the media.

In the digital reconstruction, Julie Gilliam was a petite Caucasian with wavy blond hair that was cut just below her ears. A small round face with big eyes.

We got out of the car and walked along the grassy area that led to the dock. It was late afternoon, and most fishing businesses open at dawn. A single bulb burned outside the bait shack. My eyes trailed up to a man standing on the wooden plank that ran between the two houseboats.

"Permission to come aboard?" Shooter called out, her voice upbeat.

The man was slight of stature, with curly brown hair. He wore a mechanic's one-piece in olive green and looked to be in his sixties.

"Bait shack's closed," he said. "Not that you two look like you're ready to fish."

Up close, the floating structures had seen better days. The houseboat on the left advertised the best bait to catch bluegills. The one at right was the residence, and half the paint had peeled off the side of it.

"Are you Bud Gilliam?" Shooter asked.

"I am," he said. He took the plank over toward the houseboat, and we headed in the same direction. As we got closer, I saw a shotgun laid out on a circular table on the boat deck.

"Jo," I said softly under my breath, but she had already clocked it.

"That's a classic," she said to the man. "Stevens Model 94, am I right? Sixteen gauge?"

"You know your weapons." The man rocked back on his heels. "You government?"

"I grew up hunting with my dad," Shooter said, not answering him directly. "My pop would take a Model 48 Topper that he learned to shoot with. I would use a Stevens. He gave it to me when I turned ten."

"You still have it?" the man asked.

"You know what?" Shooter said. "I sold it." She shook her head, and her strawberry-blond hair flitted from left to right. "Felt bad about it after. Went into the gun store to buy it back, but the owner had taken the Tenite off. Replaced it with wood."

The man shook his head as if someone had committed an atrocity. "Yuppies," he said. "That store owner was trying to upcharge some young buyer. Some hunter who wouldn't know a grouse from a turkey."

"We're with the Federal Bureau of Investigation, by the way," Shooter said. "I'm Joanne Harris. This is Gardner Camden."

The man nodded. Looked curious more than anything. "This gun was legally purchased, ma'am," he said.

"I'm sure it was, Mr. Gilliam," she replied.

Shooter looked to me, and I glanced back at her. She had established rapport, and I wasn't going to fight her for the right to tell this man the worst news of his life. We had been brusquer with Amber Isiah than notification policies recommended, but that was different. All we knew at the outset was that she'd been stealing a dead woman's identity.

"We understand your daughter, Julie, has been missing," Shooter said, "since March of last year?"

The man's face blanched, and he nodded. Now it was my turn.

"The police have found the remains of a young woman," I said. "Likely mid-twenties. Shilo PD put a picture out on the news."

The father said nothing for a second. Then he turned away from us, out toward the water. We had closed the distance and were at the edge of the dock, but I kept my eyes on the gun to make sure he didn't move toward it.

After two minutes, he turned back and wiped at his face. More than a year had elapsed since Julie Gilliam went missing, and no doubt her father had imagined this moment a hundred times.

He walked to the edge of the houseboat and unhooked a rope to invite us aboard. "You got this picture on you?"

I pulled out my phone and showed Gilliam the digital composite that Patsy Davitt had made. He bit at his lip, nodding. Turned and walked back onto the houseboat.

On the same deck where the gun lay were two wicker chairs, and without saying a word, he pointed for us to sit in them.

"What do you remember about the last time you saw Julie?" I asked.

"She was out here on the water," he said, his voice hoarse. "There was a local fella who didn't know much about his boat. She and I were fixing it up. It was springtime."

"You two always live here?" Shooter asked. "On this boat?"

"Since her mom died when Julie was twelve," he said. "Jules was an easy kid to raise. Good grades in school. Knew everyone on the marina. Everyone loved her."

"The last time you saw her," Shooter said, "was she dating anyone?"

"No," he said. "She had a boyfriend a year before that, a friend from high school. But no one after him."

"Your daughter was twenty-four when she went missing, sir," I said. "Was she employed?"

"She worked on the lake some. Waitressed some. She didn't know what she wanted to do yet. She'd say that a lot. But I think she just didn't want to leave me here alone."

I reflected on the professions of the women who had gone missing. A dancer. A cab driver. A nursing assistant. A motel manager. I was struggling to find a pattern and considered the statistics of college-eligible women in the US.

Two point one million high school students enroll immediately in some college, two-thirds of that number in four-year schools. But so far none of our victims had done so. And women were 12.9 percent more likely to attend postsecondary education than men.

"Julie hadn't attended any college?" I asked.

"She was considering trade school," Mr. Gilliam said.

"Healthcare?" I offered, wondering if there was some connection to nursing, like Mavreen Isiah.

"That was one thought. But she grew up on a boat fixing things, so Jules was thinking more plumbing or electrical."

So no pattern with occupation.

Julie Gilliam was also younger than the other victims, whose median age was 30.3.

Nothing on this case seemed to follow a pattern.

"That picture looks like her"—Bud Gilliam motioned at my phone—"but at the same time, it doesn't. You guys found something? Some DNA or scientific thing like on television?"

"Something like that," Shooter said, and we followed Gilliam's gaze out toward the water.

Julie Gilliam had not gone missing in Shilo's jurisdiction, so we lacked the case file on her as a missing person. This rendered the visit more of a notification and less of an interview. Still, we could dig in on some details. Shooter asked her father about the day Julie went missing.

"We're unincorporated out here," he said, pointing at the area around him. "So the local sheriff asked for volunteers to search the area. A hundred people showed up. Lotta boaters and hunters familiar with the local inlets and swamps. Sheriff divided into groups of four and broke down the whole area into grids. He and I stayed here, by the phone."

"Nothing?" Shooter asked.

"There were a lot of calls," Gilliam said. "People checking in. I half expected her to be found in some bad condition. Somewhere in the swamp." He paused and shrugged. "Nothing. Her friends put it on the internet, the social media. More calls, but nothing. Sheriff still comes by every few months to check in. Her friends do the same."

He wiped at his face again and stared out toward an inlet thick with sawgrass. A tricolored heron landed on the top of the bait shack, and I thought of something I'd heard other members of law enforcement express. That they wanted to catch a perp and watch as someone stuck a needle in their arm. I had never felt this way, but hearing Gilliam speak, I understood the sentiment.

I pulled the sketch from my satchel. "Does this man look familiar?" I asked.

He stared at the picture. "No one I know," he said. "Who is he?"

"A person of interest," Shooter replied. "It's possible he has nothing to do with your daughter's case. But we have to be sure."

I asked to use the bathroom, but it was more of an excuse to inspect Gilliam's boat. Inside was a small combination living and kitchen area, from which a tiny hallway led to two bedrooms.

"You have my girl in the morgue or something?" I heard Gilliam ask as I walked away.

"In a manner of speaking," Shooter said, her voice softer than normal.

I headed down the hallway and glanced right and left at the two diminutive bedrooms, which only had enough room to fit a bed and a tiny dresser. Gilliam's bed was unmade, but his daughter's room looked pristine. I walked inside and opened a drawer, seeing a blue hairbrush thick with blondish-red strands. Straighter and longer than Bud Gilliam's.

As I came out, Shooter mentioned that Gilliam had agreed to come to the Shilo PD the next day.

"I'm sorry for your loss, sir," she said. "Is there anyone we can call to come be with you?"

"No," he said.

"There's a blue hairbrush," I said. "In her drawer. Can we take it?"

He nodded, his voice caught in his throat.

Shooter moved out to the car to grab her crime kit and came back holding an evidence bag. While she was inside, Bud Gilliam asked me for another look at the photo. I showed it to him, and he held his hand over his mouth.

"How did you make this?" he asked, referring to the photo.

I wasn't sure of everything Shooter had told him while I was inside. But I reflected on the comment she had made in the car on the way here.

"It's computer-generated," I said. "It's not her, Mr. Gilliam. It's just a computer image."

Tears blanketed Gilliam's cheeks, and he nodded. "Her mouth looks perfect, though."

Shooter came out, the evidence bag in hand. But I was stuck on what Gilliam had just said. His words were wrong.

"Do you have a recent picture of Julie?" I asked.

"Sure," he said, moving inside and finding one in a four-by-six frame. He handed it to me, and I stared at it.

"She had a cleft lip."

"Yeah," he replied.

I looked more closely at the photo. Most cleft issues, whether to the lips or the palate, are noticed at birth in the US and repaired in the first few years of life, often in a series of surgeries. With prenatal ultrasounds, some are even detected as early as week thirteen of a pregnancy. But they would not be seen on a skull, hence our picture looking better than expected by her father.

I studied a scar mark just above her lip and could tell that she'd had at least one corrective surgery, probably as a child.

"You asked me about the last time we talked," Bud Gilliam said. "Maybe I wasn't totally honest."

"That's not abnormal," I said, my eyes steady on the man. "We just met."

"Julie and I argued," he said. "She'd talked with some guy who said he could help her. Do some procedure on her mouth. I told her she didn't need it done."

As he spoke, I looked more closely at the photo of Julie Gilliam. I couldn't help but think that something had gone wrong with the cheiloplasty surgery, intended to fix the problem Julie had been born with. Her lips showed asymmetry, and a small scar ran up toward the philtrum, the vertical grooved indent below her nose.

Bud Gilliam continued. "I mean, if she wanted to do it—sure, I told her. But she was beautiful as is. We argued, and she took off in a huff. That's the last time I saw her."

"Thank you for your time," Shooter said. "I'll see you tomorrow at the station."

He nodded and turned, his shoulders slumped.

Out in the rental car, I paged backward in my notebook, looking for contact information for the sketch artist Cassie and I had met four hours ago, thinking of this man that Julie Gilliam had met with.

Beside me, Shooter muttered something under her breath, then got out and headed back to the houseboat. As she did, I called up W. C. Walker.

"Mr. Walker," I said. "This is Gardner Camden with the FBI. Do you remember me from this morning?"

"A bird like you, brother?" he chuckled. "You're hard to forget."

"The sketch you did," I said, staring out the window as Shooter placed a hand on Bud Gilliam's arm. "You said there was a nickname in Spanish that the women used. For the man in the sketch?"

"Right," he said.

Out the window, Bud Gilliam handed his shotgun to Shooter. She said something, and Gilliam went back inside the houseboat. Came out with a revolver, which he also handed to Jo.

"You say it was *el joven*," I said to the sketch artist. "The young man. But not that."

"But something like that," he replied.

Shooter placed the two guns down on the table on the houseboat and hugged the man, something that was not covered in the death notification manual. Gilliam held on tight. When they stepped apart, she took the two weapons and headed over to our car.

"Was it *el médico*?" I asked the sketch artist. *The doctor.*

"There you go, brother," Walker said. "Hot damn, it *was el médico*. Is that a clue?"

CHAPTER TWENTY-TWO

BY 5:35 P.M., SHOOTER AND I HAD MADE OUR WAY BACK TO the precinct, first driving through the swampland, then veering south toward Shilo.

As we found a spot in the parking lot, I saw insignias from four counties on the police cruisers parked there. News of the bodies we'd discovered had attracted the attention of surrounding police departments.

Shooter and I made our way to the second floor. Cops—some in uniforms that included wide-brimmed campaign hats, others in suits—crowded outside the office of Detective Warner Quinones, who eyed us and nodded. We threaded around the open cubes toward the glass-walled conference room at the north end of the second floor.

"Everyone on Yelp raved about this restaurant," Richie said as we entered. He placed two paper bags atop a credenza and set out six cans of Coke and Sprite. "So I picked up a couple quarts of their specialty."

"Quarts?" I said.

I hadn't eaten all day and was looking forward to solid food. Still, Richie talked so often about being "a foodie, through and through" that I figured the meal would be of high quality. Or if not, some cuisine popular among Floridians under thirty.

"Minorcan clam chowder," Richie said, opening the top of the paper bag and laying out four soup containers for the group.

"What the hell is Minorcan clam chowder?" Cassie said, entering after Shooter and me, her face half-buried in a case file.

I looked to Cassie. "Are you asking me?" I said. "Sorry, I don't know everything."

"The chef gave me a taste at the restaurant," Richie replied. "It's made with seafood stock. But it's got this hot pepper in it. Called datil."

"That's an heirloom pepper," I said, opening my laptop and grabbing a chair. "It's grown in St. Augustine and belongs to the same species as capsicum, which is used in pepper spray."

"So you *do* know everything," Shooter said.

On another day, this would've gotten laughs, but the case had everyone focused. I opened my container and blew on the chowder. Across the surface, carrots and diced potatoes floated in a red liquid, along with flakes of oregano and rosemary.

"Do we have a whiteboard?" I asked Richie.

He put down his soup and hopped up. "There's a portable one outside. Let me grab it."

I turned to Shooter. She would be the senior agent once I left with Cassie for Miami. "I suggest we write out all the victims' names. Begin with a list. Then populate missing dates on a timeline. You okay with that?"

"Absolutely," she said.

Richie rolled the board into the room and closed the door behind him.

"We've got nine known victims, right?"

"Check," Shooter said. "Presuming we're counting the three women that Offerman and Quinones looked into a few years ago."

Richie jotted their names on the board.

"The first three were Maria Elisandro, Rana Delgado, and Susan Jones," he said. "Those were the ones Offerman documented."

Out the glass of the conference room, a sheriff in an olive uniform stepped off the elevator and headed toward Quinones's office.

"Then there's the six we uncovered four days ago," Cassie said.

Melanie Nelson was the one whose mother Cassie and I had spoken to in the mobile home park. Araceli Alvarez was the young lady whose family Richie and Shooter had talked to at the same time.

"Today we identified two more," Shooter said as Richie added those names to the board. "Mavreen Isiah. She was the woman we ID'd off the pin in her leg."

"And Julie Gilliam," I said, "whose father we spoke to on the way here."

Richie put up his index finger. "Our reconstruction artist is now almost certain one of the victims could be a man. More specifically, Thomas 'Dog' Herrera, who was the boyfriend of Melanie Nelson."

"So where does that leave us?" Shooter asked.

"If Dog is one of them," Richie tapped on the board, "we've got only one unknown. I'm still wading through messages and calls along with Detective Quinones."

"And these folks are all locals, correct?" Cassie asked.

"All within thirty miles," Richie said. "But to be clear, not all in the Shilo jurisdiction."

I stood up, walking over to the board as I spoke. "Let's begin with Mavreen Isiah. She worked as a certified nursing assistant in some sort of medical plaza. It's possible Mavreen worked *with* our man in the sketch. Which made us wonder if he was in the medical field."

"Amber, her sister, seemed to think no," Shooter jumped in. "But we met with Bud Gilliam, the father of Julie Gilliam, and on the way out, Gardner noticed something."

"His daughter had a cleft lip," I said, opening a pack of saltines and placing the crackers beside my soup. "It was corrected at birth but done poorly. The surgery left a gap that could be fixed as an adult with minimal scarring."

"According to her dad," Shooter said, "some mystery guy talked to Julie about fixing it the night before she went missing."

"And the pattern?" Cassie asked.

"Maybe there isn't any," I said. "Or maybe we just can't see it yet. But one victim, Araceli Alvarez—" I pointed at her name.

"She didn't like her nose," Richie jumped in. "She was the one where the ME found the nick on her infraorbital foramen."

"That seemed like an odd detail," I continued, "until we saw the cleft lip in Julie Gilliam's photo. After I left Gilliam's, I reached out to the sketch artist we interviewed this morning."

"W. C. Walker?" Cassie said.

I nodded. "He had told Cassie and me that the women had a nickname in Spanish for the man in the sketch, but he couldn't remember it." I looked to Cassie. "He confirmed it was *el médico*."

"The doctor," Cassie said.

"And Mavreen's sister," Shooter jumped in, "said our man in the sketch was doing something through back channels—like people came to him who needed things."

"So you're thinking what?" Cassie said, tapping her spoon against the edge of her soup container. "Some doctor is targeting women with offers of backroom surgery? One girl's nose? Another girl's lip?"

"Possibly someone who's had legal trouble," I said. "Dropped off the grid."

Cassie flicked her eyebrows, skeptical. "It doesn't take a lot to be *on* the grid if you're talking about a plastic surgeon, Gardner," she said. "There's the American Board of Plastic Surgery, but it's not mandatory to be part of it or even licensed in that discipline to do surgery. *Any* medical doctor can do plastic surgery."

"Presuming we haven't found every one of this guy's victims," Richie pointed out, "of the twenty-four other missing persons in Shilo, four are prostitutes."

"And you're assuming what?" Cassie said. "Sex workers are ripe for this sort of targeting?"

I took a spoonful of the soup and tasted salted pork mixed in with clams and pepper.

"They use their bodies to make their income," Richie replied. "They might understand the return on investment better than most."

Shooter turned to me, her head cocked. "What came together for you?" she asked. "The dates. When we were talking to Amber?"

I nodded and grabbed a marker, moving name by name through Richie's list, taking each woman's first name and populating a horizontal line across the whiteboard.

Rana in October of 2018. Araceli in May of 2019. Julie in March of 2020.

When I was done, there were dots next to four of the nine victims' missing persons dates.

"I'm making an assumption," I said, "that Mavreen Isiah was the girlfriend of the man in the sketch. Everyone okay with that?"

The team nodded, and Cassie leaned forward. "Oh snap," she

said, shaking her head. "You think Mavreen is more than his girl. You think she's his partner. That she was helping him abduct these women?"

"Araceli in May 2019. Melanie in September 2019. Dog possibly in December or January. And Julie Gilliam in March 2020." I looked around. "These four deaths occurred while Mavreen and El Médico were together. Amber said her sister had fallen under his spell. Like she was in a cult. It's possible she helped him kidnap the women. Or felt forced to."

"So we treat Mavreen as a victim *and* a suspect?" Richie asked.

"Maybe she wanted out, but couldn't escape," Cassie said. "Eventually she became a victim herself."

"I have a question," Shooter said. "This man? Dog? He's not El Médico, right?"

"No," I said. "We asked Melanie Nelson's mom."

Richie stood up. "Speaking of moms, I have an update. I spoke to Dog's mother today."

"Bitch?" Shooter said.

Cassie bit at her lip, repressing a smile.

"The precise term for a canine mother is actually *dam*," I said, "although that applies to many animals."

"Damn, Gardner," Shooter said, and Richie shook his head.

"Well, this *dam* saved Dog's baby teeth," he said. "I had Santos cut a piece of pubis bone from the skeleton we suspect is Dog. I overnighted that, along with one of the teeth, to Quantico."

At headquarters, that bone would be ground down to powder, which would contain millions of bone cells, and in turn, the DNA of Skeleton #6, for comparison to the teeth.

It felt like we had gone through most of what we knew about the women. I checked the time on my phone. Cassie and I needed to be on the road soon to get back to the gun case, and I had promised Poulton I would not miss our flight to Miami.

On the ride to the airport, I was also planning on checking in with my mom's doctor.

I quietly slurped down more of my chowder and felt my face going red from the heat. I glanced again at the list of victims.

"So we have Julie Gilliam, with the cleft palate, whose dad is coming in tomorrow, correct?" I said.

"I'll take that interview," Shooter said. "We had a good rapport. I'm hoping I can pull more details out of him."

"And we have Dog," I continued, "whose baby teeth are getting compared to his hip bone. That leaves Amber, who is masquerading as her sister, Mavreen. She has effectively placed herself in protective custody. As long as she stays put, she's safe."

Cassie turned to me. "What's she like?"

"Young. Scared."

She shifted to Shooter instead. "Good drip?"

"No," Shooter said. "Basic."

I looked to Cassie. She was trying to decide if we should reinterview Amber, and I knew what she was thinking. Richie was handsome and close to Amber's age. Plus, Shooter and I had conducted our interview in a moment of trauma. Now that Amber was reflecting more on Mavreen, new details might come up.

I turned to Richie. "Why don't you drive out there tomorrow? And check with the State Department. Apparently Mavreen got a passport issued. Let's see if she traveled anywhere before she died. If she did, who's sitting beside her on the plane?"

"On it," Richie said.

Shooter pulled out the pink phone we'd been given two hours earlier. "We also have Amber Isiah's cell," she said, rolling her white

Duke sweatshirt back to her elbows. "Amber told us about these phone calls she'd get from Mavreen. I took a look at her history and contacts. Amber actually labeled the numbers. 'Mavreen January.' 'Mavreen February.' 'Mavreen February #2.'"

"Those are times her sister reached out?" Cassie asked.

Shooter nodded. "And the numbers she called from. We could try to call them back, but every indication is that they were burners. So I'm not sure what the upside is to dialing them and possibly putting Amber in jeopardy when this guy sees the number. Thinks she's out there and trying to reach him again."

Richie paged through the numbers on the phone, but Cassie's face was scrunched up. "Wait," she said. "The guy in the sketch was calling Amber?"

"She called him first," I said. "But yeah."

"Does she know where he was when he made those calls? Like, was he at her sister's place?"

"Her phone would list a city," Shooter said. "But with burner apps and phones, you know that information is worthless, Cass."

"Obvi," Cassie said. "But did Amber ever know? I mean—his location?"

I squinted, curious where she was going with this. "The day Amber fled," I said. "She told us a neighbor reported that a man came by her apartment. Same thing by her old work an hour later. We can assume it was this El Médico. Why?"

"The thing with a burner is, we know the number, right?" Cassie said, her arms crossed and her head tilted up in thought. "But we don't know who owns it or where they are."

"Or whether they'll ever turn it on again," Shooter said.

"Exactly," Cassie replied, scribbling something on her napkin.

"But the Bureau's been doing a lot of data analysis lately on anonymized cell information. Layering it with stingrays."

"What's a stingray?" Richie asked.

A stingray, or IMSI catcher, was a surveillance device that mimicked a cell phone tower. Cassie explained to Richie that this device sent out signals as if it were a legitimate cell tower, the goal being to trick local phones into transmitting their locations and other data as they passed by.

I studied Cassie, not seeing the exact strategy she had in mind yet, but knowing her expertise at statistical analysis was near perfect.

"Tell us what you're thinking," I said.

"Well. Bear with me, y'all." She stood up again, walking as she talked. "Do you think this guy has another phone? A real phone. Like, not a burner. His legit phone."

"Sure," I said. "Why not?" I wanted to hear where she was going with this.

"Okay, let's assume he's got this real phone, right? It's transmitting his location on the day Amber flees. Plus any calls he makes. But when he calls Amber, he uses one of the burners. I mean, he figures she'll recognize the number and pick up, right?"

I nodded, seeing now where her mind was headed.

"If we know the day and hour where this guy was," Cassie said, "we could get a warrant for the closest cell tower to Amber's old apartment. Do a dump."

"The carrier would release that?" Richie asked, crossing his arms over his chest.

I turned to him. "They'd anonymize the data, so we're blind to who it belongs to until we can give them a reason to release more specific information."

"That's when we use the stingray device," Cassie said. "To collect current incoming and outgoing calls. And study old calls."

"Repeated calls, you mean?" Richie asked.

"Exactly," Cassie said, continuing to pace. "These are rule-outs, Richie. We eliminate neighbors and regular traffic from the data pool to get rid of the numbers we know are *not* El Médico. Then we do the same for the second location, Amber's work. If he made a call from both locations, we overlap the data and voilà—we find one specific device. His *regular* phone."

No one seemed to know what to make of this. I finished my soup. Glanced up.

All eyes were on me.

"A similar tactic was used in Denver," I said, thinking of a case in which law enforcement had identified a series of masked adolescents using only a location. "It's a valid approach."

"Geez. Love y'all much," Cassie said, shaking her head at Shooter and Richie, chastising them for looking to me to validate her strategy.

"It's a long shot," I said. "But if it works, we'd have El Médico's number. And if he's still using that phone—"

"His exact location," Cassie said.

"We'd have to get a request in to headquarters," I said. "Get it approved. Then work with a team in Miami or Jacksonville to go through the data. Let's try."

Everyone was quiet, and I glanced back at the whiteboard. The bottom name read "Body #9 / 'Jane Doe.'"

"What are we doing to ID the last body?"

"Slogging," Richie replied with a shrug. "Quinones's people have been contacted by nine nearby jurisdictions and logged over two hundred calls."

"This is the most recent attack?" Cassie asked.

"From how fresh the skeleton looks, yeah," Richie said.

"So far it's just been Richie going through all this," Shooter said. "I'll jump in tomorrow to help."

I was still hungry and grabbed a saltine packet, left it beside my laptop. "Good," I said. "Anything else before Cassie and I go?"

Richie spoke up then. "Yeah, I've got something. Straddles both cases. The victims up here—and the gun case down South." He tracked his gaze from me to Shooter. "Freddie Pecos is having a funeral."

As his handler, it was Richie's job to follow any news about Pecos, even after his death.

"You want to attend?" Shooter asked. This was standard protocol, to keep tabs on criminals at their funerals.

"I do," Richie said. "But if you recall, one of the Sandoval crew saw me a month ago."

This was another reason why Shooter and I had gone on the bed check the night we'd found Freddie dead. Richie was slightly blown.

"We still have no idea how this El Médico guy and Freddie are connected," Richie said. "They had a conversation at an ATM, and an hour later Pecos is gunned down."

"Who's organizing the funeral?" Shooter asked.

"Sarah Kastner," Richie said. "That's his aunt. She owned the property that mobile home was on."

"And when is it?" I asked.

"Monday," Richie said. "One p.m."

Three days from now.

I stared at the board full of victims' names—women we knew little about. Was Poulton right? Were two cases one too many for the four of us?

"Well, Gardner and I are spoken for down South," Cassie said. "If Richie's blown, that leaves one very special agent to go to the funeral."

We all looked to Shooter.

"Sure." She smiled. She put on the voice of a Southern debutante. "Gives me a chance to wear that little black dress I love so much."

"Great," I said. "Then let's get the op going down South on the gun case. Once that's dialed in, we'll get Tech in Jacksonville to do a simple wire-up on Jo for the funeral."

Shooter wasn't going undercover, so we'd take the easiest and most reliable approach and have her wear a transmitter and a mic, taped to her person.

Everyone agreed, but to my right, Shooter was smirking.

"What?" Richie said to her. "What are you smiling about?"

"This feels like a perfect time to tell you all. I actually don't own a black dress."

CHAPTER TWENTY-THREE

CASSIE AND I SAID OUR GOODBYES, AND I TOSSED MY empty container into the trash. The soup was tasty, like Richie had promised, but I was still starving.

We packed up our rental car and headed to the airport. Five minutes into the drive, I got a call from Detective Quinones.

"Where are you?" he asked.

"En route to the airport," I replied. "You got something?"

"A woman from one of the families just texted me."

"What family?" I asked.

"Susan Jones's."

This was the hotel manager. The one who didn't match the pattern. "We drove out to her family's cabin this morning," I said. "No one was there."

"That's her ex's place," Quinones said. "I just got off with the victim's mom. She told me some cop is talking to her *other* daughter, Susan's sister. I just wanted to make sure everything is okay."

"Detective," I said. "I can only track what my people are doing."

"That's the thing," Quinones said. "I got two detectives doing follow-up from the tip line. None of them are over there."

"Hold on a second," I said.

I texted Shooter:

> Are you and Richie still at the station?

A response came back fast.

> Yeah. Why?

I stared at the phone. Who was talking to Susan Jones's sister?

"Send me this woman's address," I said to Quinones. "Right away."

Cassie and I had to be at the Gainesville airport in forty minutes, but we got the address, and she took our speed over sixty on the state highway. Soon we were two miles away from the address. Then one mile. Then a block.

We pulled into a starter neighborhood not far from the county line. We had gotten there in eleven minutes, and a green Honda Civic was parked in the driveway. Blocking the old beater was a white Buick.

Cassie parked at an angle that jammed both cars, and we got out, drawing our service weapons. I pointed toward the back, and she moved to a wooden gate along the side of the house. She lifted it open and whistled, waiting to see if a dog came. When none did, she moved along the side yard, and I approached the front.

Outside the door, I heard a woman crying.

I tried the front knob. Unlocked.

I turned it and entered, my Glock out as I moved through the entryway and into the living room. A man stood there, his back to me. He had a bulky figure—six foot two and two seventy, at a guess. I spied Cassie approaching a glass slider on the far side of the room that led in from the backyard.

Cassie pulled at the slider.

"FBI," she yelled. "Put your hands up."

This forced the man to look in her direction, and I came at him from behind. Kicked out his legs and dropped him onto his stomach.

I swung him around and saw a familiar face.

"Offerman?"

CHAPTER TWENTY-FOUR

FORMER AGENT ED OFFERMAN SAT IN A CHAIR IN THE kitchen. We'd cuffed his arms behind his back until we could figure out what the hell he was doing in the residence of Mila Jones, whose sister's body had been found in 2019.

Offerman was dressed in khaki slacks and a white golf polo, the logo of a country club on the chest.

"What the hell?" Cassie said.

"Calm down, cupcake," Offerman said to her. His face was wet with sweat after the takedown, and the wooden chair groaned under his weight.

"What are you doing here, Ed?" I asked.

"I have every right—" he started, but Cassie put her hand on his chair, right behind Offerman's back, and pulled, jogging it backward, the front two legs in the air.

"Jesus, okay!" he said. "I got an email from my old partner, all right? Ray told me the case was live again. I flew back. On my own dime."

After the takedown, Cassie and I had separated Offerman from

Mila Jones, who reported that he'd shown up unannounced an hour before we got there.

"Did he flash a badge?" Cassie had asked.

"Not exactly," Mila Jones had replied.

"Did he say he was with the FBI?" I followed up. "Identify himself as an agent?"

No again.

The kitchen was tight with Cassie, Offerman, and me, and our flight time was approaching fast. "You're obstructing a criminal investigation," I said. "Chapter 73, Section 1510 of 18 USC—"

"I was having a conversation, is what I was doing," Offerman said.

"We could charge you," Cassie said.

"You're not gonna charge me, Pardo," he snapped. "We're old friends."

I took a step back. If Offerman had simply let Mila Jones *believe* he was with the Bureau still, there was little we could do. The woman had invited him into her home.

"I'm gonna find out where Shooter is," Cassie said, moving back to the living room.

"Hey," Offerman hollered after her. "We're on the same team, remember? This was one I left on the table. I'm back to help."

Cassie stepped out, and I heard her speaking with Detective Quinones, who had just arrived.

"Ed," I said, focusing him. "This old case. Is everything in the file? There's nothing you held back?"

"Just my instinct that it wasn't over," he said.

I nodded. "Did you ever find any connection to South Florida?"

He squinted at me, and I expanded the inquiry. "To gun fabrication or militias? Gun sales?"

"No," he said, his voice a question more than an answer. "Why?"

Detective Quinones entered the room then, his forehead a series of lines as he studied Offerman. "Ed?" he said. "What are you doing here?"

"Warner, hey." Offerman's voice was casual, even though he was still cuffed. "I was just canvassing, you know? Going over some leads. Getting back after it."

A uniformed cop had followed Quinones into the kitchen, and his eyes moved from me to Offerman. Cassie came in, too, and raised her eyebrows at me, motioning at her Apple watch.

"Agent Pardo and I need to get to the airport," I said. I pulled Offerman to his feet, uncuffing him.

"Shooter's two minutes away," Cassie said. Her face had been a shade of red since the "cupcake" comment, and now she turned to Quinones. "You requested federal help, correct, Detective?"

He nodded. "Correct."

Cassie turned to the uniform.

"Ed Offerman is not with the FBI," she said. "He's a civilian. If he does anything to undermine an open case, arrest him. He talks to a witness, arrest him. Shows up at the station—"

"We got it," Quinones said.

And we walked out. No new suspect. And still no leads pointing us toward a killer.

CHAPTER TWENTY-FIVE

THE SEAT BELT SIGN DINGED AS WE MOVED ABOVE TEN thousand feet, and I looked inside my bag. My cell phone had died an hour earlier, and I could picture my charger plug, still in the other SUV. When we'd split up and I'd gone with Shooter, I'd left it in that vehicle.

"Can I borrow your phone?" I asked, seeing that Cassie had already connected to Wi-Fi.

"Of course."

I looked up a website and clicked a few pages down.

"Everything okay?"

"Camila's science fair is tonight," I said. "I thought I would miss it, but since Poulton sent us home early . . ." I shrugged. "I think I can catch the last fifteen minutes."

"The bottles with the rotten meat and the molasses?" Cassie asked, referring to the conversation we'd had at the stakeout.

"It's a twenty-three-minute ride from the airport to her school," I said. "Figure seventeen minutes from gate to the street—"

"You want company?"

I was about to say no, but then I remembered how I'd done this in the van outside the bar.

"If you want," I said.

She smiled. "Dope."

I sent a note to Camila's grandmother Rosa from Cassie's phone, telling her I'd get Camila from school. Then I handed the phone back and grabbed my laptop. But before I could open it to begin work, Cassie started talking at the ninety-mile-an-hour pace that I had become accustomed to in the two years we had been partners.

"I was starting to worry that Frank had low-key blown it," she said. "I mean, years ago, not looking into this case. But Frank knew, you know?"

I squinted at Cassie, not sure what she meant.

"I mean, he didn't like Offerman. Who would? But Frank knew Offerman was never gonna pass the case on."

"You mean through official channels?"

"Exactly," Cassie said. "Offerman chatting Frank up in the elevator, but never formally requesting that we take it? Never passing the file to PAR in any real capacity? He wanted to control it. Still does today."

Cassie was correct. Offerman flying in from Mexico proved it.

"He asked me out once," she said, rolling her eyes, her face nonplussed.

"Offerman?"

"Well, not Frank," Cassie said, snorting. "The whole thing was kinda cheugy, actually."

This was an expression for when someone "super boomer"—as Cassie would put it—did something untoward.

"I was in the lunchroom on the second floor," she continued. "In the old office. Offerman came in with a salad in a to-go container.

Like *that guy* eats salads. He plopped down across from me. Started making small talk."

"Did you go out?" I asked.

"Pfft." She made a noise. "Do I look delulu?"

I paused. Considered what little I understood of office politics. "You don't date guys in the office . . . ?"

"I don't date *jerks* in the office. Let me think what I told Ed. . . ." She paused, cocking her head to the side as if recalling the moment. "Oh yeah. 'If you want to date me—first, go invent a time machine. Then go back to when you're thirty. But wait—I'll be fourteen, and yes, that's giving creep vibes, just like it is now.'"

"Wow," I said.

I recalled that retirement party for the outgoing FBI director fifteen months earlier. How that night Cassie had asked me if *we* were on a date. We were only four years apart in age.

"*Cupcake*," she said, making a noise with her nose. "And on a case like this—with dead women?" She shook her head. "Some generations. . . ."

Cassie got up and grabbed her carry-on, took a few things from it while balancing the bag on the edge of the overhead bin. Then she headed to the bathroom. When she returned, she had changed into a skirt, black tights, and a V-neck with an illustration I knew to be Luffy, a popular manga character from a series that Camila read.

I stared at her.

"You changed."

"This is my science fair outfit, Gardner." She smiled, striking a pose. "Part stylish. Part nerd. I can wear glasses if you think it'll help."

I studied her. Cassie always looked good. I thought of what she or Camila would say.

"Perf," I said, my voice flat.

Cassie grinned. "Good answer. You're learning."

An hour later, we touched down at Miami International and got in an Uber. Took it to the corner of Thirtieth Avenue and Seventh Street, where my daughter attended elementary school.

On a white-and-blue marquee was the school's name and below it the words "It's science time, Kensingtonians."

Cassie and I hustled through the parking lot, but when we arrived at the auditorium, I couldn't locate Camila or her project.

"Let's go around again," I said, and Cassie agreed. We passed slime exhibits and insect hotels. Saw celery sucking up various colored inks. Volcanoes spouted baking soda, and potatoes powered batteries.

I spotted my daughter then, emerging onto the stage at the far end of the large space, a brunette in her thirties beside her.

"Daddy!" Camila hollered, running over.

My daughter was dressed in a plaid jumper with a purple shirt under it. She had on her fancy black shoes that she wore to church with Rosa.

"I didn't see your project," I said.

"Yeah," she replied. "Something happened to it."

Camila noticed Cassie then, and I introduced them.

"I know you," Camila said. "You gave my dad a book for me. For Christmas. Lucy Callahan. Lightning girl." She beamed at Cassie. "Love, love, love that book."

Cassie grinned. "I do kinda eat at giving gifts." A humblebrag, as she would say.

By this point, the woman who had been standing with my daughter had reached us. She was mid-thirties and attractive, with a single braid of brown hair draped across her right shoulder.

"Veronica Lopez," she said, her voice a deep pitch, her accent rolling on the *r* in her name. "I oversee science at the school."

"Gardner Camden." I extended my hand. "This is my colleague, Cassie Pardo. Where is Camila's exhibit?"

The teacher motioned for us to follow her, and we moved in a group up a set of stairs. They led to the stage where I had seen my daughter a moment earlier. We stepped behind a green curtain. There, on a white card table, were two science projects, the leftmost one my daughter's.

"Someone smashed it, Daddy," Camila said.

I examined the project without speaking, circling the table on which it stood. The upper halves of the cut water bottles were dented and tilted on their sides, and the ones that formed the various fly traps had leaked pools of molasses and maple syrup.

"And this?" I pointed at the other project.

"This is Sheila Torre's exhibit," the teacher said. "Also destroyed."

Sheila's project was a series of cups with labels on the side, each denoting how much salt was in each cup of water. But there was no water anymore, and the plastic cups had cracks along their sides. The bottom of the project had been lined in aluminum foil, and black streaks showed where the silver was torn.

I stared at the bottom of Camila's project, which was built on a base of plexiglass. Each time I'd seen it, there had been a drawing under the plexi that was now missing.

"What happened?" I asked.

"We don't know," the teacher said. "I spoke to each of the girls right after lunch, and neither saw anything."

I circled the table again, taking in every minute detail.

"This was likely a jealous child," the teacher continued.

"Were there any witnesses?" Cassie asked.

The teacher turned to her. "No," she said. "And we don't lock up the auditorium during recess."

"Why don't I take my daughter home?" I said. "We can follow up by email or phone."

"I'd appreciate that," Ms. Lopez said.

We turned and walked away: Camila, Cassie, and me. But I told them to wait a moment and headed back. Grabbed Camila's project.

Ms. Lopez helped me lift it up.

"The other girl went home in tears, Mr. Camden," she said. "Camila was quieter."

"Thank you for this additional information," I said.

Outside, we walked down toward the parent drop-off area near the primary learning center. In the parking lot, Cassie ordered an Uber home, and I did the same for Camila and me.

"Thanks for coming," I said, walking over to Cassie as her car pulled up.

"Of course," she said. "See you in the morning."

The car drove off, and Camila walked over. Held my hand.

"She's pretty," she said.

"I agree."

We got to Rosa's in five minutes, and Camila changed into her PJs. She quickly kissed me good night and hurried to bed without asking for a story. Unusual.

Rosa had been in the shower when we got there, and now she came out in her nightgown and robe. Made me a tea with honey and placed it on the worn wooden table in the eat-in kitchen.

"The condo served me notice," I said.

"What?" Her eyes got huge.

I hadn't yet told anyone this, including Camila. That the owner who'd put us up at the Rio Rio had decided to sell his rental property.

"They're kicking you out?" Rosa asked, her eyes big.

"The market's up. The owner's taking the moment to renovate

the place," I said. "Once all the repairs to the walls are done, they're putting it up for sale."

Rosa raised her eyebrows and shook her head, almost invisibly. I went quiet. We had a complex relationship. Her husband, Saul, was my first partner and mentor. It was Saul who had invited me to Sunday dinners at his house. Dinners where I'd gotten to know their daughter, Anna, my ex-wife.

My mother used to remind me that their family was not required to accept me the way my own family did. That it was a privilege to be loved by strangers. But everything with Rosa changed after I turned Anna in to the police. Saul had two heart attacks that month, and the second one killed him.

"They'll extend the hotel another three weeks," I said. "But I don't believe it's a stable environment for Camila."

Rosa sat down at the table, and I did the same. She had her robe buttoned up; her long brown hair was damp and made wet marks on the fabric.

"You want Camila to move back here?"

In the first two weeks at the Rio Rio, my daughter had been excited about the prospect of life at a hotel. The free continental breakfast, with unlimited miniature cereal boxes. Rides on the luggage cart. At night when she was hyper, I had her run the long hallways, timing how fast she could make it from the ice maker at one end to the Coke machine at the other. But as the condo took longer to fix, and my work got busier, Camila spent more and more time locked up in room 312. It had become increasingly clear that this was not the home she needed.

"For now, I think it would be best," I said. "Until I figure something else out."

Rosa held my gaze for a beat. Camila had lived at Rosa's half her life.

"This is always her home," she said. "You know that. But when you talk about stability . . ." She shrugged. "Camila lived here. Then you uprooted her to stay with you in that condo. Then she lived in a hotel. Now back here. What's next?"

"I don't know," I said.

"Why now?"

I explained about the science project. About the conversation with Ms. Lopez.

"The shoes you dress Camila in for church," I said. "They leave small black marks on the engineered wood when she runs around the hotel. The same marks were visible on the other girl's project."

"That doesn't mean anything."

"Camila had me mount a piece of Lexan to the bottom of her exhibit."

Rosa squinted. "What?"

"It's a thermoplastic polymer," I said. "Lightweight glass. Plexi, people say."

"So?"

"Camila made a drawing with colored pencils, depicting the insects feeding on the bait traps. She worked on it for weeks. She was very proud of her work. She slipped it in between the two sheets of Lexan at the bottom. It wasn't there in the broken exhibit."

"Someone probably took it," Rosa said, her eyes steady on mine.

"On the way home, I asked Camila if anything was missing from her project, and she said no. I imagine you'll find the drawing folded up in her backpack."

"What are you saying?"

"Camila destroyed the other girl's exhibit. Then, to look innocent, she did the same to her own. But she didn't want to ruin the drawing."

"Why?"

"I don't know," I said. "But I'll find out. At the right time."

Rosa swallowed, and we sat in silence for a moment.

"You can never turn it off, can you?" she said eventually. "The way you are. This analysis."

"It's not a burden," I said. "It's a gift."

Rosa huffed.

"I will be spending more time in Hambis," I said. "Over the next week. That's why I asked about Camila. But I'll also be in Dallas. My mother woke up."

"Oh my God," Rosa said. "Why didn't you tell me?"

"I just did," I said, my voice flat.

Rosa twitched at my response. Then shook it off.

"I've been praying," she said, looking away. When she returned her gaze, there were tears in her eyes.

Camila had told me that Rosa said the rosary every night for my mother. My daughter had asked about this. About what I thought of it.

"I'm not religious like you or your nana," I'd said to Camila. "But there are triple-blind studies on the power of prayer."

"What's triple blind?" Camila had asked. I explained this in the best way I could, describing a study of infertile women in Korea whose names had been randomized and given to distant prayer groups in Canada and the US. Neither the patients nor their providers were informed of the prayers, yet the women for whom prayers were offered had nearly twice as high a pregnancy rate as the control group who had not been prayed for.

"So how is your mom doing?" Rosa asked.

"She's confused," I said. "Weak."

"Is there a chance she falls back into a coma?"

"Very little," I said. "But there's a high likelihood that her Alzheimer's is worse than before."

Rosa wiped at her eyes. "God is good," she said. She took her teacup and placed it in the sink. "I need to go to bed." She raised her eyebrows at me. "Camila is always welcome here. You know that."

"Yes."

"There's also that room." Rosa pointed down the street. "The Salinas family rents it out. It's not much. Eight by ten maybe. No kitchen. Just a bathroom and a bed. I saw her put out the sign two doors down."

"When?"

"Three days ago. It might still be available if you wanted to rent it."

I studied Rosa. She was not normally this civil to me, and in fact, she had not made a tea for me in three years, nine months, and two days.

Her eyes met mine, but I did not know what had changed.

"Thank you," I said.

Things were happening, personally and professionally—things I might be missing because I failed to see context. But I could only do what I was capable of.

Rosa turned back then to face me. "This science teacher," she said. "What you noticed with Camy's project . . . did you tell her?"

"Why would I tell her?" I asked.

"'Cause you're . . . you."

"Right." I nodded. This was an understandable assumption. I'd had the choice to turn Rosa's daughter in to the police, and I'd done so.

"Well," I said. "When it comes to Camila, I try not to be me."

CHAPTER TWENTY-SIX

I STOOD IN THE DOORWAY TO MY OFFICE AND SQUINTED inside.

Sitting in my chair was Frank Roberts, my old boss, who had run PAR for four years.

"What are you doing here?" I asked. It was 8:20 a.m. on a Saturday, and Frank's office was in Dallas, Texas, not Miami.

"Nice to see you, too," he said.

Frank is six foot one, and nearly every day, he wears a suit with a vest. He's Black, with short, cropped hair, and is impeccably neat.

He tapped at the desk. "My office in Jacksonville was nicer."

When Frank left PAR to become the head of the Dallas office, I'd inherited his old office, which looked out over the front lawn of the building in Jacksonville. I'd left the place behind the week after. Moved PAR down South so I could be closer to Camila.

My eyes moved from Frank to my desk. His workbag was unpacked, and three files were laid out in a neat line.

"What brings you to Miami?" I asked.

"You, apparently," he said. "You're a busy little bee."

Frank's computer was plugged in where I normally plug in my laptop. And his old briefcase, which has a bullet hole in the side, leaned against my desk.

"Right," I said, putting it together. "So busy that Craig Poulton asked you to come all the way here from your new job in Texas, huh?"

"Something like that," Frank replied.

I studied my old boss. "*You're* our project manager?"

"For the short term," he said, giving a sharp nod. "A two-week assignment, from what I was told."

Frank had taught me to say the opposite of how I was feeling when interacting with higher-ups. And we were both proud when I could pull it off.

"Okay," I said. "Sounds good."

Frank smiled but looked confused. "You sure?"

Craig Poulton was slowing down our work, and Frank was an effective barrier. I just didn't believe he would've arrived this fast if things were perfect in Texas.

"Absolutely," I said.

Cassie rounded the corner and stopped short. Balked at the sight of Frank.

"Hey, stranger," he said.

She gave him a big hug, and I explained how Frank would be overseeing PAR for two weeks while we juggled both investigations.

"Wow," she said. "Surprising."

I glanced at the time. We needed to be on the road to meet the DA in Farner County.

"Yes," I said. "But let's get underway. I'm driving."

CHAPTER TWENTY-SEVEN

ON OUR WAY UP 27 TOWARD HAMBIS, CASSIE AND I FILLED in Frank, beginning from day one of the investigation and running through the fire at the mobile home.

"So you burned up your own C.I.?" Frank asked.

He was in the passenger seat of my car, and I glanced over. Made eye contact. "Our dead C.I., yes," I said, noting how odd it was that everyone skipped this detail.

"And this is what prompted the search for a new informant?"

"Yup, yup," Cassie said. She moved on, giving Frank a rundown of the man that Richie had found interacting with Freddie Pecos at the ATM in Hambis. How that had led us to case number two. Ending with a description of the six bodies we'd found up north in Shilo.

"But this guy today?" Frank asked.

"Travis Wells," Cassie said, referring to our potential new C.I. on the gun case. "Hopefully he's our new BFF."

All along the highway, the king of the invasive plants, kudzu, devoured the landscape, covering electric poles and lines of cable.

"And y'all haven't seen him since he got arrested outside this Rotten Coconut place?"

"Exactly," I replied.

I took an exit, and we moved through Farner County.

The streets were filled with fast-food restaurants and Dollar Generals. Outside a discount store named Dean's, four blue kiddie pools leaned against a stucco wall.

The county courthouse building was white with an ornate relief molded into a triangular area at the top. Along the perimeter of the lawn out front, tiny blue and white pinwheels spun in the wind.

As we closed our car doors, Cassie asked me to pop the trunk, telling Frank we'd be right behind him.

I got to the back of the car and opened it manually with the keys, scanning inside. "I don't remember you putting anything back here."

"Yeah, that's 'cause I didn't, Gardner." She leaned in close to me. We were alone, without Frank for the first time that morning. "What's he doing here?" she whispered.

"He's helping us juggle the cases."

"Yeah, yeah, of course." Cassie cocked her head. "But I mean . . . what's he *doing here*, Gardner?"

I stared at her. I'd just answered this question.

"It's giving . . ." Cassie didn't finish the sentence, and I waited. *Giving* was big with her. Sometimes things were giving creepy. Or giving liar. Or giving '80s vibes.

"Gardner," she said, "how are you okay with this? You've been leading us for over a year now. We've closed seventeen cases. That's our best year yet."

"And now we can close two more," I said. "Poulton warned me, Cass. We accept help—or ditch one of the cases. None of us wanted the latter, correct?"

"Correct," she said, nodding. "Okay, I get it."

I waited to see if there was anything else.

"Well . . . at least this means *we* can work together again, right?" Cassie said. "You and me?"

"We had a strong partnership," I said.

Cassie pursed her lips, and her eyes got big. She slammed the trunk and headed after Frank.

"I'm coming," I said.

"Oh, thank God," she replied, not turning. "More *partnership* on the way!"

I heard my mother's voice then. *Read the room, Gardy. Not just the words you hear in the room. But the words behind the words.*

I caught up with the two of them, and we moved through the metal detectors in the lobby. In the elevator, I studied Cassie. Did her comment mean she was interested in something more than just us working together?

On the second floor, we found DA Justin Seethers, whom I'd spoken to by phone the day before. The man who was prosecuting DUIs as third strikes.

Seethers was five foot nine with a black beard and a thick mop of hair. He wore a golf polo and fitted slacks, which I assumed was him dressed down for the weekend.

He told us that he'd been in with Travis Wells for the last hour. "You wanted this guy in a place where he's ready to deal, right?"

"Precisely," I said.

"Well, he's primed," Seethers said. "Tell me you're gonna do something positive with him."

I looked to Frank before answering. But before I could speak up, Seethers did first.

"Listen," he said. "I know you big-city types think we're in the middle of nowhere, and I'm some hard-liner." He looked from me to Cassie this time. "But a lot of good people live out here. Unless I start prosecuting these fellas harder, the shit they pull is gonna become commonplace. And I can't have my kids growing up like that."

"If you're not a hard-liner, Mr. Seethers," I said, "we don't have a case."

"Good," he said, patting my shoulder. "I gotta run an errand. You're okay to handle your own interview?"

"What about his attorney?" Frank asked.

"Oh, he didn't call for a private," Seethers said.

"He used a public defender?" Cassie asked.

Seethers nodded, telling us that Wells's public defender had gone to Starbucks but would be back within a half hour and was reachable sooner if needed.

Cassie and I exchanged a glance. Travis Wells using a state lawyer reinforced something we'd hoped to see: that for the time being, at least, he didn't want anyone from the Sandoval gang to know he'd been picked up. Given what had happened to his buddy inside the Rotten Coconut, this made sense.

To keep the numbers down, Frank and I headed for the interrogation room, while Cassie hung back in an area labeled OBSERVATION A.

Inside, we found Travis in an orange prison jumper. His V-neck showed off a tattoo in the shape of a tiger's head that spread across his neck and upper chest. I gave him a rundown of what we already knew about J. P. Sandoval, then detailed the role that Wells himself had played as a supervisor of the two-state operation, describing how money was moved across state lines using illegally obtained debit cards. I listed the code numbers of the weapons violations that Wells was guilty of, both in Florida and Georgia, as well as the relevant federal gun laws, interstate commerce regulations, and RICO in-fringements.

Travis Wells held his gum between his teeth for most of this. Then I moved to the final summary, telling him we knew about the "buy-build-shoot kits" and their tie to a weapons manufacturer.

During this last part, Travis sat up sharply, looking from me to Frank.

"Wait," he said. "Buy-shoot kit. What is that?"

Frank squinted at him. "What do you mean 'what is that'?"

"I'm not familiar with that expression," he said.

Frank glanced at me, then back at Wells. "That expression is your ticket out of here, friend," he said. "If you don't know about that, you don't have much to bargain with."

"Wait, wait, hold on," Wells said, his hands moving toward Frank before he remembered they were handcuffed to the table. The heavy metal made a clunking noise that reverberated off the walls.

Frank stood up. "No point in talking to this guy if he doesn't know anything, Gardner."

I understood what Frank was doing and its effect on Wells. But something had always worried me about the Sandoval gang. That knowledge about the buy-build-shoot kits might be more insulated than we had anticipated. And that Travis Wells might not know the same things that our dead C.I. Freddie Pecos had.

"The other lawyer," Wells said. "He told me if I was a hundred percent honest, I was good."

"Sure," Frank said. "But it matters *what* you're honest about."

Wells looked over at me. "What's your partner talking about, bro?"

"This is a trade opportunity," I said. "If you don't know anything relevant, you lack anything to trade."

"Yeah, okay," he said, his eyes wide. "I know things, though. They're important. They're just not that 'buy-build' thing."

Frank sat back down. "So what are they?"

Wells was breathing heavily now, and any brazen attitude he'd once had was long gone. He was worried about something. Something big.

"I don't want to play games," he said.

"Good," Frank replied. "Neither do we."

Wells hesitated, and I held my focus on him.

"You're worried," I said, "that we're indiscriminately deciding which things are important and which are not."

"Exactly, yeah." He pointed at Frank. "What he said." He motioned with his eyes at me. "It's indiscriminate and stuff. How you're acting."

"Why don't you give us a rough idea," Frank said, rocking back in his chair, "of what you do know."

"I know why Sandoval is building up a stockpile of weapons," Wells said. "I know where they're headed."

This confirmed something that we'd guessed at but were never 100 percent clear on: that the ghost guns—and the gun shipment we lost track of—were two distinct and separate things.

"So tell us." Frank kept his voice casual and raised his hands, palms up toward the ceiling. "Where are the guns headed?"

"No, no, I tell you that . . . I need immunity."

"You're not getting immunity either way." Frank shook his head.

"Then get that lawyer back in here. I'll take my chances in court. 'Cause if I tell you what I know about this, not only am I getting immunity, I want ten grand. Plus, I get dropped in Baja."

Frank narrowed his eyes in a look that telegraphed pragmatism, but I was intrigued. Wells was a key member of the Sandoval crime

organization, and he was effectively asking us to leave him in another country, far from his own crew.

I wasn't the best at communicating with criminals. I thought
about what Cassie or Shooter might say here.

"Give us a tease, brother," I said, the words sounding mechanical.
"One word. A taste."

"Okay," he said. "I'll give you two initials: D.C."

My mind moved through everything we knew about the case.
As far as I was aware, there was no connection to the District of
Columbia.

I thought again about the shipment of 186 guns we'd lost track of.
A pile of weapons in our nation's capital wasn't something I wanted
a blind spot on.

I stood up. "Give us five minutes," I said. I left the room, and
Frank followed me into the observation area.

"Tell me you're not considering this," he said once we were in
with Cassie. "He clearly doesn't know a thing about these gun kits."

"Agreed," I said.

"And if he doesn't," Frank said, "then he can't lead us to a manufacturer."

"Agreed again."

Frank looked to Cassie, then back at me. "What am I missing,
guys?"

"This DA," I said, "he's prosecuted two DUIs as third strikes before, but it's—" I looked at Cassie. "What would you call it?"

"Speculative," she said. "Risky as shit. Not tested yet in the higher
courts, where it will fail constitutionally. How about that as a tease?"

Frank grinned, but I stayed focused.

"Let's roll this forward," I said. "Say we *don't* make a deal with
him. We leave the local DA to try to make the DUI stick."

"Exactly," Frank said. "Wells sits around and gets more worried about a life sentence. His attorney calls us, and he spills."

"But this guy is scared, not worried," I said. "So he makes a different call. Goes from getting repped by a public defender to a lawyer J. P. Sandoval brings in. It's a risk for him personally. What happens next?"

"Better lawyer gets him off," Cassie said. "He tells Sandoval that he was approached by two feds."

I nodded, picking up where Cassie left off. "Starts to smell like a sting. Sandoval packs up shop."

"What are we supposed to tell Poulton?" Frank asked.

"The director wanted another C.I. in the fold," I said. "Nothing more. We find out what Wells knows, and we follow where that information takes us. Poulton was dubious about a domestic weapons manufacturer making ghost guns anyway. So was Kemp at ATF."

"Wait, so no trip to Baja?" Cassie smiled. "I was hoping I could roll in a Cabo weekend. Get some sun. Couple mojitos, maybe."

"The reality," I said to Frank, "is that we seized nine hundred and eighty-one thousand dollars in debit cards before we burned that trailer. If Wells insists on a payment, I had Richie hold back twenty-five grand in case we needed it."

"You held that back in debit cards?"

"For the case," I said. "We're not going to the mall."

Cassie began laughing, but Frank looked spun. I realized he had not yet read our reports on this investigation.

"Let's go back in," I said. "Find out what *D.C.* means. We can grab our files for you to read after. Get you up to speed."

Frank nodded. "Great."

We turned and went back in to meet with Travis Wells, but he'd thought it over and wanted the public defender back to get his deal in writing first. We pinged the guy and waited ten minutes. When the attorney returned, we moved back into Interrogation.

"Damon Alicante," the attorney said, shaking our hands.

The local public defender was in his early forties and stocky. He wore a gray suit, but the arms and legs were wrinkled as if someone had slept atop them.

"My client has information he thinks is of use to the federal government," Alicante said. "To be more specific, Mr. Wells knows of a stockpile of weapons being accumulated near our nation's capital. If you want the details, we'll need a walk for him on the third strike, a full purge of his criminal record, a clean drop out of the country, and a payment of twenty thousand dollars."

"It was ten thousand fifteen minutes ago," I said.

"Right, well, fifteen minutes ago, it was also a fairly dubious DUI charge parading as a third strike."

I almost smiled. I ran a team of agents that people underestimated, and I should have known better. I had looked at Alicante and seen a wrinkled bookkeeper. He was clearly far more competent.

Purging Wells's criminal record was also a new request. Which intrigued me even more.

The lawyer lifted his hands. "Hey. I'm just a local attorney getting my hours in on a Saturday. I can always call in one of the big firms."

"No way," Wells said, not following that his lawyer was pressing us. "I want you."

Frank looked from Wells to the lawyer. "What more can you tell us before we agree to terms?"

Wells ran his tongue along his front teeth and made a smacking noise. "The guns are in a row house in Foggy Bottom."

Foggy Bottom was a neighborhood in D.C., bounded by the Potomac River to the west, Constitution Avenue to the south, and Pennsylvania Avenue to the north.

Frank glanced at me. The area was home to the Federal Reserve, the US Department of State, and the World Bank.

"I don't know the exact street number," Wells said, "but I know people who do."

"You're sure about that neighborhood?" I asked.

"A hundred percent." He nodded.

I had done nine months in D.C., but Frank had worked there for two years. If someone was storing munitions in a home in Foggy Bottom, they could walk directly across the National Mall to the US Capitol. They could be outside the White House in even less time.

"What's the plan with these guns?" Frank asked.

"I don't know that part of the op," Wells said. "But let's just say there's some supporters who think January Sixth would've gone a helluva lot different if there were less yahoos wearing funny hats, and more true patriots."

"What's it gonna take to get an exact address?" I asked.

"Two, three days."

We would need to follow Wells. Maybe even embed someone with him. It couldn't go down like Freddie Pecos.

"I don't like it," I said to Frank. "Not if he has to travel to Georgia."

"Hold up," Wells said, his eyes on me. "One of my dogs is right here in town. Not twenty minutes away. If he hasn't split with the next shipment, I can probably get the address tomorrow."

The lines across Frank's forehead read like skepticism. "What are we talking about?" he said. "A dozen guns? Doesn't sound like much of an *op*."

"A dozen?" Wells laughed. He bit at his chewing gum again,

moving it in and out of view between his teeth. "More like two hundred, old man."

Richie had lost track of a shipment of weapons on this case, and I wondered if these guns *were* that shipment. Or perhaps we knew less about Sandoval's operation than we thought, and multiple shipments had already made their way to D.C.

"There's about fifty handguns that are subcompact, so they're easy to conceal," Wells continued. "A hundred or so break-action and semiauto rifles. And a dozen AR-15s."

It was hard to get my heart rate up, but that many guns that close to key targets in our nation's capital did the job.

We needed to get there before they were gone.

"Best part for J.P.," Wells continued, "all that shit's in D.C. Ready to roll. This next run is straight ammo. So . . . they already got the guns. Soon they'll have the ammunition. Then it's just a matter of go time."

CHAPTER TWENTY-EIGHT

FRANK STARED AT TRAVIS WELLS. WE HAD LEFT THE ROOM to confer and come back.

"Your release would be heavily supervised," he said. "A device in your phone to track and listen. Daily check-ins. An agent watching you."

"I'll get what you need, boss," Wells said. "You just make sure I'm in Baja before you guys start knocking down doors."

I studied Wells. If not for us picking him up at the bar, he was facing life in prison. But a good lawyer could get him out of the DUI. Had his public defender told him this?

Perhaps. But sometime in the last hour, he'd gambled that it didn't matter. With what we knew of Sandoval's operation, he'd be going down anyway, sooner or later.

I put out my hand. "We get the address, and we have a deal."

Wells shook, his cuffs catching on the metal ring on the table as our hands met.

Frank and I stepped out again, and the attorney met us in the hallway. Told us he would write up the details in the next half hour and pass Wells back to us so we could brief him on next steps.

We turned in to the observation room, where Cassie was bouncing on her heels. She pointed at Frank.

"You didn't believe us."

Frank flashed his eyebrows at her, still skeptical. "We need to embed an agent with him."

"We don't have time," I said. I had considered a similar option already and dismissed it. "This guy needs to be out and about by morning. Briefed sooner."

"Then I need to get ahold of Poulton," Frank said. "Expedite his paperwork."

"And Wells needs a story," Cassie said.

I looked to her and nodded.

"Maybe he ran off with a girl for a few days," she said. "Ignored his phone. Drunk in the Keys?"

A tale like that would explain why Travis had dropped off the grid for the time he'd been in jail.

"So write it up," Frank said. "Then let's get Tech from Miami up here, stat. I want software installed on this guy's phone. A GPS tag on his person."

Frank had been pacing as he spoke. I watched him, then turned to Cassie. "You mind if I talk to Frank?" I said. "Alone?"

She nodded and grabbed her phone. Stepped outside of Observation A.

I waited until the door was closed.

"I'm glad you're back," I said.

"I'm here," he replied. "I don't know if I'm back."

I studied Frank. I wasn't good at laying out the perfect words in these situations.

"For this to work," I said, "we need to figure us out."

He nodded. "We could each take a case."

"No." I shook my head. "Hierarchy matters. You taught me that. And with two cases, one a serial killer that might be tied back to this investigation, the other ghost guns in D.C.? These are both heavy-weights."

"True," Frank said.

"I'll work with Cassie on briefing Wells," I said. "But in terms of both cases, you need to be Frank."

"That's all I can be." He smiled.

I hesitated. "What I meant to say is—I'll work for you. Like before."

He stared at me without saying a word, then shook his head.

"Man, I forgot." He crossed his arms and rocked back on his heels. "You don't have any ego, do you, Gardner?"

"There's no logic in it."

"So I'll be me," Frank said, motioning with his head. "Which would leave you to be you. Our secret weapon."

I smiled. Which I don't do often. My first partner, Saul, had been like a father to me. Frank was never that. But he was the best boss I'd ever had.

CHAPTER TWENTY-NINE

TECH FROM THE MIAMI OFFICE IMPLANTED LISTENING software on Travis Wells's phone, and a GPS tag was sewn into the pocket of his jacket, providing a redundancy system that allowed us to track him in multiple ways.

And while Frank ironed out Travis Wells's deal with a lawyer from Justice, Cassie and I established the details of his backstory. Travis had met a girl at a bar called the Oaks and taken her home. The next morning, the pair drove to Miami and got liquored up at a beach hotel, where they'd been ever since.

We'd been in Hambis all day, and I wanted to check in with my daughter before the op got underway. I also realized that I'd not reached out to my mom's doctor last night as I'd planned.

"I'm gonna head home," I said to Cassie. "Crash down there so I can see Camila in the morning. I'll be back here first thing."

She nodded, and I got in my car and drove toward Miami. I also needed to check in with Richie or Shooter on the other case up north. I phoned Richie, but it went to voicemail, so I left a message.

By 7 a.m. Sunday morning, I had showered, dressed, and was

unlocking Rosa's front door. My mother-in-law was asleep on the couch in a decorative gold-and-red dress that I'd seen her wear many times. Rosa was part of a local group that met Saturday evenings and practiced a mix of salsa and swing dance.

I walked quietly toward her. At her side, a heating pad was plugged in, but not hot, and on the living room table was a prescription bottle for Carisoprodol, also known as Soma. A muscle relaxer.

I moved into Camila's room and knelt by her bed. Placed a hand on my daughter's head. She rolled over and opened her eyes, a smile forming on her face.

"What happened to your nana?" I asked.

"Hip impingement," she said. "If I were more awake, I could tell you all about it."

I smiled at my daughter. More often than not, I found her reading WebMD for fun and memorizing most of it.

Was this the 2020s version of Gardner Camden as a child? I wondered as I ran my hand through her hair.

"Am I in trouble?" she asked.

"Why?"

"Grandma says I'm staying here again," Camila said. "Instead of with you."

"I'm traveling a lot right now," I answered. But I knew she was referring to the science project.

"I'm sorry," she said.

I studied her face. She knew what I suspected.

"I know you are," I said. "But why?"

"Sheila Torre is a bully," Camila said.

"She's bullied *you*?"

My daughter shook her head, and little brown hairs stuck to her forehead. "To Sophie."

This was Camila's best friend, and they were fiercely close.

"Loyalty is important," I said, referencing an emotion that I rarely felt, but admired in every member of PAR. "But you can't do something like this again."

"People will find out?" she asked.

"It's wrong," I said.

I kissed her on her head and stood. Told her I had to go.

"*Te amo*," she said.

"*Te amo* more," I replied.

I turned and moved out to the living room. Locked the door and got on the road.

I drove out of the neighborhood and past Grapeland Heights Park. The blue and purple slides of the waterpark reflected the morning sunlight, and I turned onto 953 toward the airport. Taking the on-ramp for I-27 a little later, I traveled with the canal to my left. The older Hialeah airport motels were on my right, mixed in with window tinting shops, Cuban restaurants, and banquet halls.

The highway turned vertical, and all along the roadside, hatchbacks were open. Small signs taped to car windows advertised tamales.

On my left, was the wide expanse of Florida, home to endless farms, as well as a hundred miles of wetlands and sawgrass, cypress and alligators. I broke west by northwest onto a series of state highways, cutting through one of the most diverse farmlands in the country. In Hendry County, there were fish and gator farms. The agriculture included tree nuts and berries, melons, sweet potatoes, and tobacco. Livestock ranches sold sheep, donkeys, and cattle. Some even cultivated Christmas trees.

My phone buzzed, and it was Richie, returning my call from last night. I hit the button to accept. "You got something?"

"Maybe," he said. "You remember our unidentified body?"

I pictured each decomposed skeleton in my head. Matched them up with names where we had IDs. Landed on one unknown woman. "The most recent victim, right?"

"Yeah," Richie said.

Most of the bodies were nearly skeletons, but this woman had only been in the ground a few weeks or a month. "Did you find something?"

"I'm not sure," he said. "Agent Harris called in an ME specializing in exhumations. They established a PMI of twenty to fifty days."

A PMI was a postmortem interval. The amount of time the body was estimated to be in the ground. I hit the accelerator. To my right, a bank of hard dirt led up to Lake Okeechobee.

"They tried to test for drugs and poison," Richie said. "But the decomp was too much."

"Richie, if there's something you found—"

"There were muscle groups we examined," he continued. "There's some indication the woman was in restraints."

I considered how they must have come to this conclusion. There was actually a body of scientific data on restraints causing asphyxia, mostly from police holding suspects down.

"What muscles?" I asked.

"The flexor carpi ulnaris," he said. "The tibialis anterior—"

I had been picturing this incorrectly. "Her wrists and ankles?" I asked.

"Yeah."

"You have a theory?"

"The ME couldn't test for drugs. But there wasn't any indication of starvation or dehydration. I think these women might've been held or transported. But if so, only for a short time. A day, maybe?"

"Transported?"

I heard conviction in Richie's voice. "I still think there's a connection to our gun case," he said. "Maybe this body hasn't been ID'd because the victim's from South Florida. Maybe there's another field of corpses down there."

This part was speculation. Richie holding on to his theory about bodies being moved around the state.

"Anything else?" I asked.

"Yeah," he said. "Agent Harris wanted you to know. For timing reasons. We're looking at the frequency these women were taken. The interval between kills."

Richie always used the name Joanne or Agent Harris. Never Shooter.

"You're saying he's due," I replied.

"Yeah," Richie said.

"Have you discussed some sort of public notice with Detective Quinones?"

"He made one," Richie said. "But if this guy was in South Florida a few days ago with Freddie Pecos, we should consider a statewide bulletin. Warning women."

I wondered whether this was my call or not.

"I'll take it up with Frank," I said. "He's back."

"Frank Roberts?" Richie's voice spiked.

"Yes," I said. "He's project managing us. Sent here by Poulton."

"Huh," Richie replied.

I was curious what Richie would think of Frank's return. The rookie was developing his skills as a profiler, and I wondered whether Frank leaving last year had been a positive or a negative for him, since that was Frank's specialty.

"Thanks for keeping me updated," I said.

Richie hung up, and I thought of his statement about South Florida and the gun case. If I knew one thing about working with the youngest member of PAR over the last year, it was that he had great instincts for criminality. If he suspected the cases were connected, they just might be.

Twenty minutes later, I emerged from the mix of farm- and swampland into the town of Hambis, where I'd spent sixty-three days over this past year. I parked in a vacant lot across from our regular hotel, a place Shooter had dubbed the "DisComfort Inn." Locked my car.

Walking across the street, I approached a white Ford Econoline van. Frank sat in the driver's seat, and the door unclicked when I got close.

"Morning," he said, grabbing his jacket off the passenger seat and laying it over the center console. "Interesting town y'all have been staying in."

Frank wore black slacks, a lilac shirt, and a black tie. He fired up the engine, and we sat in silence, waiting four minutes until Travis Wells, in jeans and a leather jacket, emerged from a hotel room door on the first floor.

"If you're staying awhile," Cassie said to Frank, "there's a place called Gatorama less than an hour away. Shooter and I went. Gardner passed on the experience."

I glanced at Cassie in the rear of the vehicle, who wore gray athletic pants and a hoodie. "He's been briefed?" I asked, motioning at Wells.

"'Til two a.m. last night," she said. "I hate to say it, but—" She looked to Frank and raised an eyebrow. "Okay guy, right?"

Frank shrugged. "I mean, if brains were ink? He couldn't dot an *i*. But—overall—he listened. He knows what he's gotta do."

Wells got in his Camaro then, and Frank fired up the van, following him from a far enough distance that no one would suspect anything.

I was comfortable with silence, but it was unusual from Frank, who was typically full of Texas sayings like "She makes a hornet look cuddly" and "He's overdrawn at the memory bank." With this in mind, I studied the boss. I was still curious about his arrival back here. The logic did not compute for me just yet.

"Have you checked in with Poulton?" I asked.

Ahead of us, Wells drove into an industrial area, and Frank slowed the van, pulling to the curb two blocks behind our new C.I.

"I have," Frank said. "He's not happy."

As Frank parked, I stepped over his jacket and into the rear of the vehicle.

"You told him about the deal with our new C.I.?" I asked.

"Of course," Frank replied. "But you know . . ."

"He doesn't trust us," Cassie said. "Thinks we're gonna lose this guy, too."

"He doesn't trust *anyone*," Frank said. "Guns near the White House. That could mean his job."

In the back, I took the seat next to Cassie and put on the second set of headphones. In front of us was a giant bank of listening and recording equipment.

"And the buy-build-shoot kits?" Cassie asked. "He was pretty hot on that. But it's on the back burner now?"

"Well," Frank said, "you start talking about guns on the Mall. Everything else just goes . . . poof."

Travis Wells entered some sort of machine shop, and the green lights on the main board flicked higher in volume. The software installed on Wells's cell phone was voice activated. Or, more accurately, sound activated. In my headphones, I heard the screeching noise of metal being cut by a diamond blade.

Frank stayed up front, but he turned his body to face us. In between the sounds, Cassie explained what they'd gotten from Wells the previous night. He was meeting his contact here, a man named Darren Regnar.

We listened. The sounds of metal fabrication died down, and the noises of the outside grew louder: birds, planes, the buzzing of electric wires. Travis had made his way through the shop and into an interior yard where the meeting was set to happen.

The sounds were muffled at first, as if his cell was in his pocket, but we picked up enough audio to hear that Regnar was upset that Travis had disappeared for four days.

The audio came in clearer then. Regnar's voice was gruff.

"What girl?" he asked.

"Just some fuckin' girl," Wells replied, his voice rising. "You don't know her."

"I'm not sure I know *you*, man," Regnar said. "So where is she?"

"At my place." Travis hesitated. He laughed, but it didn't sound natural. "Motherfucker, if you'd just had the couple days I had, you wouldn't let that pussy out of your sight. But what was I gonna do—bring her here?"

Regnar didn't speak for a minute, and Cassie turned to me.

He's burned, she mouthed.

I put my hands out, palms facing Cassie.

Be patient.

When Regnar spoke again, his voice was raspy. "Well, I ain't had your week, bro. I had three days of hard labor because your ass was MIA. Which means I had to do *your* shit. You know how the boss is."

Travis's voice broke. "Was JP pissed?"

Regnar made a noise with his nose. "Jesus, I didn't tell him shit about you being gone. If I told him you ran off with some girl, he'd beat *my* ass. But you know what's gonna happen now? *I'm* gonna head home. Get me some barbecue. Maybe a six-pack. And you're gonna pick up six hundred pounds of ammo from storage."

"All right," Travis said. "I appreciate you, bro. I'll do whatever it takes. You know that."

"Good," Regnar said. "'Cause I got my cousin working this now. I had to use him 'cause you fuckin' disappeared. So now he's *your* partner. I already paid him for the week. Out of your cut."

"Hey, as long as he can work."

"Oh, he can work." Regnar chuckled, the timbre of his voice deep. "He's big as a house. 'Long as you two load up his truck, he'll head for the DMV tomorrow. He's driving this time, not me."

DMV was an acronym that stood for *District, Maryland, and Virginia.* And whoever this cousin of Regnar's was, he would be driving the ammunition directly from Florida to the house in Foggy Bottom.

Cassie leaned forward, rocking in her chair. "C'mon, Travis," I heard her say. "You can do this."

"He knows where he's going?" Travis asked then. "Same house you drove to last time?"

He was fishing for the address, but doing it poorly.

"No, a new place."

"Oh shit, really?" Travis asked, and Cassie leaned forward even more.

"No, shithead. Same house."

"And should I go with?" Travis asked. "You know—in case he needs help?"

"Nah," Regnar said. "There's a protocol up there. Truck gets to the house. Cases get unloaded right away. Brought upstairs and broken down."

The conversation continued for a minute more, but there was nothing of value for us. Regnar gave Travis the address of his cousin, which Frank mapped into his phone. We heard the sounds of the machine shop resume, and Frank fired up the van, starting the trek to the cousin's place ahead of our C.I.

Cassie stayed in the back with the headphones on, and I moved up front. Frank's phone was in a cup holder between us, and my eyes watched the GPS dot that represented Travis's position to make sure he was heading to the same location that we were.

"How did he sound?" Frank asked.

"A poor liar," I said. "Not adept at disguise."

"Well, hell," Frank replied, his eyes rolling as he gripped the wheel harder.

The drive to the cousin's place took ten minutes, and we watched as the neighborhood became more rural. It was a Sunday, and school-age kids were unattended and smoking cigarettes, sitting on the decks of old swamp boats parked in driveways.

Frank let Travis's Camaro pass us. As the C.I. pulled up in front of a tan house, Frank increased the van's speed, and we circled the block.

A moment later, Cassie alerted us that she'd heard the thrum of the Camaro engine.

"Wells is on the move," she said, and Frank turned the van around, catching the sports car as it followed a black F-150 driving back the way we had come, toward the interstate.

The F-150 in front of Wells was towing a U-Haul box trailer.

Along the side was an illustration of a sailfish, flying out of an aqua-marine wave. Below it were the words GULF SHORES: GATEWAY TO WORLD CLASS SPORTFISHING.

"RT 218," Frank said, reading the plate number off the trailer. "U-Haul identifier, UV 1448B."

I took a picture with my phone, and we followed the two cars onto the state highway, then off of it two miles later. The truck pulled into a place called the Van Ness Oversized Storage Facility, and the Camaro did the same. Frank slowed five hundred feet away and parked.

The storage place was blocks long, and I imagined Wells stacking boxes inside the U-Haul as we sat here in the van, trying to listen.

"Cassie and I should go in on foot," I said, and Frank nodded. He moved to the back, putting the headphones on, while we slid open the door to leave.

Cassie and I walked toward the storage place. A blue Toyota was pulling out, and she ran ahead of me, using her body to trigger the electric eye and force the gate back open.

We made our way inside, and I sized up the place. The facility was massive, with eight lanes of storage garages ranging in size from six-by-tens to much larger, closer to the width of a two-car garage.

"This is the place," Cassie said, and I cocked my head. "Richie asked Pecos where Sandoval hides his ammo. It was some giant stor-age lot."

I nodded, continuing to study the location. All the units were accessed by rolling-type doors made of steel, and each of the ones I inspected had a padlock attached to the bottom.

Cassie had moved about fifty feet from my position, and now she waved me over. I moved closer to her, noticing that every ten sheds, there was a break between the buildings. At each of these breaks, a slim alley, four feet wide, ran between that particular row of buildings. These were not intended as pedestrian walkways but appeared to serve as areas for drainage.

"I think if we go down these"—Cassie pointed to the alley—"we'll have a view up and down each row."

I nodded, and we moved into the corridor-like space. On each side of us, the buildings rose twelve feet high, casting a shadow that left us in darkness.

After twenty feet, Cassie stopped, and we looked out. Up and down the second row of buildings. No Camaro. No truck.

We moved down the next corridor and into the third row. Then the fourth. As we neared the edge of the fifth, we pulled even with the back bumper of the Camaro and glanced to our left down the row.

Parked in front of the sports car was the F-150, and attached to it, the U-Haul with the sportfishing graphic.

I leaned in close to Cassie, whispering in her ear. "I'll double back and come down the next corridor, one building over. Get a different angle."

She nodded and held up her phone, indicating she would text me if something urgent happened from her vantage point.

I backed out the way I came. Ran down the next corridor over and slowed before peering around the edge.

While the row where Cassie hid offered an angle behind the cars, I had the opposite vantage point, looking diagonally at the front of the F-150.

I could now see a wide rolling storage door was pulled up in front of it. Inside were boxes of ammunition, stacked eight feet high. The containers were a mix of types. Most were cardboard, but there were a handful of metal canisters, as well as the red translucent polypropylene boxes that rifle ammo is stored in.

All of these were blocked from access by three rolling carts, two of which held saws with diamond blades and one of which held a set of brake rotors, pads, and four twenty-two-inch truck rims.

Regnar's cousin was a massive man. Six foot four and 290 pounds. He had a thick black beard and wore Lee jeans and a white T-shirt with an illustration of an American flag on the front. He and Travis rolled each of the carts out, one at a time, to gain access to the ammo.

I tucked my Glock into my waistband and looked up at the top of the building, confirming I was in a shadowy divot and could not be seen.

The two men pushed the carts out of the way and took the equipment off the first one, which was the easiest to unload. They placed the two circular saws on the pavement. Once empty, they rolled that cart back into the garage and began loading ammunition onto it.

Something flashed in my peripheral vision.

Cassie.

She'd left her spot in the shadows of the next corridor. As I watched, she made her way out into daylight, first to the Camaro, then toward the F-150 truck.

What the hell?

She looked around, hesitating, but could not see into the storage garage like I could. She got close to the back of the truck, and I swallowed. She was about to blow the whole operation.

Cassie came even with the F-150 and pulled open the cab door that led to the middle seat.

My eyes scanned back to the storage garage. The men were done loading, and Cassie did not have an eyeline on them.

"Get out of there," I said, but it was under my breath, and she could not hear me.

She took something from her pocket and leaned into the cab section of the truck. Her head dropped out of view, and it looked as if she was going to climb inside.

The two men began moving the flatbed cart toward the U-Haul, but they had loaded it too high and stopped, adjusting a few boxes. Then began pushing from the rear.

Cassie popped out of the truck and closed the cab door, pressing it shut softly, her hands on the edge of the door. But the dome light did not go off.

She backed away in a crouch, making it far enough to get behind the Camaro and lay down, hidden out of view as the men pushed the cart toward the U-Haul and opened the back of it, loading in the contents, which took seven minutes and fifteen seconds.

I moved along the building, my weapon in hand. Glocks do not have safeties, so I stepped carefully to the edge of the shadow, ready to move. But the men just turned and pushed the cart back toward the storage unit.

As I let out a long breath, the big guy pulled alongside his truck and stopped, staring at the dome light.

"Huh," he said, loud enough for me to hear.

He glanced around, his eyes moving up and down the row of storage units. Finally he bumped the cab door with his hip, and the light went off.

I texted Cassie when the coast was clear, and she hustled back between the buildings, into the concealing shadow.

Wells and the cousin rolled the cart out a second time, then a third. After the fourth trip, they had used up all the space in the U-Haul, and they placed the remaining two cartons back inside the storage unit.

Wells moved toward his Camaro to leave, but the cousin said something to him. He nodded and turned back, heading over to where they had left the two saws on the pavement. The men lifted the first one, placing it on the empty cart. Then the cousin's phone rang, and he answered it. He walked a few feet away, holding up his index finger to Wells as if to ask him to wait.

A text came in from Cassie.

> What's going on?

I looked down and wrote back.

> Nothing yet. You planted something?

Cassie texted back.

> A GPS tracking device. The one I keep on my keys.

In the two years Cassie and I were partners, she would routinely misplace her cell phone and keys. But this was brilliant. We'd be able to track the Ford F-150. Which meant we had the U-Haul number and license plate. We had a GPS tag in Wells's jacket. And now we had the truck. All we had to do was disappear into the shadows and contact Poulton and ATF.

The attorney general had signed off on the deal with Wells, but we knew that a better deal was coming for him, with a bigger payoff, once he agreed to testify against J. P. Sandoval in court. So it was better that Wells *didn't* go with the cousin to D.C. We needed him safe in federal custody, in Baja or elsewhere.

The cousin got off the phone and helped Travis put the second saw on the cart. The two men began pushing it back toward the shed. But the cousin stopped after he passed the threshold of the garage and motioned for Travis to do something. I squinted and watched Travis hand him an extension cord. As he did, the cousin yanked on a rope by the front of the unit, and the metal door slid down, closing the front of the garage halfway and blocking my view.

The cousin turned back to Wells, and I could only see their feet—pushing the cart deeper inside.

Their feet stopped then, and one of the men walked over toward the wall. *What was going on?*

I heard a noise then, from inside the garage—a whine of some sort. *Bvvvvvv.*

Wells was our C.I., and we had a duty to keep him safe. I considered my options. Inaction was always a choice. Or I could investigate.

Looking both ways, I ducked out of my hiding spot, darted across the alley, and cut into the shadowy space between the next set of buildings.

A buzzing noise began and slowly grew louder. With my back to the wall, I edged along until I was at the mouth of the garage, whose door was halfway down.

I crouched to look inside, and saw that Travis was in the far corner, behind the cart. The cousin's back was to me.

That's when I saw it.

A glint of something.

A diamond blade, spinning.

And then where it was headed: across Travis Wells's face.

I heard a scream unlike anything I'd ever heard before.

And a spray of red flashed across the concrete wall inside the garage.

I swallowed.

I'd heard bone cut at dozens of autopsies during my career. And a diamond blade was stronger than any autopsy tool.

I ran back to my old hiding spot in the shadows. Texted Cassie—

Go. I'm a minute behind you.

As I sent the message, the storage door rolled up, and the cousin came out into the light. He pulled a work rag from his pocket and wiped at his face. A moment later, he walked back inside the shed and came out with a set of keys. Firing up the Camaro, he drove it past his truck. Then backed the sports car into the storage unit and locked the place.

He took out his phone and held it to his ear. I heard two words— "It's done."

I cursed under my breath.

Another C.I. gone.

Craig Poulton would not be happy.

CHAPTER THIRTY

WE FOLLOWED THE F-150 WITH THE U-HAUL ATTACHED TO its rear, but hung back a good fifteen car lengths.

Since I'd joined Cassie and Frank in the van, the mood had grown quiet. Cassie sat in the back, again with headphones on, but said nothing. I imagined she was listening for some sign of life from Travis Wells that she was never going to hear.

She glanced over at me. "You're sure?" she said. "A hundred?"

"The diamond blade started smoking," I said, "and then it cooled down. His brain material and blood were lubricating it."

Cassie shook her head, her brown hair crowded inside her hoodie. "Monsters."

Frank followed the F-150 off the freeway and back toward the tan house where Travis had picked up the cousin earlier.

"So we just leave our second C.I. behind," she said, "bleeding to death inside that shed?"

We pulled to the curb ten or twelve houses down from the cousin's place, and Frank looked back at her. "Sandoval could have an employee at that storage facility," he said. "Someone who might tip them off if a squad of black-and-whites roll in and break that lock."

Cassie nodded, and I got the impression that she already knew this, and her question was rhetorical.

But it made me determined, more than before.

We had lost two C.I.s. One, we burned after death. This one, we left in a closed space to bleed out.

"Sandoval," I said, and everyone nodded. The gang's success was predicated on their ruthlessness. And Sandoval had either been the voice on the other end of that phone call, or he had green-lit the murder via Regnar.

"Dead men tell no tales," Frank said. Which was one of Frank's go-to lines.

The cousin backed the F-150 against his garage, and I took binoculars from the center console. Through them, I saw the man grab something from inside the house. He came out and crouched near the back of the U-Haul.

Cassie moved up from the back of the van. "What's he doing?"

Our view was blocked by the U-Haul. "I can't tell," I said.

The big man walked toward the front door with something in his hand, but I couldn't see what it was. After a minute, he went inside and closed the front door.

I stepped out of the van and called Barry Kemp from ATF. The stars were out, but a wetness hung in the air. South Florida humidity, still fighting the night for attention.

"You got an update?" Kemp asked, his voice hoarse.

I had emailed the ATF deputy director the day before about the house in Foggy Bottom. Now I told him what had happened to our second C.I.

"Jesus," he said. "So you don't have an address on where this guy in the U-Haul is headed?"

"No," I said. "But it's a thirteen-hour run to D.C. If I'm the driver, I'd get up by four or five a.m."

"Can you keep eyes on him until sunup?" Kemp asked, his accent ringing strong on the word *eyes* as if it had two syllables.

"Sure," I said.

"I told you I'd have an agent available, right?" Kemp said.

"Yeah."

"His name is O'Reilly. I'll have him there by four at the latest."

"Your agent will take over surveillance?"

"Not on his own, no," Kemp said. "My guess is that it'll take Homeland 'til seven to get satellite support up. Until then, you and O'Reilly are gonna have to play leapfrog."

This meant we'd surveil the F-150, but avoid the driver noticing, with one of our cars in front of the truck and the other in back.

"A lot of these state highways," I said, "they're two lanes on each side. Some two lanes total. You pass, and you get seen."

"Well, you can't be seen," Kemp warned. "Too much at stake."

"This O'Reilly," I asked, "he's briefed in?"

"No one's briefed in, Camden," Kemp said. "This is all need-to-know. Like you wanted, right?"

"Right," I said.

Returning to the van, Frank told me that the lights had gone off in the home. Cassie hung up with Richie, who had been doing research on Regnar's cousin.

"His name is Bayard Hemmings," she said. "Juvie record. Plus four years in Gulf Correctional for assault. Now he's graduated to murder."

I told them about the morning surveillance, and we set a sleep schedule.

"So this guy's got enough ammo for a small army," Frank said, "but we're not taking him down now because he's the small fish?"

I nodded, but heard the skepticism in Frank's voice and knew what was coming next.

"Yes," I said.

"Well. Obviously I'm still wrapping my head around this case." Frank raised his eyebrows at me. "But, uh . . . small fish are starting to pile up."

"Not for much longer," I said to Frank. "This house in D.C. . . . that's our endgame. We spook this guy, and we don't get there."

This seemed to quiet Frank's doubts, and I closed my eyes, resting my head against the passenger-side window.

As I drifted off, I thought of my mother. Before her attack, I would call her at odd hours like this, and she'd see my picture on her phone and pick up. Often, when she was roused unexpectedly from sleep, her mind was clearer than during the day.

I wondered: Would she return to her former self, even if it meant that the Alzheimer's would still attack her without notice? And now that she'd left her old home behind, should I move her to Miami, where she could be closer to Camila and me?

At 3 a.m., I was roused by Frank, who seemed wired. Cassie had been up for an hour, and now it was Frank's turn to rest.

"Before I hit the sack," he said, "I'm going over there. If Hemmings was scanning for some signal at the back of the U-Haul and picked up Cassie's tracker, we need to know that."

We all agreed, and Frank pointed down the street. "Gardner, you take the binocs and go for a walk. Make a triangle on my position and bring your cell. Text me if you see anything."

"And me?" Cassie asked.

Frank handed her the keys to the van. "Stay at this position. In the driver's seat in case there's a need to move."

I reached up and flicked off the dome light, then got out of the van and began walking, moving down the opposite sidewalk from Hemmings's house.

Frank took off, moving in a crouched position across the road. I was about eight houses down when he got to the space in between the U-Haul and Hemmings's garage.

I glanced back at Cassie in the van, then at Frank. As I did, a small burst of light ignited between the U-Haul and the front door.

"Shit," I said softly, taking my phone from my back pocket. I texted Frank:

Don't move.

I stayed still, waiting for my phone to light up. It vibrated, and I picked up the call without saying hello.

"What is it?" Frank whispered.

"You triggered something," I said. "Look down."

I waited, and he came back on. "It's pitch black over here," he said quietly. "What am I looking for?"

"Some low-voltage wire," I said. "Thin. Running from the back of the truck to the front of the house."

"Oh hell," Frank whispered.

From across the street, I thought I saw something stir inside the front window and held still.

"Don't move," I said and typed a response instead, wanting to keep Frank from talking.

> There might be more wires you can't see. And Hemmings probably crashed on that couch by the front window.

I had worked a case with Shooter where we'd found a device like this. If it was wired properly, a set of AA batteries or a fuse could spark a tiny shell filled with magnesium or glitter or pepper spray, causing a small burst of light that someone on watch would notice. Even if Hemmings had fallen asleep and didn't notice, he would see the evidence in the morning when he woke up and walked outside. That's why he'd set the trap. To make sure he wasn't being followed.

I headed back to the van, messaging Frank while I did.

> Is there a smell? Any powder on the ground.

My phone buzzed.

> Yes and yes. Metallic smell. White powder. I also see a battery now. Something tied to the bumper of the U-Haul.

"Damn it," I said to myself.

> Stay put. We have to reattach that line or we're dead in the water come morning.

I shook my head, surprised I'd not stopped Frank from crossing the street. There could be security lights on the house or other defensive measures. By trying to see if Cassie's tracking device had been spotted, we'd put the mission in jeopardy. Now Hemmings would see a broken wire and call off the drive to D.C.

I got back to the van and had Cassie get on the road, telling her I'd explain what happened as we drove.

"How much time do you think we have?" she asked after I'd gone through the details.

"If he gets up at four?" I said. "Forty-five minutes to an hour."

She drove through the dark, only switching on her headlights when we got near the interstate. In the meantime, I'd googled home improvement places and twenty-four-hour stores but had found only one open in the area.

Cassie pulled into an all-night Dollar General, and we split up.

"Look for anything with electrical wire in it," I said.

Inside, Cassie brought me a pair of jumper cables and an extension cord. I shook my head. "For this setup, we need a thin strand of copper. Hobby gauge."

Cassie bit at her lip, her eyes big. "At this hour?"

I walked over to the counter with some AA batteries. "Do you sell gunpowder?"

The woman laughed. "Are you kidding me?"

"How about magnesium?" I asked. "Or magnesium citrate?"

She pointed. "There's a health area over there."

I found the powder and paid for that and the batteries. Then we got back in the van, knowing Frank was still crouched by the back of the U-Haul, waiting. The sun would start coming up soon.

"Find a bar," I said.

"What?"

"Just drive," I raised my voice.

I pointed at a light down a dirt road, and Cassie headed in that direction. "Is there a plan?" she asked.

"Yes."

A mile down, we pulled up outside a small country bar, and I hopped out. Pushed open the front door to the place.

"We're closed," a voice from the back hollered.

I waited until a face emerged. A man in his late sixties wearing a gray T-shirt and jeans.

"Law enforcement," I said, holding out my badge.

"We're still closed," the man said, a hard look on his face.

The place was bathed in red light, and the ground had sawdust scattered on it. Cassie joined me, and the man's eyes moved to her. Then back to me.

"You play live music here?" I asked.

"Every night," he said, one hand on his hips, the other scratching at a white mustache in the shape of a wide upside-down *U*.

"Where?" I asked.

He walked closer. "I know a lot of the cops 'round here. That wasn't a cop badge."

"FBI," Cassie said, holding up hers.

The man walked us over to an area along the far wall. He pulled back a curtain, revealing a small alcove. "The band usually hangs out here before the show. When it's time, we pull back this curtain."

I turned on my phone light and searched the area. Electric guitar strings are made of either nickel-plated steel or pure nickel. A similar gauge to the wire we needed, but much more elastic. Which would help if we needed to attach it to the existing copper wire outside Hemmings's house.

"Nickel is conductive," I said to Cassie. "Look for guitar strings."

Five minutes later, we'd found two long strings and two short ones. I thanked the bartender and texted Frank.

> Copper or silver colored?

He responded as we got back in the van.

> Copper.

Shit. I looked at the guitar wire, trying to come up with an idea.

"My purse," Cassie said. "Look in my makeup kit. I've got a bronze eye shadow. Should be good enough to fake it in the predawn light."

My phone buzzed with a text. Frank.

> A light just went on. Hemmings is up.

"Let's move," I said to Cassie, and she got on the road. As she sped back toward the house, I used a makeup brush to paint a copper color onto the guitar wire. The phone buzzed again, and I swallowed. But it wasn't Frank.

> This is O'Reilly. I'm ten minutes away.

The ATF agent. I wrote back to him:

> Get to the address and park behind a white van. I'll be in touch.

We made our way back to the neighborhood and pulled up; it was 4:08 a.m. All the lights were on in the house.

I hustled across the street with the wire. The night was still dark, but in the corners of the sky, a purple color was forming that would soon turn reddish-orange as the sun came up.

Frank motioned, and in the predawn light, I saw a long strand of wire that lay severed on the ground. I followed it across the concrete and saw that the other end was attached to a hose bib by the front door.

I tied one end of the guitar wire to the bumper of the U-Haul, then carefully attached the other end to the lead of copper wire that ran toward the front door.

In my pocket, I felt my phone buzz. O'Reilly.

2 minutes away.

I studied the contraption shoved between the U-Haul's bumper and the body of the storage unit. Two AA batteries and a fuse. A rocker switch. I looked around and found the shell that had caused the spark. Filled it up with the magnesium powder. I placed it gingerly against the back bumper and pulled the guitar wire taut.

"I gotta meet the ATF guy," I whispered, handing Frank the batteries. "Replace these. Real slow. Then press that rocker switch."

I took off across the street. As I got to the van, a Honda Accord pulled in behind it with its lights off. I crept over to the passenger side and opened the door. A man in his thirties sat in the driver's seat.

"Jesus, you scared the shit out of me," he said.

"Camden." I put out my hand.

"O'Reilly."

The agent was white and fit with a round face and a trimmed reddish beard. "Where the hell'd you come from?"

My pulse still raced. "We're close," I said to him, motioning at the tan house down the street. "Lights just went on. You got a full tank?"

O'Reilly glanced at his dash and then back at me. "Half," he said. "What do I need to know?"

"We're just following this guy," I replied, keeping the job simple. "Playing leapfrog. Head to the Marathon station near the freeway on-ramp and fill up. I'll text you when the F-150 leaves the house."

"Do you know when we'll have sat support?" he asked.

"Seven-ish," I said.

This meant that for the next three hours, we'd have to follow the F-150 without being noticed. "You'll be up front first," I said. "Aim to be ahead of him by ten car lengths. We'll hang back by the same."

As I got back in the van, Cassie hit my arm.

I looked over. The front door to the house swung open.

Cassie and I scooched down in our seats, but we could still see Hemmings. He moved two feet out of the door and kicked at the wire. A small burst of light came to life in the dark, and he turned, satisfied. Grabbed a coffee cup from inside and locked the door.

"Unbelievable," Cassie said.

I shook my head, wondering where Frank was hiding.

Hemmings got in the truck and took off, and I texted O'Reilly.

Target's on the move.

A minute later, Frank jogged over and got in the driver's seat.

"Holy cow almighty," he said. Which for Frank was like cursing.

We got underway being the chase car, and Frank called Poulton on speaker, relaying what had happened the night before with our C.I. at the storage place.

"But you still got this guy with the ammo in your sights?" Poulton asked.

"We do," Frank said, leaving out the misadventures of the last two hours.

"Well, this goes right, and you don't lose him . . . we're all heroes,"

Poulton said. "It goes wrong and none of us are working here next week."

Which I took to understand—*we* weren't working here next week.

Poulton explained that a command post would be set up in D.C. once we knew the exact address of the home in Foggy Bottom. Our charge was to get to the Jacksonville office after the vehicle was marked by satellite, leave the van there, and fly to Washington. Check in with Poulton once we landed.

"I'd be a lot happier if we knew where this guy was going," Poulton said. "If we have to set up a command post after the truck arrives, it's too easy for someone to spot us."

He hung up, and we drove in silence, looking for the U-Haul.

"Shooter's headed there," Cassie said. When I glanced back, she clarified, "To Jacksonville, not D.C. She's getting wired for Pecos's funeral."

I registered this note, remembering that Jo was attending Freddie's funeral to dig for information.

Frank accelerated, and finally, we saw the truck and U-Haul, ahead of us by eight or ten car lengths.

We moved up 27, through south-central Florida.

The leapfrog process was one that experienced agents had been trained on. From a well-concealed position, we'd watch Bayard Hemmings from the rear while O'Reilly drove in front of him. Then, at the right time, we'd pass the F-150, and O'Reilly would get off at an exit. He'd get back on the highway without drawing attention to himself, placing his car at the rear, behind the truck and U-Haul.

This would keep up, with us alternating every forty-five minutes, until we heard that the truck was marked by satellite, after which we could drop off entirely.

The only drawback to the plan was the one I'd mentioned to

Kemp: that the strategy was best performed on larger highways with two lanes or more on each side. Three or four, preferably.

After an hour and ten minutes, the road became a two-lane, and we could no longer play leapfrog. It would be another ninety minutes before we had satellite tracking.

I texted O'Reilly.

> Just maintain your speed. He's a half mile behind you.

The area we passed through was originally swampland, but the swamps had been drained decades ago. All around us were rows of tufty plants, with tiny red dots peering through the variegated green.

"What is that?" Frank asked, making nervous small talk.

"Tomatoes," I said. "This whole area."

We crossed another river, and the road turned northeast. The area became more rural, the houses and structures farther away from each other.

A redbrick church with a white steeple sat in a clearing. A large sign above the building read OUR DEEPEST NEEDS ARE SPIRITUAL, NOT POLITICAL.

We were behind the U-Haul again, and the sportfishing picture on the side gleamed in the morning sun.

"We've been back here too long," I said. "Make a move."

Frank pushed his speed over seventy, and I texted O'Reilly to pull off and get right back on.

The road got wider, and we passed the U-Haul to take the lead spot. Began to head through farm country.

I texted the ATF agent.

> You got him?

No response.

"What the hell?" Cassie said, seeing my phone.

"Give him a beat," I said.

I typed the same question again.

Now a message came back.

> I lost him. Sorry. Looking everywhere.

"Son of a bitch," Cassie said.

I called the ATF agent up. "What do you mean?"

"I don't see the truck anymore. Don't see the U-Haul. I sped up a lot. I can actually see you guys. But he's not in between us."

I glanced in my side mirror, and there was O'Reilly's Honda, about ten car lengths behind us.

"I'll call you back," I said, hanging up and turning to Cassie. "Your tracker."

She was already logging in to the app on her phone, but we were in the middle of nowhere, and it was slow to load. "It's not showing up," she said.

"Damn it," I said. "Just pull off, Frank."

O'Reilly was calling, but I ignored him. As we slowed, he passed us, a confused look on his face.

"C'mon, c'mon, c'mon," Cassie said. Quitting out of the app and restarting.

Then she had him.

"Get off," she hollered, and Frank swerved onto the exit.

"Go right. He took an exit. Got on another state route. About two miles east of us."

Cassie directed Frank toward the location she was tracking, and he accelerated down a tiny strip of road in between two giant fields.

"We can pick up where he is from here?" Frank asked.

"If you stop driving like an old lady," Cassie said, with attitude in her voice.

The van lurched forward, and my body pressed back against the seat. I got on with O'Reilly and told him where we were headed.

"How do you know he went that way?" he asked.

Kemp and I had agreed not to share intel with anyone outside the team. "At this point," I said to him, "it's just a hunch."

We came down the next incline, and the hillsides were black, perforated with white lines. Fields of solar panels on the left and right; they rose up in front of us, too.

Frank swung a hard left and put his foot to the floor again, the van moving now at over ninety miles an hour. In the back, the recording equipment that was bolted to the floor creaked.

A mile down, we saw the U-Haul, and I let out a long breath.

I got on with O'Reilly and set a new plan. Told him we'd both stay behind the U-Haul, in case one of us had spooked the guy.

"Thank God you put that tracker in the truck," I said to Cassie.

"Yeah, remember that, will ya?" She smiled. "Like maybe when you do my annual review."

The sun came up, and the road turned north again. "If he's heading up through Orlando or around it," I said, "this was not a shortcut. He'll have to cut back to the main highway."

The area seemed to alternate: farms—then swampland—then ranches with loose numbers of cattle. In a field, a farmer used a tractor to tow a traveling gun system for irrigation from one field to the next, a boy and his dog following a car length behind.

Another ninety minutes passed. Up ahead, we saw a sign indicating we were five miles from Interstate 4.

I got a text from Barry Kemp at ATF that satellite surveillance had come online, and the F-150 was "red," as they say. Which means it was marked for good.

Frank exhaled, and I sat back. I had been gripping the binoculars hard in my hand for the last fifteen minutes. Now I placed them in the center console.

"I could grub," Cassie said, breaking the tension. "Anyone down to grub?"

"I'm sick to my stomach," Frank said, "but I could use coffee. Let's get around all these cars first."

He drove us past the tourist traffic around Orlando, and we pulled over at a diner an hour from Daytona. I told O'Reilly where we were, and everyone looked at the breakfast menu, even if we weren't hungry.

All the while, Cassie kept her eyes on the dot that represented the F-150 on her app.

"They'll have a sat operator," I said. "Watching a close-up of that truck for the next eight hours."

"I know," she said. But she kept staring at the dot anyway. "So what exactly did you see?" she asked. "Last night at the storage place."

I had avoided describing this in detail earlier, and Frank leaned in, waiting for the answer, too.

"Hemmings pushed Travis into a corner," I said. "Behind the cart they'd been using to load ammo. The saw blade got stuck in a piece of bone," I continued. "It came out the other side of Travis's head. That's why I knew he was dead."

"Geez Louise," Frank said.

"Hemmings came outside and took a rag," I continued. "Wiped blood and brains from his face. Called up somebody, probably Sandoval or Regnar. Told them it was done."

"These bastards," Cassie said. "I hope they all fry."

After we ordered, Frank got up and left for the restroom, and I looked at Cassie.

"I'm sorry," I said.

She looked up from her phone. Squinted. "What are you sorry for?"

"Your comment about 'more partnership on the way'—it made me think about my decision fifteen months ago. Shooter and I working together. You and Richie."

She held my gaze but said nothing for a moment. Then: "Richie needed a mentor, right?"

"Right," I said.

But I could tell that she knew the truth. That this had always been about her and me.

O'Reilly's Honda pulled into the restaurant parking lot, and I walked outside to meet him.

"Nice driving, Tex," he said. "I'm sorry about that fuckup. I swear I don't know how it happened."

"It all worked out," I said.

He glanced behind him. Up and down the highway. "You feds keep busy, huh? What is PAR anyway?"

"We're an analytics group," I said. "Pattern recognition. Statistical analysis."

"And this thing?" He pointed at the road. "You probably can't say, but—what if I guess?"

I put out my hand to shake and say thanks. To leave it at that.

"Domestic terror?" he pressed. "Ghost guns? If I get it right, will you blink once?"

I smiled at this.

"Serial number mismatch?" he asked.

"I appreciate your help," I said.

He shook my hand finally. "Anything comes up—you have my number."

"I do."

O'Reilly took off. After breakfast, we got back in the van and headed up to Jacksonville, toward our old office.

I-95 moved inland, and the April breeze of the salt air from the ocean disappeared, replaced by the thickness of humidity. A shimmer of heat rose off the highway in front of us, and I turned my head, counting fourteen cell phone repeaters mounted on a three-story metal tower that emerged from a bank of white oaks.

I closed my eyes for a moment, my brain exhausted, my head feeling thick.

When I flicked them open a second later, an hour had passed. A freshwater fishing pond sat beside the interstate, ten minutes from the old office.

Frank took the next exit, and I sat up, ready to focus.

As we pulled into the parking lot, Cassie was slow getting out of the van, her eyes fixed on the building where we'd all worked together, an odd look on her face.

"You all right?" Frank asked.

She nodded but said nothing at first, heading toward the overhang that led from the parking lot to the building.

"I just remembered the last time we were here," she said. "I mean, all of us, together as a group. There was a press conference . . . Richie had gone to Texas, but the rest of us were here. Craig Poulton, too."

My memory filled in the rest, and I began to walk more quickly, moving ahead of them. Cassie was recalling the day my mother had been attacked. Something uncharacteristic had happened to me that day. I went ballistic, punching holes in the walls in the break room

on the second floor. If not for the two days of investigation that followed, that would've been my last week at the FBI.

Cassie and Frank followed behind me, and we made it up to our
old conference room. Shooter wore a black dress that stopped above
her ankles, and a man in his twenties from Tech was confirming that
her wire was working.

"Test, test, funeral test," she said, leaning against the wall. Cassie
high-fived her on the way in, and the kid from Tech gave Shooter a
thumbs-up.

"Looking very nice, Joanne," Frank said.

"She looks locked in," Cassie corrected him.

Shooter gave Frank a hug. "I heard you were back, but I didn't believe it."

"He's here," I said, mimicking what Frank had said to me. "Not
necessarily back."

Frank crossed the room and put out his hand to Richie, who
worked on his laptop at the table. "Rook," he said.

"Agent Roberts."

"When do you leave?" I asked Shooter.

"An hour. Funeral's in Lucas Beach near Daytona. That's where
the aunt lives." She turned to the rest of us. "A public safety announcement: Anyone takes a picture of me in a dress, and I shoot
you. Maybe not today. I got a funeral to get to. But within the week."

Cassie laughed, and I glanced around the room. Richie was taping up the photos of the missing women, and Shooter studied them
as the tech guy left.

"Huh," she said. "Their features. I didn't notice before."

"Didn't notice what?" Richie asked.

"Their jawlines," Shooter said. "They're all a bit boxy. Their features . . . husky."

I walked closer to Richie. "Any new developments?"

"There is, actually," he said, and the others moved closer. "There's a new agent trainee in the Miami office. He's been slow, so I gave him a project. Looking around Hambis near Freddie's trailer. Ring cams from neighbors. That sorta thing."

Cassie glanced at Shooter, who smirked.

"Rookie's got a rook of his own, huh?" Cassie said.

Richie ignored the comment and pulled up a photo. We crowded around his laptop and saw a wide shot of two cars, the front one Freddie's, the back matching the vehicle we'd seen at the ATM.

"Freddie was aware of this car behind him, right?" Cassie asked.

"That time of night?" Richie said. "Middle of nowhere? He had to be."

"Where *was* this?" I asked.

"A mile from Freddie's place. Call it fifteen or twenty minutes before Freddie's estimated time of death."

This all but confirmed that El Médico was the last person Freddie had seen alive.

"I don't remember us asking this before," Cassie said, "but why didn't he take Freddie's body with him? He buried all the other women."

"And Dog, too," Shooter interjected. "Presuming Dog's one of our other unknowns."

"You have a theory on that, Agent Brancato?" Frank asked.

"I have a bunch of thoughts on all this stuff," Richie replied. "No theory."

"Let's hear 'em," I said.

"I've been contemplating what each of these two men knew about each other," Richie said. "If they're friends, El Médico knew what Freddie was into, right? With the Sandoval crew?"

"Perhaps," I said.

"Well, there were two guns in that mobile home. Let's put aside the antique rifle. That's probably a personal weapon of Freddie's."

"Agreed," I said.

"As to the handgun," Richie said, "we've been operating under the assumption that El Médico didn't take that because he knew what Freddie was doing and didn't want to cross Sandoval."

He looked to Shooter and me. "But you two didn't find the cash from the last batch of ATM pulls in the trailer that night. Per the text you found on his phone, Freddie missed a drop."

Meaning the cash was in the wind.

"But if El Médico took that cash, *that* would be crossing Sandoval," Cassie said, putting her hands on her hips. "Even more than grabbing a handgun."

"Exactly," Richie said. "It's odd, right?"

"Maybe he doesn't need a gun," Frank offered. "Maybe he has some other way of subduing his victims. His shooting Freddie was the exception. After all, in the six bodies you dug up, there was no sign of gun injury, right?"

"Right."

I glanced back at Richie.

"I believe you've tied the two men together sufficiently," I said. "Nailed down El Médico as the probable killer of Freddie Pecos. Everything else . . . is just a guess. But if we find this guy—" I pointed at the sketches of El Médico taped to the far wall.

"When we find him," Shooter said.

"*When* we find this guy," I continued, "if there's no cash on him, there's only one possibility."

"Freddie had already taken it," Cassie said. "Blew it on something else."

Which changed how we'd been thinking of Freddie Pecos.

We all contemplated this in silence. Then Richie said aloud what I'd been thinking.

"Even if these two cases aren't tied together, the two men definitely are."

"And we still have no idea how," Cassie said, finishing my thought.

Frank clapped his hands together, grabbing our attention and refocusing me and Cassie on the task at hand.

"Okay," he said. "Getting back to the man we *know* is *actually* transporting guns . . . Camden and Pardo—we leave here in two and a half hours. The U-Haul is en route still, and ATF is scrambling to find a command center without knowing where the hell that truck is gonna land."

I nodded. "I'll find a cube to work in."

We had a limited amount of time before we had to leave for Dulles. Quickly, I found and printed an assessor's map of D.C., studying a grid of the homes in Foggy Bottom.

We had spent three months getting to know the personality of J. P. Sandoval, and now I needed to predict his behavior. In his day job, Sandoval owned a chain of gun stores in Florida and Georgia. But from the notes Richie had taken on his meetings with Freddie Pecos, we knew a decent amount of what Frank would call "the color of the man."

Sandoval's operations were secretive and ruthless, and nothing proved this better than Travis Wells being brutally murdered inside the storage unit. Or Daniel Horne, drowned in a toilet at the Rotten Coconut. Still, when Pecos had spoken of Sandoval, he had done so in the same way that followers speak of evangelistic CEOs, or cult members speak of cult leaders. The picture he painted was idealized: a patriot in touch with some greater sense of right and wrong.

As I studied our written profile of Sandoval, though, something else popped out. For someone who had never served in a forward post in the military or been trained by law enforcement, J. P. Sandoval was a flawless tactician.

I taped the assessor's map to the side of the cube I was working in and placed my laptop below it. According to information Cassie had pulled from Travis Wells, three trips had been made to D.C. before today. For each, a U-Haul had been rented. The six-by-twelve cargo trailer was U-Haul's most common size, and from Cassie's vantage point at the storage facility, Wells and Hemmings had filled every inch of it.

From a quick study of the company's website, I noted the true size of the trailer's interior, one that accounted for height and discounted the area above the tires. The U-Haul measured $11'7'' \times 6' \times 5'5''$. The volume, then, was 396 cubic feet. Assuming there were air pockets and unused gaps, I estimated 350 cubic feet of usable space. Four trips meant 1,400 cubic feet of weapons and ammunition.

Next, I imagined the square footage that this much cargo would require at the Foggy Bottom property. I made an assumption that the home was meant to be operational—that a militia member could walk up, collect a weapon and its ammo, and proceed on their way. If so, storing the weapons and ammo in a giant cube in D.C. would be impractical. And J. P. Sandoval was never impractical.

I made deductions as to how guns and ammunition would be laid out in an operational manner inside the home. This allowed me, in turn, to make assumptions about the size of the house we were looking for. Delivery of the guns was also a factor. A private area to unload them, box by box, was needed, if not a service elevator from a garage level.

I clicked from a computer layout of the area to the county's parcel description of each property, then back to my map, making red *X*'s that eliminated houses that did not meet my criteria.

The Bureau and ATF would also need a location from which they could run a command center—an empty piece of commercial or residential property.

But what everyone really wanted to know was the *exact* row house the U-Haul was heading toward—*before* it got there. Only that would give us a true operational advantage.

A voice broke through my thoughts. "We're leaving in ten minutes."

I had been working robotically. When my mind operates in this manner, I tend to hear no one and lose track of time. But Cassie's voice was an exception.

She stepped into my work area, studying it. "This was my first cube at PAR," she said. "Then I moved over by you. By the window."

I glanced around. The area PAR used to occupy in this office had not been filled since we left, which I had not noticed until now. I lifted my eyes toward my old cube, one over from Cassie's. The piece of cardboard I'd carefully cut to let in 32 percent of the air-conditioning from the vent above our old desks was still there.

Cassie's eyes moved to the map. "Are *X*'s good, or are *X*'s bad?"

I took in the fifty-three red *X*'s covering homes in the grid. "The *X*'s are good because they're bad," I said. "They're rule-outs. Houses that lack a subterranean garage. Or an elevator. Or are under 2,267 square feet."

"Two thousand two hundred sixty-seven, huh?" she said, smiling.

"I'm leaning toward multistory homes between 2,600 and 3,200 square feet," I said. "But 2,267 is my bare minimum. And with the variety of munitions, I'd organize by levels if I were them. Two stories at least. Three preferred."

Frank came over and inspected the map. "The *X*'s?" he pointed.

"Bad," Cassie said. "So . . . good."

"Rule-outs." Frank nodded. "Do you have the place?"

"Yes," I said.

"Swell," he said, his eyes moving over to Cassie. "You both packed and ready?"

Frank is never surprised or impressed by what I do, and that sense of normalcy is something I have always liked about his management style.

"If you're sure of it, get on the phone with Poulton," he said to me. "The U-Haul's a couple hours out from D.C."

I called Poulton from my cell and read him the address on New Hampshire Avenue in Foggy Bottom.

"There's an empty office floor," I said, glancing at my map. "Diagonally across from the place. It's listed as available on two different real estate sites. Could be a good command center."

I hung up the phone, and we got going to the airport. As we boarded the plane, Poulton texted me an update:

> A team is in place on New Hampshire. I hope you're right about this location.

When the plane landed in Dulles, I turned on my phone and watched as the texts populated in.

> U-Haul thirty minutes out from Foggy Bottom.

> U-Haul ten minutes out from Foggy Bottom.

Then:

U-Haul just passed your address.

This was the last message, just seconds earlier, and Frank saw my face.

"What is it?" he said.

"I got the location wrong."

CHAPTER THIRTY-ONE

WE POCKETED OUR PHONES AND FILTERED OFF THE
plane. It wasn't until ten minutes later that another text came in.

> Maybe he got spooked. Circled the block and got gas.

> Then came back to the address.

> Good job, Camden.

We grabbed a rental car and got underway. I exhaled, calming
my nerves.

The space I had recommended for use as a command center
was a vacated environmental consulting firm across from the row
house. As we pulled into the garage below the building, my phone
buzzed. A note from Shooter to call her.

Jo was likely driving back from the funeral and wanting to de-
brief, but I needed to focus on D.C.

I got out of the rental and walked to the elevator with Frank and
Cassie.

"Poulton doesn't make his way out to Texas much," Frank said. "How's it been for you, Gardner? Reporting to him?"

I blinked, realizing that while Frank had been called back here by Poulton, this was his first face-to-face with the director in months.

"Challenging," I said. "There's a lot of subtext that I suspect I miss."

Frank smiled and placed his hand on my shoulder. "I miss your candor," he said. He glanced at Cassie. "You, too, Pardo. No one in Texas talks like you."

"No one anywhere talks like me," Cassie said, grinning.

As the elevator rose, Frank told us that two dozen agents from the Bureau and ATF were on-site already.

"Is there a plan yet?" Cassie asked. "To raid the place?"

"Right now, it's a wait-and-see. ATF wants to track who's coming and going. Especially if Sandoval is not there."

We took the elevator to the fifth floor and got out in a reception area with a logo that read EnviroTekk. A man in his twenties was behind the desk, and he stood as the elevator opened. We flashed our badges, and he motioned at a pair of double doors without saying a word.

The center area of the floor held eighteen cubicles, each with low walls separating them, the kind where employees could lean over and collaborate. But the only kind of collaboration going on now was between large men in tactical gear, their H&K MP5s laid out across the desks.

There are fifty-five FBI field offices, and every one of them maintains a Special Weapons and Tactics, or SWAT, team. Several have what's called Enhanced SWAT, too.

This was more than Enhanced SWAT. When Americans' lives are threatened domestically, the Tactical Operations group at the FBI is called upon, and members of the Bureau's Critical Incidence Response Group, or CIRG, are brought in. This team includes former

Army Rangers and Navy SEALs, and as we circled the floor looking for Poulton, I counted six men who by their sheer size had to be CIRG.

"Someone ate their Wheaties this morning," Cassie said in a low voice.

The windows had been covered in brown craft paper on the north and west sides of the building. The exception was one window, where two men were crowded around a scope.

My phone buzzed. As it did, Cassie pulled hers from her back pocket, too.

"Call Shooter," she said.

"I saw her note."

"She says it's urgent," Cassie reiterated.

I looked at my own cell. Shooter had texted four times since I'd gotten in the elevator. Craig Poulton emerged from an office at the far end of the room, and I turned to Frank. "I'll be back in a second."

I returned to the reception area, but three men in camo pants were standing there, speaking loudly. I moved to the stairwell and called Shooter.

"We're about to get briefed," I said to her. "What is it?"

"We've got a problem, boss."

A man came up the stairwell and nodded at me, an AR-15 in his hand. He moved past my position and opened the door that I'd come out of.

"I went to the service," Shooter said. "Told them I was a friend of Freddie's. Which they all took as a girlfriend, I think."

"Okay," I said, waiting for the problem.

"Freddie's aunt reserved some restaurant afterwards for a reception. They invited me to come, and I figured what the hell? I didn't get much at the service. So I went and mingled. The aunt's daughter was there, and we struck up a conversation."

"This would be Freddie's cousin?" I asked.

"Natalie," Shooter confirmed. "She told me Freddie would come to Lucas Beach each summer when they were kids. Natalie's mom owned a beach house."

"Jo," I said. "If there's something urgent—"

"Me and this Natalie sorta hit it off." Shooter sped up her story. "I went to leave, and she said she needed to tell me something. Could we talk outside?"

"Sure, you said."

"'Sure,' I said. Out by my car, Natalie told me she got introduced to a medical examiner in Hambis. This guy found something funny on Freddie's body."

"Wait. Back up," I said. "What's this cousin doing in Hambis?"

"Right," Shooter said. "So Natalie drove to Hambis to see what happened with the trailer and her mom's property. She went by the police station. One thing led to another, and suddenly she's in a room with this ME named Levis. He pulls her aside and tells her that the fire burned away Freddie's soft tissue. He was autopsying a pair of ribs."

"That's a candid description," I said.

Shooter's voice dropped. "The ME found a knife cut, Gardner. A slice through one of Freddie's ribs."

I blinked, remembering the night Shooter and I had been in the trailer. Before we lit the place on fire, I'd told her to work fast with her knife and get the bullet out.

"I must've cut through one of the costal cartilages," Shooter said, her voice growing quieter, as if embarrassed.

A human rib is bone, but as it moves toward the sternum, it becomes cartilage. This softer material helps with elasticity and allows the ribs to move forward, which in turn assists in breathing.

"This ME wanted to know from Natalie," Shooter continued, "did Freddie have some previous injury to his ribs?"

"What did she say?"

"That Freddie never mentioned anything to her. But it'd been a while since the cousins all hung out. Natalie wanted to know if *I* knew of an injury. You know, as his ex-girlfriend."

"What did *you* say?"

"That he complained sometimes. His breathing was labored. It sounded generic and believable."

"But your conversation was after she talked to the ME," I said.

"Exactly," Shooter replied.

"So whatever Natalie stirred up," I said, "it's stirred."

"Natalie asked this ME," Shooter continued, "could the injury have happened in the fire? He told her, 'No way.' That's why he was looking into it. He suspected foul play."

I felt my nostrils flare outward. Now I understood "the problem." And it was a big one. Cassie and Richie had established early on that at least one detective and one patrolman in Hambis were on the payroll of J. P. Sandoval.

"The medical examiner was asking Natalie's permission," Shooter said, "as a family member. Would she object if he investigated further? He'd have to cut into Freddie's chest to do so."

"She said yes."

"She did," Shooter said.

"When did this conversation happen?" I asked. "Between the ME and Natalie?"

"Two days ago. And that's not all, Gardner. This ME is smart. He told Natalie he went through the police inventory of the trailer. Guess what he found—aside from the guns being missing?"

I blinked. "The guns went missing after the fire?"

"Both of them," she said. "But I presume that's the dirty cops' work. Guess what else he found, Gardner?"

She paused. Then said what I knew was coming.

"Liquor bottles."

"He studied the engraved number on the glass," I said. "Figured out they were Everclear?"

These were the bottles of grain alcohol I had used to set the mobile home ablaze. At 189 proof, it was a natural accelerant.

"How much of a problem is this ME?" I asked.

"A big one. He's been studying fires initiated with accelerants. Spoke to someone at the state. Told Natalie about PMCT."

Postmortem computed tomography, or PMCT, was a cutting-edge tool used in forensic investigations. In the case of burn victims, the technology helped arson investigators differentiate between normal postmortem changes the body undergoes from heat—and those of suspect origins.

I pictured the ragged piece of lead that Shooter had pulled from Freddie's body and wondered if the antique rifle had left other fragments inside him.

My mind began tracking where this story went next. If the ME was not dirty himself, he would—without knowing—inform the dirty cops, telling them what he'd found. They, in turn, would tell Sandoval.

My mind moved to what J. P. Sandoval would do. One of his men had been burned alive. The other had mysteriously disappeared for three days. Given these facts, Sandoval would know he was under investigation. He'd tell the men inside the Foggy Bottom house that the feds knew they were there. That they should arm themselves and go down swinging.

'Cause cult leaders all knew what Frank had said to Cassie: that dead men tell no tales. And Sandoval *wanted* them dead because it protected *him*. That was his number one concern.

"PMCT has a particular sensitivity to metallic artifacts," I said. "Especially those of ballistic origin."

"I know," Shooter replied. "When I was at ATF, we did a double-blind study with cadavers. I was brought in to shoot them, Gardner. The examiners worked blind of me. They were charged with discerning entrance and exit wounds. In the final radiographic report, they were able to tell the projection of my weapon and guess at the type. Sometimes I'd shot with older hunting rifles that would leave behind fragments. Other times I did through-and-throughs with handguns."

"This ME," I said. "Levis. Do we know if he's clean?"

"No idea. He could have a hard-on because he's part of the gang and suspects something. Or there's the other option. He's a genius like you. Just stuck in Hambis."

"When did he send the body to the state?"

"Two days ago, on a rush. It's headed back today," Shooter said. "Levis has been texting Natalie updates. She thinks he's sweet on her."

"Today when?" I asked.

"Well, it's interesting you ask that. I reached out to a buddy at the state. Apparently they send their reports back to locals at 6:01 p.m. every day. That way no one calls them about any results until the next morning."

I pulled the phone from my ear to check the time. It was 5:03 p.m.

And 6:01 was fifty-eight minutes from now.

I had been instinctively staring upstairs as Shooter spoke. On the way in, Frank had described the operation as a wait-and-see.

But in less than an hour, this ME would walk into a detective's office in Hambis and tell them that someone had carved a bullet out of Freddie's stomach. Then burned his body. If that detective was dirty, J. P. Sandoval would get a call one minute later.

"I need to go," I said. "Are you headed back to see Richie?"

"He went back to Shilo," Shooter said. "I'll brief him on this, though. I was thinking of having him follow up with Natalie so I can play it clean. Keep acting like Freddie's ex. I'd have Richie question her officially."

"I may need you to contain this ME, Jo," I said. "Can you head down to Hambis instead, and I'll be in touch?"

"Right away," she said.

As I bounded up the stairs, I thought of what I knew about men in militia groups. Of their proclivities and ours. At the FBI, we were famous for two standoffs in the last forty years. Each of them had taken the reputation of the Bureau down a notch.

I flipped open the double doors from the lobby and saw Barry Kemp from ATF.

"There's the man of the hour," he said.

Poulton was beside him. "The head of the head cases," he said. "The genius himself. We just got food, Camden. Eat with us. We're holding the raid 'til after midnight."

But Poulton's expression changed. He'd read my face, and his patented smirk fell.

"You have new intel?" he said.

"In fifty-eight minutes, the men across the way are going to receive a phone call," I said. "When they do, they'll arm themselves and fight to the death."

CHAPTER THIRTY-TWO

I RELAYED EVERY DETAIL SHOOTER HAD TOLD ME TO Craig Poulton, and the men and women around him dug in for more.

"The police in this municipality are compromised?" a tall man asked. The question was about the town of Hambis, and it came from Ethan Mackey, the head of the Bureau's Counterterrorism Division, or CTD.

"At least one of the detectives is dirty," Cassie said. "But there are only two in town. So if one of them finds out . . ." She let her voice trail off.

"And your agent?" Mackey followed up. "He's positive about all this?"

"She," Frank said.

Kemp cocked his head. "This is Joanne Harris?"

Cassie nodded, and Kemp turned to the other men. "She was one of mine before she went to work at the Bureau. Solid agent. Crack shot. Former Olympian."

The rest of the team nodded, impressed, and Kemp moved on, discussing what activity he'd witnessed so far at the Foggy Bottom house. ATF had set up a camera in a retail location on the street. After the U-Haul had entered, three other SUVs followed, containing a total of nine men. License plates had been run. Four of the men were ex-military, three with dishonorable discharges and two with criminal records.

"We've got a lot of firepower on our side," Poulton said. "But we don't want a standoff. Even if we win the battle, we'll lose the PR war."

Within ten minutes, the number of personnel on the fifth floor had doubled, and we'd moved to a larger conference room. A man and a woman in matching suits joined us, both from the Department of Homeland Security. Five of the soldiers from tactical joined our group, as well—two from Enhanced SWAT, two from CIRG, and one from SABT, our explosives division.

I looked at my phone. Nineteen minutes had passed.

I had often wondered about Poulton's specialty, but now it was on display. He balanced the interests of each team, incentivizing them to work together.

"SRT-2 is based out of Sterling." Poulton pointed to a man in tactical gear. This was ATF's northeastern Special Response Team, located a few miles from Dulles airport. "Call someone you trust," he said. "Tell them to get a team here based on my orders and Barry's, but wait a block away. No other information."

"Got it," the man said and headed out.

Twenty-three minutes had passed.

The FBI was taking point on the raid, but six other groups were represented in the room, and PAR wasn't in the business of knocking down doors.

"I think you know everything we know now," Frank said to Poulton. "Would you like us to clear out?"

"Not a chance," Poulton said. Instead, he brought us from team to team, telling me I should analyze everything I heard and offer advice. "Don't hold anything back, Camden," he said. "That's an order."

We moved to a group of six men and two women from CIRG, who were huddled over a blueprint of the space across the street.

"This is Gardner Camden," Poulton said. "He runs the group who found this intel."

The lead CIRG agent walked us through their plans. When he was done, Poulton turned to me. "Thoughts?"

"We found .22-caliber blanks on a shipping manifest twelve days ago," I said. "So I anticipate there's a ninety-six percent chance you'll encounter trip wires."

"Copy on trip wires," a big guy with a beard said.

He seemed to move on too quickly, and Poulton's eyes met mine.

"The blanks were bought from dog breeders and are normally used to introduce hunting dogs to gunfire," I said. "But there are no dogs kept by this crew."

"Not sure we're reading you," a tattooed woman in tactical gear said.

My memory was moving fast, flipping from document to document. Assimilating more information. "The gang also bought floral wire in quantity," I said. "A black color that florists don't prefer."

"Gardner," Cassie said, and I glanced up.

I had it now.

"The floral wire is used in concert with the .22-caliber blanks and a firing capsule," I said. "You wrap one end of the wire around something. Out in the wild, it could be a tree trunk. But the black color is better for indoors. For evening, like now. You attach an unloaded .22-caliber capsule to some unseen area. Then run the other end of the wire to the capsule. Stretch your floral wire and pull it taut."

"When someone trips the wire," the tattooed woman said, "the blanks fire."

The bearded guy shrugged. "But they're just blanks."

"Causing you to return fire," Cassie jumped in. "You shoot until you've unloaded your magazine, like your training dictates."

"But all you've reacted to are blanks," Frank said. "Your enemy comes out of the shadows and shoots you while you reload."

The men and women looked at each other, nodding, then back at us. "Are you CIA?" one asked.

"No," I said. "We're PAR."

They nodded, but from their facial expressions, it was clear they had no idea who or what PAR was.

Poulton leaned in. "These three won't be with you on the raid," he said. "But they're helping stack the odds in your favor. Got it?"

The soldiers nodded, and one of them fist-bumped me.

"You think these fellas have an escape plan?" the bearded guy asked. "A tunnel or something?"

"I have no information on that," I said. "But if you corner them, they will choose to die rather than give up. Your goal should be to minimize your own casualties, but take as many of them alive as you can. Most militia members live normal lives. Hold regular jobs. They have families we can use as leverage. But only if the men survive."

"Thirty-three minutes," I heard Kemp call out.

The big group came together again, and Poulton and Kemp reviewed the details of the raid. Colt M4 carbines and H&K MP5s hung from the necks of the soldiers in tactical gear, and Glock 23s were shoved into holsters on their belts for close shots.

"CIRG is taking point on the raid," Poulton explained. "As guns

and ammunition are being collected, that falls under the purview of
ATF. Anyone taken alive goes to CTD and Homeland."

Two men in suits came through the double doors, and Poulton
and Kemp stepped out of the room, meeting with them separately.

"Who's that?" Cassie asked in a low voice.

"Justice Department," Frank said.

The FBI had a wide latitude when it came to the pursuit of domestic terror subjects. But calling Justice was the way you assured
that latitude. Or made it wider.

"When the FBI revised the rules of engagement in 2010," I said,
crossing my arms, "they made it clear that domestic terror suspects
could be interrogated without a Miranda warning when the questioning was needed to collect timely intel. Poulton also sent them
our case notes about the previous three deliveries of ammunition
and weapons."

"These guns are unregistered," Frank added. "Two men inside
have criminal records, and it's a violation for them to carry here."

The District of Columbia also required firearm registration
within forty-eight hours of arrival, and the first three loads of weapons had been here for over a month with no such filing. Add to that
the fact that assault weapons were banned in the nation's capital.

Poulton and Kemp returned, and I checked my watch. Thirty-
nine minutes had passed.

Barry Kemp cleared his throat. "Listen up, people," he shouted.
"You are facing off against domestic terror suspects. Any adult male
or female seen with a weapon will be treated as a threat, and deadly
force can and should be used. If animals are used as protection, they
should be eliminated. Any subjects presenting threats of death or
grievous harm to our team, take 'em out."

A new group of six men and women arrived, and Mackey popped

out of the conference room to speak to them. Counterterrorism in D.C. has a fly team, and he briefed them before they left the building. They were headed via jet to J. P. Sandoval's home in Georgia for an intercept and arrest, presuming Sandoval wasn't found in the house across the street.

Two FBI armored trucks moved to "position one," the other side of the building from the target house. The soldiers turned on their helmet cams and headed down the stairwell.

Tech had arrived in the intervening ten minutes and set up a bank of monitors in the conference room. We listened as Poulton engaged D.C. police via cell phone. Traffic cops were ready to block off New Hampshire Avenue, and the Bureau's Hostage Rescue Team was on standby.

Frank, Cassie, and I stood with Mackey, Poulton, and Kemp, our eyes trained on the green night vision glow emanating from eight screens that corresponded to the cameras on the soldiers' helmets. The FBI armored truck began moving through the darkness, and someone from SWAT descended on the back of the building, ready to cut the place's power.

"Time to go off," Cassie said, rocking on her heels.

Forty-seven minutes.

The armored trucks turned the corner at speed. On the monitors, we could see the jostling of men in the back.

The eight screens bumped simultaneously as the armored truck hopped the sidewalk and flew up onto the lawn in front of the house. Our only audio was from the two lead CIRG agents, but we could hear noises coming through a window that Kemp had opened.

The power was cut, and men and women in tactical gear poured out of the back of the truck and moved up the steps, the first of them carrying a sledgehammer.

I watched the monitor on this man's helmet cam as the focus swung all the way toward the street. Then it arced back to the left as the sledgehammer flew down, tearing the front door apart with a crack we could hear up on the fifth floor.

A flash-bang went off inside, and for a moment, a cloud of dust filled the green haze across six of the monitors.

My eyes followed the lead man into the house, and a sound echoed. *Crack. Crack. Crack. Crack. Crack. Crack.*

The noises were too rhythmic in nature—the breaks between them too consistent. On the audio, I heard the words *twenty-two-caliber blanks*.

Our men moved forward after this, and through the green haze, a camera found a man and gave him a verbal warning: "FBI, on the floor!"

The man fired back and was downed in two quick shots. *Pop. Pop.*

Another man. Same result.

Outside our window, we could hear an announcement sounding: "This is the FBI. Anyone on New Hampshire Avenue, stay inside your home."

More pops could be heard; the flash-bangs continued as the team took the second floor.

One of the cameras on a helmet hit the ground and went static, the view unmoving, fixed on a floor molding. Cassie stiffened, her face draining of color. One of our men, down to militia fire.

A police helicopter moved above the residence to watch any movement out a side door or back exit, and my eyes followed the lead CIRG agents up to the third floor.

Pop. Pop. Pop.

Each time a man was downed, we heard a live count. We were

already at twelve, two more than the number we'd seen enter the house, including Hemmings, who'd driven the U-Haul.

Pop. Pop. Pop.

We heard the announcement over the tactical mic that power would be turned on, and each CIRG agent took up a protective position in the house, knowing that more men might be hiding inside. The green haze turned to black, and the monitors went full color as the lights came on.

Two firefights began then, and a loud boom sounded.

"There are citizens out in the street," Cassie said, moving to the window.

My eyes stayed on the monitors. On the lower floors, CIRG agents were zip-tying militia members. I counted four injured bodies.

"D.C. police and HRT will get them inside," I said to her, my gaze still locked on the TV screens.

"Ten enemies dead," a voice came through the audio. "Five total wounded, including one of ours."

The CIRG and SWAT agents moved from room to room, checking every crevice and closet but touching nothing else.

"All clear," a voice said. "We're going to remove the wounded and clear the street. Let SABT inside to search for explosives and collect cell phones."

Two helmet cams moved outside, and the bodies of the injured were loaded into the back of the armored trucks.

Poulton had a walkie in front of him. He informed the lead agent that an ambulance was a block away and would be at Walter Reed in twenty minutes for our injured man.

I walked over to the window with the clearest view and peeled off the craft paper. A handful of citizens were standing on their stoops, holding up iPhones and filming the melee as the injured were re-moved from the residence. Two CIRG officers carried their colleague outside, and our Hostage Rescue Team moved onto the street.

The target residence was a pink row house with only two feet between its structure and the next house over. I continued to watch as HRT agents entered the homes on either side and removed res-idents for their own safety. For other citizens in the street, SWAT went door-to-door, ordering them back into their homes. Soon D.C. police arrived on the scene, using their cars as barricades to block traffic onto New Hampshire Avenue.

"First estimate," the voice from CIRG said. "Ninety-four assault rifles. Eighty-one shotguns. A hundred and forty handguns of vari-ous makes. Two thousand assorted rounds. None of this includes the twenty-two cases of ammo that just got here. That's still unloaded."

The haul of weapons was enough for an army of two hundred to head to the White House or Congress. I stepped back from the window as Poulton walked toward me. His face was relaxing now, the stress beginning to dissipate.

"I told you a year ago," he said.

I nodded. "You said we'd do great things together."

"There's that memory," he said, pointing. He took a wrapped ci-gar and stuck it in my shirt pocket. Then he turned to Cassie and Frank. "You, too, Roberts. You're a dirty dog, but you always come in clutch when needed. And the good lady as well." He motioned at Cassie, clearly not remembering her name.

Poulton's assistant Olivia tapped him on the shoulder. I heard her whisper the word *envoy*, which was the current code name for the president. Poulton told us he owed a call to the White House and began walking away.

Audio from the lead CIRG agent crackled to life from the monitor across the room, and I stared out the window, watching the soldiers exit the house.

"I'm going down to the basement," the voice said. "Check out all this ammo."

Some small, but critical detail was missing. Like a single sentence removed from a book. I scanned my brain for it, my memory flicking through every memo, email, and text about the case.

An image flashed in my head.

Sandoval, leaving the Rotten Coconut.

Dead eyes.

"Something's wrong," I said, my voice barely a whisper.

And when I found the detail, I knew I needed to move.

Fast.

Or innocent people would die.

CHAPTER THIRTY-THREE

I PICTURED THE DETAIL, A MEMORY FROM THE MOBILE home where I had been a week ago. But as I turned to look for a walkie, everyone who had one was down on the street.

I ran out the double doors to the lobby and sprinted, taking the stairs two at a time, a bigger story building in my head.

First—the words that the lead CIRG agent had just said. *None of this includes the twenty-two cases of ammo that just got here. That's still unloaded.*

I pushed out the front door and ran right into a barricade. Got up and moved around it.

D.C. police had blocked access onto New Hampshire Avenue, and I took in the activity. Portable lights had arrived, and the night was so bright that the row house glowed fluorescent pink. Tow trucks hooked up cars to pull them away from the front of the house, and cops swarmed the sidewalks.

"Hey, buddy," one yelled at me. "You can't be out here."

The automatic garage door under the pink row house was beginning to close. Inside, I could see our lead CIRG agent.

"Wait," I yelled. But the noise of a police helicopter overhead drowned everything out.

The garage door was halfway down. I took off across the street toward the row house, running as fast as I could.

"Hey," I hollered, but no one could hear me above the noise.

A cop's hand touched my shoulder. I shrugged it off, ran down the incline toward the closing door, and dove to the ground, my body rolling under the garage door just before it shut.

Inside, the CIRG agent was twenty feet in front of me, and I got up. Began running toward him.

The cases of ammunition that we'd seen from the storage unit had been taken from the U-Haul and left by a service elevator, piled in a cube-like shape. Looking at them, I recalled the question that Travis Wells had asked yesterday—about the ammunitions trip to D.C.

And should I go with? You know—in case your cousin needs help?

But Regnar had told him his help wasn't needed. That there was a protocol.

Cases get unloaded right away. Brought upstairs and broken down.

But the ammo was not upstairs or broken down. It had been left here in the garage, the F-150 and U-Haul parked three feet away.

The CIRG agent's shoulder blade lifted in slow motion, his hand close to the cube.

And I reached out, grabbing at the back of his vest.

He turned on me fast, maneuvering my hands off his body. His Glock 23 found its way to my chin, and he held me up, his other hand grabbing my neck and squeezing painfully.

"It's a trap," I said, my voice hoarse.

The soldier's blue eyes passed over me, and he relaxed his grip, recognizing my face.

"J. P. Sandoval," I said. "He's a perfect tactician. Never makes a mistake."

The bearded soldier stared at me intensely. Then let me go. "Well, he did today."

"No," I said. "In the mobile home I burned down, there were six rolls of monofilament fishing wire. A fifty-pound test, too heavy for fishing. In a neutral color not good for South Florida swamps."

"I'm not following," the CIRG agent said.

"Our C.I.," I said. "They told him there was a protocol. Everything gets unloaded and brought upstairs the minute the U-Haul gets to the house."

"So if that didn't happen," the soldier said, "there might be a new order in place from Sandoval?"

I nodded. "An extra level of caution. Maybe 'cause Sandoval got spooked. Same time he made the decision to kill Wells at the storage place."

We both turned to the cube of ammunition, our eyes moving along its perimeter.

And then we saw it. A tiny gray fishing wire led from the bottom of the pallet and moved under the U-Haul.

The CIRG agent got down on his hands and knees, and I joined him. Beneath the F-150, we saw a flashing red light on a black box.

"That's a bomb, my friend," the CIRG agent said, his voice calm.

The box was planted near the truck's gas tank . . . the gas tank Hemmings had filled up when he got to D.C., after passing the pink row house the first time. This might also be a new protocol. To leave thirty gallons of gas beside an explosive.

The CIRG soldier got up and wiped his hands on his pants, his expression turning to a smile. "Hooyah, brother," he said, "you just saved a Navy SEAL. I owe you a life, CIA man."

"PAR," I said.

"Whatever. Let's argue the point across the street while SABT defuses this thing."

CHAPTER THIRTY-FOUR

AN HOUR HAD PASSED. EACH OF THE CORNER OFFICES ON the floor held one of the four injured men. Emergency workers tended to their wounds, patching them up but not letting them near a hospital or other public place until Poulton said different.

Cassie walked from office to office, staring at each man before returning to the cube where I sat, my eyes glazed with fatigue.

"I looked for Hemmings," she said, referring to the U-Haul driver. "After what he did to Wells, I got a little satisfaction in knowing he didn't make it." She paused as our eyes met. "Is that wrong?"

"I don't know," I said, staring out the window where I'd torn off the craft paper. My mind was blank, and my body felt empty.

An image flashed through my head. Frank and I at lunch five and a half years ago. His pitch for PAR.

Frank knew that the FBI sought out genius-level thinkers. He also knew that the Bureau was not shy about recruiting those with aberrant work styles. And he'd seen firsthand the results of that combination: the best and the brightest who were also the oddest—like me—failed in a highly bureaucratic environment. So Frank went office by office, looking for the intellectual misfits. And then he served as our buffer.

But our mission at PAR was *not* to run down explosives or go undercover. It wasn't to avert deadly disasters or watch as men got their faces cut by a circular saw. Or were drowned to death in a toilet.

"Gardner?" Cassie said.

I had taken my pulse twice in the last ten minutes, and it was still rapid. My mouth felt dry, and I was lightheaded.

A larger team from Justice and CTD had arrived. Frank and Poulton stood in the glass conference room with them, going over next steps.

I got a lot of attaboys from various soldiers, as well as the lead SABT technician, who told me the bomb in the garage had held enough C-4 to take down the pink row house and the four buildings around it, along with a lot of our people in the street.

The conference room door opened, and Frank strode our way. "We can take off," he said.

"Just like that?" Cassie asked. "What about Sandoval?"

"He was picked up ten minutes ago in Georgia. CTD is taking over the questioning of these four, and one of them already accepted full immunity to turn on Sandoval."

"No cap?" Cassie said.

"No . . . cap," Frank replied, his voice signaling his lack of confidence in the term. "Justice is holding Sandoval on seditious conspiracy. Interstate gun violations. Transporting explosives. Fraud. Attempted murder. About ten other charges."

Hearing this woke something in me, and I glanced over. Started listening again.

"They checked every cell phone in that home," Frank continued. "No call went out, and that's a credit to PAR. Right now, officers are descending on the homes of these men. Wives will be arrested on suspicion of treason. Kids will be placed in foster care. Trust me. More men will talk."

It seemed strange that the case had begun with illegal debit cards and quickly ramped up to a threat on the White House. And now, as far as it concerned us, it was over.

"So these other three that got captured . . . ?" Cassie prompted.

"Whoever talks, walks," Frank said. "Witness protection for their family. But they gotta name names, or no deal."

"What about Regnar and the others?" Cassie asked. "Sandoval's crew down in Florida? The dirty cops?"

"All swept up," Frank said. "Arrested."

"Was there any cash found?" I asked, motioning with my head in the direction of the pink row house across the street.

"No," Frank said.

"And the two thousand buy-build-shoot kits?" Cassie asked.

"Not yet found." Frank shook his head. "It's part of the questioning we'll put these guys through. But this first guy at least—he didn't know anything about it. So maybe it's like Gardner thought: Information was compartmentalized in Sandoval's organization. Need-to-know, you know?"

"No," I said.

"No what?" Frank asked.

"Freddie was a hothead," I said. "He liked to go out behind his trailer and take his AR-15. Dump full magazines of ammo, unworried that the cops might pay him a visit. He constantly talked—"

"Smack," Cassie jumped in. "To Richie. To everyone."

Frank squinted, not following Cassie.

"What Gardner's trying to say is—the likelihood of *only* Freddie knowing about anything . . ." Cassie put up her hands and held them a tiny distance apart. "It's small."

Frank took this in, nodding. "Okay. I'll socialize that. Make sure everyone is clear."

The adrenaline of the raid was still pumping through my exhausted mind. It was hard to believe what had happened in the last twenty-four hours. Our deal with the new C.I. His murder at the storage shed. The raid. Half the block almost getting blown to bits.

"Shooter," I mumbled, explaining that I'd sent her to Hambis to intercept the ME.

Frank's gaze looked like one of pity. "No problem," he said. "Jo can head back to Shilo in the morning. Don't forget. We've still got another case to solve."

I looked around then, and maybe for the first time, it became clear that everyone was staring at us.

A gentle smile came to Cassie's face. "Guess we're gonna need a couple wheelbarrows, huh?"

Frank studied her, confused.

"For the size of our balls," she went on. "You know, once the president and people like that figure out what we did today?"

Frank started laughing, and I was reminded of what he'd said before. That no one talked like Cassie.

"What else?" Frank asked. "You two need anything?"

"How about a drink?" Cassie said.

The question was hanging in the air when Poulton arrived. In his hand were two more cigars. "This is for you, Agent Pardo," he said, holding one out to Cassie. He must have asked someone for her name in the intervening hour. "And for you, Roberts."

We turned and got in the elevator. No one said anything on the ride down. I knew that, medically speaking, we were in shock. Or at least I was.

Frank fired up the rental, then pulled to the curb a few miles away. We headed inside a bar called the Sovereign. A round of tequila shots appeared. Beside each was a bottle of Dos Equis Amber. I wasn't a big drinker, but I understood the need for release after a case like this.

Cassie raised her shot, then moved it down. Away from her and back. "*Arriba, debajo. Al centro, adentro.*"

We mimicked the action, downing our own shots. But my mind was still shuttling through the images of the last week. The Rotten Coconut. My mom waking up. Camila's smashed science project. The two C.I.s.

"Layla hates Texas," Frank said. "And I hate the job there."

I turned to face him. Layla was his wife of twenty-one years. Fifteen months ago, they had relocated to Texas, where Frank had grown up. He'd taken the top fed job in the state.

"You hate your *new* job?" I asked, putting down my beer.

"I do," Frank said, but he added no other context to the statement.

I kept my eyes on him. This was why he had agreed so quickly to come back and help us.

"We're still renting in Dallas," he explained. "And Layla thinks I can just come back to PAR. I had to explain to her that the top brass were shutting us down." His eyes met mine. "And that I lied to you guys. That I never told you about it."

This was a subject we'd never discussed in front of Frank—how he was about to let Shooter and Cassie be transferred away. How I was about to be fired.

"Wow," Cassie said. She was sitting on a stool by the bar counter.

Frank and I were standing, my hand resting on the dark walnut wood beside my beer.

He stared at me for a long beat, before finally speaking. "Say something, Gardner."

"What do you want me to say?" I asked. "Do you have a question?"

"Geez, I got a hundred questions. Will it ruin things if I come back? Will it take away an opportunity from you?" He turned to Cassie. "Or you? Will it destroy the chemistry y'all have been building without me? Am I a jerk, even bringing this up?"

I had an answer to each of these questions. But that didn't mean I knew Cassie's answer. Or Shooter's or Richie's. And we were a team.

At the same time, I was keenly aware that the case we had just finished would not have come to the same conclusion under my leadership. And everyone at PAR had to know that, too.

"You are an exceptional leader," I said to Frank.

"Hear, hear," Cassie said, clinking the neck of her beer bottle against the side of mine.

"And you left us to fend for ourselves," I said.

No one said anything.

I continued matter-of-factly. "You ran off on your own on that last case fifteen months ago, and I came after you. Saved your life. You still said nothing to me. That behavior was peculiar."

Frank's head was down, and he was abnormally quiet.

I considered the possibility of Frank Roberts leading PAR again, and something else came to mind—something that I'd only realized in the fifteen months since Frank was gone. That of all the special analytical skills represented at PAR, what Frank brought to the mix was the easiest to overlook. He supplied some sort of invisible glue. Sure, we were solving more cases than ever. But there was something absent from how the team had functioned prior to his departure.

Some missing element I could sense constantly, even if my mind could not name it. Even if my logic could not identify it.

Camaraderie? Chemistry? Community?

"I'll step aside," I said, and Frank raised his eyes to meet mine. "But I am not giving up the title or the pay. They'll have to invent a new title for you. And you and Poulton will have to work out those details."

"Okay," Frank said. "What else?"

"I need to be near my daughter. If we have to move back to Jacksonville, I will give my notice." He stared at me, and I continued. "It's my belief the team will fall apart without me."

Frank motioned to the bartender for another round. He said nothing for a while, then met my eyes. "They say you have no emotions."

"I've heard."

He shook his head. "What's humility, then?"

More drinks came, and Cassie made another toast. "To Frank Roberts, a great lead agent."

"To Gardner Camden," Frank countered, "the smartest man at the FBI."

I turned to Cassie. "To Cassie Pardo," I said. "If you didn't put that tracker in Hemmings's truck, we would've lost him on the interstate. And something horrible would've happened tomorrow in D.C."

"And we'd all be fired," Frank added nonchalantly.

Cassie's eyes never left mine, and I saw her bite at her lip. Then look away from me.

A few minutes later, we each took another shot before walking four blocks to a hotel that Frank found on his phone. He explained that he'd gotten a text from Poulton, saying to skip commercial and take a jet if we needed a flight in the morning.

"We're kind of a big deal," Cassie said, a singsong tone in her voice.

I smiled at her, but I knew there was still another case to solve.

Anything could happen.

The world started spinning, so I got my hotel room key card. But before I could walk off, Frank pulled me into a hug.

"Thank you," he said.

"Nothing happened yet," I replied. "You still have to talk to Poulton."

"I know," he replied. "But thank you."

I got in the elevator and leaned my head against the wall. Barely made it to my room and crashed onto the hotel room bed.

As I did, some details finally resolved in my mind. The cut in Araceli Alvarez's facial bone. Just like the cut Jo had made when she went looking for the bullet.

The answer was there, and so was another one. The *what*, even if the *why* was still unknown.

And then all the answers faded away into some black hole where discoveries made under the influence go, and I fell fast asleep.

CHAPTER THIRTY-FIVE

AT 9 A.M., I HEARD A KNOCK ON MY DOOR. IT WAS FRANK, dressed in yesterday's suit, which somehow looked pressed.

"Ten minutes," he said. "I'm walking back to the bar to find the rental car."

I looked in the mirror. My eyes were bloodshot, and my hair was sticking up. I splashed handfuls of water on my face and tried to clean up my appearance. Grabbed my things and moved downstairs.

In the lobby, Cassie was pacing the floor, headphones in, drinking a Red Bull.

"Morning, Agent Camden," she said.

"Morning, Agent Pardo," I replied.

It was an odd feeling. We had solved what would probably be the Bureau's biggest case of the year. Yet we couldn't relax. A man we knew very little about had likely killed eight women and one man.

He had also killed our first C.I., Freddie Pecos. Shot him to death in his own trailer: a case we knew close to nothing about. If we did, it might lead us right to El Médico's true identity.

The black rental SUV pulled up outside, and we got in. Headed to the airport.

An hour later, we'd landed in Gainesville via private jet and rented another SUV. Frank was driving us to the hotel to pick up Shooter and Richie.

"Shooter spent the night down South," Cassie said, leaning forward from the back seat. "She met with the ME down there and made the hike back up this morning."

"Good," Frank said, pointing the car toward Shilo.

Alongside the road were small corridors of cypress that hid waterways leading to hammocks of hardwoods that were a thousand years old.

I closed my eyes for a moment, my brain still exhausted and my head feeling thick. Everything faded to black.

When I opened them again, I was in a backyard in Miami. I scanned the faces that I saw. A younger Rosa. Saul. My ex, Anna. A handful of guys from the office who liked Saul but did not care for me.

My eyes landed on Camila, seated in a high chair, wearing a pink Mexican-style dress. My mother stood beside her, emboldening Camila to do something.

"Go on," she said, encouraging her. "Do what feels good. Have fun."

And Camila did. She lodged her hands deep inside her birthday cake and rubbed them all over her face, the icing coating her cheeks. My mother laughed, and I heard people clap.

I felt a bump and opened my eyes. Frank was slowing the SUV.

I was happy in Miami eight and a half years ago. As much as I understood happiness.

But you cannot negotiate with the past, my mother used to say. *You cannot win an argument with a ghost, Gardy*, she'd tell me.

I thought of my mom, clawing her way back to consciousness. She'd become a ghost and was trying to regain a sense of herself. Could I get back there? What would it take to return to some life that felt normal, like I had with Anna?

I sat up and found my phone. Texted my mother's doctor, who had given me his personal cell before I left Texas.

How is she?

A moment later, three dots pulsed, and his message appeared.

Better. Out of the blue, she asked about you yesterday.

Except she fouled up your name. Called you Gardy.

I smiled. Then wrote back fast before putting away my phone:

Thank you for helping her. She deserves the best.

The world seemed to be returning to normal.

We pulled into the parking lot of the Homewood Suites. Through the front window, I saw Shooter, heading out of the lobby toward us.

"If it isn't the conquering heroes," she said as we got out of the car. "Can I say I knew you when? Get your autograph?"

"Where do you want me to sign?" Cassie said, and Shooter mimed pulling down her shirt. Cassie laughed out loud. "Where's the rook?"

Shooter glanced at a set of exterior stairs that ran up to the second floor, and she shrugged. "He texted me twenty minutes ago. Said he had a big day yesterday. Thought he had a lead on this thing."

"Cassie and I can grab him," I said to Frank. "Leave one of the cars and go with Shooter. We'll catch up."

Cassie told me she needed coffee, so I headed up the stairs to the second floor alone.

As we'd left the bar last night, I had been thinking about Cassie and me. Watching her walk away now, a specific thought moved through my head.

Was there something between us still? Something that was about to develop fifteen months ago, but I had halted it? And if Frank was back, and soon he'd be the boss again . . . did this pave the way for something new?

I got to the second floor and knocked on the door.

If Richie needed time to get ready, I was going to pull Cassie aside and ask her if she felt something.

No one answered Richie's door.

Do you feel something?

No. I would not say that. That sounded like I was asking about an earthquake. Or had just flatulated.

I called Richie's phone, but it went to voicemail.

I would like to explore something with you.

No, not that, either.

Cassie made her way up the steps to join me, a Styrofoam hotel coffee cup in hand.

I turned to face her. "Hey," I said.

"Hey yourself." Cassie smiled.

I wasn't nervous. I just wasn't sure how to phrase things. But before I could speak, I heard a noise and saw a woman pushing a maid's cart in our direction.

"Did you knock?" Cassie asked, her head tilted toward Richie's door.

"Yes," I said. "And I called. Nothing."

Cassie pulled out her badge and flashed the maid. "Do us a favor, will ya? Open this door?"

The woman swiped her passkey, and I swung Richie's door ajar. Holding it open, I glanced inside. The place looked empty.

"Agent Brancato?" I hollered.

"Richie?" Cassie's voice followed mine.

That's when we saw it.

A drop of blood on the wood floor, just inches from the door.

CHAPTER THIRTY-SIX

CASSIE AND I PULLED OUR WEAPONS.

"Richie!" I hollered.

I studied the hotel room as I stepped inside. It was suite-style. The primary area held a kitchenette, living room, and desk. There were no suitcases in the room. No items on the desk or below it.

"Richie?" Cassie repeated, her voice steady.

It took four seconds to check the space. "Clear," I called out to Cassie.

I moved left, toward the closed door to the bedroom, while Cassie rechecked the rest of the room. She opened a small cabinet, but it held only a fold-out ironing board.

I stepped closer to the bedroom, and Cassie crossed the space, approaching from the opposite side. "Armed federal agents," she called, "looking for Richie Brancato."

I pushed the door open with my left foot, my Glock raised at eye level. But the only thing inside was Richie's body. He was laid out on the floor in a pair of boxers and nothing else, a white hotel towel spread across his chest.

I kicked the door all the way open, and Cassie rounded the opposite corner with her weapon out, both of us confirming at a glance that the space was empty. I tucked my Glock away and crouched near Richie on the floor.

"Jesus," Cassie said from behind me, double-checking the bathroom and moving back into the primary area before bolting the door so no one could approach us from the rear.

I was on the ground beside Richie, feeling for a pulse on the radial side of his wrist. It was weak at best, and his skin was clammy and cold to the touch.

"Nine-one-one?" Cassie said, her voice spiking.

"We'll get him there faster ourselves," I said. "Get the car."

Cassie ran out the door, and I prepared myself to lift Richie up. But before I did, I turned and scanned the space, knowing that after we left, I might not have another chance to inspect a clean crime scene.

Out in the main room was the desk where Richie would have kept his workbag, computer, and papers. There was nothing there. I scanned back to the floor by the entryway and found the drop of blood I'd first seen. Nearby were a couple more sprinkles, but not more than a quarter ounce in all.

I looked back to Richie, noticing a smear of shaving cream in his right sideburn. Beyond his body, a small pool of water lay on the floor, outside the bathroom door.

I imagined the rookie, emerging from the shower, then shaving. Maybe hearing someone inside his room.

And opening the door to find what? A person going through his workbag? El Médico, specifically?

I'd seen enough of the space. I turned to him.

"Okay, rook," I said. "It's go time."

I grabbed his body and pulled it over my shoulder in a fireman's carry. Then bent my knees to support our combined weight and stood. Moved fast toward the flight of stairs that led to the parking lot, while Cassie flew into the space below me with her SUV.

Outside, I laid Richie on the back seat of the Tahoe, then jumped in on the opposite side, my door still ajar as Cassie peeled out of the lot.

I pulled Richie's torso onto mine and examined his symptoms.

"His blood pressure is low," I said, slapping at his cheeks but getting no response.

"Richie," Cassie yelled from the front.

The rookie's lips moved, but he didn't speak. The car fishtailed as we came out of the hotel lot. Cassie hit the gas, and Richie's body pressed against mine. I held him, keeping him from rolling onto the floor as the speed normalized.

"How's he doing?" Cassie yelled.

"Not well," I said, my eyes on his pupils, which were no bigger than three millimeters.

Cassie swerved around cars, her foot pressed hard on the pedal. We emerged into a commercial area, and my eyes scanned the road around us.

"There," I yelled, and she jerked the steering wheel hard to the right, the Chevy Tahoe hopping a sidewalk as we sailed into the parking lot of a Navarro's Discount Pharmacy. A sign over the left side of the building read MINUTE CLINIC, and Cassie aimed for the front door, slamming on her brakes and leaving me two feet from a set of glass sliders.

Inside, the place was covered in SALE and OFERTA signs, screaming about deep discounts in two languages. I found the pharmacy and jumped the line, flashing my badge at a woman at the counter.

"Naloxone," I said. "Narcan. Kloxxado. Have you got any of them?"

The woman blinked. She was a brunette in her late twenties and stood behind a sheet of glass. "Uhhh—" she stammered.

"I've got an unresponsive federal agent," I raised my voice. "Narcan. Two boxes."

"Sorry. Yeah, of course," she said, hurrying over to a shelf. She returned with two boxes of the nasal spray used to counter the effects of certain drug overdoses, almost stumbling in her haste.

She turned to ring me up, but I took off and ran.

Outside the store, Cassie had the door to the Tahoe open and was beside the car, kneeling next to Richie. She turned to me. "You're thinking opioids," she asked, her eyes wide. "Heroin? Fentanyl? Methadone? Vicodin?"

We had almost no information, and anything was possible. Had an assailant done this? Had Richie shot himself up?

"There was no drug paraphernalia at the scene," I said. "Shooter said she had just talked to him. And the symptoms match up."

Cassie moved out of the way, and I inserted the spray into one of Richie's nostrils.

"Four milligrams?" Cassie asked.

I nodded, spraying the pump up Richie's nose. His body spasmed, and his mouth sputtered with saliva. But his lips were still tinged a blue shade, and his nostrils flared outward.

"Two minutes between doses," Cassie said, and I tore open the second box.

Richie was struggling to breathe, and his skin, which was cold, felt sweaty at the same time.

The pharmacist was beside me now, and her eyes moved from Richie to me. "I'm gonna call an ambulance," she said.

She left to go into the store, and I counted down the time, ignoring the crowd that was gathering, some of them holding up cell phones and filming us.

"You're sure, right?" Cassie asked, motioning at the second box of Narcan. Her lips had faded from red to a pinkish white.

I was not sure. But the voice of my mother rang in my head.

For most of life's big decisions, Gardy, you'll need to act with eighty percent of the information.

"Yes," I said.

I inserted the second bottle into the opposite nostril. "C'mon," I said and pressed the pump hard.

And Richie sputtered to life, his breathing coming back in small gulps at first, then larger ones a moment later.

CHAPTER THIRTY-SEVEN

AN AMBULANCE HIT ITS HORN, AND THE CROWD AROUND us separated.

There were two techs by my side, and my mind felt flatter than normal. A numbness I was unused to.

"Gardner," Cassie said, and a memory flashed in my head.

Richie, opening the door to my mother's hospital room. A pinprick in her neck.

And now we'd almost lost Richie.

Cassie was clearing the crowd around the Tahoe while the two men strapped Richie onto a gurney.

"I'll go with him," I said, and Cassie nodded, moving toward her SUV.

The two men loaded Richie into the back of the ambulance. Then one of them hopped out. Jumped into the driver's seat while I stepped onto the bumper and climbed inside the back.

The inside of the vehicle smelled like a mix of gas exhaust and antiseptic, and I found purchase on a shelflike structure beside Richie.

The rookie lifted his head off the stretcher and mumbled, so I leaned in close.

"Came out of the bathroom," he said. "Going through my stuff."

I inspected his eyes. His pupils were still less than three millimeters.

"Was it our guy?" I asked.

"Five ten," he mumbled. "Muscular."

"Let him rest," the ambulance tech said, and I glanced over at him. He was in his late twenties, and he placed orange foam plugs in his ears. He offered me a pair, too, but I turned him down. Richie was still talking.

"Foreign pistol. Unusual looking," Richie said. "I dunno which."

The ambulance sirens were incredibly loud, and we took a corner so fast I had to grab onto Richie's stretcher.

"Our guy, though?" I asked.

"Sir," the tech hollered at me.

"Could've been a 43X." Richie was slurring his words.

A Glock 43X was a fairly ubiquitous handgun, sold for under five hundred dollars and popular among homeowners because of its light 5.4-pound trigger pull.

"Caucasian?" I asked. "Or Latino?"

"Hey," the tech said. "Enough."

But Richie's eyes were nearly closed now, and I needed information.

"Richie," I said, slapping his chest with my hand.

"Don't hit him," the tech yelled.

But Richie opened his eyes.

"White," he said. "Bandage on his face."

"Was he the guy from the sketch?" I demanded. But Richie had gone quiet.

A few minutes later, the ambulance driver hit a blast horn, and I placed my hand on Richie's forehead. "Richie?" I demanded.

"You shouldn't have seen my face," Richie said then, opening his eyes. "It wasn't ready."

"What?"

"It wasn't ready," Richie repeated. "He said that."

The driver took a hard left and leaned on the horn again, beeping it twice in some sort of signal. A moment later, the back door to the ambulance opened. Through the gap, I saw Cassie's Tahoe pull in behind us. To our right, under a covered portico, were two containers holding a series of backboards in green and orange and yellow colors.

The tech who had driven us ran over to a sliding door marked EMS ENTRANCE. He hit a button and leaned inside, hollering something to the staff. Two nurses emerged, and the tech from the back pulled Richie's stretcher out, pausing as an accordion-like structure with wheeled legs popped out from the bottom.

I came alongside the stretcher to help, but the tech from the back waved over two security guards in black pants and fluorescent-yellow vests.

"Watch this guy," he said. "He was hitting the patient. Trying to hurt him. Step aside, sir," he said to me.

I glanced around, confused, as hospital security approached Cassie and me. Was he talking about me?

I flashed tin at the two guards and moved inside, ignoring them. "FBI business," I said. "That's our man on that stretcher. No one gets seen before he does."

CHAPTER THIRTY-EIGHT

A HALF HOUR HAD PASSED. RICHIE WAS UNDER OBSERVA-tion at the University of Florida hospital in Gainesville, where the ambulance had brought him. Cassie and I stood in the waiting room. She'd gotten a coffee for her and a tea for me, each in paper cups with blue and orange stripes along the side. The waiting room smelled like a mix of mop wax and flowers, and Cassie's face looked gray.

"I asked Richie if his attacker was the guy in the sketch," I said, trying to meet her eyes. "But he kept falling asleep."

"This is hitting hard," Cassie said.

She informed me that she needed to throw up. Which was a reminder that I'd eaten two pieces of pizza fourteen hours ago in D.C. The only thing I'd put in my system since then were three beers and four tequila shots.

"You shouldn't have seen my face," I said. "It wasn't ready."

"What?"

"The guy said that to Richie. 'You shouldn't have seen my face. It wasn't ready.'"

"What the hell does that mean?"

"I don't know," I said. "Maybe Richie was babbling. He also told me the guy had a rare handgun. Then a minute later, he said it was a Glock 43X."

I relayed the other details to Cassie, putting together a story from the limited information we had: Richie had come out of the bathroom and found a man going through his case files. He'd described the man as five foot ten. A muscular build.

Cassie stared at me, waiting for more. Or maybe she was waiting to see if I was done, so she could go vomit.

"Covering some part of his face was a bandage," I continued. "I didn't get more than that."

A doctor named Carlson came out into the waiting room then, wearing a pale blue coat. Her wavy brown hair fell to her shoulders, and she wore glasses that hung from a chain around her neck. She told us that Richie was stable but had been sedated.

"For how long?" I asked.

"It's too early to tell," Dr. Carlson said. "We stabilized him with IV fluids. Gave him heart medication for his blood pressure. But… I don't love some of the symptoms I'm seeing. I've contacted our toxicology specialist."

"What kind of symptoms?" I asked.

"Hypotension," she said, pushing her hair back behind her ears. "Bradycardia. We'll let him rest. Hopefully by late tonight or early tomorrow, we'll have better news."

Hypotension typically meant a blood pressure lower than ninety over sixty, while bradycardia referred to a resting heart rate under sixty. The two in combination was something I was not certain about.

"He was healthy before today?" the doctor asked.

"Very much so," Cassie said. "We believe he was injected with something."

"That's what I heard," she said. "And you don't know what exactly?"

"No," I said.

"We'll stay close to him, then. Begin ruling things out."

The doctor left us, and I recalled what Shooter had said when we arrived at the Homewood Suites. She'd texted Richie to say that we were driving in from the airport.

"You think El Médico was there?" I asked Cassie. "Right before *we* got there?"

"Shooter's text probably spooked the guy," she said. "Mighta saved Richie's life."

Soon after, Frank and Shooter arrived at the hospital. While Cassie filled them in, I tried to picture our suspect, present at the Homewood Suites as we drove up. Realizing a handful of federal agents were about to gather downstairs, he must've injected Richie with an unknown drug and left, taking the rookie's phone, computer, and case files. Which included sketches of El Médico himself.

And all of Richie's leads from yesterday.

"Amber Isiah," I said, snapping out of my thoughts and looking at the team.

The plumbing supply house where Shooter and I had interviewed Amber was just twenty minutes from here.

"If El Médico has Richie's notes," I said, "he knows Amber is alive and where she works. Amber is the only witness who's ever seen his face."

"Let's get a squad car there," Frank said, and Shooter nodded. "On it."

"Can you locate Richie's weapon?" I asked her. "I'm betting it's in his hotel room safe."

"Of course," she said, stepping aside to handle both tasks.

Frank turned to Cassie and me then. "Whatever Richie found," he said, "it attracted this guy's attention. You got any idea what it is, Gardner?"

"No," I said. "But he's close. We need to move fast."

"Detective Quinones is sending two patrolmen to keep an eye on Richie," Frank said. "And we got the sketch of El Médico with every cop in this county. The best thing we can do now is go through every open lead and be quick about it. Find what Richie found."

Shooter returned, telling us a squad car was rolling to retrieve Amber. "I tried calling," she said. "No answer."

"Drive over there yourself," Frank said. "You and Gardner interviewed her. A friendly face will help."

"Done." Shooter spun on her heels and strode off.

Cassie, Frank, and I waited until the two patrolmen showed up to watch Richie. Then we headed back in Frank's car and reassembled in the conference room at Shilo PD.

Less than an hour had passed since we'd found Richie. I taped up papers on the wall that represented every lead we'd had four days ago, before the gun case took the focus away from this one.

I looked to Frank. "Before we start in on these"—I pointed at the wall—"can we talk about our suspect?"

Frank Roberts is considered one of the top profilers in the country. It was the primary reason that his request to form PAR had been approved five years ago. But we'd been using him as a project manager instead of leveraging his talent at building a psychological profile of our suspect.

"We finally have some physical descriptions of this guy," I continued. "But in terms of what we typically study at PAR"—I pointed at Cassie and me—"I've looked through everything, Frank. There's no pattern here."

"There's always a pattern, Gardner," he said. "You know that better than anyone."

"Sure," I said. "But on this particular case? Our statements are missing persons reports filed by acquaintances. Our autopsies are of desiccated skeletons. Our crime scenes are dirt in the ground. And our victims are marginalized people who can offer little in the way of financial gain to their killer."

Frank nodded, seeing where I was going with this.

For years, classic FBI profiling had been the province of agents like Frank, who had a mixed background that spanned law, law enforcement, and psychology. And while there was no one singular way to practice profiling, the best professionals shared a common methodology that began with crime scene statements, moved to a list of psychological factors and personality traits, and eventually landed on variables that included age, race, and birthplace. All of which helped investigators find the monster . . . based on the method.

But when victim details were nonexistent, and when the reason victims were removed from this earth was unknown, imputing details about the monster had to come some other way.

"Instead of profiling inputs," Frank said, his eyes fixed on mine, "we have to move in a different direction."

"You mean begin with him?" Cassie said, taping up the sketch of El Médico. "Even if we don't know shit about him."

Frank nodded. "Let's work backwards," he said. "From known models and categorizations. Try to impute in reverse from his kills."

We all agreed. This was not the traditional way of doing business, but we needed to find this guy fast. And there was no other way, not with such sparse evidence.

"Let's start wide, then," I said. "Anything we suspect."

Frank took off his jacket and tossed it aside. "With organized killers, we typically find three intercept points."

"Right," I said. "Where the killer first saw the victim. Where he killed them—"

"And where they were disposed of," Frank finished.

"This guy's disposal points are all within a two-mile radius," Cassie said. "The housing project a couple years back was the first. Near the county line where Gardner and Richie found the body six nights ago was the second. And the group burial we found the day after was third."

As Cassie said this, I found the map that Detective Quinones had loaned me almost a week ago. The one upon which I'd initially drawn the circles and tangential lines—to help locate the skeletons. I circled the areas where we'd found the victims and taped the map onto the conference room wall.

"All of these bodies were found within the confines of Shilo County," I said.

"So statistics tell us that sometime in the last five years," Frank said, putting his hands on his hips and pacing, "he's either lived in Shilo or had a full-time job there."

Cassie took the whiteboard pen from me and jotted this down. "And you're assuming he's an organized killer why?" she asked.

"He must have used some ruse or charm to get these women to trust him," Frank said. "I'd also guess he's attractive and well spoken. Takes care of his appearance. Organized killers tend to live with a domestic partner or are married."

"Gardner thought Mavreen Isiah was El Médico's girlfriend during some of these murders," Cassie said, scrawling another note on the whiteboard.

"And she worked where?" Frank asked, looking at the map.

I made a mark where Alantay Medical Group was located.

"Let's circle a one-mile radius around that," Frank said.

Which I did.

"I'd bet my pension this is his neighborhood," Frank continued. "Either he lived there, worked there, or both." He pointed at me. "Now, the first two women called him El Médico, and we have a suspect who was comfortable injecting Richie with us practically at the hotel, right?"

"Right," Cassie said.

"Another victim had a cut on her infraorbital bone postmortem," I said. "Still another was offered a cleft lip surgery."

Cassie shook her head. "Guys, Richie already sent patrolmen with our sketch through every local hospital. Zilch. *Cero.* No one's ID'd this guy based on medical experience."

Frank looked back at the wall map before crossing to Cassie's laptop. He opened up a digital street map that covered the same area.

"Then he must work in some clinical setting," he said. "Just not a hospital. Gainesville has a huge medical community. Shilo's is decent-sized, too, for a small town."

I studied the street map. Two medical plazas were located inside the circled area. Each was a block and a half long and probably contained a hundred doctors' and dentists' offices.

"Let's get some patrolmen," I said to Cassie, "walking our sketch door to door in these plazas. Someone knows this guy."

"Heard," she said.

Cassie left the room to coordinate with Detective Quinones, and I suggested to Frank that we put the medical angle aside, rather than fixate further on it.

While I did this, Frank took a turn in his analysis.

"One of the things that's been bothering me, Gardner," he said, "is the why."

"Why he's doing this?" I asked.

"The bodies show no evidence of a blitz attack, based on everything in our ME reports. Also, none of the telltale signs of abuse. And like you said, the victims appear to come from economically disadvantaged backgrounds."

There was a reason Frank raised these specific points. Data told us that 62 percent of US serial killers claimed they had murdered their victims for either enjoyment or financial gain. But if we could not make some personal connection between victim and killer, and if these women were too poor to offer El Médico money . . . why on earth had they been targeted?

And if there was no pattern in picking them, how would we find their killer?

Cassie came back into the room. She told us that patrol was on their way to the medical plazas we'd marked. I stepped closer to the wall and stared at the composite sketch.

"His picture's all over the news," I said, "but no one recognizes him."

I thought of the detail about the mask on his face and how that affected the quality of our sketch. Of Richie's mention of a bandage.

Is he purposely trying to disguise himself?

It felt like we had explored everything from the killer's point of view, so as a group, we decided to switch back to another urgent matter: how Richie might have attracted the attention of El Médico. We had begun to chase down a half dozen leads on the case. Any one of them might have led Richie into the hands of a killer.

"Let's start with the pimp boyfriend, Dog," I said, pointing at the paper I had taped to the conference room wall. "Richie had the ME grind up one of the skeletal hip bones to compare it to Dog's baby teeth, which his mother had supplied. Do we know if Richie heard back on that yet from Quantico?"

"On it," Cassie said and began typing on her laptop.

I turned back to the wall. "Freddie," I said. One word.

"What about him?"

"Richie was convinced the cases were connected. If not the cases, the two men."

"El Médico and your first C.I.?" Frank asked.

I nodded, turning back to the wall. "Natalie Kastner," I said. This was Freddie's cousin, the one whom Shooter had interviewed at the funeral reception. "When I spoke to Shooter from D.C., the plan was to keep Jo's cover as the ex of Freddie Pecos intact. Jo had asked Richie to follow up on case details with Natalie. Interview her."

"Do we know if he actually did that?" Frank asked. "If he called her or drove down to Lucas Beach?"

"We were all so busy in D.C." Cassie shrugged. "I don't think any of us know."

The truth was that we'd left Richie on an island while we pursued the gun case. Left a rookie in the crosshairs of someone who'd killed nearly a dozen times.

"I'd also asked Richie to keep digging into how El Médico and Freddie might know each other," I said. "Richie looked back at the original ATM footage from Hambis. He told me that Freddie looked confused when he saw El Médico. Then surprised. Then happy."

"And?" Frank asked, his voice impatient, the veins on his neck showing.

"There's something about him." I tapped on the sketch. "People don't notice him. But Freddie . . ."

"Freddie did," Cassie said.

"And Freddie didn't live much longer after," Frank said, shaking his head.

Cassie pointed. "But the happy part."

"They knew each other," Frank and I said simultaneously.

Cassie was pacing in front of her laptop, which she sometimes did as leads came in.

"What is it?" I asked.

"Two things," she said. "One, the results on the DNA from Dog did indeed come back. It's a match. Dog is Skeleton Number Six."

"But you just found this out?" Frank confirmed.

"Yeah."

"So Richie didn't know it," Frank snapped. "It's not something we need to chase."

"What's the second thing?" I asked Cassie.

"Shooter's on her way back from the plumbing supply house. Amber is nowhere to be found."

Frank grimaced, and I guessed at what was going through his head. Richie had been compromised while we were in D.C. As lead, Frank would be held accountable. Now a witness had been placed in jeopardy.

We were running through the last of our leads, and nothing about how Richie had attracted the ire of a killer was popping.

"Guys," Frank said, frustrated. "C'mon."

I studied the note about the data analysis project that Cassie had proposed with the stingray device. This was based on the idea that El Médico had a non-burner phone—*his own phone*—that he might've used at two known locations: Amber's apartment in Gainesville and Amber's workplace in Shilo.

Cassie's theory was that we could use historical information on calls made in those two locations, along with the IMSI catcher, to collect data and rule out recurring phone numbers of locals in the area. If we got lucky, this would reduce a pool of ten thousand phone numbers down to five hundred. And if we crossed the two locations and a single number emerged, it might be El Médico's personal phone.

"Did this stingray get authorized?" I asked.

"While we were in D.C.," Cassie said, nodding. "We got a three-person tech team to sort through the data."

"Who's leading that from our side?" I asked.

"No one so far," Cassie said. "But I can. We also have a patrolman bringing Richie's phone and laptop back here. They were found on the side of Highway 24. Low-key trashed, from what I heard."

"How's Richie take notes lately?" Frank asked.

"Phone, mostly," Cassie said.

"If the computer's trashed," Frank said, "we can get his calls and texts off the cloud from his work phone."

I was half listening, half staring at the digital composite of Skeleton #9. She was a Caucasian woman, five foot eight, with wavy brown hair and a square jawline, at least according to the digital reconstruction photo from Patsy Davitt.

"We had one more body to ID," I said. "Maybe it led Richie somewhere else? There's a stack of messages he was going through from the tip line."

The whole case was in front of us. We just needed to find the right string and pull on it.

I heard a noise and turned.

Shooter was standing at the threshold to the conference room. Her face was blank.

"He crashed again," she said.

"Richie?"

"They stabilized him, but the doc told me that if we can't figure out what he got injected with by morning . . ."

She walked over to us, and I stared past her.

We needed to move faster.

CHAPTER THIRTY-NINE

THE FOUR OF US STOOD IN SILENCE, NOT SURE WHAT TO do next. By tomorrow, unless we found El Médico or figured out what he had injected the rookie with, we'd lose Richie.

"Let's split up," I said. "Jo, Cass, get on a flight to Jacksonville."

"What's in Jacksonville?" Shooter asked.

Cassie reminded her about the data project, but Shooter just stared back as if the exercise was theoretical.

"You agree with this?" she said to Frank, her voice sounding exasperated. "Taking two of us off the board right now?"

"I dunno," Frank said, looking to me.

I turned to Shooter. "Jo, there's cops walking a beat with our suspect's picture. Cops going through medical clinics. It's on the news. But what *we* do is different." I looked to Cassie. "This guy's phone number is buried somewhere in that pile of ones and zeros. Believe in your instincts. Don't try to be a great beat cop. Be a great agent for PAR."

"He's right," Cassie said and nodded, her confidence buoying the room.

Shooter still looked pale. "Okay," she said. "I'll trust you guys."

Beyond the glass, the Shilo police station was busy. Shooter and Cassie grabbed their stuff and left. I turned to the evidence I'd taped up on the wall.

"Richie is sharp," I said to Frank. "But he's one guy, and there's four of us. Whatever he found—we'll find it. Or we'll find this suspect."

Being in motion helps me think, so I grabbed half the pile of orange messages from the tip line. "I'll take these," I said. "I'm going to Lucas Beach to talk to Natalie Kastner."

"I'm coming with you," Frank said, grabbing the second half of the message pile.

We got in the car and moved east by southeast, down through Marion County. To our left were thick loblollies, and through them, I could see the dark green water of Newnans Lake.

Bodies of water in Central and South Florida often drain into a flood basin, and I remembered reading about this lake. In 2000, a drought had brought to the surface the remnants of canoes that dated as far back as 5000 BC.

Data. The past. Always inserting itself into the present.

Clues, always there, if you are looking for them.

I glanced at Frank. "So, Dallas," I said, returning to the topic from the night before at the bar. "No good?"

"Dallas was different," he said. "Spreadsheets. HR meetings. Budgeting."

For years, Frank had been trying to move back to the state where he'd grown up. He'd applied for multiple jobs, all management level.

"But that's what you wanted, right?"

He pursed his lips. "I thought so," he said. "Was this job everything *you* wanted?"

I studied Frank. I had taken his job. But seeing him back here made me realize that I hadn't. Frank had supervised us. Shepherded our careers. And handled politics. I did few of those things, preferring to solve riddles instead. I was *part* of the team, not their boss.

"I tried to focus on what I'm good at," I said. "Instead of trying to be you."

I rolled down the window, even though the climate inside the car was perfect. The hot wind outside was oppressive, and I breathed it in, my lungs absorbing the wet warmth of Florida, my right hand along the windowsill feeling as if it were wrapped in fleece.

I turned my head to look out the window. The American South is full of burned-out houses, shuttered farms, and manufacturing plants that were once central to small towns but are now rusted out and discarded, the local population shrunk down to three digits in size. I have no emotional attachment to Florida or South Carolina, both of which I have lived in for the bulk of my life. But my mother, when I was young, would take me on long drives throughout the area.

What will become of us, Gardy? she'd ask. *If we are okay with throwing away this many people and all this history?*

I didn't know the answer as a preteen. Now I hardly thought of it at all.

My mind moved back to Richie.

"How are you feeling?" Frank asked.

In my head, I kept replaying the moment Richie had found my mother, a bloody pinprick in her neck, her white comforter covering her chest and body. How the rookie's voice had cracked as he framed my mother in his cell phone while I stood a thousand miles away, helpless.

Now it was Richie in a hospital bed.

"We have 'til morning," I said. "We just need to keep moving. Checking leads. Making calls."

As we drove, Frank and I moved through the pile of messages, sorting them into priority, non-priority, and irrelevant. Hotlines and tip lines attract the oddest of society, yet among them, law enforcement usually finds its best leads. Triaging them is critical.

"You think he got Amber?" I asked Frank. "Based on our files?"

Frank sucked in the skin of his cheek. Bit it and turned to me. "I do."

"Damn it," I said.

Within an hour, we had made our way through the Ocala National Forest. As we got farther south, rain fell in a sudden downpour. The droplets were enormous. They hit the windshield and seemed to separate from each other of their own accord as if drawn away from the glass by an electric current.

A quarter mile from the shores of Lucas Beach, the rain stopped, and I could smell salt in the air. But out ahead of us, the sky showed thunderheads as we drove through a neighborhood of low-lying ranch-style homes.

"Hurricane weather's coming," Frank said. "You can smell it."

I looked around. The sidewalks were rounded and the lawns carefully manicured. Shooter had met with Natalie Kastner at an area restaurant, where the post-funeral reception had taken place. But we were heading to Natalie's home, which was on Avalon Street, fifteen blocks from the water.

We parked. Palm trees lined the road, and tiny American flags were planted in the grass near every mailbox. Our eyes landed on a two-story house painted a butter yellow color, with stacked stone running from the windows down to a line of bushes that flanked the front of the place.

It was 4 p.m.

Without our help, Richie Brancato would be dead by morning.

We rang the doorbell, and a woman answered. "Can I help you?" she asked.

"We're with the Federal Bureau of Investigation," Frank said, holding up his badge. "My name is Frank Roberts. This is Gardner Camden."

The woman's eyes widened, and she looked past us as if expecting someone else. "What's this about?"

"Are you Natalie Kastner?" I asked, confirming we were in the right place.

"Yes."

I thought of what Shooter had told me as I stood in the stairwell in D.C. after Freddie Pecos's funeral. What Natalie had been told by the ME in Hambis.

"Your cousin Freddie Pecos," I said, keeping it simple. "We're looking into irregularities in his death. Can we come in?"

The woman directed us through a living room furnished with an overstuffed white couch and into a sunroom, which let in a breeze that smelled of sand and salt air. Natalie was in her late thirties, and her hair had streaks of brown and red in it, the kind that come from sun exposure. She pointed for us to sit down, and we each grabbed a chair.

"We're looking for some background on Freddie," I said. I pulled out my phone, but instead of showing her the sketch of El Médico, I found a photo of Richie. "Before we get started, has this man come by and spoken to you?"

I handed her my phone, and she studied Richie's picture. "No," she said. "Who is he?"

"A member of our team," Frank said. "He's not in a position to confer with us today, and we thought he might've already reached out to you yesterday."

"I was at my mother's house for the last day," she said. "We had a funeral for Freddie, and she asked me to stay over."

We nodded in understanding, and Frank started in, collecting background from Natalie. First, asking questions we already knew the answer to, to establish fidelity. Then probing for information on her relationship with Freddie.

"When's the last time you saw your cousin?" he asked.

"Before we heard about his death," Natalie said, blowing air into her bangs. "Gotta be three years. My mom had a party for her seventy-fifth. Freddie was her godson, and she flew him in." She looked from me to Frank. "I gotta say, I'm confused. Why is the FBI looking into my cousin's death? I spoke to local police in Hambis the other day. The medical examiner said *they'd* be looking into it."

I studied Natalie. "Certain circumstances with your cousin's death came to the attention of the federal government," I said. "Were you familiar with how Freddie earned a living?"

"No," she said. "But I wouldn't be surprised if it was something illegal."

I looked to Frank.

The possibility of Richie talking to Natalie Kastner was the main reason we'd driven down to Lucas Beach. If Richie hadn't, Natalie could only be counted on for background information on Freddie. But if she hadn't seen her cousin in three years, what context could she provide?

Frank took out the composite sketch of El Médico and handed it to Natalie.

"Does this man look familiar to you?" he asked.

Natalie took the photo, and a sort of quarter smile formed on her face. At the same time, she shook her head.

"Take your time," Frank said. Which is something Cassie used to say a lot when we were partners. Computer scientists, I often told her, have estimated that the human brain moves at a speed of one exaflop, or about one billion calculations per second. *No one* needs to take their time.

"No," Natalie said. "Sorry."

Frank squinted. "You were nodding, though. Almost . . . smiling."

"Yeah, well, the picture reminded me of someone. A kid, from when I was young."

"From around here?" Frank asked.

"Over the bridge," Natalie said, gesturing out the open window. "One of the big beach houses. They've all been torn down. Almost all of them are resorts now. We used to go up there for parties. But . . . part of the face is wrong, so I think he just looks like a lot of people, you know? Sort of a . . . generic face."

As she spoke, Natalie rose and closed the windows, a gust of wind picking up and rattling behind them.

"We believe this is someone Freddie knew," I said, hoping that would get her to take a second look.

"Well then, for sure it's a no," she said.

I blinked. "I don't understand."

"My mother loved Freddie, Agent Camden," Natalie said. "But you know—he wasn't like us."

"Us who?" I asked.

"You know—me . . . my brother, Andrew." She paused. "Freddie was my mom's sister's kid. Her only kid. So we took him every summer. But we weren't always together, if you know what I mean."

This woman spoke in innuendo, and I was not following her.

"No," I said, my voice sounding irritated as I heard it. "I don't know what you mean."

"My mom would get us all ready in the morning, right? Swimsuits. Check. Sunblock. Check. Me, Andy, and Freddie. Leaving for the beach all together, right? One happy trio."

"Right," I said.

"Except we didn't hang out together," she said. "We had *our* people—"

"And Freddie had his," I finished her sentence.

"Exactly," she said, sitting back in her chair.

"So who *would* Freddie associate with?" Frank asked.

"Surfers," Natalie said, turning to him. "Stoners. Kids who took the bus over to the beach."

"Not whoever this drawing reminded you of," Frank confirmed.

"Exactly," she said.

I considered my own childhood. Thought of the summers I'd spent with my mom on Kiawah Island. It was hard enough making friends back home. But on vacation? If you were odd like me and found one person to connect with, you held on tight.

"Did Freddie have a best friend?" I asked. "Someone he saw every summer?"

Natalie smiled. "He did, actually. Some Polish immigrant kid. Real dreamer."

"He took the bus in?" Frank asked.

"No," she said, scoffing. "He lived here. With his mom. Above a pancake restaurant on the pier where she worked."

"And he and Freddie were tight?" Frank asked.

"Oh yeah," she said. "That kid was a real storyteller. Once told

Freddie he was the heir to some big hotel chain." She shook her head, smiling. "The billionaire next door. Living above a run-down restaurant."

"He wasn't?" Frank asked rhetorically.

"The boy was pathological," Natalie said, shaking her head. "Perfect friend for Freddie."

"This kid have a name?" I asked.

"None I would remember. And that restaurant is long gone."

I glanced at Frank. We needed to either dig in or let go, so I pointed at the sketch.

"We have good information that this man met your cousin fifty-three minutes before Freddie's death. They drove back to his trailer together. And then this man shot Freddie in cold blood. So he's not just a person of interest, Ms. Kastner," I said. "He's our prime suspect in your cousin's murder."

I'd seen Shooter take this approach, switching from witness to suspect to get a reaction.

And it did. Natalie grabbed the paper from Frank's hand and stared at it again. But after a minute, the result was the same.

"Sorry," she said, her face crumpling.

But Frank continued anyway, trying to keep the rapport going.

"Your cousin," he said. "Do you have any pictures of him?"

"Not as an adult," Natalie said, "but my mother was a photographer. After I got my own place, I inherited more childhood photos than I have space for."

She walked over to an ornately carved credenza, covered in framed pictures.

I stayed in the chair where I was, mentally moving through the nine known victims and anything we hadn't yet followed up on.

"Gardner," Frank said, and I stood. Walked over to the credenza

I got in on the driver's side, and Frank plopped onto the passenger seat. He examined the text. "You think there's anything with this Natalie woman? You got pretty aggressive there."

I glanced back at the house. "She displayed all the microexpressions of deceit."

Frank squinted, turning so he faced me. "Right up until the last minute, it looked like you couldn't get out of there fast enough."

I turned the ignition switch, and the car thrummed to life. "The plan was to talk to anyone Richie did, right? Chase what he chased?"

"Right."

"Richie was never here," I said. "Never called her."

"Sure," Frank replied. "But if you think she's holding back . . . ?"

"She flushed when she saw the sketch," I said. "Studied it for ten seconds. It might not be conscious, but she recognizes something about that face."

I flipped a U-turn to head back toward the state highway and threw on my wipers to clear away the oncoming rain, which began to fall. Frank thumbed through the tip line messages that we'd flagged as urgent.

"Back to Shilo?" I said.

Frank shook his head. "No. Drive up that way, will ya?" He pointed. "Toward the water."

"Why?" I asked.

"Because we're here, and she mentioned it." His voice rose. "It's good police work."

I swung a right where Frank directed me. We moved over the inner waterway and found ourselves on the parallel peninsula. I could smell the salt water, and Frank pointed again, directing me to go straight until we were almost at the beach. We turned left and headed up the main drag.

and stared at a framed photo of two kids outside a boa
cream shop. From their facial structure, I identified Fredd
the boy. Beside him was Natalie Kastner, their arms drap
each other.

In other pictures on the credenza, Natalie sat on the l
ious teen boys, sometimes in boats, sometimes at board
even though she did not look old enough to drink.

Frank asked Natalie if he could hold on to the picture
die in it, and she agreed.

"There's a woman missing right now," I said. "Kidn
can't tell us anything?"

"Gardner," Frank said, but I kept my focus on Natalie

"I told you everything I know," she said. "I'm sorry."

Frank thanked her for her time, and I took out a c
with her.

As we walked out to the car, a text from Shooter pop

Two women went missing from Hambis. Three days befor
Freddie's death. Quinones had searched this out for Richi

Frank was staring at the same message as I unlocked

"If this is El Médico," I said, "he's moving around. I
different areas of the state."

"Why move?" Frank asked. "No one had a lead
Shilo."

A second text came in from Shooter, who was obviou
a lead on an unsolved missing.

Two more girls with similar looks missing. Lucas Beach.
Where you guys are.

and stared at a framed photo of two kids outside a boardwalk ice cream shop. From their facial structure, I identified Freddie Pecos as the boy. Beside him was Natalie Kastner, their arms draped around each other.

In other pictures on the credenza, Natalie sat on the laps of various teen boys, sometimes in boats, sometimes at boardwalk bars, even though she did not look old enough to drink.

Frank asked Natalie if he could hold on to the picture with Freddie in it, and she agreed.

"There's a woman missing right now," I said. "Kidnapped. You can't tell us anything?"

"Gardner," Frank said, but I kept my focus on Natalie.

"I told you everything I know," she said. "I'm sorry."

Frank thanked her for her time, and I took out a card. Left it with her.

As we walked out to the car, a text from Shooter popped up.

> Two women went missing from Hambis. Three days before Freddie's death. Quinones had searched this out for Richie.

Frank was staring at the same message as I unlocked the car.

"If this is El Médico," I said, "he's moving around. Hunting in different areas of the state."

"Why move?" Frank asked. "No one had a lead on him in Shilo."

A second text came in from Shooter, who was obviously chasing a lead on an unsolved missing.

> Two more girls with similar looks missing. Lucas Beach. Where you guys are.

I got in on the driver's side, and Frank plopped onto the passenger seat. He examined the text. "You think there's anything with this Natalie woman? You got pretty aggressive there."

I glanced back at the house. "She displayed all the micro-expressions of deceit."

Frank squinted, turning so he faced me. "Right up until the last minute, it looked like you couldn't get out of there fast enough."

I turned the ignition switch, and the car thrummed to life. "The plan was to talk to anyone Richie did, right? Chase what he chased?"

"Right."

"Richie was never here," I said. "Never called her."

"Sure," Frank replied. "But if you think she's holding back . . . ?"

"She flushed when she saw the sketch," I said. "Studied it for ten seconds. It might not be conscious, but she recognizes something about that face."

I flipped a U-turn to head back toward the state highway and threw on my wipers to clear away the oncoming rain, which began to fall. Frank thumbed through the tip line messages that we'd flagged as urgent.

"Back to Shilo?" I said.

Frank shook his head. "No. Drive up that way, will ya?" He pointed. "Toward the water."

"Why?" I asked.

"Because we're here, and she mentioned it." His voice rose. "It's good police work."

I swung a right where Frank directed me. We moved over the inner waterway and found ourselves on the parallel peninsula. I could smell the salt water, and Frank pointed again, directing me to go straight until we were almost at the beach. We turned left and headed up the main drag.

As we moved farther north, I noted what Natalie Kastner had mentioned. The large estates had disappeared; in their place stood a dozen hotels and resorts of various quality levels and price points. The towers above Lucas Beach rose ten stories high. At the base of each, chunky parking garages faced Atlantic Boulevard.

We moved past them and approached a strip of large houses.

"Pull over there," Frank said.

I pulled into the bike lane, and he got out. Started walking backward, in the direction from which we'd come.

A car honked its horn at me. I was blocking a driveway to a boutique hotel. A sign read THE OLIVE in one direction, and AURORA HOUSE in the other. I put the car in reverse and moved backward ten yards. The sidewalk became rounded, and I placed my car tires up on it to keep out of the road.

"Where the hell are you going?" I said aloud, even though Frank was gone.

I turned off the ignition and followed him. The structure we'd parked beside was the back of a property. To my left, as I walked south, a tall wrought iron fence rose sixteen feet in the air.

I caught up with Frank, who had badged a man on a riding lawn mower. The man was dressed in baggy jeans and a green shirt, and a bandana covered his face. The rain was picking up, but more than that, a wind howled in from the beach.

"How many houses are here?" Frank asked him through the gate.

The man shrugged, and I tried it in my best Spanish. "*Cuántas casas estan aqui?*"

"Not much," the man said. "*Más hoteles.*"

Frank pulled out the photo of El Médico and showed it to the man.

"*Conoces?*" I asked, seeing if he recognized the man.

"No," he said.

Frank began walking farther south, away from where we'd parked, and I shook my head at him. *What the hell?*

He passed a driveway for another boutique hotel and approached the next house down, a similarly tall gate covering the back of the property.

"I can think of better uses for our time," I said, catching up.

"Really?" he snapped, turning, the rain gathered in little dots along his hairline. "Like what?"

"Like one of us going to local police and checking in on these missing persons Shooter has identified. Statistically, in serial killer cases, eventually one victim will have a clear personal connection to the killer."

Frank stopped walking. Blinked. "And where have all your statistics gotten us so far, huh? I gotta call Richie's parents. That's on *my* list today."

I examined Frank. Last year, he had been taken by a killer. Kidnapped and put in a life-or-death situation. I could see that he was starting to decompensate, the longer Richie was in the hospital.

"Frank," I said. "There's nothing here. Let's go."

Frank stared at me, his face falling before he nodded. We walked back to the car, and I looked at our group text chain. Cassie was updating us.

> In Jacksonville and going through the parameters of the dataset.

The rain began to come down harder, and I started up the engine. Frank seemed to have lost the fight and was now subdued.

"You're right, Gardner," he said. "If Richie didn't come down this

way, there's no point in me being here, either. You still want to check
on missing persons?"

"I do," I said. But more than that, I needed a place to focus. Away
from Frank.

He knew I preferred to work alone, and I wanted to look into
missing persons in Lucas Beach. For his part, Frank wanted to be in
Shilo. Closer to where we'd last seen El Médico.

Fifteen minutes later, we met with Detective Brian Johnson at
Lucas Beach PD, who Shooter had called about the missing persons. Johnson had wavy hair that reached his shoulders, and a sandy
brown mustache. He wore a suit jacket, but his shirt was open two
buttons down.

"It'll take me a half hour to pull the physical files," he said to me.
"You got something to work on?"

"Absolutely," I said.

Frank took off for Shilo, and Detective Johnson gave me a room
to work in, one that looked out over a lawn full of mature fruit trees.
I unpacked my workbag and took every item off the Formica desk.
Then placed each missing persons file in a straight line. I began taping
up a series of colored Post-its on the window—each with some note
that might help me find a pattern I had not yet seen.

In my head, a series of questions echoed:

Why does El Médico want these women?

How does he locate them?

What's his connection to the medical community?

Or Freddie?

*Why abduct Dog? Both he and Freddie were breaks in El Médico's
pattern.*

I moved back through the inventory we'd found with each skeleton. A necklace with Melanie Nelson. A custom pin made by Araceli

Alvarez's mom. The intramedullary nail embedded in Mavreen Isiah's femur.

I closed my eyes and pictured my mother's face.

"Mom," I said. "I can't do this alone."

I opened my eyes and stared at two files. The women's bodies had been buried two feet down and three feet away from each other, but there were no other personal items.

No. That wasn't exactly true.

All the victims had one thing in common: the material surrounding their buried bodies. Strips of bamboo were wrapped around the skeletons, the pieces cut in irregular patterns, some with squared-off edges at the ends of the strips. Others with curved ends to the fabric, as if stitched by machine.

Detective Johnson opened the door, and his eyes swept across the items I'd relocated from the desk to the floor so I had a clean workspace.

"I'll put those back," I said.

He held out a file. "Odette Nell, twenty-four. Caucasian. Missing eight months. No witnesses."

"From where?" I asked.

"Local from about a mile away," he said, staring at the open file. "Roommate said she had a dentist appointment last August. The office said she never showed up."

Johnson waited for some response, but I just grabbed the file and placed it on the desk. The detective closed the door, sighing, and I heard my phone pulse. A text from Cassie:

> Tell me you got something.

I wrote back, telling her I didn't. Then moved to a photo of the bamboo strips, laid out under one of the skeletons.

In religious cultures, shrouds of bamboo are used for burial, but the material is typically cut to suit the size of the body. In this case, the pieces looked like leftovers.

My cell phone rang.

"Remember Dog?" Frank said.

I looked at the time. Ninety minutes had passed. Frank was back in Shilo.

"Melanie Nelson's boyfriend," I said. "The pimp?"

"I tried a shot in the dark," Frank said. "Asked Quinones if I could speak to one of his vice guys."

Shilo wasn't a big place. "He *has* vice guys?"

"There's a pair of them," Frank said. "I met with one. He said he never busted Dog as a pimp, like the girlfriend's mom said. According to him, Dog was a dealer."

"Details?" I asked.

"Before he disappeared," Frank said, "Dog got popped for something with the street name Sleep Cut. He walked on a technicality."

I wasn't familiar with this name. "What is that, Frank?"

"It's fentanyl," Frank said, "cut with this other drug. Xylazine."

Xylazine was a veterinary medicine created in the 1970s to sedate animals for diagnostic testing. I had read reports of it becoming recreational over the past two years.

"This vice cop was trying to make a deal with Dog," Frank continued, "find out where he was getting the xylazine from, so they could get it off the street. At some point, the vice guy didn't hear back. He's been looking for Dog ever since."

"Dog was dealing animal tranquilizer," I repeated.

"Yeah," Frank said. "And there's something else. One of the tip line messages we flagged was a guy named Tony Harris. Turns out he's Dog's cousin, the one who originally reported him missing."

"Do we know if Richie phoned this cousin back?"

"I found an outgoing call on his cell," Frank said. "Nine minutes. But I can't get ahold of the cousin."

A piece of the case fell into place.

"Frank," I said. "The strips of bamboo. I know what they are."

CHAPTER FORTY

"ANIMAL BURIAL SHROUDS?" FRANK SAID, REPEATING MY words. He sounded dubious.

"The minute you mentioned the animal tranquilizer," I said, "I realized why the strips are so small. They're not for humans, Frank. They're precut for cats and dogs. They come in kits."

Mavreen Isiah had told her sister that the man in the sketch was doing something through back channels. That people who needed things came to him. Like illegal backroom medical procedures.

Or medication.

"Are you near a computer?" I asked.

"I'm in the hospital lobby," Frank said. "But I have my laptop."

This was why Frank had wanted to go back to Shilo. Not just because of leads in the area. He'd wanted to be close to Richie.

"The area we circled on the map of Shilo," I said. "Look around Alantay Medical Group where Mavreen worked. I think you'll find an emergency animal clinic."

"Our guy's a vet?" Frank asked.

"More likely some sort of tech."

"I see one business," Frank said. "Let me get over there in person. Call you from it."

I hung up and turned, my reflection catching in the darkened second-story office window. It was night. Out the window, a water feature above a small pond shot a spray twelve feet into the air, but it blew toward the building, soaking the lawn. Around it were plantings in concentric circles: wild olive, greenheart, and Chickasaw plum, all covered in rain.

Should I have gone back and stayed with Richie? If Frank were not here and I was the team lead, would I have known to do this?

I picked up the missing persons file that Detective Johnson had handed me. Odette Nell was twenty-four and white, with an athletic figure and a thick jawline. In both her pictures, she stared, unsmiling, arms crossed, dressed in a lacrosse shirt.

A single sentence that Shooter had uttered when we stopped at the Jacksonville office came to mind. That the women were of a particular type.

I glanced from picture to picture. Each of our victims had strong, almost masculine faces. Wide in the nose or mouth, just like Shooter had noted in Jacksonville.

The phone rang. Frank again. "This place is small, Gardner," he said. "Mom-and-pop operation. It's just the owner and office manager at this hour. They just finished up some emergency medical procedure on a dog."

I checked the time: 9:23 p.m.

Richie only had until morning.

"They recognize the sketch?" I asked, hoping to finally ID the man we'd been calling El Médico.

"We're in luck there," Frank said. "Donald Dom. Went by Donnie.

But the owner said the guy would hardly respond to it, and after everything that went down, it turned out not to be his real name."

"What's 'everything that went down'?"

"The owner and his wife came in one morning," Frank explained. "Their entire drug supply was gone, along with every ounce of xylazine. Surgical instruments. Anesthesiology equipment. They called the police. Had to shut down for a month."

So now we had our medical connection. "When *was* this?"

"May 14, 2019," Frank said.

This was before the deaths of Araceli Alvarez, Melanie Nelson, and Julie Gilliam, all of whom could have been anesthetized with xylazine. It also predated Dog's death.

"Hold on a second," I said. "This Donnie Dom—he worked full-time at that vet?"

"Yup."

I paced the small office in Lucas Beach. "So before 2019, he might have been stealing xylazine from them without their knowledge."

"Possible," Frank said. "What are you thinking?"

"Offerman," I said, referring to the retired FBI agent who first traveled to Shilo to assist on the case. "He came into Shilo in May of 2019. There was probably a lot of press coverage about the cops and the FBI. Maybe Donnie had been stealing the xylazine all along and got spooked."

"Decided to take the whole lot of what was left?" Frank finished my thought. "Clear out the vet?"

"Frank," I said, "how long did this Donnie guy work there—before the robbery?"

"Little over a year."

This matched my theory and allowed him access to the drug,

going back to the first two women who had been reported missing in October 2018.

"And their description of him?" I asked. "White? Thirtyish?"

"They thought thirty-five," Frank said. "Believed he was from the Daytona area."

Daytona was minutes from Lucas Beach, where I was.

"They said he was the clinic's go-to for euthanasia," Frank added. "Patients loved him. He did home visits. Even offered to bury the pets for customers."

"Thirty-six inches apart," I said to Frank. "It's a burial standard for pets."

I thought of the statistics of young men who had abused and practiced their crimes on animals before moving to humans. Ted Bundy. David Berkowitz. Jeffrey Dahmer.

"I need to look through everything again with this new information in mind," I said. "Did you check on this Donnie guy's name?"

"Police did after the robbery at the animal clinic," Frank said. "The name was bogus, but I'll have our people run it again, just to be safe. Then I'll stay near the hospital until patrol finds Dog's cousin."

The hospital.

"Frank," I said. "How is Richie doing?"

"Not well," he said. "His grandfather is flying in. I'm meeting him within the hour."

I hung up, and a new reality set in. We could find El Médico. Even figure out what Richie had been injected with and still not save him. This is why Frank had been growing frustrated. Patterns and puzzle solving . . . sometimes it wasn't enough.

"Screw that," I said aloud.

I stared out the window that looked over the back lawn of the

Lucas Beach PD. During the conversation with Frank, I had taken a dry-erase marker and written the words *vet medicine* on the glass.

I studied the words, mentally cataloging every deadly medical-grade drug or gas used in a veterinary setting. Nitrous oxide. Phosphine gas. Injectable antibiotics used to treat farm diseases.

"Talk to me, rook," I said, knowing Richie had found something that we still hadn't.

I recalled the conversation with Richie about Florida and California. The farm country where he'd grown up east of San Diego.

Central Florida was more rural than many people realized, and the more farm animals a veterinary practice treated, the wider the variety of drugs they had on hand.

Desperate times, I thought.

I called Frank back, and he picked up on the first ring.

"Frank," I said. "Have you left the vet's office yet?"

"I'm in the parking lot. Why?"

"Go back inside. Ask them if they have something called atipamezole. I'm going to text you the spelling. Get a sample, if you can."

I typed the name of the drug for Frank and sent the message. Then hung up and waited while he spoke to the vet.

Frank called me back. "Okay. I got it in hand. What now?"

"Drive to the University of Florida Health Shands Hospital."

"No, no, no," Frank said. "This is canine medication, Gardner. The vet told me."

Atipamezole was a synthetic drug used for the reversal of sedative and analgesic effects of certain chemical compounds like dexmedetomidine in veterinary medicine. It was sold under the name Antisedan and used on cats, dogs, and horses.

"If Richie was injected with xylazine," I said, "the drugs they're using on him . . . just like the Narcan I used . . . it's not gonna reverse what El Médico put in him."

Frank's voice intensified. "And this will?"

"Unknown," I said, trying to stay calm. "But the doctor reported bradycardia. Respiratory depression. These are all symptoms of xylazine overdose."

"Has this been tested on humans?"

"In very limited circumstances," I said. "Sample sizes too small to be considered by the FDA."

Frank told me he'd head back to the hospital, but didn't promise to put the atipamezole in the hands of Dr. Carlson.

A half hour later, I saw a text from him, a warning that Richie's grandfather wanted to speak with me. He'd arrived with a medical power of attorney to act as Richie's guardian.

Incoming video call. He wants to look you in the eye.

My phone rang, requesting a videoconference. I clicked the button, and up came the image of William Banning, Richie's grandfather.

"Camden," he said, his voice gruff.

I thought of a time when I'd hit him in the face as hard as I could. To save a life, of course.

"Sir?"

Banning was a heavyweight in law enforcement, and for a time, the boss to all of us at the FBI.

He didn't waste time with formalities now.

"I just got out of a meeting with this Dr. Carlson. She consulted the hospital's toxicology specialist, and they recommended strongly against the use of atipamezole."

"Yes, sir," I said. "That's reasonable."

"But you disagree?"

"Is Richie still in decline?" I asked.

"Decline?" Banning's voice was deep and self-assured. Yet he seemed to not recognize the word. "This doctor went to her board," he said. "I spoke to them, too. They have a policy as to medicines not coming from their own pharmacy."

Right, I thought. Frank couldn't just show up with something in a vial.

"But if they're losing the patient," I said, "as a last resort?"

"They're leaving that up to me," Banning said.

And what? Banning was, in turn, asking me?

An outsider might observe Richie and me and see a relationship that was akin to siblings. He, like a little brother to me. But Richie and I had no blood in common, while he and Banning did.

As I stared at the phone, a text popped up from Frank, who must've been standing beside Banning.

> You can say "I don't know."

I stared at Frank's note.

"We don't lose agents, right?" I said to Banning. "You said that once at a speech. My first year at the Bureau."

"I can't remember that," he said.

Another text popped up from Frank.

> Be careful.

"If it were my daughter, Camila," I said, "I'd administer the medicine."

"Okay," Banning said.

The screen went black. He'd hung up.

I sat in the dark after the call, but I couldn't go through any more case files.

When I came out of the office, the floor was empty. Only one light on. Detective Brian Johnson was still in his office, his window lashed with rain.

Did I just make a life-or-death decision for Richie? For his family?

"Y'all done?" Johnson asked.

I stared blankly at him, my body numb. "Yes."

"Good," he replied. "Boss made me stay until you finished. I got two kids and a wife waiting on me."

He shut off his light and guided me through the bullpen, which was now a maze of empty desks.

"Do you know the area well?" I asked.

"Grew up two miles from here," Johnson said.

"We met with a local woman earlier," I said. "Wealthy. Confident. Insular."

"Yeah." Johnson smiled. "I know the type."

"She thought she might've recognized our suspect."

The detective pulled a notepad from his back pocket. "You want me to follow up with her?" he asked.

"No," I said. "But there was something she said. That most of the places north of town got sold off to resorts or hotels in the last twenty years."

Johnson blinked. "Agent Camden, are you looking for a place to stay the night?"

Frank had left with the car, and I could hardly keep my eyes open. "Yes," I said.

"Well. As to a hotel recommendation, if your reimbursement policy is anything like mine, I'd try somewhere closer to town. Not some bougie-ass place on the beach."

He hesitated. I could tell he was about to add something.

"As to what the woman said about the resorts north of town, she's just wrong."

I blinked. "Wrong in what way?"

We reached the elevator, and Johnson hit the button to call it.

"The hotels up there," he said, "some have been remodeled in the last few years. But most of that land was sold off fifty years ago. Long before whoever you interviewed grew up."

I pictured Natalie Kastner, staring at our sketch. Some memory from her past that she couldn't shake loose.

"So there's nothing new?" I asked. "Up that way?"

The elevator door opened, and we got in.

"There's new things all the time," Johnson said. "But the families who stayed up that way—those big estates—they've been owned by the same people since I was a kid."

"How many are there?" I asked. "That never sold?"

"Mansions?" he said. "Wow, I dunno. Figure . . . seventeen or eighteen?"

The elevator door opened onto the lobby, and we walked out.

"Hell, they built *this* place," Johnson said. "Back when the local rich considered it their civic duty."

I squinted at him. "By 'this place,' you mean the police station?"

"Oh yeah." He steered me over to a framed picture on the lobby wall, commemorating the building. It was a color photo of a group of men and women from the '90s, standing on the lawn of a building. The photo was twelve by eighteen, matted and surrounded by shiny red oak.

"They bought an old Spanish-style building," Johnson said. "Retrofitted it. Donated it back to the city."

I scanned the faces of the men and women in the framed picture.

There was something familiar about one of the men. I pulled out my phone and stared from our sketch to the picture. It didn't match. It wasn't El Médico.

"What can you tell me about this guy?" I asked.

Johnson glanced from the photo to the caption below it, which listed the names of the men and women. "Paul Burrows," he said. "No idea."

I kept scanning the photo, and Johnson made a huffing noise. "I told you I got kids, right?" he said. "A wife? Folks waiting on me?"

I didn't answer him.

Johnson's shoulders stiffened, and he bit at his lower lip. He walked over to an ornate wooden information desk, twenty feet away, where a patrolman sat.

"Let me behind there, will ya, Mac?" he said to the cop, who cleared out. Johnson took his seat and began typing, moving from screen to screen.

"That particular guy's deceased, Agent Camden," he said finally. "Had one child, a son named Edward. He's thirty-six."

"Any criminal record?"

He pounded a few more keys.

"None," he said. "And there's this."

Johnson had opened a browser and found a recent article about the son of the man in the picture, Edward Burrows, an up-and-coming architect who had closed down his practice. The article featured other men in their thirties and forties, and its focus wasn't on Burrows but on a larger phenomenon. That of a generation of once-thriving professionals in the Lucas Beach area, who now never left their homes. "Professional Shut-Ins," the headline read.

I stared at the photo of Edward Burrows.

Over the last four hours, I had begun a project of taking every face on the case and breaking it into pieces, per the three principles of the Loomis method that sketch artists used. First, I reimagined each cranium as a flattened sphere, which helped me think of the top of the head in quadrants. Next, I rethought how the jawline and cheekbones attached to the cranium. Then I broke the facial features into thirds, worrying less about matching the sketch of El Médico and more about finding strips of a face that connected to any piece of evidence on the case.

Something about Burrows was familiar, but I could not figure out what.

"Your suspect gets around, right?" Johnson asked. "Shilo, you said. Also north of Miami. Maybe here."

"Yes."

"Well, this guy hasn't left his house in a year."

The detective motioned the patrolman back to his station, and we left the building. Outside, Johnson turned to face me, his forehead wrinkling into lines that indicated an emotion I read as pity.

"Listen," he said. "We just met today, so I don't wanna judge. But it feels like you're grasping at straws. Sleep helps, Agent Camden. Maybe you try again in the morning."

"I've got a colleague in the hospital," I said. "He may not make it 'til morning."

The detective looked down but didn't answer.

My phone rang, and I glanced at the screen. The number read "Blocked," and I mentally prepared myself to hear that the atipamezole had caused some deadly reaction in Richie.

"Camden," I said.

"Agent Gardner Camden?" a female voice asked. "Detective Eloise Curtis, Lucas Beach PD."

"Lucas Beach PD?" I repeated, and Johnson looked up.

I'm at the home of Natalie Kastner. She had your card in her pocket."

"What do you mean—*had*?"

"She's been murdered, Agent Camden."

CHAPTER FORTY-ONE

DETECTIVE JOHNSON GRABBED HIS KIA SEDONA AND
drove out of the gated area behind the Lucas Beach PD, picking me
up where I'd been standing when I'd received the call. The water feature outside was lit with a blue glow at night. I watched it fade into
the darkness behind us as he turned onto the state highway.

Johnson's concern for my sleep habits had disappeared, and his
body seemed tighter now.

"This is the house of the woman you mentioned?" he said.

I nodded but did not speak. The area west of the station was home
to a variety of industrial companies that made tile or bent metal, their
logos glowing and wet on the sides of the buildings at night. Past this,
the neighborhood gave way to shopping centers that housed regional
insurance companies and smoke shops with the word *gator* in the
name, each anchored by a 7-Eleven or a Family Dollar store.

I was thinking of Richie. Having faith was difficult if you didn't
grow up with it, but I knew someone who did. As Johnson drove, I
texted Rosa.

> I have a friend who is hurt. His name is Richie. Can you pray for him?

An answer came back fast.

> Right away.

Up ahead were the bridges that led to the beach. I motioned for Johnson to turn right before them. He slowed at the mouth of Avalon Street, where Frank and I had visited Natalie Kastner five hours and fifty-three minutes ago.

The neighborhood that had appeared pristine before sundown, with its curved sidewalks and American flags, was aglow in the red and blue lights of four cruisers parked at angles to each other, blocking the flow of any traffic.

Twelve neighbors stood gawking from the surrounding properties as Johnson introduced me to his colleague Detective Eloise Curtis, who had phoned me minutes earlier.

Curtis was early forties and wore the black-and-pink athletic-wear uniform of half the moms at Camila's school, save the white crime-scene booties that covered her feet and the disposable smock over her hair. She'd come from her son's ice hockey game a half hour ago, she told me.

"Ms. Kastner held what role in your case?" she asked.

"We spoke to her on background," I said. "She wasn't a suspect or a person of interest. Her cousin had been shot." I explained about Freddie Pecos and how he'd been a confidential informant on a federal case.

Detective Johnson left us then, and Curtis and I walked toward the home. She lent me a pair of latex gloves, and I snapped them on, staring at a Ring camera outside the front door.

"First generation," Curtis said, following my eyeline. "Unfortunately, it's been dead for years."

Inside the house, Natalie Kastner's body was splayed out on the white couch Frank and I had passed on the way to her sunroom, her body turned nearly all the way onto her back, her eyes facing the ceiling. She was dressed in a tan blouse and an ocean-blue skirt, but the latter was covered in dots of arterial spray that reminded me of a scattergram chart, plotting the age range of victims over time.

The fatal cut began below her left ear and ran downward and medially, before straightening out across the midline of her neck, producing the largest pool of blood I'd ever seen in person.

"It appears Natalie welcomed the perp into her home," Curtis said. "At some point, he got behind her. Cut fast and hard. She fell away from him, her body hitting the edge of the couch and turning."

The victim's hair was still damp from a shower.

First Richie.

Now Natalie Kastner.

El Médico's state of mind was deteriorating.

Eight yellow crime-scene markers were spread about the living area. I swallowed and moved around to the far side of the couch, then bent over it to study the victim. Natalie's cheeks and nose had been sliced up with the same blade that cut into her neck, but that attack had taken place after she was down on the ground. Footprints bloodied the white carpet and headed toward the front door.

"Brian says you're on the hunt for someone," Curtis said, referring to Detective Johnson. "That you have some picture?"

I recalled Natalie's prolonged stare at our sketch. Its familiarity to her, hidden somewhere in her brain.

"We have a composite," I said, finding a copy on my phone and holding it out.

Our serial killer had followed Frank and me here. If not literally, he'd used Richie's case notes to find Natalie.

Why? And why had neither Frank nor I seen the threat coming?

"Ms. Kastner mentioned a brother earlier," I said. "Named Andrew. You should consider sending a squad car over. Her mother also lives in town."

"Copy that," Detective Curtis said, taking a note on her phone. "Any idea where this killer is now?"

"No."

I needed to call Frank. He, in turn, needed to call Craig Poulton. Our killer, who had been operating in the shadows, had changed his M.O. First attacking a federal agent. Now killing a potential witness. And Amber Isiah was still missing.

"The man you're hunting," Curtis said, motioning at my phone. "Do you have a name for him?"

"Donnie Dom," I said. "But police looked it up. It's bogus."

I summarized Frank's and my conversation with the victim. Then, putting aside any apprehensions about confidentiality or jurisdiction, I told Curtis everything. The debit card case. The bodies in Shilo. Richie.

I needed to make a call, so I stepped out into the street. It was past 10 p.m. I rang up Frank.

"He's responding," he said before I could speak. "They administered the medicine, and his body is coming around."

"Thank God," I said. "Listen—"

"His vitals are stabilizing," Frank interrupted. "The doc's about to give him something to wake him up. See how he's doing."

I exhaled, a weight lifting.

Then I explained to Frank about Natalie Kastner, and he repeated the information to someone he was with.

"Where are you?" I asked.

"I'm grabbing a jet to Jacksonville with Director Poulton. He came down to see Banning and Richie."

"Why Jacksonville?"

"Cassie and Jo are still going through the data, but they're closing in on something. We're confident we'll get this guy by morning." He paused. "Gardner," he said, "find a hotel room and crash. Be ready to go tomorrow at five or six a.m."

I agreed and hung up. The local crime scene team had arrived, and Detective Curtis ordered everyone out.

I walked away, moving through the neighborhood on foot. In ten minutes, I'd left the homes behind and found a commercial street with lights on and fast-food restaurants.

As I walked, the wind increased in power. Large drops of rain touched my arms and head, but I was too tired to care how wet I was.

I hadn't eaten all day. I found a food cart. Paid ten dollars for two hot dogs that looked barely cooked, but were covered in browned bacon and grilled onions.

A taxi pulled up to drop a group off at a bar, and I raised my hand, signaling the vehicle.

The driver rolled down his window. "Where to, boss?"

I tossed the second hot dog in the trash and got in the back. "Just drive," I said, "over toward the beach."

He glanced back at me, not moving, and I held out two twenties. He put the car in gear, then drove up and over the curving bridge. It split into two parts, each a two-lane in one direction that rose over the inner waterway.

As I glanced right, lights marked the curve of the next bridge over. The docks I'd seen earlier with Frank were dark now, save one that held a party boat, moored at the far end, with lights that blinked on and off in blue and orange. Even inside the waterway, the waves crested high, causing the boat to bang against the dock.

As we came off the bridge, I directed the cabbie north, along Atlantic, where Frank and I had been earlier. Then I rang up the hospital in Gainesville, identifying myself as a federal agent and asking them to put me through to the room where Richie Brancato was.

"Hello?" a voice answered.

Richie sounded small and far away, and for a second, I stayed quiet.

"Gardner?" he asked.

"Yeah."

"Figured," he said. "No one else would call me at this hour." His voice was gravelly.

"Are you well enough to talk?" I asked.

"My throat hurts," Richie said. "But they gave me something five minutes ago, and I'm jumpy as shit. Just lying here in the dark."

I didn't reply for a second, grappling with a feeling that was unusual for me. Guilt? Concern?

"Gardner?" he said. "Still there?"

The words sounded digital and garbled. I glanced at my phone. The storm was affecting power, and I was down to one bar.

"Do you recall when you told us what happened to your sister?" I said. "It was last year. That big case. Agent Harris and I were about to jump on a copter?"

"Yeah."

"You said you never would have joined the FBI if not for her—"

"I remember," he said curtly, cutting me off.

"Then you told us how everyone at PAR flamed out somewhere else. Made some mistake."

"Is this my mistake?" he asked.

"No," I said. "I just wanted to make sure you knew. It's okay if you want to reevaluate things. If you don't want to work with us after this case is over."

Richie said something, but it was garbled.

"What?" I asked.

"Are we getting shut down or something?"

"We might have been close to that a week ago," I said. "I guess that's why we pushed the gun case so hard. But there was a cost. I left you on an island by yourself."

"Where are you?" Richie asked, and my eyes moved to the meter in the cab, which read $22.50.

"Lucas Beach," I said.

"He's from there," Richie replied. "El Médico."

Inside the cab, I sat up straight. "What?"

Again Richie cut out.

"Richie?" I said, looking around. Down one street, I saw no power on.

"Remember Dog?" Richie said then, his voice coming back in. "He was getting drugs supplied to him. Unusual stuff, Gardner. I asked his cousin where Dog got his junk from. He said a guy from some beach town just north of Daytona stole the drugs. Resold them to Dog, who cut them up. Put 'em on the street."

I swallowed. Clearly no one had told Richie yet that *he* had been injected with those same drugs. Sleep Cut, as Frank's source in Shilo vice had called it.

"I think Dog's cousin called El Médico, Gardner," Richie said. "Two days ago. Led him right to me. I was working at the hotel, and I told the cousin where he could reach me. Rookie fuckin' move."

"Did you tell Poulton this?" I asked.

"No," he said.

"Don't."

Richie exhaled loudly. "My point is—you didn't leave me on an island, Gardner. I screwed up. You can act nice and all . . . act like I didn't, but . . . it's not your style."

Richie was right. It wasn't my style. But he was wrong about the assumption that went along with this. That I didn't make the kind of mistakes he had.

"I left Frank last year, and he almost got killed," I said. "I turned my wife in to the police nine years ago. I say things to Craig Poulton I should never say to anyone. And you know what?"

"What?"

"The way my mind works—I remember every single detail about those mistakes."

He went silent for a moment, and I did not fill the space.

"Cassie is close," Richie said finally. "She's tracked phone numbers and narrowed it down to the same place you're headed."

My mind felt thick and dull. I was exhausted. "The project with the stingray?"

"I heard Frank and Poulton talking," Richie said. "They said 386. After they left, I asked a nurse to look it up on her phone. It's the area code for Lucas Beach."

This was why Frank had flown to Jacksonville. The team must've had a bead on El Médico. But night had come, and they needed to put in a request with the specific phone carrier to ID a device. That took legal paperwork. The kind that had to be done during working hours, even if you were the FBI.

"Richie," I said. "Did you or Jo make any other time estimates as to how long this guy holds his victims?"

"No," he said. "But the ME found no signs of dehydration. We thought it was a day. Why?"

"Amber Isiah," I said. "She's been gone almost twenty-four hours. With Natalie Kastner murdered—"

"He's tying up loose ends," Richie finished my thought. "You think he takes them to Lucas Beach?"

"Maybe," I said.

Then the phone went dead.

A few seconds later, Richie called me again. "What have you found down there?" he asked.

"Not much," I said. "This case has no patterns. The perp, no clear motive. No reason why he moves from one geography to the other."

As I said this, a thought occurred to me.

El Médico had worn a mask.

When the sketch artist mentioned this, we understood it through the prism of infectious disease. Things like the flu or Covid-19. I had assumed he was a careful medical practitioner or even a germophobe. But El Médico didn't work with humans. He worked with animals.

So maybe it was to cover his face.

My head pounded. I computed the sleep I'd had recently, between the raid in D.C. and taking turns sleeping in the van. Five hours over the last two and a half days.

"Do you know what I was injected with?" Richie asked.

I was incapable of lying to anyone on my team.

"Xylazine," I said. "It's a tranquilizer. Used in veterinary practices. And lately cut into other drugs and sold on the street."

Richie went quiet then.

Of all the drugs El Médico could have stolen from an emergency vet clinic, why had he taken xylazine? Why had he used *this* on his victims?

The medicine acted on the central alpha-2 receptor and suppressed norepinephrine release from nearby nerves. It caused central nervous system depression and eventually respiratory depression, both of which would start within minutes and last for four hours.

What was he doing to his victims that took four hours but didn't show up on their skeletons?

The taxi driver had burned through most of the forty dollars. He glanced back at me. "Buddy," he said. "Am I dropping you at one of these hotels? Or somewhere else?"

I saw the pair of signs where I'd pulled over earlier with Frank. The Olive. The Aurora House. Something clicked.

"The Olive," I said to the driver. "That's fine." The cabbie turned onto the drive, and I held the phone to my ear again. "I have to go, Richie."

"You figured something out," Richie said, his voice a mix of surprise and curiosity.

"I might have a lead," I said. "A riddle that, until now, I didn't notice."

"What?" he asked. Then the phone went silent again.

"You there?" I inquired.

"Be careful," Richie said. "I was close, and he got away. He's been a step ahead of us this whole time."

The phone cut out again, and I raised my voice, hoping Richie could hear. "Rest up," I said. "I'll be fine."

I hung up, and the cab driver pulled off the palm tree–lined drive, just past the place where Frank had hopped out of the car earlier. The cabbie slowed at a turnaround, where a white Mediterranean structure was lit up, surrounded by windswept banana palms.

The Olive was a three-story boutique hotel that couldn't have held more than twenty rooms. Large hand-cut casement windows lined the second and third floors. I opened the cab door, but a rush of wind shoved it shut again on my face.

"Geez," I said, pushing it back open.

Entering the lobby, I headed toward the check-in desk with just my workbag in hand.

A teenage girl with reddish hair and green eyes stood behind a desk. I told her I'd like a room for the night. After she checked me in, I badged her to wake up the night manager.

A few minutes later, a man who identified himself as Clive came out from a pocket door. His hair was combed, but his suit jacket and pants bore wrinkles.

I needed to crash and be up by 5 a.m. like Frank had said. But I needed information first. I asked Clive who owned the estates on either side of the hotel.

"To our south is a gentleman by the name of Renning," Clive said. "Some tech guru from Silicon Valley. Bought the place three years ago. He's here maybe twenty days a year."

This was the property where Frank and I had spoken to the man on the lawn mower.

"And the other direction?"

"That's the Burrows estate," he said. "House passed down in the family."

The man whose father's photo I'd seen at the police station. The professional shut-in.

"Have you met Mr. Burrows?" I asked.

"Two years ago," the manager said. "He doesn't leave the place often. We deliver him room service at times."

"That's convenient," I said.

The Olive property was of some size. Out a window, I saw a small pond with a wagon wheel that circulated water, the wind blowing it toward the hotel. "Your people walk the food over?" I asked. "Take a golf cart?"

"There's a space between the bushes out front," Clive said. "You probably passed it as you turned in."

As we spoke, the place went dark, and I looked around. A gas generator kicked in, and the lights flickered back on.

"He allows them into his room?" I said, not missing a beat, my mind thinking of the article on Burrows. "He's not a germophobe?"

"Sorry about that," Clive said, putting on a good face amid the storm. "And no, not from what I've heard." He glanced around at the hotel, the wind whipping against the large windows that looked out through the dark toward the beach.

I thanked the manager and checked into my room on the second floor. Dropped my workbag on the bed and stared around the room.

Frank had told me to crash. To be ready by 5 a.m.

I washed my face and lay down on the bed. But something caught my attention. A black-and-white photo on the wall. The Olive was one of two structures in the picture. Between the two stretched a large pool.

I sat up. Stared at it, then walked back downstairs.

Clive was still at the front desk.

"This place," I said. "And the one next door—the Burrows house. It was once one big property?"

"You saw the pictures in your room?" Clive smiled. "Yeah, the Burrows Family Trust owns the Olive, Agent Camden. Fifty years ago, they knocked down a couple tennis courts. Covered the pool. Made this hotel its own place."

"Mr. Burrows," I said, referring to the shut-in we'd discussed earlier, "when's the last time he ordered?"

The manager walked over to a computer and punched some

keys. "Actually, it's been a while. Two months of radio silence. Guess maybe we should make sure he's all right."

I stared in the direction of the neighbor. Frank had said to get some rest. But something was itching at my brain.

Amber. Almost two days gone.

I thought of what Richie had said. About El Médico being one step ahead of us.

Edward Burrows was somehow involved. El Médico's next victim, perhaps? Or was he our killer, parading as a shut-in?

Had he taken Amber Isiah captive? Would morning be too late for her?

I mentally double-checked my work, my mind shuttling through every face I had seen in the last week. Natalie Kastner. Detective Johnson. The men and women in the police station photo. Freddie, in his childhood photo.

And then one last set. Every boy Frank and I had seen Natalie Kastner in a picture with.

In doing this, a face matched. Not completely, but in pieces.

"I'll follow up on the neighbor," I said to Clive.

I turned and headed out onto the valet drive. A teenage boy sat there, a rain hat on his head. I moved past him. Found the gap in the oleander bushes and stepped through it, onto the property of Edward Burrows.

CHAPTER FORTY-TWO

AS I WENT THROUGH THE HEDGE, THE RAIN FELL THICK ON my arm. I glanced up and saw cumulus clouds the color of slate. Heavier rain was coming fast. I emerged onto a back lawn, the patter of water on my forearms loud.

If Burrows owned dogs, surely they would find their way through the hole in the hedge and over to the hotel. With this in mind, I moved freely across the thick Bermuda grass.

The property was enormous. A line of banana palms had gotten so big they were growing sideways—the diameters of their leaves at least four feet, with burn marks running down the centers and giant orchids growing all around them.

It was almost midnight. I stepped from the lawn onto a pathway that led east between the Olive and the Burrows estate and pulled my Glock, raising my voice.

"Mr. Burrows," I called. "FBI on your property."

But I heard nothing.

The rain came harder now. An oversize banana palm leaf broke off and flew across the yard, hitting a second-floor window with a slapping noise.

I studied the house but saw no access from the rear yard and no lights on. Moving farther east, I came alongside the structure toward the water. Giant purple jacaranda trees lined this side of the house. They'd formed a canopy over the walkway and seemed to be choking each other. I padded carefully past them, coming out onto the beach.

There was no moon on the water, but I could hear the waves crashing hard. Somewhere to the north, boats banged against a dock. I turned to my right, sure I'd heard a noise, but saw nothing.

In front of me were the bright red flowers of a royal poinciana, a tree my mother would point out when she visited Anna and me years ago. Through the dark, I could smell the fragrance coming from the spoon-shaped flowers.

Pieces of the puzzle were coming together, but giant parts were still missing.

I thought of the drug Richie was injected with. It caused hypotension, or low blood pressure. It also caused respiratory depression, which would calm the victim almost to the point of immobility. All of that began at injection and lasted for three or four hours.

El Médico needed that time to do something. What?

I came along the beach side of the house and saw the front of the estate. A pair of enormous double doors with decorative wooden moldings loomed on each side. One of the doors was hinged closed at the bottom, and it rattled with every passing gust of wind.

But the other door swung wildly on its hinges, open, then closed. *Slam.*

A black rectangle of darkness marked the inside of the house each time it swung inward.

A twenty-million-dollar estate—open at night?

I glanced up. No lights on in the house. It might not qualify as exigent circumstances, but given the death of Natalie Kastner and my concerns about Edward Burrows, I moved forward, onto the concrete landing.

I felt for my penlight.

Nothing. I must have left it on the bed when I put down my bag.

The wind flung the right side of the door open. Then bang. Closed.

I stepped closer.

Another gust. The door swung inward, and I stepped across the threshold.

Just inside, someone had taken flowers from the royal poinciana and trimmed them, placing them in an enormous round bowl. But weeks must have passed, because the flowers were rotten and shriveled.

"FBI," I hollered.

The house creaked under the storm, the interior dark with shadows. I took a step forward, my thoughts assembling and disassembling.

El Médico had some medical experience we didn't know about, apart from his veterinary background. He must have. I recalled the nick on the orbital bone of Araceli Alvarez. The cut was on the wrong side of her nose, and a thought came to my mind. An article I'd read about a doctor with spatial dyslexia whose license had been pulled for operating on the wrong side of the body.

In my pocket, my phone buzzed. I must have picked up one bar again. But I kept my eyes ahead, scanning the dark areas all around me.

"Edward Burrows?" I yelled.

The house was a Florida mansion from the 1930s, and the huge foyer held two curving staircases that began side by side at the bottom before moving to the left and right, then rejoining at the top.

Leaves littered the ground, but in the distance, the floor looked clean of debris.

How long had the door been open?

My Glock was out, and I looked for an electrical switch to provide more light. But I could not find one that worked.

The details came faster now. The nick in the orbital bone. The gauze Richie saw across El Médico's face. Our interview with Amber Isiah—her noting the eyes from one sketch matched, but the others were off.

El Médico needed these women, and I finally knew why.

"He's practicing," I said to myself, moving into the enormous foyer of the mansion.

Lightning flashed across the windows. I looked left and right, scanning two giant rooms opposite each other: a library and a bar.

"Anyone home?" I hollered, but my voice just echoed off the walls. "Ms. Isiah? Amber?"

At the foot of the stairs was an elevated slab of marble that sat between the two large rooms. I stepped up onto it. Took two paces along it and stepped down from it and into the library. Shelves of books ran from floor to ceiling, and antique sliding ladders gave access to every volume.

The room was empty. I moved back to the marble. Then down into the other large room, wanting to clear the entire first floor before I went farther.

El Médico.

He's pulling them onto his lap.

Practicing first.

The other large room looked like a speakeasy built a hundred years ago, from the curving wooden bar at the far end to three tables, closely surrounded by chairs. Rich mahogany covered every inch of the room, with hand-drawn inlays. The dark wood ran along the bar and up into the moldings that covered the ceiling, giving the feeling that you were in the body of an old sailing ship.

Lightning flashed to my west, and I recalled my mother teaching me about the storms that blew though South Carolina when I was a child. The heat of a lightning discharge caused the air to expand. As it cooled, the contraction created a wave of sound that we perceived as thunder.

Mom taught me to count between lightning and thunder. To determine the distance away. Fifteen seconds was three miles. Ten seconds, two miles. Five seconds, one mile.

I found another light switch, but flicking it did nothing. The crack of thunder reverberated, a noise so loud it sounded like a transformer blowing.

Lightning flashed across the windows again, and my eyes moved fast. The bar was empty. In my mind, I said, *Clear*, and turned. Circling back to the staircase.

One one-thousand, two one-thousand.

Something caught my eye. Across the room on a marble pedestal. A brightly colored blue lamp.

Except it wasn't a lamp.

"Mr. Burrows?" I raised my voice.

The place went dark, and I patted my side, looking again for my penlight.

I heard the thunder as I got to ten and knew the storm was close. Light crashed through every window again, and the blue color glowed.

A more emotional person might have jumped at what I'd noticed, but I held still and moved closer, seeing what had caught my eye.

Darkness fell, and my mind moved the story one step forward.

He's practicing on others, so he can cut himself.

And suddenly, I thought of what El Médico had said to Richie.

You shouldn't have seen my face. It wasn't ready.

I reflected on the process I had developed with faces. Breaking them into planes and quadrants. Of what had been familiar to me when I'd seen the picture at Natalie Kastner's house. The dimpled chin and nose.

Natalie Kastner had dug into her past. Identified something, but she didn't know what.

More lightning. I moved toward the glowing blue item.

One one-thousand.

The story Natalie had told of Freddie's childhood best friend.

Two one-thousand.

The same man he'd run into at the ATM. The person who'd shot him.

Three one-thousand.

Was this friend related to someone well known? The heir to a hotel chain?

Four one-thousand.

Perhaps Freddie's friend was right. Perhaps he *was* the progeny of some backroom affair: a rich local and a restaurant waitress.

Thunder nearly shook the house, the rain lashing sideways against the windows.

I moved closer to the blue jar.

The victims had all been petite in frame, but with husky faces, and now I knew why. He wanted women he could overpower, but with more masculine facial features. I also knew why the bodies had not been blitz attacked. He didn't want them bruised.

I pictured xylazine being injected. How the muscles would become soft. The body loose. Perhaps then El Médico lifted the women onto his lap. Pulled them onto his own body, a mirror positioned in front of the pair, the incapacitated victim laid atop him.

Cut you, he'd threatened Amber Isiah.

I imagined the victims, unable to move. And El Médico with his dirty veterinary tools. The women draped atop him. How he'd control his breathing. Take the knife and begin cutting into their faces, pulling their skin taut. Watching and learning as the human body reacted. Adding fillers to plump the skin outward. And unknowingly scraping at the bone below, as he had done with a number ten scalpel on Araceli Alvarez.

All to practice.

All to be ready for the *real* surgeries.

Lightning flashed through the house, and I imagined what El Médico had done next. After these practice sessions.

He'd taken a surgical knife and cut into his own face.

Remodeling himself step-by-step into someone different.

And that's when I understood everything about the case.

The thunder was deafening, a mile out from the beach at most. I moved closer to the marble pedestal.

Lightning came once again, and the place lit up like daylight.

On the table was a large jar, filled with some blue solution.

Inside it?

The face of Edward Burrows—cut clean off his skull by the man I now surmised was his half brother, known to us as Donnie Dom or El Médico.

CHAPTER FORTY-THREE

I PLACED MY GLOCK DOWN ON THE MARBLE PEDESTAL where the face floated in the colored solution. I pulled my phone from my back pocket and saw a text from Cassie.

> We got something.

I took a few steps toward the window to see the words better in the dark. *Yeah, me, too,* I thought.

Another text came in:

> Where are you?

I walked back toward the jar with my phone. Held it up to take a picture of the face and show them *exactly* where I was.

But something was wrong.

My Glock. I had put it down on the pedestal, but now it was gone.

That's when I felt something hard hit the back of my head.

And everything went black.

CHAPTER FORTY-FOUR

WHEN I AWOKE, RESTRAINTS HELD MY ARMS DOWN.

I turned my head. By the position of the horizon out the window, I could tell that I was in an upper room in the same estate that I'd entered downstairs.

"I'm sorry to leave you for so long," a voice said. "I needed to take a walk. Think about my options. Our options."

My mouth had been taped over, and I slowed my breath, inhaling though my nose. At the same time, I used my tongue to un-adhere the tape from around my lips.

"I told your friend," the voice said.

"Your face wasn't ready," I replied, although the words came out as a mumble.

"Yes," he said. "It wasn't. It's not. But I'm improving."

I got my tongue out through the top of the tape, and a sliver of it peeled away, enough for me to try to communicate. Even if I was speaking to a disembodied voice in a dark room.

"I'm a federal agent," I called out.

"I'm aware," the voice said. "You also had a card key in your pocket. I hope you're enjoying your stay at my hotel."

I swallowed, my eyes searching the room.

"You've got a little problem, Agent Camden. Nobody knows you're here."

My head was aching from where I'd been struck. My best chance, I decided, was to scare this guy off. "Freddie Pecos," I said. "We know everything."

He came closer, and I examined part of his face. His nose and mouth were concealed with a medical mask. Above this, his forehead was half covered in gauze, as Richie had described.

"What *about* Freddie?" he asked.

"Mavreen Isiah," I said.

"You're just gonna list names?" He shook his head. "Wait. Is this a game? Can I name the category? Is it people I've killed?"

"We know about the vet," I said. "About the xylazine. Your attack on Natalie Kastner."

He stared at me, brown eyes visible under the strip of gauze across his head. I was on an adjustable bed, I had determined, cranked up at an angle. The straps that held me down were familiar from visiting my mother. They were the kind used to tie down dementia patients.

"You were out for a half hour," he said. "If anyone knew you were here, they'd have raided the place. This is why people call for backup, Agent Camden. But you didn't call, did you?"

I strained my head to look around. To see where I was. Was Amber Isiah here, too?

"Your phone will show a GPS signal at the Olive. But after you arrived, you went for a jog, remember? They'll find your cell down the beach."

I tried to move my legs, but they were strapped down, just like my arms.

"I have a question," he said then. "I'm curious. Do you know the average life expectancy of a male in Florida?"

"What county?" I asked.

"What?"

"What county?" I repeated.

"Here," he said. "Volusia."

"Seventy-four-point-six-nine," I said.

He blinked, the strip of visible forehead showing lines across it. "I didn't expect you to have that so . . . readily available."

"Why did you ask?"

"Well, half of seventy-four is thirty-seven," he said. "The age I am today."

I wondered how long he'd been staying in this house, making himself look like Edward Burrows.

"So you're Edward's older brother," I said.

"By eight months. Don't get me started on primogeniture."

When he spoke, he overarticulated every syllable, a forced formality of the type Amber Isiah had described. Putting on the affect of someone well educated.

Outside, the rain slapped the windows, and I turned my head. Trying to see where he'd disappeared to.

"I imagine you were the smarter brother," I said, trying to build rapport.

"Sure," he said. "But who got to grow up on the beach? I lived above a restaurant as a kid."

In the distance, lightning cracked across the horizon, brightening the churn of the dark water.

"He went to a good school?"

"Yale," he replied. "While I went to a state school."

But Donnie Dom knew how to talk to Araceli Alvarez about her nose. How to spot the defect in Julie Gilliam's cleft surgery.

"But you went to medical school?"

In the distance, I heard the acoustic energy of thunder cracking.

"The only one I could afford was in the islands, Agent Camden. When I came back, there were no residencies that would take me for the specialty I wanted. Not based on *that* school."

This was how El Médico had learned Spanish. And why he had a skill set well above that of the average vet tech.

"Edward, though." His voice dropped, becoming angrier. "He moved to Boston. Got a master's in architecture. But I'm a patient man. So I waited. All that time."

I had been working more of the tape free from my mouth, and I turned to see he was beside me again.

"Then one day, I met him," he said. "He invited me here, Agent Camden. Here! That's when he told me he was scared to leave this house."

"Donnie," I said.

"My brother and I are one life, Agent Camden. Edward took the first thirty-seven years. I get the next."

Lightning broke against the sky and lit up the dark room. In its flash, I saw him unfold something from his pocket. A picture of his half brother. He pulled down his mask for me to compare his surgeries to the photo of Edward Burrows.

"What do you think?" he asked, his face earnest, his eyes searching mine.

The dark marks the sketch artist had drawn, I saw now, were scars left from earlier surgeries. Filler had made his nose wider. And sure, there was a family resemblance to begin with. But only a madman would have thought he was getting better at the craft of plastic surgery.

I turned my face away, and he grabbed my hair and pulled me back.

"What. Do. You. Think?"

"You look nothing like him," I said.

He struck me across the face.

From the beach side of the house, the storm gained energy.

"I'm gonna cut you for that," he said. I heard him move across the room. There was the noise of a medical tray shifting. Of instruments being moved around.

"You buried Edward here on the property?" I asked.

"He didn't want to leave the house." He was yelling over the storm. "I gave him his wish."

I heard a screeching sound. A tray of scalpels, being dragged closer.

I swallowed. I didn't want to be found with my skin cut away from my skull. My face floating in some solution.

"Those women were innocent," I said.

"Who?" he asked, his voice still coming from across the room. "Mavreen? Dragging her sister around without a care? She was one of the most selfish people I ever met."

"And Natalie Kastner?"

Lightning came again, and his grotesque face appeared above me, smiling.

"She dated him," he said, his look incredulous, his head shaking. "My half brother."

This was the face that had helped me connect the pieces. A strip of Edward Burrows's eyes and nose in the article about professional shut-ins. The same eyes from a photo Frank and I had seen in Natalie's home.

"Did she tell you that?" he asked. "She lost her virginity to Edward. If she had told you that, you would've run here this afternoon. Arrested me. But she didn't, did she?"

I studied El Médico's face without the mask. The cinch marks of a botched nose job. A scar along his jawline. It was a face of horror.

"And Julie Gilliam?" I asked.

"She was a sweet girl. If I could fix that lip, I knew I could take my own philtrum." He motioned at the strip between his nose and the top of his lips. "Make it like Edward's."

"But you didn't," I said.

I knew he was going to hurt me, and I pulled my head away as he held up a syringe.

"I've been hearing a lot about a new type of operation, Agent Camden. It's very hip here in Florida. Drugless plastic surgery."

The options for rescue cycled through my mind. Frank and Poulton were on a plane to Jacksonville to meet Shooter and Cassie. And I had checked in to a hotel for the night.

No one was coming.

His expression changed then, his head cocking. "Or maybe you could tell me something, and I give you an easy out. How did you know to come here? If Natalie didn't tell you?"

He stared at me, and I swallowed. Seeing the future. Camila crying. My mother confused. A closed-casket funeral.

"Natalie said Freddie had a best friend," I said. "A Polish kid."

He blinked.

"The vet where you worked," I continued. "You told them your name was Donnie Dom. Obviously a fake name."

"Obviously."

"Don, I changed to Dawn, another word for Aurora. *Dom* is the Polish word for 'house.' Dawn Dom. Aurora House, the name of this place. It's on the sign between here and the Olive."

"Smart," he said.

"Your birthright."

"And where I'll be living long after you're gone."

"You killed your best friend," I said.

Was I buying time? Because no one was coming.

"I didn't want to," he hollered over the storm. "Freddie saw me holding this dead woman's ATM card. I was there for a similar reason as him. But much darker. We got talking, and . . . he told me he was working for the FBI. I couldn't risk it."

"He trusted you," I said. "He hadn't told anyone else."

His face contorted in pain, and I thought of something my mother used to say. That inside every evil man was a small boy whose life had not gone as he dreamt. My job was to uncover those details: to strip that boy down to a confession. And in that moment, let him find grace.

But I didn't think I was capable of that task. Or that Donnie Dom was interested in forgiveness or peace.

"Are you ready, Agent Camden?" he asked, holding up a scalpel.

Under the arm straps, I balled up both fists, preparing to take the pain.

I focused everything on a single image in my head.

My daughter, at the beach. Laughing in the shallow water. Splashing me unexpectedly.

Te amo, Daddy.

Te amo more.

Then something odd happened.

CHAPTER FORTY-FIVE

WHILE RICHIE AND I WAITED FOR THE POLICE TO ARRIVE, he explained that Frank had left Richie's phone by his hospital bedside. And although the screen was cracked, it was still usable. And Richie had been watching the group text messages go by ever since he woke up after being administered with the atipamezole.

He had also overheard me talk to the taxi driver about the Olive.

When Cassie narrowed down the list of phone numbers using the stingray, she'd landed on one single number. A set of digits that AT&T had left partially anonymized, the only section of the number showing being the area code that designated Lucas Beach.

She needed to wait until business hours to get an exact location from the phone carrier. Then she'd arrange with SWAT for a morning takedown.

For the night, though, everyone presumed I had crashed already, something I'd told Frank I was about to do. And knowing I'd been up for two days, they were leaving me alone.

But not Richie.

Thunder and lightning came at once. A blast of light so whit lit up the room.

My ears rang, the acrid scent of propellant filling the air.

And a heavy weight crashed down on me.

I turned my head.

Richie Brancato, in a hospital gown, a Glock in his hand. And t body of El Médico, aka Donnie Dom, collapsed atop me.

Richie got a feeling.

He told the local patrolman who was watching him in the hospital that he was going to Uber to Lucas Beach, like it or not. And the blue-suiter, who had been told not to let Richie out of his sight, drove him there instead.

The pair arrived at the Olive and banged on my hotel room door, expecting me to open up. When I didn't, Richie woke the night manager, asking him to repeat the contents of our conversation. Which sent him to the Aurora House.

We sat outside on the curb, side by side, sirens ringing in the distance.

I felt the shape of something in my back pocket. Reached in.

Over the last day, the cigar I'd been carrying, the one Poulton had given me, had broken in half. I gave one part to Richie and took the other for myself.

He took out his lighter and set fire to the butt of his. Then mine. We both puffed away in silence for a minute.

Richie took his half from his mouth. "Good quality."

"Craig Poulton," I replied. "He gets some things right."

Richie puffed again. Then glanced over. "Hey. Maybe now that I've saved your life, you can all stop calling me 'rookie.' You know, since I stopped being one like four months ago."

I considered this. Nodded. "Sounds fair," I said. "I'll talk to Shooter and Cass."

The rain slowly let up, the thunder and lightning dying away.

"So," Richie said.

"So," I repeated.

"Probably a mistake, going in there alone, huh?"

I thought of the conversation we'd had an hour ago.

"I mean, no one knows except you," I said. "So . . ."

Richie laughed and looked up at the house where the dead man was. "I'm pretty sure the others will find out soon enough."

"Yeah," I said. "So mark me down again. For anyone who thought I was perfect."

"Gardner Camden," Richie said. "Another demerit."

CHAPTER FORTY-SIX

WE REGROUPED IN MIAMI ON THURSDAY TO GO OVER THE details of the case's resolution.

Amber Isiah came up for air sometime late Wednesday and called Shooter. Mavreen Isiah's sister had heard the news about the bodies being dug up in Shilo and decided not to stay put as we'd directed her. Instead, she drove to her mom's in Boston and didn't call anyone until she felt safe.

The case made big news across the southeast, and the following day, Detective Quinones announced that his team had identified one more body, that of Tony Harris, Dog's cousin. We could only assume that what Richie had suspected was accurate: Harris had called El Médico, aka Donnie Dom, not realizing he was more than just someone who had sold his cousin xylazine in bulk. Years earlier, Donnie was likely the one who had killed Dog—worried that Dog would rat him out for the xylazine sale.

On the grounds of Aurora House, Lucas Beach Police went digging and found the rest of Edward Burrows.

As for Donnie Dom's story? His mother, Gracia Smolak, was a first-generation immigrant who worked as a waitress in a restaurant called Proof. When Smolak was twenty-three, she found herself pregnant and had the child, deciding to raise the boy herself. Records showed she received financial support—at first $5,000 a month. Then, over time, $8,000 a month.

In 2007, a local real estate magnate gifted Smolak a two-bedroom cottage five miles from the beach. She and her son moved there from the apartment above Proof. And she told her son that he would be in the will of the Burrows family, but not until the father and mother were both dead. This was a story his mother told Donnie to keep quiet about, and Donnie was a good listener. The one exception appeared to be a friend who lived far away, Freddie Pecos, who Donnie saw only four weeks every summer.

Donnie's mother was diagnosed with lupus in her forties and passed away. A year later, Jennifer and Paul Burrows were killed by a drunk driver.

Upon their passing, the entire estate went to their son, Edward, leaving Donnie Dom with nothing.

Why Donnie Dom—or Donnel Smolak, per his birth certificate—chose to kill Freddie Pecos was harder to determine. Freddie was a criminal himself. Was he about to rat out his best buddy from youth—and if so, why?

Freddie was a curious guy, we all knew. And a big talker. As a C.I., he'd peppered Richie with questions about law enforcement. He would tell Richie over and over, "I'm a cop now, just like you." Which was endearing to hear from a C.I., but of course untrue.

So maybe after they'd met at the ATM, Freddie had picked at the situation with Donnie more than he should have. Maybe he suspected something illegal was going on and thought of himself as a cop, looking for the truth. Or maybe, seeing Freddie's hand-guns and cash on hand, Donnie Dom shared more than he should have.

And suddenly, the two were at odds.

CHAPTER FORTY-SEVEN

TWO WEEKS LATER, AN EVENT WAS HELD IN THE MIAMI office.

Craig Poulton and Barry Kemp flew down to give commendations to each member of PAR, including Frank, for our work on the gun case.

I brought Camila. Rosa got her ready in a pink dress with dark tights and her black church shoes.

We also stopped on the way and picked up my mother.

The Sunday before, I'd moved Mom to a place called the Garden Palms, a nursing care facility in Miami that specialized in Alzheimer's patients. I toured a condo on the same street with a two-bedroom unit for rent. The place was a hundred years old, and two stories tall, and Camila climbed inside an old dumbwaiter and pulled herself upstairs, falling in love immediately. I found it acceptable.

As for the ceremony, it was held in a side garden at the office on a Thursday night. Each of the members of PAR, including Frank, were called onto stage and pinned with the FBI Medal for Meritorious Achievement.

"This award is given for extraordinary service in a duty of extreme challenge and great responsibility in connection with national security," Poulton announced, once we were all pinned with our medals. "These five agents put their own safety behind the larger goal of protecting Americans wherever they live, including members of law enforcement, Congress, and the White House."

As he said this, I glanced at my mom, who had tears in her eyes. Then I looked at my team. Cassie and Frank. Shooter and Richie. I was proud to have run PAR during these investigations, and I was glad to have Frank back at the helm, too.

After the awards, Barry Kemp from ATF came over to congratulate me. "You celebrating tonight?" he asked.

"The team is," I said. "But I'm here with my little girl, and I'm not much of a drinker."

Cassie approached us as Barry moved away, and Camila recognized her from the science fair.

"What'd you think of the award?" Cassie asked her.

"The medal's cool," Camila said. "But the talking went on and on."

Frank mentioned the bar the team was heading to, but I had to get my mom home, and I'd promised Camila frozen yogurt in exchange for her being quiet during the speeches.

As I loaded everyone into my car, Cassie found me in the parking lot.

"You're leaving without me?" she asked.

"I have to get these two home," I said. "I'm not going out."

She waved at Camila in the back of the car. "I think I'll take yogurt over shots."

"Really?"

Cassie looked at her watch. "It's early," she said. "Maybe after yogurt we can grab a drink."

I hesitated. *Was Cassie asking me out?*

"It's a school night," I said. "So. Camila's bedtime is in ninety-one minutes."

"So . . . minutes ninety-two and on . . . you're available?"

"Yes."

"Perf."

She jumped in the back seat, and we drove to my mother's place. Got Mom inside and tucked in. Then the three of us—Camila, Cassie, and I—headed to Camila's favorite ice cream shop. Cassie got a matcha frozen yogurt, and Camila got a mixture of Snickers, Oreo, and peanut butter, with gummy worms buried under each layer. I got a one-scoop vanilla cone. My daughter also conned me into three packs of chocolate coins, which I had seen everywhere at Rosa's place lately.

We grabbed a table and ate. Camila seemed fascinated with Cassie.

"Can you show me how to do eye makeup like that?" she asked.

I held Cassie's gaze.

"Nope," Cassie said.

"Why not?" Camila asked.

"Too young," Cassie said. Then she changed the subject, picking a candy wrapper up off the table. "You like Monedas Mexicanas?"

"It's my fave," Camila said.

"A company just like that had a flavor when I was growing up," Cassie said, smiling. "Salted chili lime with chocolate. I was the only girl who liked it."

Camila looked around the ice cream shop. "I've never seen that here."

"This was in California. There were not a lot of kids in my neighborhood who liked chili powder mixed with chocolate. My dad drove me to Oakland to get it."

"They had Monedas way back then?" Camila asked. "When you grew up?"

Cassie glanced at me, then back at Camila. "How old do you think I am?"

"I dunno." My daughter shrugged. "My dad's age, I guess."

"Well." Cassie moved on. "They had chocolate coins back then, but not the Monedas brand. What makes them so special?"

"It's not the taste," Camila said. "I mean, they're good, but . . ." She flipped the packet over and ran her fingers along the back. "See, my friend Sophie and I—that's my best friend—we're trying to win chocolate for life."

"Now I understand," Cassie said.

"They have scratchers on the back," Camila continued. "Just like my nana's lottery tickets. We keep getting the ones that say, 'Buy one, get one free.'"

"That's the trick," Cassie said. "There's probably only one 'chocolate for life.'"

"Sure," Camila said. "But we have a system."

Cassie chuckled. "Spoken like a true gambler."

"I told Sophie that there *has* to be a way they keep track of the packages." Camila motioned at a long string of numbers on the back of the chocolate wrapper. "It's nineteen digits," she said, "but it's broken into four groups of numbers. We noticed a couple packages ended in 588. They were all 'buy one, get one free.'"

Cassie leaned in close to Camila, the grin on her face half-wonder, half-amusement. "So you avoided any that ended in 588?"

"Exactly," Camila said, "but then Sophie found some that ended in 124 and 763 that were also 'buy one, get one free.'"

"The numbers aren't what you're thinking, Camila," Cassie said.

My daughter frowned. "What are they, then?"

"It depends on the company. You ever see numbers on the bottom of a can of food?"

"Yup."

"There's this thing called the Julian calendar. Food companies use them to convert dates into long strings of numbers. Like January 15, 2021. That becomes 21015," Cassie said, "21 for the year, 015 for fifteen days into the year. December 30, 2021, would be 21364, because it's one short of 365 days."

"You know a lot about numbers, don't you?"

"More than your dad, even," Cassie said, her eyes sparkling.

"So how would you do it?" Camila asked. "How would you hide the one chocolate-for-life package? 'Cause I'm determined to win."

"I guess if I worked at Monedas, I'd start with whatever system we had at the company," Cassie said. "Let's say it was the Julian calendar system. And then I'd purposely mess it up."

"Why?" I asked, and they each turned to face me.

"Oh—you're listening?" Cassie smiled. "I thought you'd disappeared into that place you go."

Camila grinned at this.

"Why would you mess it up?" I repeated.

"First," Cassie said, "for people like Camila. I'm sure she's not the only one trying to win. And I don't want to just break her system. I want to break her faith. Her feeling that there *is* a system. I want her to throw it all out the window in frustration."

I stood up from where we'd been sitting and nodded.

"You have a plan, Daddy?" Camila asked.

"I have a thought," I said.

"About chocolate for life?" Camila's eyes were huge.

"Finish your ice cream, hon," I said. "I'll be right back."

As I walked outside, I heard Camila say, "Daddy's gonna get me chocolate for life."

"I don't think so," Cassie replied.

On the sidewalk outside, I found a number in my cell phone. A guy by the name of Manny, who ran our Evidence Recovery Team in Miami.

Details of one of the cases still had not made sense to me. But Cassie's words to Camila had triggered a notion.

"It's Gardner," I said when Manny picked up. "Hey, I know Lucas Beach PD took possession of that crime scene up north, but you looked around first, right?"

"More than looked around," he said. "I saw the face of the guy who almost killed you. Yikes."

"You take pictures at the scene?"

"Yup."

"There was a gun," I said. "In the upstairs bedroom."

"There was *your* gun, which he took off you. But you got that back, right?"

"I'm speaking of a different weapon," I said. "One he had."

"Yeah," Manny replied. "I saw that."

"You have a photo of it on your phone?"

"You want the serial number?" he asked.

"I do."

Manny told me to hold on. A moment later, he returned. "It's a Venera," he said, referring to the Czech manufacturer of the gun. Then he read me the serial number, stopping every few digits.

When he finished, I thanked him and turned back toward the ice cream shop. But before I entered, I froze. A thought became a suspicion.

What to do about it was another matter.

Think like you. Act like other people.

I found a number on my phone and penned a text, channeling what Shooter would say.

> Yo, it's Gardner Camden. Up in your area. Seeing if you wanted to grab a beer. Talk shop.

I stood there, waiting for a response. Three little dots animated:

> Sorry. Busy on a case. Rain check?

I wrote back:

> Sure.

I pocketed my phone and returned to the ice cream shop, my mind cycling through a conversation from two weeks earlier.

"I need to drop you off at Nana's," I said to Camila.

"Already?" She gave me a look.

Cassie stood up, realizing the mood had changed, but not alerting my daughter. She motioned at the yogurt pulls. "Should we bring her something?"

"Huh?"

"A dessert," Cassie said, flicking her eyes at me. "For Rosa."

"Yeah." I turned to my daughter. "Camy, why don't you get your nana something she likes. And a couple more of those chocolate packages for you. Have Cassie look at the numbers. Give you a fighting chance at this sweepstakes."

Camila ran off to fill a yogurt cup, and Cassie turned to me. "What's going on?"

"The gun case," I said. "It's not over."

CHAPTER FORTY-EIGHT

I RETURNED TO ROSA'S, AND CASSIE WAITED OUTSIDE.

As I tucked my daughter in, she smiled at me.

"I'm so lucky," she said.

"Yes," I replied. But I wasn't sure of the context.

Camila pulled her covers tight. "Two grandmas here now. And Nana Rosa told me she's gonna take your mom to lunch. So they can get to know each other better."

A gesture like this was not unusual for Rosa.

I stood up, turning on Camila's purple night-light. Thinking about how I'd taken my daughter's mother away from her. Robbed her of a youth with Anna. When Camila understood the breadth of my actions, she would never forgive me. I'd lose her for good, and I'd deserve it.

"Your eyes, Daddy," Camila said. "What's wrong?"

"Nothing," I lied.

I hugged her again, squeezing the air out of Camila's lungs before letting go. Turning without looking at her. Walking out to meet Cassie.

CHAPTER FORTY-NINE

"DIRECTOR POULTON," I SAID, RAISING MY VOICE AS I banged on a hotel room door.

Cassie and I had driven to the Dolce, a hotel twenty minutes south of the office where she had heard Poulton would be after the ceremony.

"Why doesn't he stay at the Fairfield?" I asked, referring to the hotel a block from the office which visiting agents used for lodging.

"He doesn't want to consort with the muggles," Cassie said.

We'd badged the front desk and received the director's room number. But when we banged on the door, there was no response.

"He might have a six a.m. flight," I said, wondering if Poulton was asleep already.

Cassie bit her lip. "I saw a rooftop bar from outside," she said. "Maybe he's schmoozing with Kemp from ATF."

We moved to the elevator. Took it up to a bar on the top floor. Across the highway, the giant guitar of the Hard Rock Cafe danced with color.

Music played loudly, and I scanned the rooftop. A few chairs

hung from swings. and in between them were pillars filled with bou-
gainvillea.

At a marble table that faced toward the street sat Craig Poulton
and Barry Kemp, both still in suits but without the ties.

"Oh shit, it's the dream team," Kemp said as we approached.
"*Now* it's a party."

He pulled out a brown wooden chair for Cassie. But Poulton did
not look as happy to have us join him.

"What is it?" he said.

Cassie sat down beside Kemp at the four-top, and I grabbed the
seat beside Poulton.

"A development," I said. "Maybe it's more of a matter for ATF
than FBI."

Kemp sat up straighter, and Poulton kept his eyes on me.

"In the mobile home we burned down, we found some guns. Before we left, Agent Harris read me a serial number off the handgun
slide."

"Okay?"

"It didn't match with the numbers Gardner memorized for that
particular gunmaker," Cassie said.

"What gunmaker?" Kemp asked.

"Venera," I said. "I assumed when we got to D.C., we'd find serial
number mismatches. Or blanks on weapons. But we didn't."

"Maybe you made a mistake?" Poulton said.

"There's no way to tell that now," I said, "because of what went
missing at the crime scene in Hambis."

Kemp squinted. "The guns went missing from that trailer?"

"We imagined the dirty cops took them," Cassie said.

Poulton's forehead was crisscrossed with lines. "Where are you
going with this, Camden?"

"Do you remember," I asked him, "how our initial C.I., Freddie Pecos, said he saw an invoice? A two-thousand-quantity gun order. Pre-built striker-fired pistols?"

"Of course."

"We never found those in D.C.," I said. "And our second C.I., he didn't know anything about them. So I assumed the same as everyone else. That it was dark, and Jo or I got the serial number wrong."

"What changed?" Poulton asked.

"We found a gun in the house in Lucas Beach," I said. I turned to Kemp, unsure as to how much he knew of our other case. "Donnie Dom had it, the man with the cut-up face. It was a Venera. I just called about the serial numbers."

"They don't match up?" Kemp asked.

"They're nonsense," I said.

"And it's a real Venera?" Kemp followed up. "Or some hobbyist's ghost gun?"

I thought about this. We hadn't contacted the manufacturer yet, but it would be a massive risk for them: one that would put them out of business in this country.

So my gut was that it was a mix of the two. Legal gun components from Venera were being purchased and boxed up, along with eighty-percent lowers, all milled out and ready. All someone had to do was assemble the pieces. No additional machining necessary. Ghost gun at the ready.

"I think Pecos had *two* guns," I said. "Two Veneras. Both privately made weapons that he put together from a kit. Donnie Dom stole one of them the night he shot Pecos. The dirty cops removed the other—the one Shooter saw the serial number on that night in Freddie's trailer."

"And you think these gun were, what?" Poulton asked. "Some advance on this two-thousand-quantity order of buy-build-shoot kits? Samples?"

"If it *were* a sample," I pointed out, "Sandoval would've been the one to get that, not Pecos. *Sandoval's* the gun dealer. Or in the least, one of the men we captured in D.C. would've talked about the buy-build-shoot kits. But no one has, right?"

"Right," Kemp said.

"That's been bothering me," I said. "Why wouldn't they know? Only one possibility."

"Freddie had a side gig, all his own," Poulton said.

I nodded. "And right before his death, Freddie missed a money drop to the gang. It was in their text chain when we came upon him that night in the trailer. Our assumption was that whoever shot Freddie took the cash."

"Except we didn't find any money with Donnie Dom," Cassie said. "So maybe Donnie *didn't* take the money. Maybe it was Freddie's seed money for the gun buy."

"For the two thousand kits?" Kemp asked.

"Exactly," Cassie said. "And it'd already been spent."

"Freddie was covering his bases," I said. "Blaming the gun kits on Sandoval when he talked to us. That's why no one else in Sandoval's organization knew about the buy-build-shoot kits. It wasn't part of Sandoval's operation."

Kemp had been listening carefully, but now he sat back. "One thing doesn't make sense, though, Camden," he said. "Why go to the trouble of putting serial numbers on a weapon at all, if they're the wrong serial numbers?"

"And that's the other thing that's been bothering me." I pointed at Kemp. "It's why I never brought it up before."

"Now you have an answer?" Poulton asked.

"We were just eating ice cream with my daughter. Who is trying to win chocolate for life in this silly sweepstakes."

Barry Kemp squinted, and I focused.

"International sales of American-made weapons have been sky-rocketing," I said. "Correct?"

"Correct," Kemp said, nodding.

"And there's confidence between you and Canada and Mexico that you'll trace guns, even amid shooting incidents. Because foreign countries are using ATF's eTrace system."

"Yup."

"Same with domestic incidents, correct? School shootings. Assassination attempts." I hesitated. "Even if it's in the rearview mirror, we can always trace a properly sold gun."

I paused again, and the music changed. Beyond the table, a light-show played by the rooftop pool. "But what if we couldn't?"

"Couldn't trace a gun?" Kemp asked.

"What if someone released guns with serial numbers that meant nothing? Gibberish."

"Other countries would stop using eTrace," Cassie said. "Domestically, people would lose faith in our ability to do investigations."

Poulton's whole body had become rigid. "You think someone is trying to do that?"

"I do," I said. "I think they're doing a dry run of guns south of the border. A test before they dump more guns like this on American soil."

"That would take a real insider," Kemp said. "Someone who knows how to trick the system. Who's worked with manufacturers."

"When we first spoke," I said to Kemp, "everything was need-to-know."

"I remember," Kemp said. "You were worried about a leak."

"And when I asked you—is your guy O'Reilly briefed in—you said no one was briefed in. Per my request."

"Right again," Kemp said.

"So you never told O'Reilly what we were tracking in that U-Haul?" I asked. "Or why?"

"I made something up," Kemp said, crossing his arms over his chest. "What are you getting at?"

"After the leapfrog process, your agent met me in a parking lot of a restaurant. He started pinging me with questions. Were we after domestic terror? Ghost guns? Militia?"

"You tell him anything?" Kemp asked.

"Nothing," I said. "But he started guessing. One thing after another. Before I walked away, he said, 'Serial number mismatch.' I didn't think much of it at the time."

"What are you implying?" Kemp said. "O'Reilly is dirty? He and Freddie were together?"

"Is he on a case?" I asked.

"No," Kemp said. "He's home in D.C. A week off. Told me himself."

I held out my phone. I had texted Agent O'Reilly a half hour ago, outside the ice cream shop.

"You just said it would take an insider. Flooding the market with guns. All serial numbered. Seemingly legit. They get out into the world. Start coming up in shootings."

"And our ability to chase them," Cassie said, her voice tight, "starts shitting the bed."

Kemp took out his cell and made a call.

"Yeah," we heard him say. "Well, get his ass up. Have him call me."

He hung up.

"You're waking O'Reilly?" Poulton asked.

"Our head of Tech," Kemp said. "I want a trace on O'Reilly's phone. Before this goes any further."

"Is he on any other cases?" Poulton asked.

"He wrapped yesterday," Kemp said. "So if he's anywhere other than his home in Maryland, I'm concerned." He glared at Cassie and me. "Otherwise, this is a smear job."

I swallowed, and we all waited. A minute later, Kemp received a call. He requested a trace on the agent's phone. Ten minutes after, he found out O'Reilly was at the Port of Miami, specifically the cargo end down by Fishermans Channel.

"If Freddie had the guns down in Hambis," I said, "that's the port he'd ship from."

"Can we scramble a copter over there?" Kemp asked Poulton.

The director went to work, finding one that was available and directing it to the next building over.

"You guys can take that," Cassie said. "Gardner and I will head over by car."

On the way, she glanced at me as we moved around nighttime traffic. "So this is a date with you, huh?" she said. "Feels a lot like work."

I slowed as the traffic came to a standstill. Cassie's face was turned away from me, her eyes on the side window. Before the cars moved again, I leaned across and gave her a kiss on the cheek.

"Well, that doesn't happen at work," she said, glancing over.

"No," I replied. Facing forward still. Got onto the highway.

Should I have done that?

We moved into the tunnel that brought us under the water. As we emerged onto the Port of Miami, I scanned the docks. To our left was a curving glass structure that marked where Norwegian Cruise Lines departed from. And over to our right were hundreds of ship containers.

At a guard gate, I flashed my badge at a cop, and he motioned us inside. While we'd been stuck in traffic, Poulton and Kemp had beaten us here by a solid twenty minutes. The director had mobilized port police, and a Miami PD helicopter sat on the asphalt nearby. In the distance, a cargo ship was docked under a set of freight loaders, the blue and red containers piled four stories high.

Someone moved a police van out of the way, and I saw the figure of Barry Kemp standing near an enormous cargo container with its door swung open. Cassie and I got out and identified ourselves. But the cop told us to hold where we were.

Ten minutes later, Poulton walked over. "You two did good," he said.

In the distance, I saw Kemp hold something in his hand. A box. He took an object from it, and against the night sky, we could see the distinct silhouette of a handgun.

"O'Reilly?" I asked.

"In the wind," Poulton said. "But we'll find him."

Cassie shook her head, and a thought moved through mine. That of all the C.I.s we'd gone through, O'Reilly was the real inside man. I wondered if my text had spooked him.

"Why don't we let ATF take this from here?" Poulton said. "I'll stay with Barry. He might want a presser. Or he might want to handle this privately."

Poulton had that sharkish grin on his face, and I could tell he was prepared to go either way. Collect a favor from ATF if the decision was to sweep the news of a dirty agent under the rug and handle it internally. Or be here for a press conference if Kemp decided to spin this as a positive about guns seized. A joint op between the FBI and ATF. Either way, a personal win for Craig Poulton, as always.

"Is there anything else?" he asked me.

"No," I said.

"Then you guys are free to go."

But I stood my ground, waiting. This was *our* case. PAR's case.

Poulton studied me, squinting almost, curious. Unused to me being stubborn.

"Gardner," he said. "At what *you* do, you guys are the best. But you know . . ." He looked over his shoulder. "There's a time for the brilliant misfits. And a time for those who know how to work the crowd." He paused. "Politics. It's a skill, too."

I swallowed. A very different version of me would've taken a swing at him.

But I just nodded, watching as Kemp kicked the side of the cargo container in frustration. I felt bad for Barry Kemp.

"Enjoy your night," Poulton said. "I got this."

He turned, and Cassie and I walked back to the car. We got in and headed down inside the tunnel. Away from the port. As we emerged, the Miami sky was lit up with a thousand lights.

I didn't want to talk about Poulton or the FBI. About the political end of this job, which I knew I would never master.

"Night's still early," Cassie said, her voice breaking into my thoughts.

I reflected on the moment with her and Camila in the ice cream shop. Cassie was sweet with my daughter. And she was smart with numbers. I glanced over at her. Smiled.

"Are you hungry?" I asked.

"I could eat," she said.

There were good things to focus on. I had run PAR successfully for fifteen months. My mother had woken from a coma. And we had solved two huge cases in just the last few days.

I studied Cassie. Technically, I was still her boss. But Frank would connect with Poulton, and they'd figure out a new hierarchy. PAR was too important to the Bureau, even if Craig Poulton acted as if we weren't.

Which meant anything could happen with Cassie and me.

Or maybe nothing would happen.

I computed the statistics and decided it was fifty-fifty.

"Let's find a place, then," I said. "Grub, as you say."

"Perf," she said and smiled back.

And we drove off into the Miami night.

ACKNOWLEDGMENTS

AS USUAL, I LOVE TO HEAR FEEDBACK ON MY BOOKS OR just meet readers, so please email me with any thoughts or drop me a note to say hello at: McMahonJohn@att.net. And a big thanks to everyone who's reading this series—as well as my P. T. Marsh series, which begins with *The Good Detective*.

The more I write, the more I find that each book is unique, like different children raised in the same household. And what a writer first strikes fire with in one book cannot be repeated in the next ('cause that would be boring for readers). As an illustration, to me this book is more gritty and action-oriented—and less voicey—than its predecessor, *Head Cases*. But I enjoyed writing both. Put simply, in each I find something different, so as a reader, I hope you do, too.

As usual, I want to start by thanking my family: Maggie, Noah, and Zoey; my editor, Kelley Ragland; and my agent, Simon Lipskar. That's the team I go to battle with . . . and with them, how can you lose?

I used to say that Book 2 in my other series was the hardest thing I'd ever written. That was in 2018, and I was coming off major changes in my day job and my dad passing away, which was really tough for me. But more than those things, I was writing under contract and deadline for the first time, so I had to figure out how to write a book a year, while also working full-time in advertising. Flash forward to Book 2 in *this* series, the book you've just finished, which is my fifth overall. I had a lot of time to write it, but had four spine surgeries between January of 2023 and May of 2024. Each surgery set me back in some way. The one in December 2023 took me down hard, and there were days when I wasn't sure if anything was making sense, if I could write on that many pharmaceuticals, or if I wanted to keep going at all. Through all this, my family was a rock. My mother would text me every couple days telling me that things were about to turn up with my health. My writer friends Alex and Bev constantly encouraged me. My wife and kids would tell me the book was working, even if they had not yet read it. My friend Todd would pragmatically remind me that progress only moves in one direction. And my writing coach Jerrilyn kept pushing for me to just keep showing up. And all of that was enough to keep me going. So thanks, everyone.

I have always had amazing chance meetings in life, and one of those happened a couple years ago at a critical junction in my writing career. To give you the backstory, I had written some early version of *Head Cases* and been signed by a famous agent. I gave my previous agent notice, and I was over the moon. But one day I was fired by the famous agent for no reason and found myself floating around, unsure if I was done writing. A lot of people were not getting deals, and I reached out to a lot of agents, many of whom described me as "a project." A woman named Genevieve Gagne-Hawes in editorial at Writers House, however, intercepted an email because someone was on vacation. She thought I was the type of writer they should have at their agency, so she helped me set up a meeting for weeks later.

Everyone at Writers House was so earnest in their treatment of me, and when one agent was struggling, Simon Lipskar, the president, took *Head Cases* out himself. Throughout this whole time, Genevieve was a constant. She gave me rounds and rounds of great notes, until *Head Cases* became the fun read you know it as (if you've read it). Long and short, this helped me get back on track as a writer, and this long story is to say thank you to Genevieve.

This book is dedicated to my brother, Andy, but it comes with a huge thanks to the McMahon family: my mother, Betty McMahon; my sister Kerry Archbold; and my sister Bette Carlson. Sorry, everyone else. I have the most supportive family around. And thanks to Bette for reading an early draft for medical expertise.

Additional thanks to my team at Minotaur and St. Martin's Publishing Group. Steve Erickson gets me graphics before I can say, "Steve, can you…" Sarah Melnyk is always on it for tours and PR opportunities. Mac Nicholas is on his game for advanced marketing. The proofers crush it on those little details. And Katie coordinates everything to keep us on track. On the St. Martin's audio team, Guy and Emily produced an amazing audiobook. Additionally, for those of us who read mostly on audio (like myself), I was blessed to have Will Damron be the voice of Gardner Camden (for which I've only heard raves).

Shout out to Vic Reynolds, formerly of the Georgia Bureau of Investigation. Vic was kind enough to read *Head Cases* and *Inside Man* and offer thoughts on both. And a delayed thanks to Matthew Quirk for his blurb on *Head Cases*, which was inadvertently left off my last acknowledgments.

Lastly, I want to thank all the readers who shared stories of their beautiful neurodivergent family, friends, and kids. In your life and travels, please embrace those who think differently.

As of this writing, the folks at Berlanti Productions, John Gold-wyn Productions, and HBO Max are still intent on bringing this series to TV, and I hope that keeps up. If you shoot me an email, I'll put you on the list to be the first to know about that, as well as future books. Speaking of emails—to the gun fanatics—you're hard-core when I get things wrong, but I love you guys. Keep the notes coming. I promise, I'll do better. And if I don't, Ryan, you're now at fault as my gun consultant.

I was able to visit a few cities on tour—new places like St. Louis, where I hosted a great talk at the library, and familiar places like the Tucson Festival of Books, at U of A, where I went to school. But I wanted to note a few great bookstores I visited, too. At the top of that list is Murder By The Book in Houston, Texas, where I signed about 150 books. A life highlight. Two others I adore are The Poisoned Pen Bookstore in beautiful Scottsdale, Arizona, and Book Carnival in Orange County, close to where I went to high school and where Anne Saller declares that "John belongs to us."

At the time of this writing, I'm not sure what is next for me. I have a police procedural that's been on hold for two years, and in my downtime I've completed it. And I also finished a family story that is in a completely different genre, but when I read it, I think it's my best work. Both stories have been waiting patiently for a long time to be heard by readers. But then there's this pesky group referred to as the "Head Cases," and there's more stories to come there. It's excit-ing, and it's hard to keep up. As someone with a day job that's never under fifty hours a week, it's hard to tell all the tales. But as far as the ones that have made it to print so far—many, many thanks to every-one who's read them. You keep this thing going. So on to the next . . .

ABOUT THE AUTHOR

Nathaniel Chadwick

John McMahon's debut novel, *The Good Detective*, was labeled "pretty much perfect" by *The New York Times*, which listed it among their Top Ten Crime Novels of 2019. The book was also a finalist for the 2020 Edgar Award and the ITW Thriller Award, both for Best First Novel. *Head Cases*, his fourth novel, is currently in development with Warner Bros TV for a streaming series on HBO Max. John currently lives in Southern California with his wife, two kids, and a rescue dog. He splits his time between crime-writing and his day job in advertising.